Each & Every One

RACHAEL ENGLISH

An Orion paperback

First published in Great Britain in 2014
by Orion Books
This paperback edition published in 2015
by Orion Books,
an imprint of The Orion Publishing Group Ltd,
Carmelite House, 50 Victoria Embankment,
London EC4Y 0DZ

An Hachette UK company

1 3 5 7 9 10 8 6 4 2

A CIP catalogue record for this book is available from the British Library.

ISBN 978-1-4091-4699-5

Printed and bound in Great Britain by CPI Group (UK) Ltd, Croydon, CR0 4YY

The Orion Publishing Group's policy is to use papers that
are natural, renewable and recyclable products and
made from wood grown in sustainable forests. The logging
and manufacturing processes are expected to conform to
the environmental regulations of the country of origin.

www.orionbooks.co.uk

For Tony and Ruth

Rachael English has such an impressive way with words, her
amazing and unique writing style is definitely part of the greatness
of this story. If you haven't bought this book yet, you should'

Librarian Blog

Rachael English is a presenter on Ireland's most popular radio show, *Morning Ireland*. During more than twenty years as a journalist, she has covered a huge range of national and international stories for RTÉ Radio's leading current affairs programmes. Her first novel, *Going Back*, was nominated in the *Sunday Independent* Newcomer of the Year category at the Irish Book Awards. Follow Rachael on Twitter @EnglishRachael

Chapter 1

Gus Shine had always wanted a big house. Not a sprawling, ten bedrooms and even more bathrooms type of place. But somewhere with high ceilings, tall windows, room to breathe. No doubt a lounge-bar psychologist would say this was explained by the way he'd grown up: ten of them in a terraced cottage near the Markets Field in Limerick, forever clamouring for an inch of space or a second's peace. Gus believed this was too simplistic. After all, his brothers and sisters had never shown the same desire.

Twenty years ago he had got his wish. After a decade in Dublin, the family had moved to Palmerston Park, and to the house he had renamed Garryowen. To his eyes, it had been three storeys of red-bricked perfection. When asked about his home, he'd tended to lapse into estate agent speak. 'Exceptionally well proportioned,' he would say, with 'period features' and 'delightful gardens'. Joan, his wife, would laugh, but he'd known how proud she was to be living in such a magnificent spot. Her own start in life had been no more prosperous than his.

Somewhere along the line, however, the joy had ebbed away. That afternoon, as Gus paced the sitting room, he saw only the flaws. He saw the black mark on the cream wall where one of the grandchildren had taken a biro for a walk. He saw how the fabric on his favourite green armchair had faded. He thought of the maintenance costs, the property tax, the heating bills. Somehow, the house felt out of control.

That wasn't all. For years, Gus's life had followed a blueprint; his business had prospered; his investments had soared. Lately, though, he'd come to realise that life had gone awry. Too little had turned out the way he'd planned.

Half an hour before, he had stood at the front window and watched their youngest child, Tara, walk down the street, her shoulders slumped like she was carrying a hundredweight of coal. Earlier in the week, he had almost told her. He'd come as close as dammit to saying, 'This life that you and your brothers and sister are used to, it can't continue. It's coming undone.' But Tara's face had been filled with a disarming trust, and he hadn't been able to follow through. Still, he couldn't put it off for much longer.

It was funny, he'd often asked how the children could be so different from each other. Certainly, this was how the four saw themselves. He remembered Veronica, a disturbing sincerity on her twelve-year-old face, wondering how she could *possibly* be related to the others. 'You really should check with the hospital,' she'd said. 'I'm sure there was a mix-up.' Now, the more he thought about them, the more he realised how similar they were.

Eventually, Gus stopped pacing and ran a hand through his hair. These days it contained more silver than sand. He was lucky, though, that age had not yet done its worst. His chin remained firm, his shoulders broad. For the thousandth time, he considered the consequences of what he was going to say. But he had already weighed and measured every possibility. There was no other option. Of this much he was sure.

Tara Shine's patience was starting to fray. The only reason she had called around to her sister's house was because she was worried about their dad, but Veronica was intent on talking about herself. That was the problem with Veronica – or Vee, as almost everybody called her: she could win the Nobel Prize for self-absorption. Right then, she was twirling around the bedroom, modelling a small black dress that to Tara looked exactly like the one she'd tried on five minutes before. In her wake she left a trail of black tissue paper and grosgrain ribbon.

Tara decided to have another try. 'So, like I was saying, it's Dad. He's gone all . . . strange.'

'What, even stranger than usual?' said Vee, as she jutted out one hip and balanced on her toes like she was wearing five-inch heels. 'Shoes please, Tara,' she added, waving in the general direction of a heap of footwear.

'Ah Vee, you haven't listened to a word. Will you quit the prancing around for a moment?' She sighed. 'Please?'

Slowly Vee lowered herself onto the edge of the bed; her dress didn't allow for sudden movement. 'Go on then. What's he done?'

Tara wrinkled her nose. 'It's not that he's done anything as such. It's just that he's quiet – way too quiet. No shouting. No laughing. No singing. "Limerick, You're a Lady" hasn't been heard in weeks.'

'Be thankful for small mercies,' said Vee.

'Seriously, sometimes it's like he's about to say something only then he checks himself and walks away. And last night I walked in on him and Mum, and they stopped talking and acted all awkward.'

'He is getting on, you know.'

'He's sixty-two, Vee,' she replied. 'These days that's young.'

'Maybe the years of obsessive money-making are beginning to take their toll.'

As she spoke, Vee flexed her toes. Tara noticed how the nails were painted a flawless caramel. This month's top shade, no doubt. Her own, which were getting their first outing of the year, had not wintered well; they were ridged and yellowish in colour. Occasionally she imagined a room in which the world's most beautiful people held regular gatherings. They would determine what was stylish and pass these pronouncements straight on to Vee. How else could her taste be so perfect? From the thread count of her sheets to the perfume on her dressing-table to the flowers in the hall, everything was as it should be. Even thinking about the effort – and the expense – made Tara's brain hurt. Rather than saying anything, she cast what she hoped was a withering look towards her sister's internet shopping.

Eventually, Vee took the hint. 'Well, perhaps you should ask him if he's OK. Or ask Mum. Tread carefully, though. Don't go suggesting he's about to croak or anything.' She eased herself off the bed and resumed her posing. 'Anyway, to more pressing matters: what do you think? I had planned on sending one of them back. Only all the re-parcelling is a terrible pain in the arse, especially when they're both so divine.'

Tara couldn't stop herself. She reached into the pile of cardboard that sat in the middle of the bed and pulled out a receipt. 'Holy moly, Vee! That dress costs a thousand euro. I mean, it's lovely and everything but . . .'

'Ha! And the other one isn't much cheaper.' Vee appeared to be enjoying Tara's discomfort.

'You're unbelievable. If Ferdia knew, he'd have kittens.' Vee had been married to Ferdia Boyne for three years. He was a junior barrister with a suitably plummy voice and pin-striped appearance. As far as Tara could make out, his demeanour masked the fact that his earnings were pitifully small. Once when she'd had too much to drink, his wife had admitted as much. 'Maximum attitude, minimum wage,' she'd laughed. Not that this state of affairs seemed to bother her. As long as the money was there to be spent she didn't care which direction it came from.

'Don't get judgemental on me,' said Vee as she stepped into a pair of black stilettos. 'There's no reason why Ferdia should ever know the cost of anything. It's not as though I'm asking him to pay for them.'

Tara was tempted to point out that she was unlikely to be paying for them herself either. Chances were the money had come from their parents. They were incredibly generous.

'And I need something appropriate for Thursday night,' continued the elder sister. 'I've a mobile phone launch so I'll have to look business-like.'

Vee worked in public relations as an event-management

4

specialist. Once upon a time, business had been brisk, but the bust had hit hard. These days, there were fewer events to manage. Like the asteroid that had wiped out the dinosaurs, the recession had put paid to the days of showy consumption. Tara listened to all of the talk about recovery, but sometimes she felt like the entire country was holding its breath. Trust was in short supply.

'I thought extravagance was out of fashion,' she said. 'Isn't it all about thrift now – frocks from jumble sales and such?'

'God, you're innocent. Oh, I'm sure lots of people have to live like that. But people *we* know? Take it from me, when they say their dress came from the supermarket or a charity shop, they're lying. They spend as much as they always did. It's just they no longer boast about it.' Nowadays, according to Vee, a serious woman was supposed to look subtle. Achieving this was complex. It was like Dolly Parton claiming that looking cheap was actually very expensive. 'We can't all get away with behaving like you,' she said, giving Tara one of her extensive range of condescending looks, 'clodhopping around the city in a pair of sandals you've owned since you were at school and a skirt that even a charity shop would reject.'

Tara ignored the barbs. She'd had plenty of practice.

The walk home from Vee's house in Mount Pleasant took little more than twenty minutes, and this was a day for relishing every step. Tara dawdled past swathes of red brick, occasionally veering onto the road to avoid the groups of homebound schoolchildren. The older ones looked as though they were aching to shed their school uniforms. The younger ones wore new sandals and had shiny pink knees. Dublin was at its best at this time of year. In the May sunshine the city felt renewed. The trees were in full blossom, their delicate white petals scattered along the pavement.

At Belgrave Square she stopped and raised her face skywards, allowing the sun to tickle her skin. If Vee was with her, she'd start warning about wrinkles. Talking to her sister had been a mistake. It wasn't that there was any real hostility between them; the situation was more complicated than that. They were a pair of parallel lines; they could go on forever without connecting.

Neither did they look like sisters. When the family genes were shared out, Vee had got the tall, thin, glossy ones. What was left had gone to Tara. Height, build, skin: you name it – she was thoroughly average. Her eyes were a wishy-washy green; her nose a small snub of a thing. Oh, and she was cursed with the type of red hair that needs no encouragement to turn into an explosion of frizz.

As the youngest of Gus and Joan Shine's children, Tara liked to think that she was the most perceptive. It stood to reason, she believed. From the moment you were born what choice had you but to watch and listen to the rest of them? Their lives were already in full-flow while you were dismissed as the baby in the corner. Despite Vee's scepticism, something was definitely up with their dad. Normally ebullient, he looked and sounded squashed. The other night, when they'd been talking – shooting the breeze about her day and his – she could have sworn there were tears in his eyes.

She was nearly home now, the park's familiar green railings coming into view. Giddy squeals drifted from the playground, and the breeze carried a faint tang of suncream. Her job as a newspaper reporter meant she often worked Sundays. The upside was that she got a day off during the week. She was looking forward to returning to her lair and cooling her feet on the kitchen's granite floor. Tara and her boyfriend, Craig Fitzgerald, lived in the basement flat of the family home. A freelance journalist, he was editing a radio documentary, so she'd have the place to herself. This was just as well. After an encounter with Vee, a little calm was called for.

Today she was out of luck. As soon as her key turned in the lock, she could tell that Craig was home. He was in the sitting room, flat out on the beige sofa, a bottle of beer at his side, Judge Judy in full voice. Appearing slightly sheepish, he zapped the volume on the television.

6

'Uh, hi,' she said, doing her best not to appear put out. 'I didn't expect you until later.'

'Ah yeah, there was a bit of a snag so I got home early.'

'Oh?'

Craig hauled himself upright and took a swig of his drink. 'Nothing for you to fret about. Get yourself a beer and we can talk about it later.'

'Is everything OK?'

'Let it go, babe, would you?'

Not entirely sure she had anything to let go of, Tara stepped into the kitchen, kicked off her sandals and took a bottle of water from the fridge. When she returned to the sitting room, Craig was patting the sofa, beckoning her to sit beside him. He was wearing his most charming face.

Tara had met few men – or women – who could do charming as well as her boyfriend. And she was a sucker for it. Not that she liked admitting this. It made her sound shallow. Actually, it made both of them sound shallow. She consoled herself with the knowledge that he had plenty of other gifts. Like his intelligence and his imagination and, let's be honest, his good looks. He was lean and dark, and even after three years together she still found herself thinking, *Am I really with him?* She was under no illusions about his faults, mind. There were times when she wished he had a touch more drive, a shade more purpose.

Sensing that this was one of those occasions on which it was best to tread lightly, she sat down and waited for an explanation.

'Well,' he said eventually, 'I don't think the Irish public will have the pleasure of hearing my programme.'

'That's a shame.' She stopped in the hope that he would fill the silence.

'Me and the guy in charge . . . we had what you might call creative differences. He wanted to make all these nonsensical changes, and of course I couldn't allow that. So I told him what he could do with his poxy documentary slot.'

Tara made a steeple shape with her hands. *Keep your voice level,*

7

she said to herself. 'And he – the documentary guy – what did he do?'

'Let's just say we didn't part on the friendliest of terms. In fact, I don't think I'll be back his way any time soon.' He paused. 'You've got to realise, Tara, these guys are barely adequate. Muck-savages, most of them. They do a couple of years in local radio or producing some middle-of-the-road current affairs crap, and they think they know it all.'

Craig's documentary was about a day in the life of an economics professor. The man in question was a particularly dusty character and, to her, the idea had never sounded promising. As her boyfriend sometimes pointed out, however, imagination was not her strong suit. 'Economists have become the new rock stars,' he'd claimed. A fleeting image of Dr Roland Dooley in leather trousers and Cuban heels had given Tara a fit of the giggles. Craig had not been impressed.

'What happens now then?' she asked. 'I mean, don't you already have the money?'

'Yeah, and he wants it back. I suppose I'll have to give it to him too. Otherwise he'll be on my case, and you know how much I hate hassle.'

She searched for the correct response. Craig, looking unfazed by the loss of one of his few sources of income, looped an arm around her shoulder and squeezed. 'Anyway, I reckon it's for the best.'

Tara was confused but didn't get the chance to say so.

'We should see it as an omen,' he explained. 'For as long as we've known each other, we've been talking about travelling. This could be the time.'

He was right about the talking part, at least. The pair had first met on a journalism course. Back then, they hadn't been in the same orbit; he'd been far too cool. After college, Tara had spent a couple of years working on a local paper in Limerick. On her return to Dublin she'd bumped into him, they'd gone for a pint or several and shared their first drunken kiss. She remembered how that very first night they'd spent hours discussing all the places they would like to see, especially India (her) and Brazil (him). But work, or inertia, or something had taken over, and they'd never been further than a package holiday to Greece. Tara had quietly abandoned her plans. Lately, however, Craig had resurrected his. He was forever harping on about dusting down their rucksacks and hitting the road.

'We're twenty-nine,' he was saying now. 'Time is ticking on.'

'I know, only I'm not convinced that going away right this minute is a good idea.'

'Oh?'

'I'd prefer to wait another small while.'

Craig's brown eyes narrowed, he withdrew his arm and raised his palms to the ceiling. 'Right, so we should wait until we're too old and decrepit to enjoy ourselves? What is it we're hanging around for?'

Tara didn't like where this was going. 'I hear what you're saying. Except with Niall away, it would upset my parents if I disappeared too – I know it would. And what about my job? I can't just jack it in. There's no guarantee it'd be there when I got back.'

'So?'

'So what else would I do?'

'Jesus, Tara, I don't know. Does it matter? You'd find something. I don't understand why you're so scared of upsetting somebody or having a second's insecurity. You're the queen of caution, terrified of taking a chance.'

'And then there's my dad.' She swallowed. 'He's not himself. I have to find out what's wrong.'

Craig made great play of throwing his eyes to the heavens. 'Go upstairs and ask him then. I'll bet he's absolutely fine. You're a terrible woman for worrying when there's nothing to worry about.'

'I—'

'Let's face facts,' he said, getting increasingly cranky. 'You're only looking for an excuse. You want to stay at home, living as

9

boring a life as possible, while your brothers and sister take advantage of you.'

'I don't think that's fair. So what if they boss me around a bit from time to time? I'm the youngest; that's how families work.'

'From time to time? Vee treats you like a dogsbody, Damien sees you as an unpaid babysitter, and Niall thinks you're the Bank of Tara, handy for a few bob when the old folks won't cough up. And you? I swear, it's like you get some kind of kick out of it.'

Tara stood up. 'You're out of line here, Craig. Somebody else has annoyed you, and you're taking it out on me. I'm not going to get into an argument, though.'

'You see, that's your problem. You won't fight your own corner.'

'You're being silly now,' she said, as she swivelled on one heel and walked towards the bedroom. Craig could never grasp that her ways were different to his. He was all bluster and rage. His temper went from nought to ninety in five seconds. And he enjoyed these explosions. Tara was slower, her anger almost methodical. She hated raised voices, reddened faces, scenes.

'I'm just being honest with you,' he shouted after her.

In the bedroom, Tara shed her composure. Her eyes stinging, she pulled the duvet over her head. Her boyfriend had gone too far, but it wasn't just the harshness of his words that hurt; it was the fact that they might be true.

One floor up, Gus had resumed his pacing. Joan was on the sofa, knitting a small white jacket for one of her conveyor belt of grandnieces and grandnephews.

'Sit down, Gus,' she said. 'All the tramping up and down is making me seasick.'

'Give me a moment, love. I'm thinking.' Five, ten, minutes passed before he flopped into his armchair. 'Is tomorrow all right with you?'

'Will you invite them round here?' Joan replied, her neat head peering up from her knitting.

'That's the best way, I think. I'll have to ring Niall, but I can do that later. I'll ask the others not to say anything.'

Her green eyes met his. 'Will I call the police and tell them to expect trouble?'

Gus smiled. Even in the trickiest of times, she made him smile. 'Will you be here?'

His wife rose from the sofa, walked across the room and clasped his hand. 'Where else would I be? We're in this together. You know that.'

Chapter 2

Tara hadn't been completely honest with Craig. The main reason she didn't want to go travelling was because, right then, she was content with her lot. She was enjoying her job. Not that it was perfect, or that she was the greatest reporter of all time. But she gleaned a certain satisfaction from being out and about, meeting all sorts, and soaking up the banter of colleagues.

Even when she'd been too young to know exactly what a journalist did, Tara had carried vague notions that this was the life for her. What a serious child she'd been, listening to radio programmes with Gus, trying to make sense of the voices in the ether and of the comments her dad made in response. He'd been mightily amused. 'How's my ace reporter?' he would laugh.

How did Tara feel about her work? Well, the way she saw it, one of the main attractions of being a journalist was the access it gave you to the lives of others. She could dress this up and claim to have a curious nature or an inquisitive mind. Or, she could be honest and admit that, like most hacks, she was plain nosy. Plus, she wanted to write something that would make a real difference. Make a difference to what, she wasn't quite sure, but there had to be something. In the meantime, she was content to highlight small injustices. Not that she would ever say any of this out loud. It sounded too earnest, too old-fashioned. These days all the talk in the newsroom was about platforms and digital strategies and content curation. Tara just wanted to write stories.

Still, no matter how much she valued her job, there were times when the work was so grim that she would gladly do *anything* else. This was one of those days.

At eleven in the morning, she was standing in front of a garda, focusing on his ruddy face and weary grey eyes, trying not to think about what he was saying. They were in the south inner-city, at the edge of a warren of flats – one of those complexes that had once been earmarked for renovation. The problem was, the boom had come and gone and the flats had received little more than a coat of emulsion. The developer had gone to the wall, she seemed to remember.

The morning was clear, the temperature climbing steadily. The breeze was gentle, but it was enough to rustle the white and blue scene-of-crime tape.

Tara wondered whether the policeman giving the media briefing considered the precise meaning and impact of his words. Or, like her, had he learnt that sometimes the only way to do this was by rote? Follow the procedure; tick the boxes; return to being human at the end of your shift. Alongside her, other reporters jostled for position. All of their faces were familiar. Most were young, still enthusiastic enough and, let's face it, ambitious enough, not to mind a job like this.

The officer spoke in the robotic tones favoured by his profession. 'I can confirm,' he said, 'that the deceased was a local youth. 'At approximately eleven fifteen p.m., he was shot once in the head and once in the back. It appears the shots were fired from a passing vehicle. The boy died at the scene. A post-mortem is currently being carried out.'

'Can you give us his name?' one of the pack shouted.

'You know the drill,' came the answer. 'There'll be no name until all the family have been informed.'

'Will you confirm his age?' Tara asked. 'Fifteen, the report on the radio said. Is that right?'

Before replying, the policeman gave a tiny shudder and looked down at the tarmac. 'No, I'd like to correct that. Having spoken to the deceased's mother, it appears he was thirteen.'

'Jesus,' said a lone voice.

'Only recently thirteen,' continued the garda. 'The lad made his confirmation last month.' Tara thought she heard a break in his voice. A ripple ran through the group. She would like to say it consisted entirely of revulsion, but there was excitement there too. This was a front page, top-of-the-bulletin story, for sure.

That was when she first spotted the boy. He had close-cropped fair hair and a nose that was made for freckles. From the size of him, she guessed he wasn't much more than seven or eight, but the look of pure concentration on his face suggested he was absorbing every word. Tara was sure he should be at school. She glared at him, as if to say 'Scram'. As brazen as you like, he grinned back, revealing a mouth that was more gaps than teeth. She shook her head before returning her focus to the briefing. Someone had asked whether the murdered boy was 'known to the gardaí'. 'No,' was the terse reply. *Lord almighty*, thought Tara, *he was only a child; he was barely known to himself.*

After making the obligatory comments about keeping an open mind on possible motives, the policeman accepted that the murder might well have been a case of mistaken identity. He appealed for witnesses to come forward, warned the hacks about pointless speculation, then shuffled off. Tara noticed that her paper's crime correspondent had arrived. This meant that he would do the main story while she'd get the task of talking to neighbours and anyone else who was willing to give an opinion. Most likely too, she'd have to track down a photo of the dead child. First, she needed to file copy for the website.

Beside her, a local radio reporter, who was new to the beat, made a tutting noise. 'We should have guessed your man would show up,' she said. She cast her eyes in the direction of a thin fellow in a purple T-shirt, his reddish-brown hair in need of a pair of scissors. 'Where there's misery, he's never far behind.'

'Do you not like Dublin's leading left-wing councillor?' replied Henry from the *Evening Post*, a teasing tone to his voice. 'Scourge of the rich. Defender of the poor. Supporter of a million causes – most of them lost. I reckon he's not the worst of them.'

'Do you know him well then?' asked the girl.

Henry smiled. 'Why don't you ask Tara here? I've a feeling she can mark your card.'

'Is he a friend of yours?' the girl said.

'Damien? Ahm . . . yes and no.' Tara paused. 'He's my brother.'

Only a couple of miles away, Gus was polishing his speech and checking his figures. That morning the head office of Shine and Company Accounting Services was quiet. That was OK. Soon enough he'd have plenty of noise to contend with.

Gus had founded Shine and Co. in Limerick in the late seventies. With the country on the cusp of a recession, it had been a foolish time to start anything. But somehow his enterprise had flourished. In the blink of an eye, he'd had satellite offices in Ennis and Thurles. Next, he'd set up in Cork. Finally, in 1983, he had moved the family to Dublin. At the time, Damien had been about to start school, Vee had been a toddler and Niall had been in the pram. Tara had yet to make an appearance.

As much as Gus loved Limerick – and he would never hear a word against his home city – he loved Dublin more. He cherished the bustle, the noise, the craziness. He treasured the fact that you could spend a day walking past hundreds, no *thousands*, of people, and recognise not one face. But you might yet get to know these men and women; the promise was there. He rarely spoke about his feelings for his adopted home; it might sound disloyal, and Limerick people despised disloyalty.

The night before he'd called Damien and Vee about his plans for a family meeting. How they'd cribbed and moaned; you'd think he was asking them to climb Carrauntoohil in their bare feet. 'Seven thirty,' Gus had said, 'and I'll take a dim view if you're not there.'

Afterwards he had gone downstairs to talk to Tara, who was wrapped up in an old dressing gown, her eyes glassy, her nose pink. 'Hay fever,' she'd explained. 'Hay fever, my backside,' he'd wanted to say. It was clear she had been crying. A pound to a penny the boyfriend was to blame. Unfortunately, Craig had been sitting on the other end of the sofa, so Gus held his tongue.

In front of him now was a mound of paper. He knew that these days he was considered a bit of a relic. 'Gus and his paper records,' his colleagues would say with a smirk and a sympathetic shake of the head. But, as he never tired of telling them, he was proud to be old school. 'School of hard knocks,' he would say. 'Never did me any harm.' Oh, he could reel off all the clichés about old dogs and hard roads. He enjoyed ribbing the youngsters. He enjoyed being the boss.

His tastes were irredeemably old-fashioned too. Gus liked it when the singer hit the note rather than warbled around it. He didn't believe that raw fish could be called a meal. He couldn't understand why pretty girls wore ugly shoes.

In his view, a lot of what was trumpeted as progress actually amounted to a step backwards. Take modern televisions: you pressed the button and they took forever to come alive. To his mind, they were no different to the televisions of the sixties and seventies, when you had to wait for the set to 'warm up'. 'Mark my words,' Gus liked to say, 'before we know it, we'll be thumping the top of the set to stop the picture from rolling.'

Nobody listened to him. Then again, they probably couldn't understand him. He certainly couldn't understand them. The previous week one of his younger employees had told him that it was – and this was an exact quote – 'hashtag pissing rain'. He was still trying to figure that one out. *What would I be like if I lived to eighty or ninety?* he wondered. Maybe he should take a few lessons from his mother. At eighty-six, she maintained her enthusiasm for life. 'You've got to understand,' she'd once said, 'I was an old woman at thirty-five. In those days we all were. I'm having a belated youth.'

Swivelling his chair around, Gus looked out onto the day. From his second floor window he had a perfect view of the perfect early summer scene. Women sauntered past, their pastel-coloured clothes fresh from the back of the wardrobe. The men, still trussed-up in winter suits, looked cross and uncomfortable.

A volley of knocks on the office door disturbed his wandering.

'Come in,' he barked before turning round. 'Ah Rory,' he said, his tone softening. Rory McNamara was the sharpest young accountant in the practice. It was hard to imagine him coming out with a phrase like 'hashtag pissing rain'.

'Sorry to be bothering you with this stuff, Gus,' he said. 'Only I've been going through the figures for Geraghty's Light Engineering, and they really are in serious grief.'

Gus nodded at Rory to sit down. God love the boy, but that was one cheap and nasty suit he was wearing. 'And?'

'I've a notion they'll go wallop any day now. The thing is,' he hesitated, 'they owe us a lot of money. And the chances of getting it . . . Well, you know yourself.'

The elder man leaned back and closed his eyes. 'I've been too lax, let too many people get away with too much.'

'What do you want me to do?'

Gus's eyes snapped open. 'I'll take care of it. I've a few things that need addressing. I'll add that one to the list.'

Tara would say this for Independent Dublin City Councillor Damien Shine: my, but he could talk. Her brother had vocal chords of steel and the confidence of a man who was accustomed to an audience. Damien had been addressing the journalists for ten minutes or more and, just then, he was at full throttle. One hand was in his jeans pocket, the other whipped through the air like he was herding cattle.

'Obviously,' he bellowed, 'the blame for this crime rests squarely with the thug who pulled the trigger. But, have no doubt, there are others who share the blame. I'm thinking especially of the authorities who have abandoned the people of this area. Who have turned decent citizens into the pawns of drug gangs. Who have kowtowed to the greed of builders and developers.'

Fearing that the running dogs of international capitalism would be next to get a lash, Tara switched off her tape recorder. She would throw a line from Damien into her story. Time was moving on, though, and she wanted to find some people who had known the dead youngster. First, she needed to have a quick word with her brother. She tried to catch his eye. As she did, she felt a sharp tug on the hem of her cardigan.

'I know him,' a child's voice said. 'The lad who got done.'

It was the little boy from the garda briefing.

'Do you now?' Tara said, part-horrified that so small a child should be caught up in this, part-amused by his bravado. Looking at his round blue eyes, she got the sense he was telling the truth. 'How did you know him?'

'Because he lives two doors down from my nan's flat. Redser Lynam's his name.'

She was struck by the way the boy kept referring to Redser, or whatever his real name was, in the present tense. 'And what's your name?' she asked.

'Ben. Ben O'Neill. I'm seven and a half.'

'Should you not be at school this morning, Ben?'

'Holy Day,' he said, without so much as a pause for breath. Tara couldn't rule out this possibility. She wasn't so hot on religious feast days.

'I'll show you his flat if you like,' Ben continued. 'Only, it'll cost you.'

She was tempted to smile. 'How much?'

He twitched his freckled nose and thought for a second or two. 'A hundred euro.'

'Well, Ben, unfortunately my boss won't allow us to pay our sources, even one as good as you.'

'Bummer,' he said, and turned to go.

'But,' added Tara, thinking all the while, 'I don't know if there's any rule against buying a boy an ice cream.'

'Hmmm.'

'And if you brought me to your nan's place now, the police wouldn't see you and they wouldn't go asking any questions about school or Holy Days or anything.'

Ben looked as though he was smart enough to understand that

he might not get a better deal. 'All right,' he said, a touch of disappointment in his voice, 'only there would have to be sweets as well as ice cream.'

'You're on,' said Tara. Another thought occurred to her. 'You do know how to get to your nan's flat, don't you?'

He gave her a stare that suggested she was the thickest woman on the planet. 'Duh, it's 426 St Monica's Mansions. That's where I live too. Me and my sister, Jenelle. She's four.' He hesitated. 'Will I be on the telly?'

'I'm afraid not. I work for a newspaper: the *Irish Tribune*.'

Ben looked confused. To begin with she assumed this was because he didn't know the *Tribune*. Then she realised he might not be sure what a newspaper was. 'I tell you what,' she said. 'When we go to the shop to get the ice cream, I'll show you my paper.'

'Oh, OK.'

'Will you come with me for a tick while I talk to this man over here?' She pointed towards Damien.

The boy looked her brother up and down. 'Is he a cop?'

'Nope,' she said. 'Just somebody I know.'

'You should tell him to get his hair cut.'

She smiled. 'That's what my mum says too.'

'All right, Tara?' said Damien as they strode towards him. 'Rough business, huh? I hope the *Tribune* will give it proper coverage, not relegate it to page eight like you usually do with stuff out this way.'

She rolled her eyes. 'Do you know any more about what happened?'

'Not much,' he said with a shrug. 'The poor kid was called Eric Lynam. Known as Redser, apparently. It seems he may have had an elder brother who got into trouble with a dealer.'

Ben gave Tara an 'I told you so' look. It was only then that Damien appeared to notice him. 'What's the story with the ankle-biter?'

'Work experience,' she replied, not wanting her brother to ask any further questions. That this was highly implausible didn't seem to occur to him. If he knew the truth, he'd drone on about child exploitation. To be fair to him, he was usually pretty good with kids. 'Anyway,' she said, 'what I really wanted was to talk to you about Dad. I gather he rang.'

'Mmmm. I told him I probably wouldn't be able to make it this evening. I've too much work on my plate.'

Tara sighed. When Damien was engaged in political matters, which was most of the time, it was hard to get him interested in anything else. 'I think it's serious. Like, I think something might be wrong with him.'

'What happened? He fall off his wallet?' He tittered at his own wit. 'I guarantee you, Tara, it'll be nothing of any importance. Maybe he's decided to retire and he wants to rabbit on about how shameful it is that none of his useless children are fit to run the family empire. Anyway, Niall won't be around to hear what he's got to say, so how serious can it be?'

'He might plan on getting Niall up on Skype or something.'

'This is Dad you're talking about. Two tin cans and a piece of string are more his level.'

'Very funny,' she said. 'I still think you should be there.' Beside her, Ben was throwing restless shapes.

Damien checked his watch. 'Got to go. I've a radio interview lined up.' He started to walk away. 'I'll see you if I see you.'

During the short journey to his grandmother's flat, Ben dropped his Holy Day pretence. While he retrieved his schoolbag from behind a cluster of bins, Tara concocted a story to explain how she'd come across him. 'You've got to promise me you'll go to school this afternoon,' she said. In response, Ben gave her a toothless grin and licked his multi-coloured monstrosity of an ice cream.

Along the way he chatted about his family. He lived with his nan, he said, because his mam was in Australia. 'She has a great job, but,' he added, 'and she'll be back soon for me and Jenelle.' Tara wondered whether this was really the case, then chided herself for her attitude. *Why shouldn't the little fellow be telling the truth?*

As they climbed the steps of his four-storey brown and white building, she spotted two gardaí – a sure sign they were heading in the right direction. Doubtless, another officer would be stationed at the Lynams' door, making sure that Tara and her colleagues didn't go bothering the family. Number 426 was on the top floor. It had a red door and thick net curtains. The door was slightly ajar, but she knocked anyway.

Almost instantly, a small, fine-boned woman with thin blonde hair appeared. A blue and white checked tea-towel hung over one arm. She peered down at Ben. 'What's he done?' she said to Tara. As an afterthought, she added, 'And who are you?'

Tara explained who she was and what she was doing. She'd met Ben walking home from school, she said. He was on his lunch break, and he'd been very helpful.

The woman didn't appear convinced. 'I'm Carmel. You'd better come in.'

Tara was perplexed. 'Ben told me he lived with his grand-mother. Is she here?'

Carmel tilted her head and fiddled with the tea-towel. 'That's me. Carmel O'Neill. Ben's my daughter's son.'

'I'm sorry. I . . .' Tara scrutinised the elfin woman in front of her. Her face was slightly pinched, and Vee would probably find fault with her muscle tone, but in her pink vest top and denim skirt, she didn't look old enough to be anyone's granny.

Ben had had enough of the doorstep shilly-shallying. 'That's my nan,' he said. 'Can we go in now? I need a glass of water. Ice cream makes me thirsty.'

Inside, the flat was immaculate but basic. It took Tara a couple of minutes to work out what was wrong. There were few family touches. Save for a doll-sized pink buggy and a plastic box containing an assortment of dinosaurs, there was little to tell you who lived here or what they did with their lives. The one other exception was a photograph on top of the television. It featured a slightly younger Ben – his baby teeth were intact – and a girl, who she presumed was Jenelle. The girl was thin and pale with wisps of white hair and a fearful expression. Next to her brother's healthy, cheer-filled face, she appeared almost ghostly.

'Go on into the kitchen, Ben, love,' said Carmel. 'Get a glass of water, wash your hands and I'll be with you in a mo.'

'That's not—' he started. His nan glared in his direction, and he scooted next door.

She switched her attention to Tara. 'I don't have a lot of time. I'll have to get his lunch and I've his sister to collect. What is it about Eric that you want to know?'

'A bit of background about his family, I suppose,' said Tara as she took her tape recorder from her bag.

Carmel confirmed that he had been thirteen. 'Massive for his age, mind. In the dark, you could easily have mistaken him for fifteen or sixteen. Not the brightest star in the sky either, the poor fella.' She'd heard that his sixteen-year-old brother, Warren, had stolen, then torched, a car belonging to a drug dealer. Rumour had it that there'd been money stashed in the car. 'Here, you won't be saying I told you this, will you?' she said.

'No, you're fine. Would you be able to give me your reaction to what happened, though? Or maybe you could say how local people feel about it? I'd need to be able to quote you on that.'

Carmel raked a hand through her hair while she considered her reply. 'All right,' she said. 'The way I see it is like this: killing a kid is disgusting, of course it is. But whatever I say is a waste of breath. Oh, for a day or two, the whole country will be on about it. Your lot will be swarming around here, and the papers will be full of stories about 'gangland', wherever that is. And politicians we've never seen before will be promising us the sun, moon and stars. By the weekend, though, you'll be gone, and the rest of us will have to go back to raising our boys and girls as best we can. And nobody will give a shit.' She paused. 'I'm sorry, love. Take the swearing out, would you?'

Tara squirmed with embarrassment. She couldn't challenge a

word that Carmel had said. 'Yeah, no problem. I . . .' She realised that Ben was standing at the door. Listening.

Registering her grandson's presence, Carmel gave a half-smile and nodded in his direction. 'Seven going on twenty-seven, that boy.'

'Seven and a half,' said Ben.

Tara switched off her recorder and got to her feet. 'What you've given me is a great help. I'd better leave you in peace.'

'Peace?' said Carmel. 'Chance'd be a fine thing. By the way, if you want to make yourself properly useful you should write about the state of these flats. For years the Corporation has been promising to fix the damp. *Years.*'

Tara plucked her notebook from her bag and tore out a page. 'If you give me your phone number, I can get back in touch. I could write something over the summer.'

Carmel wrote down her number.

'I'll call you,' Tara said.

'No you won't.'

As Tara crossed the courtyard, she stopped and looked back at the flats. Ben was standing on the landing, waving goodbye.

Chapter 3

By comparison with the bare walls of Carmel and Ben's flat, the Shine house was like a photographer's gallery. Weddings, christenings, communions, confirmations, graduations: the walls of the sitting room were a monument to the changing fashions of the past thirty-five years. There was Gus with ridiculous sideburns; here was Vee with straightened, highlighted hair; beside them was Niall, at the entrance to Trinity College, beaming like a thing let loose.

Tara's favourite photo was of her granny Phyllis – Gus's mother. It had been taken more than six years before at her eightieth birthday party. Phyllis's picture was like a snowy-haired version of the Laughing Cavalier; wherever you went her eyes followed. 'Art imitating life,' Gus would joke. Even now, she kept a close watch on her sons and daughters. And on her grandchildren.

Despite his posturing, Damien had shown up for the family meeting. As had Vee and Tara. Now they were cooling their heels, waiting for their parents. Damien and Vee, sitting side by side on the sofa, were taking the opportunity to play their favourite game: arguing. Usually their combat was mild. A little bit of niggling, a moderate amount of baiting, a few catty comments. Sometimes, however, they forgot when to stop, and the insults would grow in intensity until he began thumping the table, or she flounced out.

Vee tossed back her dark brown hair. 'All I said was, "You'd wonder what his parents were thinking – letting him out at that hour of the night." That's all. The way you're carrying on you'd swear I accused his mother of pulling the trigger.'

'It wasn't what you said. It was the way you said it, like he was some sort of lesser life form, like he'd had it coming.' Damien grunted. 'He was thirteen years old – still a child.'

'Spare us the amateur dramatics, would you, petal? You're not emoting for the TV cameras now. Anyway, I'm surprised we haven't got to the bit where you tell me it's all the government's fault.'

'Of course there's a link. It's all about how the government chooses to spend money – on communities like Eric's or on dead banks and the like. It's the same story the world over.'

'Oh, get over yourself,' said Vee. 'Why can't you just blame the scumbag who fired the gun?'

Around and around they went. Damien's certainty seemed as impenetrable as chainmail. Neither would Vee concede an inch. Tara never knew how much of this was posturing and how much was real. They were like method actors, immersed in roles they'd been playing since their teens. Although they made her head throb, she had more sense than to intervene. Instead, she thought about what she had been doing at thirteen: singing along with the Spice Girls, chain-reading Agatha Christie books, wishing her hair was any colour other than red.

'So what about you, Tara? Whose side are you on?' Damien was asking.

'I think you both have reasonable points to make,' she replied.

'You should know there's no point in asking Miss I-agree-with-everybody,' said Vee. 'You'd want to be careful out there in the middle of the road, Tara. One of these days, you'll get knocked down.'

Damien sniggered. At least she'd managed to unite them. It was a pity that Niall was away. With only eighteen months between them, they had always supported each other. But Niall was in Croatia, the latest stop on what felt like a never-ending world tour. He was the restless Shine, forever finding excuses to be anywhere other than home.

She had expected their dad to sweep into the room with great purpose. That's what he usually did. This evening was different.

Gus slouched in, with a distracted-looking Joan a step or so behind, a mug of tea in one hand. She sat in the farthest corner of the room. He flopped into his green chair.

For a short time they chatted about the weather and the news. Vee's high, fluttering laugh punctuated the conversation. So she was nervous after all. Tara said little. She tried to decipher her father's face, but it was inscrutable. By now she was convinced he was unwell. After work she'd spent half an hour googling cancers. Thyroid wasn't so bad, it seemed. Prostate, bladder, colon – these were manageable; lung, stomach, pancreas – not so much. Craig told her she was being silly, but Tara liked to be prepared. All these ideas swirling around her brain, she came close to missing what her dad was actually saying.

'You're probably wondering,' said Gus, 'what this is all about. Well, I won't do any beating about the bush. The news isn't good.'

Here we go, thought Tara.

'It's not catastrophic either, though. The problem is ... the money. It's no longer there.'

'What money, Dad?' she asked.

'*The* money. The cash, the income, the savings, the stuff that keeps us all afloat.'

The room lapsed into a puzzled silence. Tara knew she should be relieved. She should be happy that he wasn't sick. And yet, she couldn't quite grasp what he was telling them. She was caught in one of those strange, uncomfortable moments where she had to keep reminding herself that this was real and this was now. Letting her mind drift was not an option. She looked towards her mum, but Joan's gaze was rooted to the floor. She was studying the carpet like its Persian flowers and motifs held the secrets of the universe.

'I'm sorry, I'm not with you,' said Vee, who never shied from the blunt question. 'Are you saying the business is in trouble? And, if it is, why didn't you tell us before now? Why are we only finding out today?'

Gus bristled. 'To be fair, Vee, you've never shown any great interest in the accountancy game. I recall that when I did try to involve you, I was told you didn't want your head wrecked by "all those boring numbers". That accounting was for nerds and people who didn't have the imagination to do anything else.'

'Oh for pity's sake, Dad, I must have been nineteen when I came out with that.'

Joan intervened. 'Your dad and I . . . we didn't want to worry any of you. It wasn't like you could have done anything about the situation. And we kept hoping things would get better.'

'Have you gone bust?' said Vee. 'Will you be all over the news?' Her tone suggested that she found this second possibility more upsetting.

'Do you know, I hadn't thought of that,' said Gus, his voice heavy with sarcasm. 'No, it's . . . it's more complicated. We haven't gone to the wall. And, if I have anything to do with it, we won't either.'

Joan resumed her examination of the floor. Vee cleaned one manicured nail with another, while Damien picked at an imaginary hole in his jeans. Tara decided it was up to her to say something reassuring.

'Um, we're all really sorry to hear this, Dad.' She glanced at her brother and sister for affirmation but they continued with their fidgeting. 'But, I think we're a wee bit surprised. I suppose we figured . . . well, I figured . . . that if you'd got this far without shipping any serious damage then the firm must be OK. I mean, isn't everything supposed to be getting better?' Her voice sounded odd. It was too insubstantial somehow.

'Only for a small few,' mumbled Damien.

Tara ignored him. 'How much trouble is the business in?' she asked.

Gus leaned back into his chair, like he was drawing comfort from its scruffy green fabric. 'Ah, there's the thing,' he replied. 'It's not just the company I have to worry about. There's more to it than that. Now, I'm going to be on the level here, but I don't want any of the details to go further than this room.'

Vee raised an eyebrow.

'Tell Ferdia, of course. And Felicity,' he said, nodding at Damien.

It was Tara's turn to make a funny face.

'Oh, and I suppose Craig will have to know too. Only that's it. No blabbing about the town, or gossiping or moaning. We'll handle this our way.'

'By which you mean your way,' said Damien.

Gus looked like he was about to fire a caustic comment in his son's direction. He must have thought better of it, though, for all he did was clear his throat.

'To give you the full picture,' he said, 'I need to go back a bit.' He paused. 'For years, money was easy to come by, and the more you had the more you made. And, like everybody else, I came to believe that this was the way life was meant to be. The natural order of things, if you like.

'Then, I began to notice small differences. Clients um-ing and aah-ing about paying bills. Fellows who always stumped up on time asking for another couple of months. So I became more diligent. I scrutinised more accounts and thought hard about the numbers in front of me. I saw that everybody was in hock; up to their tonsils in debt. One bad month was all it would take for them to fall over the edge.'

Vee sighed. It was a sigh that said, 'We've heard all this a million times before. Hasn't it been on the radio every blessed day for the past five years?'

'Anyway,' said Gus, 'the next I knew, clients were bargaining with us, giving me the full rigmarole about hard times and cutting costs. And, to begin with, I argued back. "A job's a job," I said. "We agreed a price." On and on it dragged until finally their business was no more. The bill had never been paid, and all I'd done was waste time and money pursuing people for cash that wasn't there.'

Tara realised that her dad wasn't looking at any of them. He was addressing the painting of a racehorse that hung on the far wall.

'So, I took this on board,' he said. 'I kept a close watch on every account, and convinced myself that the fellows who'd gone bust were the flaky cases; the guys who should never have been running a business in the first place.

'For a long time, we rolled with it. I discovered there was no point in me giving anybody the poor mouth. People had too many problems of their own. Worse, they somehow imagined I was immune to the crash. "Sure weren't you around in the eighties, Gus? Weren't those times way worse? We hadn't an arse in our trousers. And aren't we still here?" They repeated those lines like a mantra.'

Tara feared he was about to get emotional. 'It's all right, Dad,' she said.

'Hear me out, lovey, would you?' Gus shifted slightly in his chair. 'When the situation showed no sign of improving, I knew other measures were called for. "We'll lay people off," I said. Except I looked around and most of the staff had been with me since God was a boy. Even if I'd had the heart to let them go, it would have set me back a fortune. And the youngsters? They cost half nothing anyway. They're only dying for the work. For them it's a case of take this job at half the boom-time salary, or feck off to Australia.

'Next, I found myself saying, "I'll shut an office. That's it." Only which office? And at what cost? Because of the way our leases are arranged, I'd still have had to pay the rent. So another plan bit the dust.

'In the meantime, the number of clients continued to dwindle. Every day of the week, someone else went out of business. And even the long-established ones, the guys I reckoned were safe, were demanding discounts, threatening to bring their business elsewhere. "There's a fellow out in Swords," they'd say, "operates from his mammy's box room. He'll do the books for a couple of hundred euro." What could I do, only drop the price? Then they were asking us to do tricky stuff. Not smart tricky stuff, but half-arsed schemes that would've had the taxman on their case in no time. The thing is, though, when people are in a panic, they won't listen to reason. When we wouldn't play ball, they were off to the fellow in Swords or some other chancer.'

Gus released a long sigh, like the weight of his worries was pressing hard on his chest, squeezing out all the air. He scanned the room. Presumably he was expecting Vee or Damien or Tara to say something. But they were quiet, grappling with the implications of his words. The air of confusion that had engulfed the room was being replaced by something else. Perhaps it was fear. Outside, the sun was setting, its violent crimson colour promising another fine day.

Finally, Joan spoke. 'Go on, pet,' she said.

'So, that's where we were,' said Gus. 'Chasing our tails, working flat out, losing money, losing clients, but muddling along.' He paused. 'That's when I started to take risks.'

Although it might have been her imagination, Tara thought there was a slight hesitancy to his voice, like it might break.

'Oh, I'd heard every joke about Gus Shine still having his communion money. Mr Canny – that was me. Never lose the cool. Never gamble. Or, if you do, don't be flash about it. The problem was, that philosophy was no longer paying dividends. I figured this was the time for the ballsy guys to come to the fore, pick a few investments, make a quick killing and move on. Only . . . it didn't work out that way. Every investment turned out to be dicier than the one before, the company was haemorrhaging cash, and every bet I placed was a loser.' This time, there was a definite break in his voice. 'And that brings us to today. The business is in a bad way. This house is mortgaged from top to bottom. And our savings are wiped out.'

An awkward hush followed. A minute or more passed before Vee spoke. 'But what does this *mean*?' she asked. 'Like, why are you telling us now? It's not as if we can do anything. None of us have any money.'

Damien nodded. 'My earnings as a councillor are tiny.'

'Believe me,' replied Gus, as deadpan as you like. 'I'm well aware of that.'

'Anyway,' continued Damien, 'you should've had more sense than to go gambling on stock markets or whatever. Those things are pure evil. They're for the stupid and the greedy. Even if you'd come out on top, the money would have been tainted.'

Tara dug her nails into the soft part of her palms. Sometimes Damien forgot that not every gathering needed to be addressed like a public meeting, or a session of the city council.

Joan glared at her firstborn. 'Funny how your principles have never stopped you from taking your father's money.' Almost immediately, as though she regretted her candour, her gaze returned to the floor. Damien's jaw appeared to loosen, but he said nothing.

We're doing what we always do, thought Tara. When they were together, they had an instinctive need to be difficult; to get each other's backs up; to say something that was guaranteed to irk someone else. In other company, they were all more flexible, less argumentative. She wondered if every family was the same.

'What are you going to do, Dad?' she asked.

'I think, Tara, it's more of a case of what are *we* going to do?' He was on his feet now, stalking to and fro. 'I haven't got everything worked out, but the way I see it is like this: if a client came to me, and he was staring into the abyss, what advice would I give? I'd say to him, "Cut costs. Slash and burn. Every last cent you can save, save it. No favourites. No sentimentality. Otherwise you'll end up like the rest of them, parading in and out of the courts, desperately trying to hold on to some part of what you thought was yours."'

'I'm still not with you,' said Vee. 'You've already told us you tried to cut costs at Shine and Co., and it didn't work.'

'I'm going to be more ruthless. That's only part of the story, mind.' He stopped pacing and rested his hands on the back of the green chair. He looked at his wife, his son and daughters. 'The way I see it, we're all in this together, and the cuts will have to begin here. I've been going through my outgoings. You could run a handy-sized country on what this family spends. The amount of money going out every month? It's nothing short of obscene. That stops today.'

'But—' started Vee.

'Oh shush, Veronica, would you?' said Joan, who was gripping her mug so tightly that her knuckles had turned white.

Tara blanched. The use of her sister's full name was rarely a good sign.

The sun had dipped below the horizon, and the five were motionless in the gloom. The room was perfectly quiet. An austere cast to his face, Gus reached into the pocket of his grey suit trousers and plucked out a folded sheet of paper. As it unfurled, Tara realised she was holding her breath.

'I have a list here,' he said, 'of suggested cutbacks. No, let's be blunt, they're not suggestions. Starting this evening, I intend to implement every single measure on this list.'

Chapter 4

Niall Shine was halfway up the street when he paused to look back towards the harbour. The hill on the other side of the water – Srd it was called – had turned pink, every building, every space reflecting the glow of the setting sun. He stood there, ignoring the noise: the giddy kids, the shrieking teenage girls, the puttering rasp of a scooter. For five minutes or more, he inhaled the beauty. Then, beach towel thrown over one shoulder, flip-flops slapping against his heels, he meandered towards his apartment.

Niall had been in Dubrovnik for three weeks, and so far everything was ticking along nicely. A bit more company might be welcome, but usually he was careful not to form strong attachments. In his experience, when you got to know people too well, they expected you to behave in a certain fashion. They thought you should answer your phone, reply to your e-mails, attend their social rituals. To Niall, this all sounded like hard work. And he was not a man for unnecessary work. Keep on moving was his motto.

The snag was that most people, especially his family, didn't understand. The previous Christmas when he had spent ten days at home, he'd had to endure a stream of jibes from his old man, culminating in a lecture about him being 'a bit old for traipsing around the world like a tool'. His brother Damien, a man who would cross the street to be offended, had joined in. 'Real life isn't like *The Beach*, you know,' he'd sneered. 'A good job too,' Niall had replied. 'I'm not sure I'd be able to handle all those sharks and machetes. Damn fine book, though.' He had left for Rajasthan the following day.

The bust-up with his father had been a shame. Gus was a decent sort, even if the 'we had it hard in my day' speeches had become tedious. Damien? He was a monumental pain in the arse.

In so much as he had a plan, Niall planned on spending the summer in Europe. Here, in Croatia, would do for a while. The weather was pleasant, the women were top class and his family owned the apartment so the lodgings were free. There was half a chance a stray aunt or two might appear at some stage. Around here was elderly aunt heaven; they could top up their tans as well as seeking a few indulgences at the shrine in Medjugorje. Actually, 'aunt' was a rather loose term for the women in question, since half of them weren't relations at all. They were contemporaries of his mum who, at some point, had succumbed to the lure of religion (Joan had no such weakness). The previous year, one had told him how cable television was transforming her life. 'Imagine,' she'd said, 'there's a channel where you can watch several masses in the one day.' In the main, though, they were grand women. Indeed, if one or more of them turned up over the coming weeks, he'd be happy to do the dutiful nephew routine.

There was another reason for sticking closer to home. A few days previously he'd received an e-mail from his sister Tara, who was all het up about their dad. 'There's a problem. I can feel it,' she had written. In the unlikely event she was right – Tara was an Olympic-grade worrier – Niall was within striking distance of Dublin.

It was with these (mostly-cheerful) thoughts in his head that he climbed to the first-floor apartment. Theirs was a modern low-rise building with a white facade and cream-tiled landings. When he reached the top of the stairs, Niall did a double-take. The door was swinging open. So much for all the stories he'd heard about this being as safe a place as you'd find. He was being burgled! And more than that, he was going to catch them in the act, for he could hear somebody talking. For several seconds he listened. There was only one voice. Male. It sounded like he was on the phone.

Ordinarily, Niall would have had no reservations about tackling an intruder. He was, after all, an experienced world traveller. A man who had been shark-diving in South Africa, who had backpacked through western Pakistan *on his own*, who had survived a bout of typhus in Borneo. Such a man would not be fearful of a Dubrovnik burglar. What he lacked, however, was weaponry. No sane person would go into battle with a beach towel, a pair of damp togs, a half-eaten cheese sandwich and a slightly soggy paperback. He decided to knock.

'Uh, hello there,' he hollered. '*Dobra večer*, even.'

No answer came. In fact, he was pretty sure the intruder was still on the phone. Bracing himself for confrontation, he took a hesitant step forward. 'How are you doing? Niall here. *Govorite li Engleski?*' Again, there was no answer. He inched into the hall. *Stay in by the wall*, he told himself, *and you'll be fine*. It was at this point that he saw his enemy. A giant of a man with a dark crewcut and a navy business suit, he was standing in the middle of the kitchen. In one hand he held a mobile phone; in the other, he carried a tape measure. He gave Niall a careful once-over before waving his tape measure hand, as if to say, 'Give me a minute'. Then he returned to his phone conversation.

This was one laidback, and unusually dressed, burglar. In other circumstances, Niall might even have admired his chutzpah. But, when all was said and done, the guy had broken into the apartment. 'Eh, hello?' he said. 'I think we need to talk about a couple of things – like, what you're doing in *my* kitchen.'

Tape-measure man gestured again, more impatiently this time.

'Ah here,' said Niall, 'get off the phone, would you?'

With that, the intruder muttered some hurried words and hung up. 'Yes? How can I help?' he asked.

'You could start by telling me who you are and what you're doing in my gaff.'

'Your gaff?'

'My apartment, flat, whatever. You know, the place you've just broken into? I hope you didn't damage the lock. The old fellow will go spare.'

The intruder knitted his luxuriant eyebrows while he gave Niall a further examination. 'Tomislav Kovac is my name, and I'm here to sell this property. According to my measurements it comes to seventy-three square metres. And the condition, I'm glad to report, is excellent.'

Niall dumped his bag and towel on the floor. 'Woah, boss, hold on a second. Nobody's buying or selling anything.'

'That's where you're wrong, my friend.' He pulled out his wallet from an inside pocket and removed a business card. It confirmed that he was an estate agent, the managing director no less, of a firm called Kovac and Kovac.

'Just because you're in the business, it doesn't mean you can march into somebody's house and sell the place. There are laws, you know,' said Niall, who grew more bewildered by the second.

'You seem to be under some misapprehension,' replied Mr Kovac. 'I have the keys for this property. They were given to me on behalf of a Mr Gus Shine – an Irish gentleman, I believe. I've been instructed to sell the apartment, and while I wait to do so, I'm to put it up for rent.'

The wind taken from his sails, Niall stayed quiet.

'So, forgive me for being confused,' continued Mr Kovac, a smile on his face. 'But where do you fit into this picture?'

A bead of sweat trickled down Niall's spine. 'That,' he said, 'is a very good question.'

Although the light was almost gone, Gus stood by the window, watching his son and daughters leave. He had hoped the evening's news would bring them together, but they lingered just briefly by the gate, before going their separate ways.

Had they been close as children? Closer than this, certainly. Even though each of them had been determined to assert their difference from the others, they had walked to school together, played together, enjoyed holidays together. OK, they'd squabbled, but isn't that what children do? Gus didn't reckon that any one event had soured their relationship. Rather, they had drifted apart. *Drift*, he thought: *the enemy of us all*. He had stressed that they were all in this together, but he wasn't sure they understood.

From his vantage point, he studied their reactions. As usual, Tara was the most transparent. One hand pulled at her hair; the other was clenched into a fist. He guessed that her brain was working overtime. Damien was harder to pin down. The boy had perfected an air of indifference, acting as though even the gravest family matters were too trivial to arouse his passions. Still, Gus saw that his son's shoulders were hunched, like he was sheltering from a storm. And there was Veronica – beautiful, brittle Veronica, gliding down the street in a trance-like state, her face preoccupied, her movements slow.

In the kitchen, Joan was doing what she always did during times of crisis: making tea and toast.

'You'll have a cup,' she said. 'You must be parched.'

Gus was about to answer when he surprised himself by wrapping his arms around his wife. He kissed the crown of her chestnut head, breathing in the apple scent of her shampoo. She was continuing to hold back the grey and she was right. As you got older, people treated you differently. They found a thousand ways to categorise and patronise you. He hated the idea of anyone treating Joan like that.

'Well?' she asked as they pulled apart.

'I suppose it could have been worse. Or perhaps I'm kidding myself.'

'I'm not sure the full implications have sunk in yet.' Joan sat down and bit into her toast. She had small, sharp teeth.

He nodded. 'When Damien and Vee get home, though, when they have time to think and to talk, it'll hit them then.'

'And Tara?'

He let the milky tea wash down his throat. 'I'd say she was the most upset. Mind you, she was probably the only one who gave a second's consideration to anyone other than herself.'

'Ah, Gus.'

'You can "ah Gus" me all you like, love. I'm telling the truth.'

'Speaking of Tara, did you have to be so snide about Craig? Making it sound as if this was none of his business. He's as entitled to know as Ferdia and Felicity.'

Gus took another mouthful of tea. 'I remember, a year or two back, hearing a soccer manager being asked why he wouldn't give his opponents the name of the team before the match. "Give them the name of the team?" he said. "If it was up to me, they wouldn't get the time of the kick-off." That's how I feel about the lad downstairs.'

Joan gave him a flinty stare. Craig was one of the few topics on which they disagreed. It wasn't that she was overly keen on him, but in her view they had to accept that he was Tara's choice. Gus had tried. Truly he had. But he couldn't fathom someone as bright as his younger daughter wasting her time on someone so . . . he struggled for the right word. *Insubstantial*: that was it. Craig was a lightweight. The first sign of trouble and he'd melt away like the wicked witch in *The Wizard of Oz*.

Gus raised an eyebrow. 'Right enough, there's nothing wrong with the boy . . . well, nothing that wouldn't be cured by a good kick up the backside.'

He chuckled as he spoke. He glanced at his wife, expecting her face to grow flintier. Instead, he saw mirth in her eyes. She tried to suppress her laughter, but it broke free, rising up from her throat like a cat's purr. He joined in. His laugh was deep and raucous. For a minute, they were convulsed.

'This is hysteria. I'm sure it is,' said Joan, as she spluttered to a halt.

Gus smudged away a tear. 'Either that or sheer badness. We're definitely going down below – laughing at a time like this.' He reached across the old-style wooden table and squeezed her hand. Joan squeezed back. Both knew that this was only a momentary respite, that the anxiety and guilt would return tenfold.

'Throw on another slice of a toast, would you,' he said.

In the hall, the telephone started to spew out those ugly sounds that phones make nowadays: a discordant symphony of beeps and bells.

'You can put it on yourself,' she replied. 'I'll see who that is.'

He got up and slipped two thick pieces of bread into the toaster. Then he stood at the door, eavesdropping on a one-sided conversation. 'Yes,' Joan was saying. 'I'm sure it was,' she soothed. 'You're not serious, pet,' she added, her voice rising a notch. Gradually, Gus realised that it was Niall on the phone. He should have called his younger son earlier in the evening.

Some time passed before Joan returned. Placing her hand over the mouthpiece, she handed him the phone. 'It's Christopher Colombus,' she said. 'You'd better talk to him. He's in a wee bit of a flap. It seems the estate agent in Dubrovnik jumped the gun.'

Ideally, Tara would have liked an hour on her own. She needed time to digest her dad's revelations, and space to unpick her thoughts. Craig, however, was making an all-out effort to atone for the previous night's chippiness. This explained why she was lolling on the sofa while her boyfriend massaged her feet.

Since the crash, Tara had become accustomed to spectacular falls from grace. For a while, every week had brought new tales of the journey from rags to riches and back to rags again. She had reported on many of them, and had spoken to the friends and foes of former tycoons. Often, this was a thankless task. Friends tended to regard you as a modern-day Madame Defarge, the type of person who revelled in the misfortunes of the previously prosperous. Enemies wanted you to go in harder. To draw blood.

Never had she expected her own family to become part of this national saga. Thankfully, they were unlikely to feature on the television news or to attract the attention of the Sunday tabloids. The story was too small-scale. But their lives were going to change.

'Rent,' Craig was saying, as he pressed hard on her big toe. 'How much rent?'

'The market rate, he said. For a furnished two-bedroomed apartment around here, that's about eighteen hundred euro a month.'

'You're having me on.'

'I wish I was. On top of that, there'll be all the bills. Electricity. Gas. Bins. Cable TV. Broadband. Our share of the property tax. It's quite a list.'

Craig stopped his kneading. 'Is he mad? We can't afford that.'

We can't, thought Tara, *but I can*. Plainly, this was not something she could say. 'He pointed out that we're adults, and that he's no longer in a position to subsidise us. He said we need to ask ourselves whether we can afford to live in a neighbourhood like this. If not, he'll have to get tenants who can. Or, he suggested we let out the spare room and get some of the cash that way.'

'Oh, wonderful, a gang of strangers rambling about the place. Wouldn't that be fantastic?' said Craig.

She swung her legs off of the sofa. 'You should have seen him. He's devastated. Wrecked. There's no other way – that's what he kept saying. And Mum is crushed too. Most of the time she couldn't even look me in the eye.'

'All right, I hear you,' he replied, clearly anxious to avoid another argument. 'When does this regime kick in?'

'Um, now?' said Tara, the statement sounding more like a question.

He pressed his fingers against his temples. 'Jee-sus.'

'It could be worse,' she said. 'Imagine being in Vee's position. Or Damien's. I don't know how they'll cope.' She was searching for a diplomatic way of saying that she would pay the bills. For a small while, at least. Although Tara had endured a couple of pay cuts, she had squirrelled away sufficient cash to get them through the next four or five months. The words were taking shape in her mouth when she realised it was time for the late news. 'I hope you don't mind,' she said as she switched on the TV. 'I'd better see if there've been any developments in the story I was covering today. The dead child, you know?'

'Yeah, cool,' said Craig, who seemed relieved to be taking a break from the rent discussion.

There were no developments. Everybody was flailing around, trying to find an appropriate response. There was a weary predictability about the script, like the reporter had run out of ways to describe bad news. As they watched, the screen filled with images of the spot where Eric had been murdered. By now the site was buried beneath a carpet of flowers and toys. The shots cut to the police briefing. The officer looked even more beaten-down than Tara remembered. Her own hand was at the left of the screen, holding out her battered tape recorder.

Then she spotted him. She picked up the remote control and rewound the pictures. Ben was at the edge of the reporters' scrum, standing on tippy-toes, trying to follow proceedings. She smiled and pointed at him.

'There's my friend,' she said.

'Sorry?'

'Ben. He was my assistant.'

'What did he do – offer to hotwire a car for you?'

'Craig!'

'Try to sell you some knock-off fireworks?'

'You're an awful messer. He was a topper of a kid. A real help.' Tara told him about her morning. She sensed his attention was elsewhere.

In the corner, the television flickered, bathing the room in blue light. When she refocused, the report had moved on. Politicians, including Damien, were giving their reaction. Unlike Vee, Tara was tolerant of her brother's politicking. Surely he wouldn't get so agitated about all those causes unless he genuinely did care? She only wished he had some empathy left over for his own family.

She was lost in these thoughts when Craig kissed her cheek. 'I've been thinking about your father's news,' he said. 'Don't take this the wrong way, but you could see it as a positive development. For us, I mean – not for him. Obviously not for him.'

'How do you work that one out?'

'First off, he's not sick. From the way you were carrying on earlier I was convinced the man was facing imminent death from a combination of Ebola and the Spanish flu.'

'A slight exaggeration.'

He rubbed her arm. 'And it was very sweet ... the way you were so worried. But now we have an opportunity.'

'We do?'

'We can't afford the rent on this place, not long-term at any rate. We'd be throwing money away.'

'I wouldn't put it quite like that,' said Tara, a sickly feeling in her stomach. She didn't like how this was going.

'Seriously, babe, we'd be doing Gus and Joan a favour if we moved out. That way they'd be able to charge full whack for the apartment.'

'Well—'

'And rather than wasting whatever money we have renting some dingy kip in Dublin, we could go travelling.'

Craig's face was swallowed up by a satisfied beam. Tara's head churned. *How*, she thought, *am I going to tell him? How am I going to say that my dad's troubles make it even* less *likely I'll go away?*

She smiled a polite smile and prayed that her eyes didn't reveal the truth. 'You could be right,' she said. 'You could be right.'

Chapter 5

Vee was talking to the radio again. And who would blame her? Some of the people who rang the talk shows were so irritating. Coming on with their hard-luck stories. Pretending they weren't looking for anything when really they were angling for a cheque to wipe away all their worries.

'You don't fool me,' she said. 'And if you can't afford to look after all those children, why did you have them in the first place?'

The day after the shooting, the radio and television were convulsed with stories of children like Eric 'Redser' Lynam. People from the flats spoke about how hard it was to keep teenagers on the straight and narrow. Even if you raised a good kid, they said, some low-life could come along and take him away. There were drugs everywhere. And not just heroin; youngsters were taking pills and cocaine and this crystal meth stuff that you could make in the bath. And there was no funding for anything. No money for playgrounds or community schemes or youth clubs.

Vee wasn't able for any more. 'Guess what?' she said to the radio. 'Life is officially unfair.' Then she unplugged the blasted machine and put it in the bin. She would rescue it later. She always did.

The newspapers too were filled with reports about Eric and the thugs who might have killed him. Journalists gave the criminals ludicrous titles, like 'The Rhinoceros' and 'The Generator'. A while back, Tara had explained that while everybody knew who these men were, the papers were scared to use their real names. 'Legal reasons,' she'd said. This made no sense to Vee. 'If the police know who they are,' she'd asked, 'why don't they arrest the toe-rags and put them in jail?' Her sister had insisted that it wasn't that simple. Her husband said something similar, except his explanation was three times as long and obscured by courtroom jargon.

Tara was on the front page of the *Irish Tribune*. Her by-line photo was as cringe-making as ever; a quick look, and you'd think the girl was a first-cousin of Worzel Gummidge. Her hair was at its explosion-in-a-mattress-factory worst, and her eyes were all squinty and confused. 'I had a sinus infection,' she'd said when Vee had tackled her. 'Anyway, what does it matter? People don't buy the paper to gawp at me.'

Patiently, the elder sister had pointed out that unless Tara got her act together she was never going to be on the television. Tara had replied that she'd no great desire to be on the telly. 'Tuh,' Vee had said. '*Everybody* wants to be on the telly.' Her sister had shrugged before wittering on about some fascinating series she was writing. Knowing Tara, it was probably about local government reform or fish quotas or septic tanks. In Vee's considered judgement, the more attractive you were, the more life had to offer. She remembered her first PR company boss saying that when faced with two equally well-qualified applicants, he would always give the job to the better-looking woman. That was how the world worked, he said, and there was no point in fighting it.

Oh, what am *I doing?* she thought. *A city creaking with discontent, my own family in turmoil, and all I can worry about is my sister's hair.* Truth to tell, there was a great deal more on her mind. Experience had taught her, however, that when the going got tough, her brain sought refuge in the superficial.

Vee wasn't proud of how she'd behaved the night before. Shock at her parents' money woes had made her sound snippy and selfish. She recalled Joan's sagging shoulders and her tight, worried mouth. She thought, too, of Gus's flat eyes and the way his corrugated hair had appeared to grow whiter by the minute. She remembered all of this, and she felt wretched.

It had been during her walk back to Mount Pleasant that the full implications had sunk in. A noise like someone stamping on dry twigs had gone off in her head. *Snap, snap, snap*, it went. By the time she reached home, Vee had been disconsolate. For a few seconds she stood and admired her house: the spotless white front, the green Georgian door topped by a stained-glass fanlight, the glossy black railings. It wasn't a very big home: one of the bedrooms was a glorified cupboard and the back garden was barely worth mentioning, but Vee and Ferdia had lavished so much time and money on the place that she couldn't imagine anywhere else feeling so special. They'd been lulled into thinking of it as their own, and now they would have to face the truth: Gus had stumped up the deposit, Gus paid the mortgage. To all intents and purposes it was his property, and he wanted it back. Or, at the very least, he wanted his daughter and son-in-law to start paying their way.

Before going in, she tried to compose herself. Ferdia had spotted her, however, and was waiting at the door. He guessed the news was bad.

'It's your dad, isn't it?' he said. 'What's wrong?'

For what felt like an age, she barely said a word. Just blubbed like a child, fat tears spilling down her face. Her husband held her, rubbing his hands up and down her back. 'What is it, darling?' he kept saying. 'Is it cancer? Or his heart? You've got to remember that old Gus is a sturdy character, Vee. He'll come through this.' Still she wept, until Ferdia reminded her that the mobile phone launch was taking place the following evening. 'You wouldn't want a swollen face for that, would you?' he said. She did her best to stop, and slowly, carefully, she told him what had happened.

'No money *at all*?' he asked.

Her head swayed from side to side. 'Not a cent,' she sniffled.

'But . . . my earnings . . . and your earnings . . . we . . .'

He paused, and Vee guessed he was swallowing what he'd been about to say. Ferdia was scared to voice the truth. Between them, they didn't earn enough to pay for the house and everything else as well. It was then that any concerns about puffy cheeks and red eyes evaporated. Vee surrendered to her sorrow and wailed like a feral cat. Poor Ferdia sat there in his barrister's pin-stripe while she wept all over him.

Now she regretted her meltdown. Seventeen hours on, she was a crumpled wreck. She was sitting in their kitchen – their *exquisite* kitchen with the white marble island and the gleaming work-tops. An icy muslin cloth covered her face. Fingers crossed the cloth would work its magic and she would look normal for her big evening. Shortly, she would have to get ready: put on one of her new dresses, paint her face, seize her clipboard and become calm, efficient Veronica.

She was convinced that the other three would muddle through. Tara was resilient and, more importantly, she was thrifty. Moving into a cupboard in some far-flung suburb wouldn't cost the girl a thought. Craig was unlikely to be so enthusiastic, but he'd live. Knowing Niall, he wouldn't notice that anything was amiss until the money stopped arriving. He'd have to give up the good life and go back to earning a living. All the same, he'd had his fun. And Damien? Their dad's predicament might put a minor dent in his do-goodery, but his wife would revel in the extra austerity. As it was, Felicity was a terror for all activities cheap and alternative. She was the type of woman who would knit her own underwear and wash her hair in nettles and rainwater before taking a sinful amount of pleasure in informing you of her superiority.

No, it was Vee who would bear the brunt of the Shine family's straitened circumstances. Ferdia, bless his heart, had been brilliant last night. Repeatedly he had assured her that they would find a solution. This hadn't prevented him from tossing and turning until the small hours. She was lucky to have him; she knew that. Everybody remarked on how well-suited they were. 'As close as lips and teeth,' her mum liked to say.

Vee removed her muslin mask and peered into the mirror she had propped up on the kitchen counter. She still looked rough.

She wondered whether her husband would be so kind if he knew the full scale of her debts. How much did she owe? To be frank, she wasn't sure. What she did know was that her lifestyle was ruinously expensive. Credit cards, debit cards, store cards, short-term loans, longer term-loans: you name them, she had them. She'd spent the past several years robbing Peter to pay Paul. If any of the lenders got shirty, she would scramble together a payment and send it their way. Lately, though, she'd been getting worried. She'd even thrown the odd unpleasant-looking letter in the bin. And this was despite regular support from Gus and Joan. Now her supply line had been cut. She was a junkie who'd lost her dealer.

And then there were the parking fines. Oh Lord, the parking fines.

Vee's eyes began to well up again. *Stop it*, she said to herself. *You have a job to do this evening.* For a few hours, she would have to shunt her problems to the back of her mind.

The first time Tara saw Rory she knew one thing: he worked for her father. The look was unmistakable. They all had eager faces, wore cheap suits and walked like they were out in the fields inspecting livestock. This guy's hair was a dull Irish brown – the sort of hair that could be grey it looked so flat and lifeless.

He was walking down the steps of the family home. She was just back from work. It was a cracking evening with only the occasional puff of pink in a pale blue sky. The sweet smell of their neighbour's lilac tree hung in the air.

'How are you going on?' he said. 'Rory McNamara's the name.' He thrust out his right hand.

Tara introduced herself.

'Ah, the boss man's daughter. You have the look of him all right.' He smiled. 'In a good way, of course.'

Now that he was right in front of her, Tara noticed that Rory had two chicken-pox scars, bang-slap in the centre of his forehead. No doubt he was a pleasant guy – they usually were – but she wasn't in the mood for banter about her dad. She pulled her keys out of her pocket and rocked on her heels, as if to say, 'I've engaged in the social niceties, so I'll be off now.'

Rory failed to read his cue. 'I was dropping off some documents,' he explained. 'I was going to e-mail them, only you know your dad – he isn't overly fond of the old computer.'

Reluctantly, Tara realised she would have to engage. 'He's terrible. If it has a plug, a battery or a screen, he gets all fidgety. "Write it down, lovey, would you?"' she said, making an attempt at Gus's Limerick accent.

Rory laughed. 'He's down in Cork today, visiting the office there.'

The mention of the office gave Tara a jolt. Was her father telling them about his troubles? She wondered whether Rory was in the loop yet. She guessed not. He was too jaunty.

'He talks about ye all the time,' he was saying. 'You most of all.'

'That sounds worrying.'

'Nah, it's all positive. He even tells funny stories about the lad – Niall, is it? – who used to work in the place.'

Alone among the family, Niall had studied Business at college. He'd trained as an accountant, and Gus had been delighted to welcome him into the family business. He would talk openly about the future and about all they could achieve. Niall had other plans. Three tension-filled years later he moved on, leaving a trail of havoc and incompetence in his wake. He'd been gadding about the globe ever since.

'Poor Dad,' was all Tara said. She looked down at the pebbled path. 'Not a useful child among us.'

'Ah, here,' replied Rory, 'you can't be thinking like that.'

'Oh, I can,' she said.

Vee was feeling more buoyant. Not only was her mobile phone launch zinging along, she had a plan: she would get a job. She already had a job of sorts, except it was part-time. Very part-time. For the past four years she'd been working on a freelance basis for a woman called Aileen Duignan. Aileen and her sisters, Agnes and Annabel, had their own public relations business: Triple A PR.

Now and again Vee went into the office. Not as much as she should, she'd admit that, but those places sucked the life out of you. She was convinced they were bad for the skin. Besides, this was the twenty-first century; everything that needed to be done could be done from home. Still, as she kept telling herself, these were desperate times and desperate measures would have to be put on the agenda. She would offer her services to the Duignans. A solid full-time position, that's what she was after. Account Director level sounded about right. She had no desire to be stuck in one of those dreary jobs where all you did was put the staples in the press releases and fetch the coffee.

Aileen was an uppity cow, with a voice like a chainsaw and a badly-filled face. Seriously, whoever did her work should have their licence revoked. She was, however, the controller of the purse strings. And, as far as Vee could tell, business was picking up. Lately when she'd gone into the office she had felt a renewed buzz. New girls sat at new desks. And the little thing who'd been helping with this event claimed they were just *flying*.

Vee had her own theory about the current mania for filling in faces and smoothing out lines. She had studied Art History at UCD, and remembered discussions about how being fat and pale had once been an indicator of great wealth. Later, women had flaunted their money by being ultra-tanned and ultra-skinny. Now, she reckoned, the best way to display your wealth was by having the face of a twelve-year-old. The younger your appearance, the less you looked like somebody who had to toil for a living. A face without wrinkles suggested that work was merely a hobby, nothing to get stressed about. She'd said all of this to Ferdia, who'd pursed his lips and thought for a moment before replying, 'Or, maybe, it's just vanity.' He was a surprisingly funny man, her husband.

Looking around, she felt a tingle of satisfaction. The room she'd hired for the event looked stunning. Silver balloons floated overhead while the mobile phone images that decorated the walls were crisp and bright. The catering, alas, was only so-so. The white wine was lukewarm and the canapés were soggy. Given the paltry nature of her budget, however, she reckoned she'd done a more than reasonable job. The place was teeming with models and assorted beautiful people. A smattering of journalists lingered. Anything for a free drink, she supposed. There was even a chance that one or two of them might write a few lines about the product she was there to promote.

The models would definitely get their mugs in the *Evening Post*. One of them had tweeted about getting a new pair of shoes from her soccer-star boyfriend, and the rest were all over her. 'They cost *how* much?' one girl shrieked. 'Twelve hundred euro,' her friend replied. '*And* you can't buy them in Ireland. They're covered in gold sequins, like a Christmas decoration. It's a shame I can't walk in them.'

Vee was wearing a heavy coat of makeup and her hair was scraped back into a severe ponytail. She wasn't at her absolute best, but she would do. She had worn the shorter of her new dresses, figuring that if she displayed enough leg, nobody would notice her face. Now she feared she'd made the wrong decision. Perhaps the other dress would have been more businesslike. 'Businesslike' and 'serious': from here on in, these would be her buzz words.

Unfortunately her regime was getting off to an uncertain start. She kept forgetting the precise name of the phone. And as for the technical details – the hardware and software and apps and megapixels – those weren't her scene at all. Mercifully, a nice man from the company was on hand to answer questions about that sort of thing.

Vee was having a sneaky swig of wine when she saw Aileen sailing in her direction. The old dragon looked frightful. She was poured into a gaudy cerise suit that was at least two years out of date, and her shoes were *all* wrong. *Now, now,* Vee said to herself, *remember your buzz words; you can think about Aileen's woeful dress sense later.*

'There you are, Veronica. Looking frightfully smart as usual. Are you happy with tonight?'

Hell, thought Vee, *how do I answer that?* 'Oh gosh, yes, Aileen. Huge interest in the company and its products. A roaring success, I'd say.'

'Yes, as long as that interest and all this ... jollity ... translates into positive coverage. Column inches – that's what the client wants nowadays. Bang for their buck. Quality *and* quantity.'

Ordinarily Vee would have been playing cliché bingo in her head, but this was not the night for such frivolity. She tried to look impressed. 'Could I have a word? Out here if possible.' She gestured towards the adjoining room. It was quiet there.

'Make it a quick one, poppet, would you?'

'I promise you, this will only take a tick.' As they walked, Vee began her pitch. It wasn't an easy task. She needed to sound flexible but not woolly, enthusiastic but not desperate. They came to a standstill beside a burst balloon and a box of unused glasses.

'So correct me if I've got this wrong,' said Aileen, 'you're looking for work?'

'Um, yeah. I mean, yes, I am.'

The woman's next response wasn't especially reassuring; she whinnied with laughter. 'My dear, you can't imagine the number of girls – and, indeed, boys – who want to come and work with us. I could paper Liberty Hall with the CVs.'

'I'm sure you could, except I have experience. And you know me.'

Aileen's face suggested that this latter fact wasn't necessarily an advantage. 'Experience?' she squeaked. 'These kids have experience by the tonne. And qualifications? Oh me oh my, you should see them. First Class this and Grade A that. And the hilarious part is, most of them are willing to do the job for a pittance. Obviously I've been making the most of their skills. Never waste a good recession, that's my motto.'

There was a metallic taste in Vee's mouth. 'I wouldn't be expensive. Plus I have so many contacts. And—'

'I don't think so, dear. In fact, I've never been convinced that work is your forté.'

'But—'

'Listen, Veronica, I didn't plan on saying this tonight. But we – Agnes, Annabel and I – have decided we can't afford you any longer. Clients these days, they don't want glitz or swanky launches. That stuff is passé. We've entered a new era.'

'I thought the economy was on the up,' she replied, her voice sounding disgustingly needy. 'You know, corner turned, green shoots of recovery and such like.'

'Veronica, you don't get it, do you? It's time for you to move on. Pastures new await.' Aileen gave a sliver of a smile, but her tone was pure ice. 'By the way, I'm not doing anything illegal or untoward here. Our arrangement has been entirely freelance. We don't owe you anything.' She shifted slightly on her ugly stilettos, a sure sign the conversation was over. 'And we'll give you a more than acceptable reference.'

As Vee opened her mouth, a peal of laughter rang out from the function room. What she wanted was to go back in there. She wanted to shout, 'Do any of you have any idea how much money I owe?' Instead, she fixed her gaze on the woman who had just fired her.

'A word to the wise, Aileen,' she said. 'That suit may be acceptable for Ladies' Day at a country race meeting, but the boss of a PR company really should have more style. Mind you, I'm sure it must be difficult to get decent clothes in your size.'

Then she gathered up the remnants of her dignity and walked out into the night.

Chapter 6

Niall was roused from his sleep by the sound of high-speed Croatian. He reckoned one of the voices in the hall belonged to Mr Kovac. He reached over and retrieved his watch. Eight thirty. Good God almighty, did the man go to bed at all? He slipped into his shorts and T-shirt, released a generous yawn, and went to see what was going on.

'Ah, good morning, Niall,' said the estate agent. 'I have here three people who might like to rent the apartment. Good news, yes?'

'Depends on how you look at it,' he mumbled.

Tomislav Kovac was one fast mover. This was the fourth group to view the place. The first prospective tenants, a crotchety-looking couple, had dismissed the price as too high. The second lot, two lecturers from the nearby college, had been put off when they'd learnt that the apartment was for sale. They wanted a long-term rental, they said. The third group had consisted of three elderly women. Chances were they'd only been there for a nose around.

From what he could tell, these latest contenders were more serious. A young couple and their female friend, all three were from up north and had moved to the coast to work in one of the big hotels. Two were accountants. Niall had been on the verge of confessing his own interest in that area, but decided to keep his counsel. The last thing he wanted was to get mired in a discussion about accruals or retained earnings. The thought made him shiver.

Two days on, he was still coming to terms with his father's bad news. He wouldn't be able to stay in the apartment, that was for sure. Neither would any elderly aunts be stopping by to bring him for pricey seafood lunches in the Old Town. And never had a man been more in need of a generous aunt. Increasingly he'd been relying on his parents to throw some cash his way. Now the pipeline had run dry.

Three years before, when Niall had walked away from Shine and Co., he'd done so with a reasonable cache of savings. He'd sold his car, waved goodbye to his disappointed parents and begun his search for . . . well, for what exactly? He'd never had a grand plan, a list of treasures he hungered to view, a culture he wished to absorb. Neither had he been seeking enlightenment. Niall had no patience for this 'finding yourself' malarkey. He knew himself only too well.

What he had wanted was to slip his reins, to feel the sun on his face and to have a brain free of responsibility and obligation. What he had underestimated was how addictive this freedom would be. Others seemed capable of doing their tour and then returning to what they called 'the real world'. He remembered meeting a Mancunian engineer around a campfire in the Masai Mara. The guy had given a wistful sigh and confessed to being bored. 'Time to return to the nine-to-five,' he'd said. Niall's reply, asking if he was a bit simple, had probably been over the top, but the ensuing ding-dong had been the talk of the Great Rift Valley. The man guarding the campsite had warned that if they didn't stop roaring they would attract a lion.

The three apartment-viewers were examining the parquet floor. Niall had scuffed it up a little, but Mr Kovac was assuring them that these were only surface marks. His other efforts to make the apartment less appealing were similarly half-hearted. He'd left coffee rings on the table and tea bags in the sink. He'd allowed one of the bathroom taps to drip, so that the sound echoed through the apartment. Last night, with a few beers on board, this had seemed amusing. But in the morning light it felt petty, and he had an urge to start tidying. Instead, he opened the front blinds and slunk out to the balcony.

The morning was predictably beautiful, the sky that shade of cobalt blue you rarely saw in Ireland. With the summer still in its infancy, the trees were a fresh, pale green. The bougainvillea looked untouched, as though this was its first day in bloom. He tried to recall which flower smelled better: the white or the deep pink? But he could get no purchase on the day. No matter how often he told himself to think positive thoughts, his brain wouldn't co-operate. He kept hearing Gus's flat voice and Joan's stilted jollity. The business in jeopardy; their savings wiped out; the future un-certain: Niall had been genuinely shocked by the news. Although his father's unhappiness had been obvious, listening to his mother had been worse. She had performed her 'never say die' act. 'We'll sort it out, love,' she'd said more than once. 'Stop it, Mum,' he'd wanted to reply. 'For once in your life, it's OK to be upset.'

His first instinct had been to talk to one of the others. But who? The chances of getting any sense out of Vee were slim. Tara would urge him to come home. And he didn't know if he'd be able for a dose of Damien. The guy was so sanctimonious, such a Holy Joe – in a secular, non-sectarian sort of way, of course. Besides, it had been a long time since the brothers had had a proper conver-sation. It wasn't like there was a fully-fledged rift between them, more an acknowledgement that they were better off keeping their distance.

For a brief time – OK, a very brief time – he considered going back to Dublin. But what would he do when he got there? On leaving school, Niall had done his parents' bidding and studied Business. He'd ended up in a job that he absolutely loathed. He didn't want to make the same mistake twice. No, he'd stick it out here for a while. Some days he went to the beach and sketched cartoons of northern European tourists. It wasn't a lucrative busi-ness – mostly he got paid in beers and dinner invitations – but it was better than standing outside a Dublin dole office in the lashing rain.

As a teenager, Niall had loved drawing. Not that he would ever be an 'artist'. He had no grand vision. He wasn't a man for concepts or contexts. He just liked mucking about, really. Gus had been unenthusiastic. 'You'll end up like one of those lads chalking pictures of The Last Supper on the pavement near Trinity College,' his dad had said. 'Take it from me, there's no money in art.'

After what felt like a hundred years, the three apartment-viewers went on their way. They hadn't expressed a definite interest in renting the place, but their bright eyes and cheery nods suggested they would.

Niall trudged to the bakery where he bought a slice of apple strudel. At the nearest café he ordered a white coffee and lit a cigarette. Not exactly the breakfast of champions, but it would do. For a small while he attempted to read a discarded newspaper. Unfortunately his Croatian didn't stretch much further than the weather forecast. He smoked another cigarette and ordered a second coffee. He was watching a cat, an angular fellow with stripes of black and marmalade and the satisfied smirk of a Tom, when his phone rang.

'Niall?' said Mr Kovac. 'I have excellent news. The three people you met earlier? They want to rent the apartment.'

'Grand,' he replied, running a hand through his thicket of sandy hair. 'When do they hope to move in?'

A gaping pause followed. 'Ah, that's the slight complication. They're insisting on tomorrow. Not ideal, I know. But I told them this should be possible.'

'Shit.'

Mr Kovac wasn't without pity. 'I'm sorry, but your father instructed that I move quickly. What will you do?'

What will I do? thought Niall. *What will I do next week? Or what will I do with the rest of my life?* The reality of his predicament hit him like a double-decker bus. Here he was, thirty years old with no home, no partner, no career.

'To be honest with you, Tomislav,' he said, 'I haven't a clue.'

Damien liked certainty. He believed in right and wrong, good and bad, us and them. Frequently, this lead him into tricky situations.

At that moment he was chained to the railings of the

Department of Education. He and a colleague, Canice Considine, were there to protest against cutbacks in Damien's council area. Having tipped off the media, they had arrived at a decent hour. The interest had been underwhelming. A bored-looking photographer from the *Evening Post* aside, no one had turned up. Damien didn't trust the *Post*. Not that long ago, in a front-page story, they'd managed to switch the 'n' in his surname for a 't'. He called Tara to see if he might get somewhere with the *Irish Tribune*, but she said they were all under pressure because of the big murder story. He'd also asked her to babysit on Friday night, and she'd given him a sermon about being taken for granted. All the same, she hadn't said no.

A man from the Department was dispatched to listen to their grievances. 'Fair play to ye, lads,' he said, in that amused tone favoured by a certain level of civil servant, 'only, if it's the Minister you're looking for, you'll get no joy today. He's in Brussels.' Other than this, they were attracting scant attention. Well, scant attention from sane, sober people; they seemed to be a magnet for every drunk on the northside. And for most of the pigeons. The time had come to cut their losses and move on. There was only one problem: Canice, the dozy idiot, had forgotten the keys.

'Ah, hell,' Damien said. 'Do you know where you left them?'

Canice had the decency to look shamefaced. 'I've a feeling I might have put them down on the kitchen counter. You know the way it is in the morning, man. I was under pressure.'

'Under pressure? What was it you had to do?'

Canice attempted a shrug but his chains were too tight. Trying to get his mobile phone out of his jeans pocket proved no easier. Five minutes of wriggling and squirming followed. In the end, Damien managed to edge closer to his fellow protester and to pluck the phone from his pocket.

'Here boys, you should keep the kinky stuff for the bedroom,' shouted a passer-by.

With some difficulty, Canice tapped out his partner Jacinta's number. Holding a conversation involved further contortions.

Jacinta was not pleased. Damien could hear her adenoidal voice giving Canice a lecture. The phrase 'useless tool' was used more than once. She would go home and get the keys, she said, only they'd have to wait until lunchtime. She was a teacher in one of the schools whose plight they were meant to be highlighting, so she could hardly up and abandon her class.

Just then, a woman with a tight grey perm and a tartan shopping trolley decided to stop and have a word. 'What are ye up to?' she asked.

'Seeking justice for the disadvantaged,' Canice replied.

She scrunched her eyes into slits.

'We're speaking up for those with no voices,' explained Damien.

'Ye'd want to speak a bit louder,' she said, her face creasing with scepticism.

Up next was a young guy with a thatch of orange hair and a pair of bright red jeans. 'Are the pair of you politicians?' he asked.

'Independent Councillor Damien Shine,' was the reply. 'Standing up for the underdog.'

'What are you going to do about the situation in South Sudan?'

Damien thought for a minute. He drew a blank. To be fair, lack of a specific policy rarely prevented him from offering an opinion. He'd crafted a range of all-purpose replies. 'I'm against imperialism in all its forms,' he said.

The guy with the orange hair looked nonplussed, so Damien chipped in another of his favourite phrases: 'I support the right of indigenous peoples to self-determination.'

Mr Orange hawked a great gob of spit onto Damien's left boot. 'You lot are all the same,' was his parting shot.

Damien sighed. Until Jacinta turned up there was nothing they could do. Across the street, the devout, most of them elderly women, shuffled in and out of the Pro-Cathedral. Young guys with lolling eyes and mossy teeth mooched past. Many of them looked like they were in search of a fix. He craned his neck and discovered that he could see the very top of the O'Connell Street spire, stark and slightly ridiculous, against the pale sky. He let the babble of city life wash over him and surrendered to his thoughts. This was turning into one bad day at the end of one miserable week.

Wednesday night's conversation had brought him up short. Normally Gus and Joan were filed at the back of his busy mind. Contact revolved around Damien's children: Willow, Aifric and Rufus. Otherwise, relations were perfunctory at best, strained at worst. Their worst clashes tended to be about the most trivial matters – like forgetting Joan's birthday. In Damien's view, birthdays were for the under-tens. Why anyone would want to celebrate being sixty-two was beyond him. His father saw things differently and had let rip for half an hour or more about the ingratitude of the younger generation.

All the same, no matter how tiresome the old pair could be, Damien felt an obligation to stay in touch. Several times over the past day and a half he'd toyed with the idea of giving his father a call, but the timing never felt right.

Their predicament had left him with dilemmas of his own. He was a full-time councillor on a part-time salary. Until Gus had produced his list of savings, Damien hadn't really appreciated the myriad ways in which he relied on the family money.

For starters, there was the cost of the car. While Damien was content to walk or to career around town on his bicycle – indeed, that's what was expected of him – three children made a solid vehicle a necessity. He didn't like to use the letters SUV (too many Celtic Tiger connotations), but he supposed that's what it was. And running the thing: petrol, tax, insurance? You wouldn't do that on a councillor's wage. Gus had also been a good man for helping with the bills, like the gas. Well, who could afford the price of central heating nowadays?

It didn't end there. There was the occasional holiday. The odd dig-out with medical expenses. And there was … he found it hard to use the words … the other matter. The matter over which a veil was drawn. A nightmarish image flashed into his brain. He was sitting on a grey plastic chair, surrounded by political foes.

They were demanding that he reveal his secret vice. 'My name is Damien Shine,' he would be forced to say, 'and my children go to fee-paying schools.'

Now, let's be straight about this: Damien was not a supporter of private education. A two-tiered system was not to be applauded. It was abhorrent. Part of everything that was wrong with Ireland. But his wife, Felicity, had gone to St Attracta's and had thrived there. It had not been unreasonable for her to want her own daughter, Willow, to go to the same school. Three years later, Aifric had come along, and sending her anywhere else wouldn't have made sense. And then there was Rufus. A shy little lad, he was starting school in the autumn. He wouldn't be well-suited to one of those schools where thirty boisterous youngsters were crammed into a class. As Felicity liked to point out, it was a parent's duty to give their children the best possible start in life, even if that start cost thousands of euro a year.

All the same, this was not information that Damien would want spilling out to the wider world. The papers would lap it up. Didn't they already make hay from the fact that *he* had been to a private school? Along with his opponents in the big political parties, the media relished any opportunity to use that most wounding of words: hypocrite.

The one bill that Damien and Felicity had always met was the mortgage. They'd managed to buy before everything went completely mental. Admittedly, they could never have done so without an uncharacteristic burst of generosity from Felicity's father, who had provided the deposit. It rankled with Damien that his brother Niall had dodged all the madness of the boom. He remembered how the previous Christmas, Niall had sat at the dinner table expressing faux-concern for the couples he termed 'negative-equity slaves'. Then he'd winked and said, 'But of course, all property is theft, isn't that right, Damo?' Smugness had poured off the idle so-and-so, and Damien had wanted to swing for him.

Vee and Ferdia were among the slaves. They hadn't just embraced the madness, they'd wallowed in it. As bad as Damien's problems were, theirs must be far, far worse. Consoling himself with this thought, he rested his head against the railings. In front of the cathedral he spotted a poster for an anti-austerity rally organised by another independent councillor, Maurice Tully. The guy was supposed to be an ally, but this was the first Damien had heard of the gathering. The double-dealing rat. They would be having words.

'In all fairness, Canice,' he said, 'what's keeping Jacinta?'

'Your guess is as good as mine, man. She's probably on a deliberate go-slow. She can get kind of awkward.'

You're telling me, thought Damien. Jacinta was a great woman for the hypocrite word. Her own school was so chronically under-funded that the very existence of private education brought her out in hives. More than once Damien had endured a lecture about phony socialists who didn't practise what they preached. On the last occasion, Felicity had silenced her with an acerbic swipe. 'Wait until you have one of your own, dear. Then you'll understand,' she'd said.

So, what to do now? Gus's announcement had come at the worst possible time. With Rufus about to start school and Willow entering secondary school, they were facing a sharp rise in fees. They could hardly send Willow to another school, could they? The night before, Damien had raised this possibility. Felicity's face had taken on a stubborn look, and her voice had risen an octave. 'Out of the question,' she'd snapped. 'We'll have to find another way.'

What that other way might be was also the source of disagreement. They would have to revisit the issue tonight. In the meantime, he wished Jacinta would get her rear-end into gear. A stray dog, a mangy mongrel of a beast, was eyeing him up like he might make a useful alternative to a lamp post. A posse of school children passed, their giggling suggesting that Damien and Canice were the funniest things they'd ever seen.

The dog was doing his worst as the man from the Department reappeared. 'I'm off to lunch, lads,' he said. 'By the way, a word to the wise: the next time you want to highlight an issue, would you not arrange a meeting? You'll find it's easier.' He peered down at the dog. 'And drier.'

Joan was rummaging through the ironing. She'd start with something easy, a pillowcase maybe, or a T-shirt. She hated ironing, *loathed* it, and the pile that teetered out of the laundry basket and spilled onto the kitchen table made her feel slightly unwell. To be fair, she was out of practice. More than a decade had passed since she'd last tackled all of the housework on her own. But, like she'd said to Gus, they couldn't expect the children to pare back their spending without suffering a few privations of their own.

Of course, she would prefer to relax with her knitting or have a potter around the garden, while the cleaner did the hard work. But, just at the moment, that wouldn't be right.

Joan was fond of the kitchen in Garryowen. It was bright, spacious, warm: all the things a kitchen should be. And it was a practical place where she could prepare and serve meals without feeling like her very presence made it untidy. Too many modern kitchens made Joan feel as if she was disturbing their symmetry, roughing up their perfect edges. The worst example of this was in her elder daughter's house. For someone who wasn't particularly given to cooking, Vee was obsessive about her kitchen. It had been the first room she'd renovated, a process Joan would never forget. A general preparing for war wouldn't have shown as much attention to detail.

How the brochures had tickled Gus. Joan recalled one of them promising a kitchen to 'carefully reflect the owner's personality and lifestyle'. 'What's it going to do?' her husband had asked. 'Go toddling around the town looking for over-priced frocks?' She could still hear him reading out extracts, the two of them falling about with laughter at the manufacturer's grandiose claims. When Vee presented them with the bill, their mirth had come to an abrupt end.

As she squared up to the ironing, Joan's mind shifted back to her own first kitchen: a functional little place with brown tiles, a yellow Formica table and an old-style washing machine with a ringer on top. Nowadays a young couple would not be impressed, but back in 1976, the newly-wed Joan and Gus had had no complaints.

They'd met in a dance hall three years before. Gus, bless him, had pursued her with the determination of a salmon returning to its spawning ground. Joan's upbringing on an East Limerick farm had been strict, and Gus – long-limbed, sociable Gus with his red Ford Cortina and his plans and schemes – had provided a welcome escape. 'City boy,' her father had dubbed him, like he was from London or Manhattan rather than twenty miles out the road. Not that her dad wasn't pleased with the match. He just wasn't the sort of man who could admit to pleasure or contentment.

What had Joan been like as a young woman? Pretty, certainly. But more than that, she'd had an unusual sophistication about her. She'd known it too. She remembered standing in the big newsagents on O'Connell Street in Limerick, flicking through the English magazines, scrutinising skirt lengths and hairdos and makeup trends, then going home and dispensing unasked-for advice to her sisters. Years later, she'd listened to Vee do exactly the same thing to poor Tara. Joan hoped that she hadn't been quite so overbearing.

Of late, she had thought more and more about what she'd passed on to the children. Gus's attributes were easy to spot. She saw them in Niall's good nature; in Damien's determination; in Tara's capacity for work. But what had they inherited from her?

She fixated too on all that she and Gus had got wrong. Joan loved her children, of course she did, but frequently she worried about the lives they had chosen ... or the lives they had drifted into. And why did three of the four always have to be so bloody awkward? They were in their thirties now, so why was keeping the peace as tricky as juggling chainsaws?

She was midway through the tower of shirts, skirts and bed linen, the iron hissing and gurgling, when Gus returned from work. He kissed her on the cheek, deposited his ever-present sheaf of paperwork on the counter and sat down.

'That estate agent out in Dubrovnik's no slouch,' he said. 'He's already got three tenants lined up for the apartment.'

'So I gather,' said Joan as she attempted to de-wrinkle a particularly stubborn shirt. (It always baffled her when women claimed to find ironing 'therapeutic'. Clearly, they hadn't done enough of it.) 'Niall sent me an e-mail saying he'd have to move on.'

'I suppose getting on a plane and coming home didn't occur to him?'

'You suppose right. He said the estate agent – a Mr Kovac, is it? – had found him somewhere new. A room in a house, I think. By the sounds of things, it's not the smartest spot in the world.'

'Oh?'

'He mentioned a "mosquito issue". In my reply, I said not to worry, a few bites would be no bother to a seasoned traveller like him.'

'You're a hard woman,' said her husband, a smile in his voice.

While Joan wouldn't go so far as to use the word 'hard', she had long seen herself as tougher than Gus. For all his ambition and drive, he was more given to sentimentality than her. In business he could be ruthless, but he left this at the office door. When it came to the children, he'd invariably been hopelessly soft. Oh, he could vent and pontificate for Ireland, but when there was a row, he was usually first to back down. He had always avoided the tough decisions. Until now.

'You look like that ironing is getting the better of you,' he was saying. 'Sit yourself down there, and I'll make us a cup of tea.'

Joan pushed her hair from her face. 'I won't say no. I reckon I've done enough for today.'

'You don't *have* to do everything on your own, you know.'

For the briefest moment, she wavered. She asked herself whether she *did* have to suffer. *Besides, would the children even notice that Edita the cleaner was no longer there?* Then she got a grip of herself.

'Thanks, love,' she said, 'but a deal's a deal. I'll soldier on.'

Chapter 7

'Would you look at it?' the woman said. 'Now, be honest with me, pet, would you want your children having a wash in the likes of that?' The woman, Nuala Timmons was her name, gestured towards the bath, which was dotted with black, furry mould. Its spores infected the air. Nuala knocked the wall over the taps and a chunk of plaster fell away.

Tara put her hand over her nose while she got the guided tour of 317 St Monica's Mansions. She'd also been to 128 and 304. They were no better. She'd been shown desiccated walls, slimy pipes and windows awash with condensation. The fetid odour caught the back of her throat and made her want to throw up. It was impossible to believe that the outside world was mild and dry.

Nuala turned on one of the taps. 'It mightn't happen this time. Sometimes we're OK ... Oh no, here we go.' The water emerged in brackish brown spurts. It gurgled down the plughole, leaving a dark residue in its wake.

'Is that ...?' asked Tara.

'Shit?' replied Nuala. 'It is indeed.'

'And how long has it been ...?'

'Coming in like that? Well, we moved here when I was expecting my eldest lad, and he's ten. So, all that time.'

'And the ...' Tara paused. 'I'm sorry, would you mind if we went outside?'

Carmel O'Neill, Ben's nan, who was acting as tour guide, chuckled. 'I warned you,' she said. 'I told you you wouldn't be able for it.'

Nearly three weeks had passed since Tara's last visit to St

Monica's Mansions. Weeks during which Carmel's prediction that she wouldn't return had lingered in her thoughts. She'd been determined to prove the woman wrong. Not because she had any great desire to do a story about damp flats, but because she knew that every word Carmel had said was based on past experience. And because she'd found Ben's mixture of innocence and precociousness so endearing.

The problem was, getting free rein to go out and do stories you wanted to do was easier said than done. Tara was no star hack with a licence to choose where she went and what she wrote. For all that she valued her job, she was one of journalism's drones. Once, when Vee had been in especially snarky humour, she had dubbed her 'a bottom of page-eight specialist', and it was hard to argue. Eventually, most reporters moved on. They went to work in PR, or they found other jobs in journalism. Jobs that provided less hassle and more money. From time to time, Tara worried about her status, only she wasn't sure what else she could do. She didn't want to be a columnist. Just imagine having to summon all that vehemence, having to pretend that every half-baked controversy heralded the end of civilisation. Neither could she see herself as one of those interviewers who believes that after thirty minutes of chat in a hotel bar they can read someone's soul.

Since their dad's bombshell, Vee had been unusually subdued. There'd been no hectoring about Tara's by-line photo, no badgering about her dress sense. Neither did she look like her normal self. Tara had long assumed that Vee's elegance was effortless; that she got up in the morning, tossed a few items together and, hey presto, there she was, straight from the pages of French *Vogue*. Even as a girl she'd had a homing device for the cool people: the girls with straight teeth and frizz-free hair, the boys in the band, the students with year-round tans. Vee was one of those rare creatures who could make a school uniform appear glamorous, and her glittery presence had made Tara feel all the more drab. At the moment, though, she appeared slightly awry. Only half put together was probably the best description.

Tara had a notion that there was more going on in her sister's head than Gus's reversal of fortune. Surely between her and Ferdia they'd be able to meet the mortgage payments? She knew that asking would be a waste of time. The only response would be a lot of hair tossing and tut-tutting.

Anyway, Tara had her own life to negotiate, and some days this was far from easy. Those were the days when she longed to shout at Craig, 'Just leave me be, just give me time and space.' But she didn't shout. She didn't say much of anything. Sometimes she felt she was being smothered by his single-mindedness. The fact that he was normally so laid-back made this determination doubly hard to handle. She'd also come to realise that he didn't grasp the gravity of her family's plight. Craig, she feared, saw Gus's problems not as future-threatening but as a minor hurdle.

Would his wanderlust ease if he found a project that engaged him? Although he was working in fits and starts – a review here, a magazine article there – most of his projects lacked substance. That was Tara's view, anyway. Needless to say, her opinion remained unvoiced. She wished she was braver. There were days when she felt like a bystander in her own life.

Challenging as he was, Tara did love Craig. You had to love someone whose physical presence made your stomach fall away, didn't you? OK, he was difficult, but so were most of her family. Difficult was what she knew best. In recent days, she'd taken to speculating about what else was on his mind. Did his plans signal that he was ready to take their relationship to the next stage? She was sure – well, almost sure – that this was what she wanted. At twenty-nine, you had to start thinking seriously. At the same age, her mother had been married for the best part of four years. Damien was already bouncing around the place, and Vee was on the way.

'You look a bit green around the gills, love, if you don't mind me saying so.' They were sitting on the balcony, Nuala studying Tara's face with a mixture of merriment and concern.

Tara was about to insist that she was grand, then thought

better of it. 'Do you know, Nuala, I don't know how you do it. The damp . . . and everything . . . they must have an effect on your health.'

'An effect?' said Nuala. 'Where do you want me to start? Stomach bugs, bacterial infections, every type of illness and ailment, we've had it.'

'And then there's the asthma,' chipped in Carmel. 'Half the kids around here have inhalers.'

'And the bronchitis.'

Their conversation was brought to a temporary halt by a roar from the yard below. Two young lads were shaping up to have a go at each other. Their arms were raised, their chins sticking out. 'I told you I didn't bleedin' take it,' yelled one of them. 'And I told you, I don't fucking care,' came the reply.

'Cop yourselves on, boys,' shouted Carmel. The two glared up, gave her the finger and marched away the best of friends.

'So,' said Tara, 'have there been any attempts to fix any of this? You know, any promises from the council about ventilation or repair work?'

'Promises,' said Carmel, 'we've had a million promises. And, from time to time, a fella comes out and has a poke around.'

'Always a very nice fella,' added Nuala. 'Says "God, that's shocking, missus" or words to that effect. Then, off he goes.'

'And nothing happens.'

Nuala was absentmindedly shredding a piece of paper into tiny squares. 'You see, we were supposed to be renovated and regenerated, but the money ran out.'

'Would you move somewhere else?' asked Tara.

'Move where?' replied Nuala. 'If the council has a vacant flat, it's likely to be in an even worse state than this place.'

'Isn't that the madness of it all?' said Carmel. 'We live in a country that's stacked with empty houses and apartments, only they were all built in the wrong places.'

Nuala nodded. 'I saw a thing on the news the other night. They were knocking down a block of flats in Longford. And they were lovely. Says I to the telly, "Why don't you take down those flats brick by brick and rebuild them here?"'

'No doubt,' said Carmel, 'the powers that be will get around to this place one day, only we'll be dead and gone.'

'In the meantime, I know what I'd like,' said Nuala, her piece of paper torn to flitters.

'Oh?' asked Tara.

'Shares in a disinfectant company,' she said with a laugh. 'We use so much of the damn stuff trying to wash the dirt off of the walls, they must owe us something.'

Afterwards, as they walked back towards Carmel's flat, Tara promised that a photographer would be out the following day. She hoped the piece would be in the paper before the end of the week.

Carmel nodded. 'Listen, I've got to go and collect Ben from school. He has a half-day, and I want to stop him from wandering off. Have you time to come with me? I'm sure he'd love to see you. He took a real liking to you.'

'Did he?'

'I think you remind him of his mam. Rosanna's hair's a bit like yours.'

'Grows in four different directions, you mean? The poor woman. I feel her pain.' Tara waited, wondering if Carmel would drop a hint as to where her daughter might be. But on that subject no more was said. She did, however, reveal that her husband was dead, and that she had a son called Jack, who was working in London.

A giddy Ben greeted them at the school gates. 'A whole half-day, and no homework,' he said to Carmel, just in case she imagined he was going to spend the afternoon with his copybook and pencil.

'I'll give you this much, Ben,' said his nan, although her words seemed to be directed at Tara, 'you're a real throwback. You know these kids who only want to sit in front of the telly or play on those games machines? All this lad wants to do is be out and about. He'd have the town walked, if I'd let him. It's either that or he has his head stuck in a storybook.'

'Is Tara having her lunch with us, Nan?' the little fellow replied.

'I think that's up to Tara.'

'I should probably head for the office and begin writing—' Carmel interrupted. 'For fear you're worried, we don't have the same problems as Nuala. The water in our place is fine. You won't be sick.'

'Oh Jesus, Carmel,' said Tara, mortified that the woman might think she was too high and mighty to have her lunch with them. 'I never meant . . .' She looked down at the boy who was wearing his 'aw, please' face. 'I'd be delighted to have lunch with you, Ben.'

'Deadly,' he replied. 'You can have jam sandwiches like me.'

'He'd have bread and blackcurrant jam for every meal if I'd let him,' Carmel explained. 'It's a miracle he has any teeth.' She paused. 'Well, now that I think of it, he hasn't.'

Ben flashed his gappy grin, and they all laughed.

Back in the flat, he set about demolishing his sandwiches with gusto. 'It'll be the summer holidays soon. I'll get to do lots of stuff, and my mam might even come home for a visit. Isn't that right?' he said to Carmel.

She tousled his hair. 'I don't know if it'll be that soon, pet.'

'For my birthday then,' he said, through a mouthful of bread and jam. 'In September.'

Carmel's face tightened. Tara decided to intervene. 'Your mum's a long way away, though, Ben. You told me, remember? And very busy, I'd say.'

His round blue eyes met hers. 'Everyone has to come home sometime. She'll need to see Jenelle too, 'cos of her being sick and all.'

'Now, Ben,' said Carmel. 'Eat up your lunch and stop being a nuisance. Tara'll have to go back to work in a minute. And anyway, weren't you talking to your mam on the phone the other night?'

'I was. She didn't say very much, but. She kept asking was I

OK, and calling me baby.' Ben pulled a face. 'Do you have kids, Tara?'

'Nope.'

'Do you have a husband or a boyfriend?'

'A boyfriend. He's called Craig.'

Ben gave her a solemn look. 'I don't know as I'll have children either. I reckon I'll have other things to do.'

Tara smiled. She was making heavy work of her bread and jam. 'Do you want to finish this?' she asked him.

'Aw yay!' He took a slurp of milk and a small, tanned hand shot out for the plate.

'What do you say?' asked Carmel.

'Thanks, Tara,' he chirped.

'And by the way, Ben, your sister's not sick. She's at playgroup right this minute, as well you know. She's just not as strong as you.'

Figuring that it might be best to move the conversation away from other members of the O'Neill family, Tara asked Ben about his plans for the afternoon. He would probably go out, he said, but they'd given him a book at school and it looked really good so he might read that as well.

'Do you like reading?' she asked, anxious for fear there was a note of surprise or, worse, condescension in her voice.

Ben crammed the last of the bread into his mouth and gave a thoughtful chew. 'I do, most of the time. Once it's not a book for babies.'

Carmel gave his hair another ruffle. 'You're a star at the reading, aren't you?'

'I'm OK.'

'Top of the class,' she mouthed to Tara.

'I like it when my nan reads to me too,' he said. He gave Carmel one of those looks that children give before they learn to mask their emotions. The look said, 'I think you're brilliant.'

She smiled. 'When Ben grows up, Tara, I want him to have a job like you.'

'Oh, I'm sure he'll do better than that,' Tara replied.

Vee and Ferdia were sitting at the dining room table surrounded by statements and invoices and assorted scribblings. Her head felt heavy, her eyes scratchy. She urged herself to concentrate, but her thoughts insisted on flitting away.

Ferdia didn't appear to notice her distracted state. 'All in all, then,' he said, in his sonorous courtroom tones, 'it seems to me that we can manage the mortgage for the next quarter. After that ...' His voice tapered off. He was waiting for her to fill the silence. When she said nothing, he cleared his throat and continued. 'You'll have to find full-time work, Vee. As quickly as possible.'

'I'm *trying*. Heaven knows I'm trying. Only that witch, Aileen Duignan, was right. The city is filled with perky twenty-two-year-olds with first-class honours degrees and a willingness to work for pocket money.' As she spoke, Vee clung to the edge of the antique mahogany table, as though its solidity would provide support. Her nails were chipped. She would have to ... No, of course, she couldn't have a manicure. She would have to wipe the polish off and get used to having Tara-like hands.

Over the past few days, Vee had come to realise that she'd crossed the line from being too young to being too old. She was only thirty-two, but already some doors were closed to her.

'There has to be *something*,' Ferdia said. 'Doesn't your father know anyone in need of a small bit of assistance?'

'Assistance?' Vee replied, her voice sounding shrill. 'I'm not a cleaner or a general dog's body.'

'I know, darling. I know. Only if we're to have any hope of meeting the mortgage payments, let alone paying back the deposit, we'll need two incomes.'

She felt herself getting huffy. 'You'll have to up your earnings too. I hope you understand that.'

'I do, I do,' Ferdia said.

He gave a conciliatory smile, and she asked herself if this was the time to come clean about her debts. Then she looked again at his preoccupied face. And she thought, *not now, I can't do it now*. Before she did anything else, she had to get her own head in order. The contours of her life had gone all wobbly, and she needed to straighten them out again. When her thinking was clear, she would talk to Ferdia.

Vee feared opening herself up to the scrutiny of others, even her husband. While on the surface she was all attitude and flounce, inwardly she craved approval. Whatever his foibles and affectations, Ferdia was a good person; a good person who loved her. Vee may have had a thousand suitors, but she'd chosen someone who was kind and honest. She was terrified that if the true extent of her problems emerged, she would lose him.

Two days previously, a truly frightening-looking letter had arrived. It was from one of the credit card companies. Vee had been about to open it when she'd decided that she wasn't strong enough. She hadn't wanted to leave the letter lying around either. So she did the only sensible thing. She took a pair of scissors from the drawer and hacked it into narrow ribbons. Then she placed the ribbons in a plastic bag, walked down to Ranelagh village and tossed the bag into a bin.

As she did, her heart beat a rapid tattoo, and her mouth felt like she was gargling vinegar. She saw a neighbour and ducked into a doorway to avoid her.

Right now, Vee found that she couldn't talk to anyone.

Chapter 8

Gus thought of himself as a gregarious man. There was one important exception: he loved the solitude of trains. As was his custom, he arrived early at Heuston Station, bought a ticket and a newspaper, then boarded the seven o'clock to Limerick. His seat chosen, he deposited his jacket and briefcase in the adjacent space. This, he hoped, was a signal to chatty travellers to sit elsewhere. Sometimes, a last-minute passenger would arrive, and with a hassled puff they'd ask, 'Is that seat taken?' Today, however, he was in luck. As the train pulled out of the station, he was on his own. He relaxed into his seat, turned off his phone and savoured the rhythmic *click-clack*.

He had considered taking the car. These days, with all the bypasses and whatnot, it was quicker to travel by road. But there was something about the train, and its steady progress through the flat fields of the midlands, that Gus enjoyed. He could allow his thoughts to drift. It was hard to remember a time when his mind had been in greater need of rest.

In the immediate aftermath of his announcement, the children had been disturbingly quiet. Even Tara had kept her distance. Then the special pleading began.

'School fees,' Damien had said. 'We can handle everything else. Felicity is a genius at economising, and leading a spartan existence will be no bother to us. But the children have got to go to school.'

'Indeed they have,' agreed Gus. 'And you of all people should know that the city has plenty of public schools.'

'Is that really what you want?' Damien said.

'I don't think you understand where I'm coming from here. This isn't some whim I've taken. There is no money.' Gus voiced these last words in staccato-style, as though his thirty-four-year-old son was actually a particularly slow teenager. 'Why don't you ask Felicity's old man?' he added. Amby Power had plenty of cash. He was also one of the tightest, most reptilian figures on God's earth.

'Perhaps I will,' a petulant Damien replied.

'Or . . . you could always earn the money. I mean, you could get some more work. Or your wife could get a job.'

The lad did an amount of sighing but said no more.

'Time' had been top of Vee and Ferdia's list. The previous night they had called around, and an unusually subdued Vee had promised that they would take over the mortgage repayments straight away. They'd also do everything within their power to return the deposit, she said; they just weren't in a position to do it now. Gus stressed that this was far from ideal. 'But I'm not an unreasonable man,' he said. 'I'll give you a short while to raise the money. I'm sure you're both in good standing with the banks.' Was it his imagination or did his daughter blanch?

Niall had been his usual self: an infuriating mix of warm-heartedness and dizziness. Oh, he was a good-natured fellow, there was no denying that. He'd been especially kind to Joan, e-mailing or ringing nearly every day. 'Just seeing how you're bearing up,' he'd say. There was no sign, however, of him coming home to see for himself how his family was coping.

And Tara? She was easy to keep tabs on, at least. There she was in today's paper. A big piece, it started: *These are the squalid conditions in which tragic teenager, Eric Lynam, lived his final days.* Gus scrutinised the pictures. The place looked rough, although the women seemed decent. They reminded him of women he'd known as a child, defeat tattooed onto their faces before they'd reached their thirtieth birthday. Their words full of fight; their eyes telling a different story.

The flats complex appeared to be one of those places where a pair of runners hangs from every length of telephone wire. According to Tara, this meant there were drugs for sale. Mind you, Gus had noticed that you could see the same tomfoolery pretty much anywhere you went these days. Young buckos having a laugh, he supposed. If you asked him, it was an awful waste of perfectly serviceable runners. Or tackies, as they'd been known when he was growing up in Limerick. *Listen to me*, he thought, *what a curmudgeon I've become.* He laughed to himself, which seemed to alarm the young woman clanking past with the refreshments trolley. He decided he'd better buy a coffee.

He was glad to see Tara doing well at work, which was why he'd been doubly put out by the latest news from her boyfriend. A couple of days back he had bumped into Craig. 'You'll be able to rent out the basement soon enough,' the fellow had said. 'Tara and myself are going travelling.' Gus had been so shocked that he'd only managed a splutter in reply. He'd gone straight upstairs to talk to Joan. 'First I've heard of it,' she'd said. So, what was Craig up to?

He sipped his coffee and gazed out onto one of his favourite places: the rolling expanse of the Curragh. In the near distance, past a collection of furze bushes and a small mob of sheep, he saw a string of racehorses out for their morning gallop. Gus was fond of horses. He didn't have any particular interest in betting, and he knew nothing about breeding or bloodlines. He just liked the look of them. They were such elegant, powerful beasts. By comparison, humans seemed ungainly and inadequate.

Horses had also given him a start in business. As a boy, he had cottoned on to the demand for a bookies go-between, someone to run back and forth between the pub and the betting shop. A nifty runner, he'd made a tidy sum. As he got into his teens, it wasn't unknown for him to hold onto the stake rather than placing what he reckoned would be a losing bet. Only once had he made a spectacular mistake. He'd been given five shillings to put on a sure-fire loser. The horse romped home at twenty to one. Biddy's Flyer, the nag was called. Gus would take the name to his grave.

As he finished his coffee, the train pulled out of Portlaoise and chugged past an estate of yellow houses. Every town in the country seemed to be encircled by similar houses, all built in the space of a decade, most mortgaged from top to bottom. If nothing else, the years of prosperity had improved the appearance of the country. He remembered as a youngster watching people emerging from hovels and wondering how they managed to survive. Joan was always amused by novels set in charming Irish villages. 'God bless those writers and their imagination,' she'd laugh. 'In my day, half of the villages looked as though a tornado had passed through.'

Gus had a busy day ahead. First off, he would go to the office. He needed to keep them up to date. The smart boys in Dublin told him there were modern ways of doing this, that he didn't have to go gallivanting across the country. He didn't agree.

He also planned on calling to see his mother. Phyllis lived with Gus's sister, Majella. His father, Gus Senior, had been dead for thirty years. At sixty-three he'd been claimed by lung cancer. The following November, Gus Junior would reach the same age. The significance of this weighed on his mind. His wife aside, he didn't expect anybody else to appreciate the importance of the day. After all, three of their four children had forgotten Joan's last birthday. Gus believed he had never been so angry. Three months on, his anger still simmered.

The rest of his siblings were scattered around the country and beyond. Rita was in Cork, Frances in Sligo, and Bernie in California. Pauline and Phonsie lived in London. Their eldest brother, Fintan, had died more than twenty years ago; too little work and too much drink sending him to an early grave.

When Gus was a young man, he had railed against Phyllis. Like many women of her era, she'd had no time for messing. You got up on time; you polished your shoes; you went to work; you showed respect. He must have been fifty years old before he truly understood what she was about. Bringing up four children was testing. How hard must it have been to raise eight on one mill worker's wage? He was even older when he started to think about what really went on in his mother's head. How well did he actually know her? He was sure that his own children thought he had always been just the way he was now. That is, if they thought about him at all. Sometimes he had to fight back the urge to say, 'I was young too, you know. I was impulsive and passionate. I didn't always wear a suit. I wasn't always the responsible one.'

At Ballybrophy, Gus reached into his pocket to check that his instructions were still there. Joan wanted him to call into a wool shop on William Street. A specific shade of lemon was called for, and she was adamant that no shop in Dublin had exactly what she needed.

He changed trains at Limerick Junction. Ah, the Junction – the bleakest place in Ireland. Everywhere else might be enjoying balmy weather, but on the Limerick–Tipperary border a breath-taking wind would be whistling up the platform and travellers would be dashing for shelter. This was Joan's part of the world. Gus had met her in the spring of 1973 in a packed ballroom – a place where the walls sweated and the clouds of cigarette smoke never cleared. Back in the era of brown suits, flared pants and flock wallpaper; the Waltons on the telly, Elvis in Hawaii and mayhem in the North.

As he recalled it, Joan had been wearing a red mini-dress and silver platform sandals. Gus had been mesmerised, and two hours had passed before he'd gathered the courage to approach her. Later, he'd learned that the sandals belonged to her younger sister and were killing her feet. What he remembered most was her air of assurance, as though she knew life would get better. Not that long ago, he'd heard a phrase on the radio: the extravagance of aspiration. He liked this, had written it down. In 1973, aspiration was not a word they used, but it was what she'd had – what they'd both had.

In those days, Gus had worked in the office of a huge metals factory on the outskirts of Limerick. By night, he had studied accountancy. There had been no college for him or for anyone he knew. In the sixties and seventies, you were expected to get out there and make a living. Whether you enjoyed what you were doing was neither here nor there. Joan's upbringing had been no different. During their courtship she had worked in the drapery section of Cannock's department store. When he got the chance, he would go in and watch her. How he had loved to see her at work, gossiping with customers and attacking bolts of cloth with an ungainly pair of scissors. Even on her worst days she'd radiated cheer and efficiency. He admired that.

Nowadays, youngsters didn't feel the same pressure to grow up and make themselves useful. Gus didn't want to return to all of the old ways, but he found the attitude of the current generation hard to understand. There was Vee, a married woman, still intent on living the life of a young dolly-bird. And worse, there was Niall, a man with qualifications galore, behaving like a teenager. Surely your children should be prodding you from behind, impatient to take over, not lounging around waiting for opportunity to fall from the sky?

The city wasn't far away now, the train trundling past small, marshy fields. Cattle gathered in the corners. The land might make a beautiful watercolour but it wouldn't feed snipe. Say what you like about *Angela's Ashes*, thought Gus (and Limerick people said plenty), Frank McCourt had been right about the damp. It got into your bones at an early age and never really left.

At Colbert Station he gathered up his jacket and briefcase. The walk to the office would take less than ten minutes. Gus strode across the black and white tiles, descended the grey steps and prepared himself for another day of saying what needed to be said. Of crossing his fingers and hoping for the best.

'You have a sheepish look about you,' said Phyllis as she polished and re-polished her bifocals. 'There's something you're not telling me.'

She was sitting, back straight as a wall, in a purple floral armchair. Majella, who was at work, had adventurous taste in furnishings. Throw in a mish-mash of ornaments and paintings, and the room had the air of a back-street bazaar.

'Honest to God, Mam, there's nothing to tell,' lied Gus. 'I've never been able to keep secrets from you, and I'm hardly likely to start now.'

His mother put on her glasses and dug her teeth into her bottom lip. Her face had the latticework lines of a long-time smoker. Despite her husband's death from lung cancer, she had smoked until ten years before. Then, a protracted bout of pneumonia had forced her to concede that, like mini-skirts and lie-ins, cigarettes were for young people. Her voice still contained a tell-tale rasp. Otherwise she was in robust health. Once a week she went into town to get her hair washed and set, and she went for a stroll almost every day. 'Our family never wear out,' she would say. And she was right. They hadn't a dodgy knee or a replaced hip between them. Neither did she have any time for anyone, young or old, who spent their life slumped in front of the television. 'Mark my words, that box kills more folks than smoking ever did,' she liked to claim.

There were days when she pretended that she'd had enough. She would complain that she was exhausted. Gus paid her no heed. 'You're like Peig Sayers,' he'd laugh, referencing the book that had tormented generations of schoolchildren. In the opening line, Peig talks about having one foot in the grave and the other on its edge. She lived for another twenty-three years.

'Well, I hope you're telling me the truth, Gus,' said Phyllis. 'Secrets are never a good idea in a family. They only come spilling out at the worst possible time. That's been my experience, anyway.'

Deciding that he'd had enough of his mother's prying and folksy wisdom, Gus reached into his briefcase and pulled out a paperback. At an age when some might expect her to favour large-print Barbara Cartlands, Phyllis had an endless appetite for crime novels and thrillers. The Scandinavians were her current favourites. Serial killers, torture chambers and twenty-page interludes on Swedish politics were grist to her mill.

She smiled at the book. 'Ah, I like that fellow. Fair play to you, Gus. I always said you weren't the worst of them.'

'Thanks, Mam,' he replied, like he was seven years old.

'So, then,' she said, 'what are your lot up to this weather? Any hope of any more weddings or grandchildren?'

'I don't think we'll be getting any days out in the immediate future, no.'

Phyllis frowned, but before she had the chance to say any more, Gus returned to the briefcase and fished out the *Irish Tribune*. 'There's Tara for you, now. Some days she seems to write half the paper.'

His mother looked the story up and down before turning her attention to Tara's by-line picture. 'The photo does her no favours.'

He took a deep breath and rolled his shoulders. 'Well, I think she's doing very well.'

'Hmmm,' said Phyllis. 'I couldn't tell you the last time any of them came to see me. Do you know, if Damien's young ones walked in the door, I wouldn't recognise them.'

'I'm sure that's not true. Anyway, he's very busy – or so he keeps telling me.'

'I take it he's still rabble-rousing and going to meetings about potholes.'

'I don't think that's quite how he sees the job.'

'That doesn't mean I'm wrong. Did you hear about Rita's lad, Fergus? He's after getting a big promotion at work. Rita says he'll be running the place soon. And her youngest fellow is hoping to study something called "International Geosciences" in the autumn. Needless to say, I don't even understand the title. But it sounds impressive.' She nodded. 'Very impressive. Did any of your crowd ever think of doing anything like that?'

Phyllis was a competitive grandparent. She liked to know what and how everybody was doing, and she enjoyed collating and passing on the news. Mostly, Gus brushed her comments aside. He told himself to be grateful that she still took such an interest.

Occasionally, though, and this was one of those occasions, she irked him.

'Our crowd, as you call them, are doing fine,' he said. Of course, he didn't mean this, but he wasn't in the form for a dissection of his family.

'I suppose,' replied his mother, mischief on her face. 'But I still say there's something you're not telling me.'

Tara could never understand why some news stories grew legs and others simply withered away. Her piece about conditions in St Monica's Mansions had taken off in a way she hadn't expected. The morning radio shows had picked up on it, and politicians had spent the day issuing statements. Damien called in a snit because she hadn't sought a quote from him. Distracted by work, she gave him short shrift. 'Why? Do you live there?' she asked. Her brother gave her a brief lecture on representative democracy before hanging up.

Much more welcome was a call from Carmel. A group of men from the council had descended on the flats and were talking about immediate remedial works. There'd be cleaning and painting and damp-proofing, they insisted – the whole shebang. Carmel said everybody was sceptical. There was a bit too much talk about the 'constraints of the budget'. But they were grateful to Tara all the same. 'You never know . . .' she said.

The flats were where Tara was heading now. Just a quick detour, she promised herself. She'd bought a present for Ben: two books, filled with ghosts and ghouls, which the woman in the shop assured her would be devoured by a boy of seven. By rights, Tara should have gone straight home. Craig was cooking dinner. The suspicion lurked, however, that the meal was a pretext for another talk about travelling. Even though she was coming to the conclusion that they could reach some sort of compromise – maybe she could get leave of absence from work and they could go away for three or four months – she wasn't in the humour for a heart-to-heart.

Armed with Ben's books, plus a colouring book and a box of crayons for Jenelle, she climbed the steps of St Monica's. Teenagers in regulation sportswear milled around. Fleetingly, she worried about her car. Then she chastised herself, and worried she was turning into Vee.

A frayed-looking Carmel met her at the door.

'If it's a bad time . . .' started Tara.

'Not at all, not at all,' said Carmel, ushering her in. 'It's one of those evenings, you know? Jenelle's been playing up. I only got her down a few minutes ago. And Ben's not here, I'm afraid. He's gone to stay with his friend, Tadeusz.'

'Well, I can just leave these.' She held up a paper bag. 'I saw a couple of books I thought he might like. And there's something small for Jenelle.'

Carmel beamed with pleasure at the gifts, before launching into a string of stories about her day, the council and the kids. In the blink of an eye the kettle was on and a pot of tea was made, and after another couple of deft movements, a plate of biscuits appeared and the television fell silent. Clearly she was desperate for adult company. Tara settled into an armchair. Carmel perched on the sofa. It was of a type you rarely saw anymore. With its thin brown cushions and scuffed wooden arms, it reminded Tara of the sofa her own granny had owned when she was a girl.

They'd barely started talking when they were interrupted by a thin wail. Briefly it faded, before rising up again. This time it was even more piercing.

'Sorry,' mumbled Carmel as she rose from the sofa. 'Give me a minute, would you?'

When she returned, she was carrying a fragile blonde girl in soft, pink pyjamas. Jenelle had stopped crying, but her face shone with tears and her eyes were full of fear. One look at Tara and she tightened her grip on her nan.

'It's all right, chicken,' cooed Carmel. 'Tara's a friend of yours. She even brought you a present.'

Jenelle's bottom lip wobbled.

'I really should go,' said Tara. 'I'm in your way here.'

'No,' said Carmel, her voice so brusque that Jenelle quivered. 'Sorry, that came out wrong. It's just that this little thing,' she kissed her granddaughter's head, 'has got to get used to meeting new people. You're a bit of a scaredy-cat, aren't you, love?'

The child whimpered.

'She has terrible nightmares. Brutal. And usually Ben sleeps through the lot. I've a feeling World War Three could break out in the yard and he would snooze away.'

Tara smiled.

'I'm sure you're wondering where their mam is,' said Carmel. 'Or their dads, for that matter.'

'In Australia, Ben said.'

'And you believed him?'

'Well, I wasn't sure. But it's no business of mine.' Strangely, Tara was far more awkward than Carmel.

'I'll tell you if you want.'

For a second, she considered Craig and his dinner. Then she looked at Carmel. She got the sense that Ben's nan was keen to tell her story. 'Thanks, I'd like that.'

While Carmel put Jenelle back to bed, Tara sent her boyfriend a quick text. *Won't be long*, she tapped, before pressing the off button.

Chapter 9

'I need to go back,' said Carmel, as she lit a cigarette. 'Back to when Rosanna was small. Myself and Willy, my late husband, had been married for just over a year when she was born. July eighty-eight, it was; as wet a month as I can remember. I was twenty-one. Twenty-one and a half, as Ben might say.' She smiled. 'And, really, life wasn't so bad. We weren't that flush but we weren't poor either. Willy was working in a warehouse in Tallaght, and I'd been working in a supermarket. I planned on going back too. I reckoned my own mam could mind the baby. Oh, I had great plans.'

Carmel paused and blew a curl of smoke towards the ceiling. 'Unfortunately, my mam had other ideas. She told me she'd had enough babies to do her a lifetime – she'd had six of her own – and she'd no intention of raising mine as well. So, I stayed at home with Rosanna, and dear God, I resented it. I was only young; I wanted to be out having a laugh. Instead, I was stuck here with the unhappiest, whiniest baby in Dublin.'

She looked at Tara, as if she was daring her to disapprove. 'I'm sure I shouldn't say that, except it's true. Every girl I knew seemed to take motherhood in her stride, and I started to worry that something was wrong with me. Now, I realise I was depressed, but we didn't talk about those sort of things then. Life was meant to be all pink babygros and cute smiles and "isn't she lovely". And she *was* a pretty child: strawberry blonde hair, eyes as blue as Ben's. Otherwise, she was a demon. Into everything. Never a second's peace. "I want, I want, I want." And if I didn't deliver? I'd say they heard the screams in Cork. In the years since, I've asked myself if, even then, it was obvious that something was up. Or was I to blame? Should I have been more patient? Paid her more attention? Paid her less attention?'

Tara didn't know where this was going, but she felt she should say something, offer some reassurance. 'I don't know that you can blame ...' Realising she couldn't complete the sentence, she sought refuge in her mug of tea.

Carmel stubbed out her cigarette. 'Two years later, Jack came along.' She gave a slight smile. 'All the Jacks. It was like the way half the boys born after the Pope's visit were called John Paul. That year every lad was named after Jack Charlton. Italia ninety, you know? There were six of them in his class. Three Nialls – for Niall Quinn. And even a Toto after ... what was the Italian fella's name?'

'The one who knocked us out of the World Cup?' said Tara. 'Toto Schillaci.'

'The very man. Anyway, what a blessing he was. A happy scrap of a boy. The sad thing is, I probably didn't give him nearly enough attention. I was too busy chasing after Rosanna, and going half-crazy because I wasn't coping.'

'Was anybody able to help you?'

'Maybe they would've done – if I'd let anyone know there was a problem. Except I was all bluster. I insisted I was flying.'

'And your husband?'

'God rest him, he turned a blind eye. Willy liked to pretend that everything was OK. Sometimes, like if she'd been bawling for hours, he lost the rag. But mostly he'd disappear. He'd go to the pub, or walk around the neighbourhood, doing circuits in the rain to escape the noise and the tension.

'There was more hassle when Rosanna went to school. She wouldn't sit still, wouldn't stay quiet. The worst of it was how she treated the other kids. You know when you see people on the telly talking about how their child was bullied?'

Tara took a mouthful of tea and nodded.

'I know this is a terrible thing to say, but I envy them. It's surely better than knowing your girl *is* the bully. To look at her, you'd think butter wouldn't melt. The roundy eyes on her and the curls – she was a regular Shirley Temple. But I'd a path worn up to that school. If we'd had money, if the school'd had money, there would have been counselling and special help, but we just had to get on with it.' Carmel pressed her fingertips against her cheekbones. 'At least Jack was great. Still is. He's like Ben. Perhaps not as bright as Ben, but real good-natured and chatty.' She swallowed. 'Jesus, I miss him. There's nothing for him here, though, and he's doing well in England. He's working as a plumber, and going out with a lovely girl. Nicole's her name – she's real London. To tell you the truth, I can hardly understand a word she says.'

Carmel closed her eyes, and Tara thought she might cry. Certainly her voice had changed. It was more muted, less certain.

'You're probably asking yourself where all this is going, aren't you, love? Don't worry, I'll get to the point.'

'You're grand. I'm grand. I've lots of time.' This wasn't true, but what could she do? Craig would have to cope.

'As Rosanna got older, I worried about her getting into trouble. There was all sorts going on around here. To be honest, I never thought we'd stay in the flats. I grew up not that far away, but we had a house. That was different. The problem was, Willy and myself didn't have the money to buy a place. And with only the two children, the council said we weren't entitled to anywhere bigger. Anyway, by the time Rosanna reached ten or eleven, she'd calmed down a bit. She wasn't so noisy, but she was sulkier. Willy was convinced this was an improvement. I wasn't so sure. She took to wandering off. She'd never say where she was going or what she was doing. Again, Willy was content enough. Jack was his boy. He'd take him to the football and that. The pair of them were as thick as thieves.

'I don't know when she first took gear ... smack ... heroin, whatever you want to call it. She can't have been any more than fourteen, though. I should have seen it coming. The place was awash with the stuff. You'd see these emaciated kids with vacant eyes and grey skin and they'd hardly be able to speak. And you'd remember what they'd been like a couple of years before: rosy-cheeked, talkative, full of schemes and devilment. Not saints, but normal. Sometimes, I'd come down the steps in the morning and there'd be a spoon or even a works sitting at the bottom.' She flinched at the memory. 'Usually I cleaned them away. It was a horrible job, and I'd be terrified of touching a syringe. For fear of the virus, you understand?'

In the fading light, Tara watched as Carmel thought through what she had to say. In her striped T-shirt and khaki trousers, her feet bare, she looked as vulnerable as her granddaughter. Her face was tense now, her body hunched, as though unseen forces were crushing her. She focused her blue gaze on Tara.

'I had myself convinced that Rosanna was too clever. And she didn't look rough. I knew what a junkie looked like, and that wasn't my daughter. Plus, she still went to school. Well, some of the time she went to school. The rest of the time, the Lord only knows where she went.' Carmel was quiet while she drank the rest of her tea. 'In the end, someone called to the door and told me. My fifteen-year-old daughter, my little girl, was taking heroin, and I hadn't even noticed. Rosanna denied it. They all do. Then she half-admitted it. She said she didn't inject, only smoked it, and what else was there to do in a hole like this? Willy fetched her a ferocious slap across the face. I swear I can still hear the sound: *thwack*. She ran out, and we didn't see her for a week.

'She was seventeen when Ben was born, just turned seventeen. To begin with, it felt like a fresh start. Imagine! I believed that. Of course, it was chaos here. All of us tripping over each other. But Rosanna was on methadone, and the baby seemed grand. A perfectly normal lad, he was.'

'And his dad?' Tara asked tentatively.

'A complete and utter God-help-us. You couldn't have left him alone with Ben for five minutes. He was strung out all the time. Lee Halpin was his name. I say "was" because he's long gone. He

OD'ed when Ben was two. Poor Ben thinks he was killed in a car crash.' Carmel shook her head. 'What must you think of us?'

Tara didn't know what to say so she asked another question. 'And Jenelle?'

'By that stage, Rosanna was back on the gear in a big way. She didn't care if I saw the track marks on her arms, or if she came home hardly able to speak. She had little enough to do with her son – until she got pregnant again and, somehow, managed to get a flat of her own. As for Jenelle's dad? Your guess is as good as mine. I doubt Rosanna knows herself. Ben was three by then, and she was determined he was going to live with her. Everything would be cool; she'd get clean; turn over a new leaf; be a proper mother; blah, blah, blah.

'Willy said we had to give her a chance. And we did. Needless to say, social workers were involved, and doctors and experts. Except nobody on this earth can lie like an addict. Jenelle was born a month premature, addicted to heroin.' Carmel hesitated. 'I've no idea what that baby endured. No idea. There she was, a small wisp of a thing, having to go through withdrawal, screaming and shaking.'

Carmel was rocking backwards and forwards. Tara did the only thing she could do. She got up, walked over to the sofa and put an arm around her. Although Carmel's body had been overtaken by tremors, there were no tears. She was too practised at swallowing them, Tara supposed.

'I'm sorry,' she kept saying. 'I'm sorry. I'm not normally like this. And you've been so kind.'

'Shhh now,' Tara said. 'Shhh.'

'No, I mustn't keep you any longer. You'll have things to do. I'm sure your fella is waiting for you and—'

'I'm in no hurry. You take all the time you need.'

After a minute or two, Carmel righted herself. She lit another cigarette before telling the next part of the tale: how Rosanna was given one last chance; how she was supposed to be monitored all the time; how, gradually, she unravelled again.

'I'd call around and she wouldn't be there, or she'd pretend not to be there. One day, I'd had enough. I got a young lad to break in for me. I paid him a fiver. Oh, Tara, the state of the place.' She winced. 'It was rancid. There was scarcely a stick of furniture, and there was dirt and mess from floor to ceiling. And it was *freezing*. Rosanna was passed out on the bed. Ben's clothes were manky. Jenelle wasn't even wearing a nappy. My grandson gazed at me with those massive eyes of his. "Mammy's sick," he said. I looked at him and thought, *Ben, you're old enough to understand now, and I'm not having you living like this. I'm not losing you as well.* So I checked that Rosanna was in the land of the living, and, just like that, I took Ben, by the hand, picked up Jenelle and left. "You're coming to stay with your nan," I told them.'

'What did Rosanna do?'

'When she came to, she erupted. She stalked over here, screeching and roaring, a face on her that'd cut sticks. Called me every kind of bitch and worse. There was an unmerciful rumpus out there on the landing. I didn't care.'

'And your husband?'

'By that point – this is two and half years ago – poor Willy was unwell. He had pancreatic cancer. He was only forty-five when he died.'

'I'm sorry,' said Tara, who remembered her own internet searches of a few weeks before, when she'd thought her dad was ill. How long ago it seemed.

'I'll never know for certain,' continued Carmel, 'but they say these things – cancer, I mean – can be brought on by stress. So, to me, it felt like Rosanna had taken his life, as well as ruining her own. Well, I can tell you, it made me doubly determined she wasn't getting those kids back.'

'Where is she now?'

'Where she belongs – in prison. Best place for her. She can't hurt herself and she can't hurt anyone else. I'm sure that sounds very hard, but it's the truth.'

Tara had heard stories like this before. Maybe not as extreme.

But similar. This was different, though. Carmel wasn't an interviewee. She was a real person.

'Do you mind me asking—'

'Dealing. The cops raided her flat and found a stash of heroin. Don't get me wrong – Rosanna wasn't any criminal mastermind, but she was holding on to the gear for some guy who was. In the eyes of the court, she was a vital cog in the wheel. She got six years, the last two suspended. That was a year and a half ago, so unless she does something stupid, she's likely to be released next year.'

'Do you have much contact with her?'

'In the beginning, she didn't want to know. "I'll manage on my own," she said. Then she changed her tune and demanded to see Ben and Jenelle.' Carmel blew a curl of smoke towards the ceiling and took a deep breath. 'I said no. "They don't know where you are, and they're better off that way. You get yourself clean, and I'll have another think." Surprisingly, she agreed. She calls and gets emotional – well, Ben told you about that the other day. So far, she's been willing to play along with the Australia story, only I'm petrified she'll let something slip. It wouldn't take a lot for Ben to start asking questions.'

'And do you go and see her?'

'I visit, all right. Usually she's frosty but we exchange a few words.' She turned towards Tara. 'You probably think I'm an almighty wagon.'

'Anything but; I think you're incredible.'

'I'm hardly that. I'm just trying to do my best for the two of them, trying not to make the same mistakes. Not that long ago, Ben picked up a phrase, except he got it slightly wrong. Instead of putting his best foot forward, he maintained he was putting "his best shoe forward". I say it all the time now: I'm putting my best shoe forward.'

She reached into her handbag and plucked out a creased picture. It showed a girl of thirteen or fourteen, pale red hair in a ponytail, laughing at the camera. She looked like Carmel; she looked like Ben. 'My last good picture of Rosanna, before I let her slip away.' She traced a finger around her daughter's face. 'I'll never say, "She was led astray" or "It was her surroundings". Thousands of children grow up in the same way. They never take heroin. They never sell it.'

Carmel spoke like someone who had spent countless days and nights trying to figure out why her daughter's life had turned out the way it did. She spoke like someone who was accustomed to being judged.

Tara glanced away. She didn't want Carmel to see that her eyes were wet. 'You can't go on blaming yourself. It's like you said, you have another child, and he's never done anything wrong. And your grandkids adore you.'

'I wish it was that simple, pet. The thing is, even if Ben grows up to be president and Jenelle runs the United Nations, I'll never stop thinking about what Rosanna has done. And about what she could have been.'

Afterwards they stood on the balcony, watching the to-ing and fro-ing below. The sky was clear; a swing-boat moon hung over the city. Tara was preparing to make a move.

'It's a gorgeous night,' said Carmel. 'Look over there – there's still a small streak of light in the sky.'

'A grand stretch in the evenings,' replied Tara. 'My mum's fond of saying that. Only she starts saying it in mid-January.'

Carmel laughed. She had a chugging laugh that somehow felt older than the rest of her. 'She's an optimist.'

'She says you have to be. "Every day above ground's a good one," she likes to say. Although I'm not sure she always believes it.' Not at the moment, anyway, Tara almost added.

'I know where she's coming from. If I didn't tell myself that things'll get better, I'd take to bed and never get up again. That's why I only have pictures of Ben and Jenelle in the flat. I had photos of Willy everywhere, but they just reminded me of what I'd lost. I have to think of the future.' She ran a hand through her hair. 'Which is not to say I don't fret. When Ben does his wandering act, I do a lot of fretting. I worry he'll go the same way as his mam, you know?'

Tara squeezed Carmel's hand. It felt bony, yet warm. 'I think he'll be absolutely fine.'

'Most of the time I think that too. But there are days when he's with me, chirruping away – you've heard him – and I wonder about the times I wasn't there. When he was in that kip of a flat with Rosanna and her junkie friends. He's such a clever lad, he must remember some of it. I find myself wanting to say to him, "What did you see, Ben? What did you see?"'

In the car, Tara switched her phone back on. Immediately it jangled to life. There were four texts from Craig and three voice messages. First he sounded annoyed that she was late. Then he sounded concerned. By the third message, his anger had been restored. 'What are you playing at?' he asked.

The phone also told her that it was twenty to eleven. She hadn't dared look at her watch while Carmel was there. It would have been rude. No, rude didn't begin to cover it. When somebody tells you something so big, so heart-scaldingly honest, everything else feels inconsequential. Even her own family's travails seemed tiny by comparison.

Tara tried to picture Carmel's daughter in jail. She'd once done a feature on life in prison, and what struck her was the difference between the men and women. Many of the young men were still full of bravado, but almost without exception the women were sad and beaten-down.

The more selfish part of her hoped that Craig might be motivated by her late arrival. That he might see how much her job mattered to her, and go easy on the travelling plans. She dialled his number. No answer. She dialled again. She'd leave a message, explain how sorry she was, assure him she'd be home in fifteen minutes. This time, he picked up.

'Craig? I'm really, really—'

'So you're still alive, then? Jesus, Tara, I was worried about you. Much longer and I'd have gone to the guards. Where are you?'

'You know Carmel – the woman I met in St Monica's Mansions? Well, I went to see her and—'

'I can't believe you chose to work when you knew I was making dinner. Would it have killed you to call and let me know what was going on?'

'No, only—' She realised she was talking to a dead line. She drove home at a frantic speed, one half of her brain formulating apologies, the other half reeling from Carmel's story. She was doing calculations in her head. Carmel was forty-six, she reckoned. Only forty-six.

She barrelled in the door, flustered and agitated, a hundred explanations on the tip of her tongue. A note sat in the middle of the kitchen table. *Dinner ruined. Gone to pub*, it read. The meal was in the bin. By the looks of it, Craig had made chilli. Throwing it away had been stupid. If she'd been three days rather than three hours late, it would still have been perfectly edible. That was Craig, though: a man for the theatrical gesture.

By now, Tara was edgy. If there was going to be a scene, she'd prefer to get it over with. She considered trying to find him, but he could be in any one of a dozen pubs. She called, except his phone was switched off. There was no choice. She would just have to wait for his return.

Chapter 10

Tara shut the front door and walked out into a featureless morning. During the night, the sky had clouded over: that layered milky cloud that looks like it goes on forever. The street was curiously empty. It reminded her of childhood mornings when she would walk along a deserted street and worry that some catastrophe had struck. She would picture herself as the last person alive.

At two o'clock, Craig had rolled in. Tara lay motionless while he banged and clattered around. Eventually she heard him stomp into the spare room. After ten minutes, she realised he planned on staying there. Her apologies prepared, she got up and padded in to talk to him. He wasn't ready to listen. 'Tomorrow, OK?' he said, only it was more of an instruction than a question.

Knowing Craig, he had probably stayed awake most of the night nursing his grievances. She was almost ashamed to admit that she'd enjoyed a perfect sleep. She was like Ben; the house could fall down around her and she would slumber on. It was a wonderful gift.

She had received an e-mail from Niall who was sitting tight in Dubrovnik. Reading between the lines, he wasn't doing much else. She got the impression that he'd run out of money and his options were limited. He was as full of silliness as ever. He had adopted a cat. Or rather, the cat had adopted him. *Luckily enough*, her brother wrote, *the cat – I've called him Seedy because that's how he looks – is happy enough to eat leftover pizza. He's a bit low-rent. Like me.*

Oh, come home, Niall, she thought. *I could do with a few laughs. So could the rest of the family.*

As she started the car, Tara cobbled together a plan of action. She would knock off work early, go to the supermarket and cook a fancy dinner. While she was at it, she'd tidy herself up a bit. Maybe even get her hair done. Strictly speaking, she shouldn't be wasting her money. New bills were popping up every day like noxious weeds. Yet, as pathetic and girly as it might sound, tamed hair always made her feel more confident.

Then she would sit down with Craig and have a proper talk.

Amby Power was in constant motion. Even when he sat down, one knee jiggled and his fingers tapped a beat against the side of the desk. Occasionally he picked at his teeth.

All this movement made Damien nervous. Perhaps that was the plan. He was a canny old buzzard, was Amby. Damien was outlining his father's predicament. Scratch that, *his* predicament. No, better yet, his *family's* predicament. He had never played the role of supplicant before. But then he'd never needed money before.

Amby's craggy face was impossible to read. At random intervals he would make a clicking noise or go, 'Hmmm', but that was it. The man was worse than Gus for the 'growing up the hard way' act. He was from Waterford, or 'Wawderfurdth' as he liked to pronounce it, for fear you doubted his authenticity.

'So, that's about it,' Damien said. 'The funds aren't there for your grandchildren's education, and I don't know what we're going to do.' He decided not to mention all the other bills that needed paying. They could wait for another day.

'I went to the tech, myself,' Amby replied. 'It did me no harm.' He scratched his head through his grey comb-over. 'In those days, mind, you cut your cloth according to your measure. And a man with a family to support would scrounge around for any work he could find.'

Damien said nothing. He couldn't afford a falling out. In his view, Felicity should have asked her father for the money, but she didn't agree. 'It'll sound better coming from you,' she'd insisted.

'Daddy thinks money matters are for men, and it's best to humour him.' In Amby's world, men did the providing. Damien had never thought of his own dad as a feminist but, by comparison with the man in front of him, he was practically Germaine Greer.

They were in the office of Powerful Parties, his father-in-law's business. It was hard to believe, but the dourest fecker in Dublin, a man for whom the phrase 'charismatic deficit' could have been coined, organised children's parties for a living. If you wanted puppets, clowns, magic or general giddiness, he was your man. Right then his eyes were clamped shut, his knee still jitterbugging away. Whether he was engaged in serious thought or simply pretending, Damien wasn't able to tell.

When at last he spoke, his voice was laced with false concern. 'One more time, Damo,' he said, 'remind me how this unfortunate situation came about.'

The bastard was really milking it, but what could Damien do other than go through his story again? He was about to emphasise how hard he was working as a councillor, then quickly changed tack and focused on the children. Amby was suspicious of politics of any kind. Just like Gus.

In his more introspective moments, Damien wondered whether his father's antipathy towards politicians had made that life seem more appealing. Even as a teenager he'd had no truck with the sex and drugs and rock'n'roll version of rebellion. Protest marches, all-night vigils: they were his world. He liked reading Noam Chomsky and listening to Rage Against the Machine. Fidel Castro and Enver Hoxha were on his bedroom wall. Actually, that last bit wasn't true; it was a story made up by Niall. When people accused Damien of being humourless, he recounted it. 'See, I can laugh at myself,' he'd say. Growing up, Niall had been the raucous son, the tester of the patience of saints, but Damien had been the one who received all the head-shaking and lecturing. 'Don't worry, Joan, he'll grow out of it.' How often had he heard his father say that?

For Gus, politics was a necessary evil. The only time he showed any interest was when debate spilled over into spectacle. He loved election coverage, especially count day, which he viewed as a cross between the All-Ireland Final and the Eurovision Song Contest. Frequently Damien was asked whether he believed in everything he said. To him, the question was nonsensical. Of course he did. He believed in his argument over his opponent's argument, his policy over their policy. Politics was an all-or-nothing world. There was no room for shades of grey or respecting your adversary's point of view. Every day you set out your stall and did your damnedest to undermine your enemies. If you started seeing merit in the views of others, you might as well give up.

Amby heaved himself around in his chair, stared at the ceiling, scrunched up his mouth. Damien gazed at a pile of party detritus: a scarlet acrylic wig, a pirate's hat, a magic wand. He wished the old miser would get on with it. A busy day of council activity lay ahead. Briefly, he imagined what his opponents would make of this scene. Even the thought made him wince.

Eventually, the answer came. 'No can do, I'm afraid, Damo,' said Amby. 'No can do. Between ourselves, cash is as tight as the duck's proverbial.'

Damien rubbed the knuckle of one thumb across his forehead. He was sure the finances of Powerful Parties were far more buoyant than his father-in-law would have him believe, but he wasn't going to grovel. He would have to come up with another plan. 'If that's the way it is . . .' he started.

'However,' said Amby, a hint of a smile passing across his face, 'I am keen to come to the rescue, so I have a small proposal that may help both of us.'

'Felicity, I said I'm not doing it.'

'Is that what you told Daddy?'

Damien's elbows were resting on the kitchen table. His head was in his hands. 'Not in so many words, but I think he got the message.'

'The offer's still there, then?' said his wife as she whirled around the room, wiping, straightening, tidying. When the mood took her, she could be as restless – and as irritating – as her bloody father.

'I suppose.' He was having second thoughts about his decision to cancel a meeting with a local residents group. At that moment, even the worst head-wreckers, the most recalcitrant moaners, wouldn't be as hard on the ears as Felicity. He noticed her old sewing basket sitting on the counter. One hole-filled sock was placed on top. A saucepan of butter beans simmered on the hob, the steam giving the small kitchen a claustrophobic feel. He couldn't say for sure but Damien suspected that both were there to underline their indigent status. To let him know he had failed.

Felicity was a complex woman. It wasn't that her public image as a champion of protest politics was false. Her politics were impeccable. Palestine, pesticides, China, climate change: whatever the issue, she was on the appropriate side. Rather, the older she got, the more certain she became that her own childhood was the model by which all childhoods should be measured. She was determined that Willow, Aifric and Rufus would have the same experience. Neither was she perturbed by charges of hypocrisy. 'I'm doing the best for my family,' she'd say. 'Isn't that every parent's duty?'

The couple met as teenagers. He remembered her shimmering into a protest meeting in a diaphanous purple skirt and green Doc Martens, thin plaits at the front of her long blonde hair. Strangely, he couldn't recall what the meeting was about. What was big back then? Shutting Sellafield, perhaps, or bringing peace to Bosnia. At twenty-one – straight after college – they had married. At the time, this had seemed like the most outrageous path possible. He could see Vee's puzzled stare and hear her exclaiming, 'Settling down? Are you completely crackers?' Neither had their parents been impressed. Gus had taken him for a 'talk'. 'No call for anything hasty,' he'd said.

Deep down, Damien wondered how much of his political

career had been dictated by a desire to please Felicity. Sure, he'd always been passionate about causes, but it was her insistence that he run for office that had spurred him on. If they had never met, what would he be doing now?

Once, Damien had planned on becoming a teacher. He'd had this image of a class of teens, all spellbound by his enthusiasm, their lives transformed by his skill. It would be like *Dead Poets Society* (if *Dead Poets Society* was set in inner-city Dublin). Like so many youthful notions, he couldn't remember discarding his ambition. It had just been superseded, he supposed.

His wife reached up to one of the cupboards, pulled down a pile of documents and plopped them onto the table in front of him. 'These came today,' she said. At the top of the first page was the St Attracta's logo. The following sheets listed an avalanche of items that both Willow and Aifric would need for the new term: books, uniform, specific shoes, specific bag, sports kit, hockey stick, tennis racquet, gum shield . . . On and on it went. He didn't dare look at the page listing the fees. He felt ill enough as it was.

She didn't utter a word, just stood there, her shoulders square, her face saying, *Now do you get it?*

'Can't Aifric use Willow's old books?' he asked.

'What planet are you living on, Damien? The books change all the time.'

'I'll bet she could wear Willow's old uniform. That would save a few bob.' He was, he figured, on safer ground here. Surely this would be the environmentally-friendly approach? Felicity placed a high premium on being a friend to the environment.

'Pfft,' came the instant reply. 'Do you want your daughter to be a laughing stock? To wear something all faded and hokey-looking?'

'Well obviously I don't, only . . .' Damien's thoughts were see-sawing. The idea of humiliating his daughter made him feel awful. The prospect of doing Amby's bidding made him feel worse.

'Perhaps you should think again about Daddy's offer.' One by one, Felicity gathered up the pages and fitted them back into their envelope. 'That's all I'm saying.'

For once everything was going to plan. Having told her news editor a convoluted lie about a broken wisdom tooth, Tara managed to escape work early. She made a quick sweep of the supermarket before calling Craig to tell him about her dinner arrangements. If he wasn't effusive, he wasn't hostile either. 'I'll explain what happened,' she said, 'and we can talk about . . . well, we can talk about travelling or whatever you like.'

While Craig was uppermost in her thoughts, Carmel, Ben and Jenelle were there too. At work she'd spent half an hour doing internet searches about babies born to drug-addicted mothers. She watched a video of a newborn shivering and shuddering and imagined what it must have been like for Carmel to see her granddaughter go through that. As was so often the case, the medical websites were vague about the long-term effects. Some children suffered developmental and behavioural problems; some didn't. She recalled Jenelle's screams and fear-filled face and guessed that her painful entry into the world had left its mark.

As she scuttled to and fro, she honed her words and perfected her arguments. A chicken was roasting in the oven, a pot of new potatoes was coming to the boil and a bottle of wine was chilling in the fridge. A small vase of sweet peas, snipped from the back garden, decorated the table. She'd gone to trouble over her appearance too. She was wearing the short black dress that Craig liked (men were so predictable) and her one pair of heels. Cooking in heels made her feel like a fifties housewife, like she should be setting out her man's slippers and ironing his newspaper. Even the thought made her giggle.

At what moment did Tara's plans fall apart? Was it when Craig sloped in the door an hour late? Was it when he picked at his dinner like she'd served up a plate of toenail parings? When he sniffed his wine like it was battery acid? Or, more likely, was it when she started to tell him about Carmel? His initial ill humour failed to ruffle her. In their time together, a pattern had formed. Craig would huff and puff until his anger blew itself out. Afterwards, he would barely remember what it was that had caused him to lash out. He'd get slightly embarrassed if the subject was raised. Slowly, Tara came to realise that this time was different.

'What I don't get,' he said, 'was why you had to do this interview last night. How many stories can you do about one dilapidated set of flats? And, with the greatest of respect, is that heroin stuff not kind of dated? If you ask me, people have little enough sympathy for junkies. You can't have a pint in town without some muppet hassling you for cash. Why would you want to read about them?'

Tara, believing he was being deliberately obnoxious, refused to rise to the bait. 'It wasn't like that. I wasn't talking to Carmel for a story. She was confiding in me.'

'Confiding in you? What are you – a social worker? Or were you helping Damien with his "good works in the community"?'

'I know you don't mean that. I was talking to a woman who needed to talk. That's all.'

Craig sipped his wine. 'Is this about the child, the boy you showed me on the news? Do you think you can rescue him or something?'

'Aw Craig, please . . .' She couldn't allow this to deteriorate any further. 'Listen, this is daft. Talking to Carmel . . . it was, well, even though it wasn't for an actual story, it was like part of my job. A responsibility, you might say.'

Ten, twenty seconds passed. She heard the buzz of a lawn-mower, the swish of an expensive car, the whoops and guffaws of teenage boys: the signature sounds of the red-brick suburbs.

'Responsibility,' Craig repeated.

The word hung over them like a bad smell. Tara wanted to explain. Truly, she did. But while sentences tumbled into her head, none of them felt right. So she sat there, digging her nails into the table's soft wood.

Finally he spoke again. 'You're a funny girl. You've no intention of going travelling, have you?'

She attempted to outline her compromise proposal. Leave of absence, she said. Three or four months, or a bit longer even. That was just a holiday, he replied, not what he'd meant at all. 'You've got to realise,' he added, 'that for some of us work isn't the be-all and end-all.' Up and down, back and forth, they went for the best part of fifteen minutes until neither was listening to anything the other said. She mentioned her dad, how worried she was, how she wasn't sure that Craig appreciated the magnitude of his problems. He accused her of being scared of adventure, of becoming staid. That's when she snapped, and the truth spilled out.

'Maybe I don't need to go anywhere,' she said. 'Maybe my adventures, my challenges, are right here. I know it's not fashionable to say this, but I like my job. I get a buzz from it, probably more of a buzz than I'd get from traipsing aimlessly around the world.' Warming to her theme, she stood up and began walking around the kitchen. 'I've heard everything you've said about the importance of going away, about it giving us perspective. But I've got plenty of perspective right here. Buckets of it. Talking to Carmel made me realise how lucky I am to be surrounded by family. I mean, can you *imagine* being completely on your own?'

Craig shrugged. She was in full flow, however, and wasn't going to stop now. 'I know my family drive me around the twist at times, but at the minute ... with the way things are ... this is where I have to be. And before you talk about me "living my own life", I've thought about that, and for the time being this *is* my life. I'm ...' She faltered slightly. 'I'm sorry if you can't understand.' As Tara spoke, any other plans flew away. She felt reckless with honesty. This wasn't just about being straight with Craig; it was about being straight with herself.

'I understand,' he replied. 'Believe me, I do. I understand that this isn't about India or Brazil or Timbuk-fucking-tu. It's about the fact that we've nothing in common anymore. That's if we ever had.' He knocked back half a glass of wine in one showy gulp, then got to his feet. 'I need to think,' he said as he picked up his leather jacket.

One part of Tara cringed at how clichéd and churlish his response sounded; another worried that she'd gone too far. Had she expected Craig to change his mind? Probably not. But, perhaps naively, she had hoped for a proper discussion. 'Will you be back later?' she asked.

'I don't think so. I might go and stay with my folks.'

'You can't walk out. I was trying to be truthful. That's all. I—'

'I'll call you, OK?'

He was halfway out the door. Tara felt her blow-dried hair reasserting its independence. 'But—' she began.

'I said I'd call you.' Quickly, he crunched across the yard.

From the doorstep she shouted his name, yet even as the word left her mouth, she knew he wasn't listening.

As chance would have it, Gus saw the activity below. These days he spent a lot of time at the window. He liked monitoring the comings and goings and the passings-by.

Did the day ever come, he wondered, when you stopped losing sleep over your sons and daughters? When you said, 'Mission accomplished. Time to relax'? He thought back on their childhoods. How he worried that Damien was too earnest; that Niall was too frivolous; that Vee was too secretive. And Tara? For some reason, what stuck in his mind was this crazy concern he'd had about her ears. When she was a baby they had stuck out, and he'd taken to pinning them back with masking tape. For an hour or so in the evenings, that was all. 'Can't do any harm,' he'd say. 'Indeed it can,' Joan would reply. 'Who knows what neuroses you'll give the poor girl? And if the social services catch you, there'll be hell to pay.' But there had always been laughter in her voice.

He turned around to see her standing behind him. 'I'll have to get you some net curtains,' his wife said, 'and a set of binoculars – so you can be a proper snoop.'

'Ructions downstairs,' he replied, before outlining what he'd seen.

'I don't reckon you should read too much into it,' said Joan. 'Everybody gets into a strop at one time or another.'

'Should I go down, do you think? To see if Tara's all right?'

'She won't thank you for interfering, Gus.'

He gave a reluctant nod. Besides, it wasn't as if they hadn't interfered already.

Chapter 11

Vee lurched between panic and malaise. Some days she flew around, making numerous – mostly futile – attempts to get her life in order. Other days, she was so heavy-hearted she could barely get beyond the front door. She felt like her every waking minute was spent trying to climb up a down-escalator.

A month after Aileen Duignan's abrupt goodbye, Vee remained without work. Eventually she decided to do something that would have been anathema to her even a few weeks before: she decided to claim the dole. But misfortunes never come singly, and she was stunned to discover that she was entitled to ... nothing.

'Nothing?' she repeated to the bored-sounding man on the official help line.

'Technically speaking,' he replied, 'you were self-employed. So, technically speaking, you're not eligible for any benefit.'

'But, technically speaking, how am I supposed to live?' she asked, trying – and failing – to keep the sarcasm from her voice.

'To be blunt, your options are limited. I mean, you *could* always ask your local community welfare office for emergency assistance. From what you've said, though, your husband is working, so ...' He faded away, as if he'd already wasted enough time on her trivial little life.

'I don't think we have community welfare officers in Mount Pleasant,' she said. 'It's not that sort of area.' At this point Vee would like to have hung up, but Mr Technically Speaking had beaten her to it.

Even before her feet hit the ground in the morning, she was obsessing about what she owed. She was also increasingly anxious about day-to-day spending. Although she'd always shared the household bills with Ferdia, they had separate bank accounts, and her husband appeared to assume she had cash put by to tide her over. The innocence of the poor man. Worse, she had snaffled the money he gave her towards their last electricity bill. To be fair, her hair had been in dire need of care and attention, and her eyebrows had gone wild. There was no way she'd get another job looking like that. She was putting out a sprat to catch a mackerel, or so she told herself.

Vee had decided that before she came clean to Ferdia, she would make an effort to tackle her personal debt mountain, to slice a bit off the top. After that, she'd address the parking fines situation. She wasn't unduly worried about those. A trawl of the internet yielded countless testimonials from people who'd got one over on the traffic wardens. Every day of the week, it seemed, cases were struck out – and often for the flimsiest of reasons. No, there was no hurry there.

There were things she'd be able to sell; she was sure of that. For a start, most of their wedding presents could go. They'd spent the last three years languishing in the garden shed. There were some monstrosities out there: crystal vases and china figurines and assorted items that hadn't been in vogue since her parents got married. The gifts from relatives were bad enough, but the presents from her father's business associates were beyond tacky. Following their honeymoon, in Vietnam and Bali, Vee had sent courteous letters to the donors of these geegaws, only now she didn't remember who had given what. No matter; she would lash it all up on eBay. Some of it must be retro enough to attract bidders.

Then there were her clothes and shoes – designer from tip to toe. They would raise a tidy sum. She would have to be cautious, though. Many of the items in her wardrobe were too beautiful to be appreciated by the women who scoured the second-hand designer stores. Vee had never been in any of these places, but she could picture the insipid creatures they attracted. No, a judicious edit; that's what was called for.

One evening, when she was stewing over another rejection from another PR company, Vee felt the urge to go out. What she wanted was to spend the night in town. She visualised herself surrounded by acquaintances, a glass of icy white wine in hand, gossip in the air. They would be in one of those bars where even the smell spoke of money. But, with her pockets empty, and no desire to talk about her troubles, this wasn't an option. Instead, she went visiting. Damien and Felicity lived in Harold's Cross, which was close to the council area he represented, but not within its actual boundaries. Vee was in that itchy, antsy humour where she fancied, if not a full-on row, at least a bit of a skirmish. And who better to provide it than her elder brother and his wife?

Their kitchen was the antithesis of her own. From what she could tell, somebody had once spent a great deal of money there. The problem was, this must have been thirty years before, and not a penny had been invested since. It was a testament to the durability of Formica, lino and pine. As if this wasn't bad enough, Felicity was one of those women who felt the need to possess all of the planet's spices and condiments plus a bewildering range of aging pots, pans and cookery books. On a cupboard door hung a photocopied list of ethically dubious products. *Don't Buy It, Don't Eat It, Don't Wear It*, it read.

The three were sipping camomile tea – nothing else had been offered – and dissecting Tara and Craig's relationship. This was the first that Vee had heard about the bust-up. In fairness, she'd been too busy trying to tackle her own problems to notice what was going on in her sister's life.

Felicity blew across the surface of her tea. 'I always reckoned he'd scarper when the going got tough.'

Damien's eyes widened. 'He hasn't, has he? Scarpered, I mean. I thought they'd just had a row.'

His wife adopted a superior look. 'I'll be stunned if he's back. He's not the type to tough it out.'

'Really?' said Vee. 'What type is he?'

'Vain, work-shy, fond of spending other people's money.' Vee feared this jibe was also aimed at her. She didn't get the chance to dwell on it, however, because Felicity was continuing her character assassination. 'To my mind, he's always had this air of laziness about him, this sense of entitlement. Not like Damien here who's got a new project on the go with my f—'

Damien pulled a funny face, and Felicity's sentence came to a halt. Vee was dying to learn more. She was sure Felicity had been about to say 'my father'. But that wouldn't make sense. No sensible person would have anything to do with Amby Power. The man was as tight as two coats of paint. Unfortunately, Rufus chose just then to ramble in.

'Can't sleep,' he mumbled. He was wearing blue pyjamas with a cartoon penguin on the front. Vee was no child expert, but it looked like he was actually having trouble staying awake. She'd been the same at his age: desperate not to miss anything.

He hopped onto his mum's knee and she kissed his sandy head. 'What do you say?' she asked him.

''Lo, Aunty Vee,' he said.

'Hello, Rufus.'

Her nephew was a sweet child, and for a moment Vee felt something uncomfortably close to envy. Quickly she banished this emotion and occupied herself with more familiar concerns. She was surprised to notice that even though Felicity was wearing Birkenstocks, she had shaved her legs and painted her toenails a pretty pale green; a *fashionable* pale green. Actually, now that she thought of it, weren't Birkenstocks having a moment too? Vee was disappointed. She hated it when her stereotypes were challenged. To tell the truth, her sister-in-law was an enigma. For years, the rest of the family had tended to dismiss her as little more than a regurgitator of right-on platitudes. 'As thick as month-old milk,' Niall liked to say. Of late, however, Vee had been revising her opinion. The woman's image might be all peace, love and organic lentils, but, when pushed, she had a waspish turn of phrase that could floor opponents. She also had an astounding knack of getting what she wanted.

'So Vee, how are you coping?' Damien was asking, a provocative tone to his voice. 'I'd say your lifestyle isn't the same since the old man's money ran out.'

For some reason, perhaps it was Rufus's presence, Vee's desire for an argument had waned. 'Oh, you know,' she said airily, 'getting by. You?'

'Fine, fine. We've always kept the frivolity to a minimum. And, of course, compared to many people in this city, we're incredibly fortunate.' Damien continued with his exposition on the plight of the poor, yet an uneasiness in his voice, coupled with his earlier interruption of Felicity, suggested to Vee that she wasn't getting the full picture.

Her own money-making schemes were foundering. Her eBay items were only attracting token bids, and when she'd brought some of her cast-offs to an upmarket secondhand shop, the weasel-faced woman behind the counter had recommended that she try 'Cash for Clothes' instead. The cheek of her! In despair, she'd visited two or three money-lending websites. She got no solace there; the sums they offered were small, and even Vee balked at the interest rates.

More accustomed to squabbling with her brother, she thought she'd see if she could coax out the truth. 'I agree with you,' she said, although the unfamiliar words threatened to stick in her throat. 'I don't know how people cope, really I don't. Everything's so expensive. Like, the price of food is just bananas.'

'Be thankful you don't have a family to feed. Or educate,' said Felicity, as she ran a finger along her son's chin. His eyes were fluttering with sleep. 'We were thinking we might have to cut back in some areas. Get a smaller car, maybe.'

On and on she went with her cash-saving options, but Vee was no longer listening. A thought was germinating in her brain. She would sell her car. She wasn't entirely sure how she'd explain this to Ferdia, but that was a worry for another day.

They'd had fights before. That's what Tara kept telling herself. Craig had stomped out before, had failed to answer her calls before. This time, however, he'd been gone for three days. Now here she was, on Friday evening, walking up Grafton Street, hoping that soon he would get in touch.

In an attempt to play it cool, she had rationed her calls to one a day. She knew the row was partly her fault, but she didn't believe that grovelling would be right, especially when she had no intention of changing her mind about travelling. This didn't mean she *was* cool; she was ill with anxiety. Each evening when she finished work she switched off her phone. Some silly superstition convinced her that, this way, he was more likely to ring; that when she turned the phone back on, an affectionate, apologetic message would be waiting. As she threaded her way along the street, a similar superstition caused her to drop coins in front of a man with a dog sculpted from sand and a busker whose repertoire was stuck in the mid-nineties. She hoped her generosity, phony as it was, would bring her luck.

By rights, Tara should have been at a retirement party. One of the *Tribune*'s correspondents had reached sixty-five and was moving on. With Tom's drinks in mind, she had left her car at home. But she'd spent the afternoon on the brink of tears and feared that even the tiniest amount of alcohol would tip her over the edge. She contemplated ringing one of her friends. She'd known Stephanie and Niamh since school, and they had twenty years of shared secrets. Both were in steady relationships, though, and the bonds of their friendship no longer felt so tight. Would they want to spend a Friday night listening to her woes? Besides, she was tired; jaded from uncertainty. What she wanted was to go home, get a takeaway, have a bath and wait for Craig's call.

While she was on the Luas, the sky began to spit with rain. Just the occasional fleck rested on the windows of the tram, but the steel-coloured clouds promised more to come.

She was at the garden gate when a single magpie landed in

front of her. He was agitated, making an *ack*, *ack*, *ack* sound, like a machine gun. Tara looked at the bird, and mad as it was, she felt like he was taunting her; like he was announcing more bad luck. She gave him a lacklustre salute. This, she told herself, was a superstition too far. Still, there was no point in courting ill fortune. And no one had seen her.

'You'll have to be more enthusiastic than that,' said a man's voice. 'The salute doesn't work unless you mean it.'

Damn, thought Tara. She looked up to see . . . oh, what was his name? The fellow who worked with her father? Something with an R? Rory, that was it. 'Uh, hi there.'

'Hi again.' He grinned before giving the bird a showy greeting. 'And hello to you, Mr Magpie. Pay no heed to our friend here. She's only pretending not to believe in your powers.'

Tara felt the heat rising up from her neck. 'I don't normally go around waving at birds.'

'Shhh,' he replied, mischief on his face. 'He'll hear you, and then we'll be in serious trouble.'

Feeling like a total idiot, she smiled. 'Um, nice to see you again.'

'Don't worry, I'm only messing with you,' Rory said.

'You're grand. I'm a bit distracted. One of those weeks, you know?'

'Don't I just? At the moment, every week seems like one of those weeks. And by the looks of things,' he peered into the sky, 'we've a wet weekend in store.'

Tara sighed. 'I think somebody somewhere made a rule. In any given year, one sunny week is all we're allowed. For fear we lose the run of ourselves.' The rain was gathering momentum, the occasional spit threatening to become a persistent downpour. Dark splotches were gathering on Rory's pale grey jacket. The magpie had had enough and, chattering all the while, he flapped away. 'I better let you go,' she said, 'before it gets any worse. I hope you're parked nearby.'

'I'm on the Luas, but the station isn't far . . .' It was then that the clouds surrendered to the pressure, and the true deluge began.

'And they call this summer,' said Tara as she made a lunge for her front door. She waved a hand at Rory. 'Come on, would you? You're going nowhere in this.'

'Eh, OK,' he replied. Not that he had any choice. The rain had become a wall of water, giant drops hurtling to the ground.

And that was how she found herself, on a June Friday night, sitting in her front room with a stranger. They were eating pizza prised from the back of the freezer (she didn't dare look at the best before date) and drinking Craig's fancy artisan beer. 'Did you ever notice how this stuff always has a ridiculous name?' asked Rory. 'Bishop's Underpants or some such?' And bizarrely, inappropriately, she was enjoying herself. Oh, she kept making references to Craig, for fear the lanky fellow across the room had any funny notions. Almost immediately, she'd laugh at herself for being so presumptuous.

Rory told her that he was twenty-eight and originally from Clare. 'Not the touristy part,' he said. 'I'm from Shannon, near the airport and the factories.' He lived in Dundrum with his brother, Aidan, who was a trainee solicitor, his other brother, Finian, a librarian, and Aidan's girlfriend, Janey, who did 'a bit of this and that'.

Initially, Tara was going to quiz him about the business. Here was her chance to find out more about her dad's struggles. Then they had another beer, and she decided that this would be a mistake. She didn't want to discuss her over-burdened dad or her subdued mum. She wanted a night off from her moody sister, her awkward brothers and her relationship limbo. What she did do was tell him about Carmel.

'That's quite a tale,' he said. 'The woman sounds like a marvel. What's she going to do when her daughter gets out of jail?'

'We didn't talk about that. I presume she'll have to give Ben and Jenelle back. That's if Rosanna wants them. It'll be a shame, though.'

'But whatever Rosanna's done in the past, they're her kids.'

'True, only after the way she treated them, how would you ever be able to trust her? And Ben's as sharp as they come. When he gets to know the truth, how will *he* be able to trust her?'

'Hmmm, I hear what you're saying. Makes the rest of us appreciate how fortunate we are ... if that doesn't sound overly schmaltzy.'

She smiled. 'You've been spending too much time with my dad. He comes out with lines like that. Seriously, though, I know what you mean. I feel the same.'

Rory swallowed the last of his beer. 'I should hit the road.'

'I think we've two bottles left. What do you reckon?'

'Go on, then. You've convinced me.'

Tara was in the kitchen when she thought she heard the click of the front door. 'Dear God, no,' she whispered, 'not now.' She definitely heard voices. She took a deep, trembly breath and went back into the living room.

Rain dripped down Craig's face (he maintained umbrellas were for girls), and his jacket was dark with water. He shook like a dog, sending drops spraying in all directions. 'I was just saying hello to your new friend here,' he said. 'Is your phone broken or something? I've been ringing all evening.'

'Ahm, hi there. My phone? I've been keeping it switched off because ...' She didn't know how to finish the sentence. 'This is Rory. He works for my dad. He got caught in the rain, so I invited him in. And with the state of the weather, he kind of got stuck here.'

'So he tells me.'

Please, Craig, she thought, *be polite*. 'I wasn't sure if ... when ... you'd be back.'

'Obviously.'

'Shocking old night, isn't it?' said Rory. 'Any sign of it easing off?' From the geniality of his tone, Tara assumed he was either unaware of the bad vibes being sent out by Craig, or was choosing to ignore them. She hoped it was the former.

But her boyfriend appeared determined to vent his irritation. 'Stuck here,' he said. 'Are the taxis all on strike?' When neither answered, he bent down and picked up an empty bottle. 'Any of these left? No, I guess not. And there was I looking forward to coming home and having a beer.'

'I was in the kitchen getting two more. You can have one and—'

'Nah, I can see I'm surplus to requirements here.'

'Listen, man,' said Rory, who seemed properly perplexed. 'I think you're getting the wrong idea. Like Tara said, I was only waiting 'til the weather cleared.' He was on his feet. 'Anyway, it's probably time I made tracks.'

Craig had a scowl on his face like a toddler just woken from a nap. 'No, no – you stay where you are. I'd be wary of this one, though. She's far more cunning than she looks.' He turned to go.

Tara felt like a valuable ornament had slipped from her fingers and she was frantically trying to reassemble the pieces. 'Ah, Craig,' she said, 'will you quit the messing? You're deliberately being thick, and there's no need for it.'

'I'm not the one who's messing,' he said. 'I'm not the one who's being thick either.' And, as suddenly as he'd arrived, he was gone.

Chapter 12

After Rory had left – in a cloud of embarrassment and apologies – Tara rested her palms against the wall. She tried to remain composed, but her breathing was shallow and jagged. Tears pooled in her eyes. In the end, she succumbed. For an hour, perhaps more, she cried, sobbing and shaking until there was nothing left. As her head cleared, she knew what she had to do.

She thought about the relationship she knew best – her parents' marriage. Tara wouldn't claim that they never fell out. And sometimes when they fell out, they were *loud*. When she was a child they used to have the same argument over and over again. Joan would start complaining that Gus was never home, and he would say she had no idea how hard it was to run a business. She'd counter with, 'Well, you should try bringing up these four, *then* you'd know what hard is.' So he'd say, 'Righty-ho, I'll stay at home and let you take care of the office.' Then she'd make offended noises and accuse him of being smart. Around and around they'd go, until one of them – usually her dad – would say, 'This is stupid.' And before you knew it, they'd be laughing and joking about something that only the two of them would find funny.

So, no, Tara couldn't say that her parents never fell out. But there was an ease about them, an understanding. She was reluctant to say, 'They belong together.' It sounded so corny. But, when you thought about it, they did.

Did she belong with Craig? That's what she'd wanted. She'd wanted it so much she'd been unwilling to acknowledge just how shoddy their relationship had become. She thought again about what had happened earlier, about her boyfriend's tantrum and about her willingness to accommodate it. And she cringed. She couldn't spend her life like this. Watching every word; trying to bend herself into shapes to suit someone else; fooling herself that this was normal. This was not to say she didn't love Craig. If Tara understood nothing else, she understood that it was impossible to understand the relationships of others. How often had her friends held her boyfriend up to scrutiny and found him wanting? And yet, for her, he had provided excitement. He challenged her, made her life more interesting. But it wasn't enough.

She slept fitfully, the empty bed a reminder of what she had resolved to do in the morning. When the morning came, she wasn't able to eat. Even her coffee tasted sour. Outside, the day was unexpectedly bright. Light cloud had broken into a thousand pieces, like a shattered windscreen.

Tara was surprised when Craig answered his phone. Without saying very much, they arranged to meet in a café. Neutral ground. Finding it too crowded, they bought takeaways and went for a walk. All the while, their conversation was stilted, more like an uncomfortable first date than a looming break-up. Save for a man and a little girl throwing hunks of bread to the ducks, the park in Ranelagh was empty. They found a bench where they could sit and say what had to be said.

Craig started by apologising. 'I haven't slept,' he said. Tara didn't doubt him. He looked all wrong, his face baggy and unshaven. 'You know me,' he continued, 'that's how I am – forever opening my mouth without thinking. I suppose it must be difficult for you to grasp. You do enough thinking for ten people.'

Tara clasped her hands together. 'By the way, just so you understand, there really was nothing going on. What I said about us sheltering from the rain, that's how it was.'

'Yeah, I believe you,' said Craig with a half-smile. 'He didn't look like your type. For a few minutes I thought you'd invited him in just to annoy me, to show me how easily you could get another guy.'

'Ah, Craig!'

'I know, I know. I was being stupid. But, like I said, my mouth was open before my brain was full engaged. Anyway . . .'

He paused, waiting, no doubt, for her to say he was forgiven. They could spend the day like this, she thought. Getting within touching distance of honesty and then pulling back.

'So . . .' she began.

'So?'

'I've been thinking about what you said the other night . . . about us not having anything in common? Well, you were right. The two of us . . . it's not working anymore, is it?' *Was it possible*, she asked herself, *to split up with someone without saying things that, in any other context, would make your toes curl?* She studied Craig's face, which was surprisingly impassive. It took him twenty seconds or more to respond. When he spoke, his voice was quiet.

'What are you saying to me?'

'I—'

'Is this the end of us? Is that what you're saying?'

'I—'

'Because, you know, Tara, I am what I am. You can't expect me to change.'

'I'm not asking you to change.'

'Why now then, huh? It's not like we've never fallen out before. Are you looking for a bit more wheedling and apologising? Is that it? OK, I was way out of line last night. Way, way out of line. That poor gobshite . . . Richie or whatever his name is . . . the guy looked petrified.'

Craig gave a smile that would have ranked highly on the all-time charm-ometer. But for once, Tara wasn't swayed. 'Rory,' she whispered. 'His name's Rory.' She paused. 'Anyway, that's not what I want. Apologising won't make any difference. I doubt you're happy either, are you?'

His smile wilted and he lifted one shoulder. 'I won't pretend everything's good. I'm just saying let's not do anything rash, y'know.'

Once more they fell into silence. Increasingly, Tara got the sense that Craig's words were motivated by pride. He didn't want her to do the breaking up. If there was going to be hassle, he needed to be its instigator. Her brain was bombarded by reasons to stay together. She remembered good times, lots of good times. At their best, they'd had that exhilarating sense of conspiracy that a relationship can bring; that sense that you're the only two to see the world as it really is. And that wasn't all. They had invested three years in being together. *Invested*: it sounded wrong, too business-like, too clinical. But wasn't that what you did? You gave a relationship your energy and commitment and, in time, you expected a dividend. If she walked away now, had she squandered those years?

Tara almost capitulated. She almost said, 'You know what? Let's not do this. Let's give it another go.' But she didn't. She took a long breath and told him it was over.

The only reaction she noticed was a minute twitch in his left cheek. 'If you're sure,' he said, his voice so expressionless you'd swear they were discussing what to have for dinner.

'I am,' she replied, her stomach flipping over. 'You have things you're itching to do . . . travelling and that . . . and I'd only feel like I was holding you back.'

'If you're sure,' he said again.

In front of them a horse chestnut tree shook. The entire tree was filled with birds. From the deepest caw to the highest twitter to the throatiest coo, they were all in full song. Tara was grateful for the noise. They exchanged a chaste goodbye kiss and for some time they held hands, periodically letting their grip loosen then tightening it again. Neither said anything. Finally they let go, and Craig got up to leave.

'My stuff?' he asked.

'You can collect it whenever you like. Right now, if you want. I'll probably sit here for another while.'

'Not now,' he said. In a couple of days, they agreed. He said he'd text her when he was calling round so she could make herself scarce, if that's what she'd prefer. 'And about your dad?' he said. 'I hope his problems get sorted. Really, I do.'

For the first time, Tara feared she would cry. *Best not watch him walk away*, she thought. She sank her teeth into her bottom lip, closed her eyes and counted to two hundred. When she opened them again, he was gone.

To begin with, she told nobody. She was well aware that her dad didn't like Craig, and that her mum was, at best, indifferent. Their reaction would be carefully modulated, yet she was sure their pleasure would seep out somehow. Her phone went unanswered, her e-mails unchecked. Vee called at least five times. Doubtless she was looking for something. Tara couldn't find the energy to cope with her. She felt flat and anchorless and she didn't expect anyone to understand.

On top of this, she started to fret that Rory would tell her father about Craig's outburst. Eventually, having worked herself into a lather, she found her mum and gave her a sanitised version of the break-up. 'Tell Dad,' she said. 'Only promise me you won't let him gloat too much.'

Joan released a series of familiar clucks. 'Oh, Tara, I'm not going to lie to you. I won't claim your dad has any great time for Craig. But he wouldn't want to see you unhappy. I swear he wouldn't.'

Tara didn't argue, but she could picture Gus's reaction to the news. He'd have to stop himself from dancing around the garden singing 'Zip-a-dee-doo-dah'.

As the days passed, she rationed her moping. She was determined not to wallow in break-up misery. She was twenty-nine; it wouldn't be right to behave like she had at twenty. Back then, even the most minor romantic rebuff had seen her and her friends gathering around a bottle of wine. They sat in the candlelight and listened to Snow Patrol albums while assuring each other that their wasters of boyfriends didn't deserve them. When she thought about it, it was like they actually enjoyed their misfortune. This was different. Mostly she kept it together. She focused on her work and on tidying the apartment. She would have to find a new tenant. Or maybe she should move on. She was loath to say the place had too many ghosts; it seemed overly dramatic. But that was how she felt.

Tara's romantic history was less than glorious. If it hadn't been for Vee's interference, she would have spent her teenage years alone. Her sister had insisted on fixing her up with a range of boys who she considered to be Tara's 'type': usually the excruciatingly dull brother of one of Vee's large circle of friends.

At college, she had fared slightly better. Her first serious relationship was with a physics student called Nathan O'Keeffe. Nathan was as steady as a mahogany table, and about as animated. At the mention of his name, Niall would pretend to fall asleep, and Vee would give a condescending smile. Damien would bring up the subject of his father, Turlough O'Keeffe, who had the habit of writing long, right-wing letters to the newspapers. Tara had been very fond of Nathan. Hand on heart, though, she couldn't claim to have felt anything stronger than fondness. When he went to London to a do a post-grad, their relationship ran out of steam. Last she heard, he was engaged to a doctor and living in Perth. In her early and mid-twenties, there had been a range of similar men. In most cases, she had done the breaking-up, prompting a litany of lectures from Vee. 'You might come to regret your pickiness,' her sister had said with the smugness of one who'd never known a day when men weren't clamouring for her attention.

One morning that week, Tara was in the newsroom about to start work on a story about refuse collection (she always got the glamorous markings), when a cardboard tube arrived. Inside was a picture that only a seven-year-old would paint. The sky was a thin blue line, the sun a lopsided disc. In the centre were two stick figures: a boy with a huge grin and a girl with lots of yellow hair. Along the bottom a message read: *To Tara, thanks from Ben and Jenelle O'Neill.* Tara could see the pencil marks where Ben had written out the words before using his paintbrush. She pictured him at work, concentration on his freckled face. Accompanying the painting was a note from Carmel that explained how Ben had wanted to say thank you for his books. *I don't think we'll make an artist of him!* she added.

The boy's thoughtfulness hit Tara like a jab to the stomach. Why was it that a kind act could overwhelm her with sadness? Carefully, she fitted the picture back into its container. She folded the note and placed it in her handbag. Only then did she go to the bathroom, lock herself into a cubicle and allow her tears to flow.

Niall smiled at the sign over the café. *Internet, Cocktails, Breakfast*, it said: three of life's essentials in one spot. Alas, he had money for only one, and, on this occasion, it would have to be the internet. The e-mails he received from home were becoming increasingly strange. Depending on who was writing, Niall found himself fascinated, or worried, or completely flummoxed.

Outside, the Dubrovnik afternoon was white hot. Over the road, beside the water, new arrivals lumbered by, buckling under the weight of their rucksacks. With a loud scrape, Niall pulled up a chair and opened his account.

Gus was first up. For the old man, e-mail was like a telegram. Keep it tight, keep it terse was his motto, as if any superfluous words would cost him. *I assume you've nothing else to do*, he wrote, *so I want you to keep an eye on the apartment. Things aren't getting any better here, and I need to get the maximum price for the place.*

Joan viewed e-mail as just another way of sending a letter, and she wrote letters in the old-fashioned way. To begin with, there was a lot of chatter about the weather (*we've had worse*). This was followed by some minor gossip about various relations (*your cousin Cyril failed his exams; your aunt Greta is in hospital with her gallstones*). At last, she wound herself up to the real news. She was concerned about the rest of the family, although her reasons for worrying about Damien and Vee were rather odd. Apparently Damien had got his hair cut and didn't look at all like himself, and a neighbour had spotted Vee on a bicycle. *Your sister on a bicycle – whatever next!?* she wrote. *Even as a child, I couldn't get her to do anything that might mess up her hair.* The headline item was that Tara and Craig had split up. Unfortunately Joan didn't give much away about how or why this had happened. Instead, she confined herself to a series of banalities about it probably being for the best.

As was her way, his mum said nothing about herself. Even though by no means a stereotypical Irish mammy, she was of a generation that didn't like to complain. Equanimity was her defining characteristic. If something really annoyed her, she would clomp about the house for a bit or go out to the garden and weed and dead-head with a vengeance. Rarely did she raise her voice. Although she'd been disappointed by his decision to leave Shine and Co., she'd said little. The only thing he recalled was a coded speech about what she might like to have done with her life if she'd had the opportunity. 'Opportunities weren't for the likes of us,' she'd added. Niall had been confused. 'Didn't everything turn out well for you?' he'd asked. 'You're not getting me, pet. I would have liked an education,' she'd replied, her voice wistful. He wondered what it would take to get Joan totally riled.

Gus, on the other hand, had no qualms about expressing his anger. When his dad was annoyed, his voice could strip paint. Back in March, Niall had forgotten Joan's birthday. So had Vee and Damien. Gus had been incandescent. Niall, who was in Goa at the time, would never forget the phone call. The mildest insult was 'ungrateful pup'. 'A disgrace' and 'two ends of a bollocks' had also featured.

Next was an e-mail from Vee. *Busy, busy, busy here*, she wrote. *I was hoping you could help me with a couple of questions.* A page of queries followed. Among her more intriguing requests, his sister wanted to know the quietest and quickest way of selling a car without it appearing on a garage forecourt ('a friend' was looking for advice), the number of parking fines you needed to accumulate before being prosecuted (another friend), and the amount you had to save with a Credit Union before they'd lend you, say, twenty thousand euro (she had lots of friends). Niall figured that Ferdia was well-placed to answer all of these questions –

certainly better placed than him – so that's what he advised.

As he typed his reply to Vee, he thought about the e-mail he hadn't received. This was the one that concerned him most. He'd written to Tara several times now. Lighthearted stuff mostly – about the exploits of Seedy the cat or local people he'd encountered or tourist portraits he'd drawn. More than a week had passed since he'd last got a response, and even that had been disjointed. Craig's departure must be causing her more pain than she was letting on.

Tara tried to wipe away the residue of her tears, but she was a blotchy, shiny mess. Scared that someone would notice, she slouched back into the newsroom, eyes welded to the floor. The news editor was standing at her desk. She tried the hay fever excuse, only you'd have to be a simpleton to swallow that, and the news editor was no simpleton. Neither, thankfully, was he without empathy.

'I don't know what's up with you,' he said, 'but you're no use to me or anyone else like this. Would you not take a few days off and sort yourself out?'

When she protested, he replied that it was an order not a request. Smothered in embarrassment, Tara went home. At regular intervals she gave herself a talking-to. Everybody else couldn't be wrong. She was better off without Craig. She was only twenty-nine. She'd meet someone in no time.

She couldn't continue to avoid people either. The last conversation she'd had about something other than work had been three days previously when she'd spoken to her mum.

Just then she noticed that Joan was in the back garden, pulling and prodding at weeds.

'Hi there,' Tara called. 'Would you like a hand?'

Joan put down her trowel before sitting back on the grass. 'Ach no, you're fine. I'd welcome some company, though. I've a feeling I'll be out here for a while.' She waved one hand along the bed of sweet peas and petunias.

Now that Tara examined the garden, she could see that it was unusually unkempt. The beds and borders looked ragged, and the lawn needed a cut; clover was starting to peep above the grass. 'Has Hughie not been?' she asked. For more than a decade, Hughie, a taciturn giant from County Donegal, had been doing the rough work in the garden, allowing her mum to concentrate on nurturing the flowers.

Joan tucked her bobbed hair behind her ears. 'Did I not tell you? With the way things are, we've had to let Hughie go.'

'Oh?' said Tara, as she sat down beside her mum.

'Edita too, unfortunately. She's been gone a few weeks now. They were both very good about it.'

Tara was annoyed with herself. She'd been so preoccupied with her own troubles that she hadn't noticed what was going on up-stairs. 'I'd no idea,' she said. 'Why didn't you tell me? No wonder you look so worn out.'

'Thanks a million, love. That's *just* what I wanted to hear.'

'You know what I mean,' Tara replied, as she rubbed her mum's hand. 'You always look great. But taking care of the house and the garden on your own? That's an awful lot of work.'

'Didn't I do it for years?'

'Except you were . . .' Tara didn't want to finish the sentence.

'I was younger then? Is that what you mean?'

'To be blunt about it, yeah.'

Joan closed her eyes and angled her face towards the sky. 'No money means no money, Tara. I thought you understood that.'

'Will you let me cut the grass then? And I could do some iron-ing or hoovering for you. Whatever needs doing, I'm your woman. Just give me a shout.'

'Your dad promised to do the lawn, and I'm determined to hold him to it,' said her mum with a smile. 'Anyway, you've your own flat to look after, not to mention your job.'

Tara explained that she wouldn't be going into the *Tribune* for a few days. As she did, she watched a bee sip at clover. He looked so velvety, she wanted to reach out and stroke him.

Joan picked up her trowel and absentmindedly passed it from one hand to the other. 'Would you not consider going away? I'm sure that'd be better for you than hanging around here.' She paused. 'I'm assuming you have the money?'

'I do, only with the way things are, I don't know that it'd be right.'

'Let me worry about what is or isn't right. A few days in the sun would do you a power of good.'

'I think you're forgetting something here, Mum. I don't have anybody to go away with.'

Joan sighed. 'OK, I just think you should take a break while you can. Things aren't going to get any easier for your dad. In fact . . .' she hesitated. 'There's a danger they'll get worse.'

'Then I'm definitely staying put,' said Tara, twirling a lock of hair around one finger. 'What's gone wrong?'

'Nothing for you to worry about,' said Joan. 'Not right this minute, anyway. Forget I spoke.' She looked away. 'Of course, you *can* hide away here with a long face on you, if that's what you want. Or . . . well, there is a way you could make yourself *really* useful.'

'I'm not with you.'

'There's Niall in Croatia, staying away just so he can prove some mad point about being a free-spirit or not conforming or some such nonsense.' She shook her head. 'Why he can't behave like an adult and get a job, I don't know. In my day, we were all in a huge hurry to be grown-ups. Now, the likes of Niall want to be kids forever. How can that be right?'

'I still don't follow you.'

'At a time like this, the lad should be here with his family. There's plenty he could be doing. Plenty.'

Tara was beginning to grasp what her mother was suggesting. 'So?'

'Why don't you go on over there and persuade your brother it's time to come home?'

Chapter 13

'I'll only need you for a month or two. Three tops. And once or twice a week, that's all. You have my word, Damo, and I can say no more than that.' After he made his pledge, Amby spat on his hand and expected Damien to do the same.

They shook on it, but a week later, as he prepared for his first job, Damien was still asking himself whether he could trust the old tightwad. Not that he had a choice; he had promised Felicity he'd raise the money for the school fees, and no matter where he looked he couldn't find a viable alternative. A degree in English and Politics wasn't of much use in an emergency, and he possessed no practical skills. His only work experience was with lobby groups and political campaigns. To begin with, he had considered other possibilities: some hours in a 24-hour shop, maybe, or behind a bar. But as much as he hated having anything to do with Amby, at least the job was anonymous. There would be no constituents having a gawk or a laugh. No sarky comments or public humiliation.

Damien had got his hair cut – a number three blade all around – so that it would fit neatly beneath his wig. Even so, the damn thing was eye-wateringly tight and already his head was pounding. The makeup was equally troublesome – thick and oily with a smell that reminded him of over-perfumed aunts. Amby had taught him how to apply it. 'Let's keep it traditional,' he'd said. 'I've no time for any of that new-fangled scary stuff. A clown ought to look like a clown.'

Ordinarily, his father-in-law relied on two unemployed actors to do his clowning. But one of the pair – a 'big useless gom' according to Amby – had got drunk and fallen down the stairs. With one leg in plaster, he wouldn't be fit for children's parties until the autumn. Damien was stepping into the breach.

No one was to know: that was his one stipulation. Not Canice or Jacinta, not Joan or Gus, and certainly not his brother or sisters. He could picture the smirk on Niall's face if he found out. Neither did he want Felicity to tell the children. With the best will in the world, one of them would say something to someone and his cover would be blown. She insisted the job was nothing to be ashamed of. 'It's my daddy's business,' she said, 'and it put food on the table when we were growing up.' He tolerated his wife's musings, until she came out with some line about clowning being honest, hard work. 'It's not,' he snapped, 'it's fucking humiliating.' Her sulk lasted for two days.

His instructions were simple. 'Clown around for a while,' Amby said. 'Make a fuss of the children, especially the birthday boy or girl. Blow up some balloons, pop one or two, act like a complete fool, pocket the cash, leave.' Special emphasis was placed on the word 'cash'. There was no place for cheques or credit cards in Amby's life. Damien agonised over whether the man paid any tax. He suspected not. Clearly, this was a heinous way to behave, symptomatic of Ireland's afflictions, not something he should be supporting. Then another surge of pragmatism would hit, and he'd decide he had no option but to play along.

The council elections were approaching. Last time out, Damien had scraped in, taking the fifth seat in a five-seat ward. Next time, he aimed to top the poll. Most people he encountered had no regard for either government or opposition. 'A crowd of shysters,' they'd say. Felicity was convinced that the opportunity was there for an independent candidate – a *strong* independent candidate – to come to the fore. After that, the country would be heading into a general election, and who knew what chances might present themselves?

The problem was, elections were expensive. Posters, leaflets, advertisements in the local paper, lifts to polling stations, pints for canvassers – the list was endless. He couldn't see how he'd be able to mount an effective campaign. Gus was unlikely to have the funds, that was for sure. He would have to work on Amby, convince him that becoming a political benefactor was a sound idea.

Damien examined the bathroom where he was getting changed. Garryowen had nothing on this place. There was enough marble for a medium-sized graveyard, and a family of five would fit into the bath. He'd been in smaller flats. Fortunately, most of his bookings were out this way – in Killiney or Dalkey or Glenageary. In Dublin's far southern suburbs nobody was likely to recognise him.

He took a minute to adjust the straps on his multi-coloured dungarees (Damien prided himself on being ascetically thin, and the suit fitted only where it touched). Then he popped on his shiny nose and checked the laces on his long red and yellow shoes. From the back garden he could hear the sound of children squealing with excitement. His audience was waiting.

'Stolen?' said Ferdia, raking a hand through his floppy fringe. 'When?'

'Eh, two days ago,' replied Vee, praying that she sounded convincing. 'I came down in the morning and it was gone.'

'Why didn't you tell me?'

'I knew you'd worry. And there was nothing you could do, so I said to myself, *Don't distract Ferdia from his work. The news can wait until he gets back.*'

Ferdia had spent the week at a circuit court sitting in the west. Now he was striding around the kitchen, while Vee told him about her stolen car.

'What did the police say?' he asked.

'You know the gardaí. A guy called around, scribbled down the details, drank a cup of tea, made sympathetic noises. Then he said that by that stage the car was probably a smouldering wreck in a field somewhere. Oh, and he gave me a tonne of forms to fill in.'

'And the insurance?'

Vee shifted on her high stool. 'They were fine,' she lied. 'It'll take a while for the money to come through, though.'

'You poor thing,' said Ferdia, breaking off from his pacing to rub his wife's shoulders. 'Bad luck seems to be following you around. Did any of the neighbours see anything strange?'

'Not a thing, I'm afraid.'

In truth, there was every chance that one of the locals did see Vee's dark blue Volvo leaving the street for the last time. They wouldn't have noticed anything amiss because she had been driving. There had been no policeman and no insurance claim. She'd received ten thousand euro from a garage near the airport. Not a great price, she knew, but cash was cash, and there was only a tiny chance of anyone she knew spotting the vehicle. Afterwards, she had distributed the money among her creditors. The sum wasn't nearly enough to pay off what she owed, but a thousand here, two thousand there, would be enough to get them off her back for a while. She held on to a small sum, a thousand euro to be precise, for her parking fines. Then, buzzing with a blend of relief and guilt, she arranged to meet one of her best friends, Lottie Bond.

Lottie's husband, Ross, was something important in technology. He earned a fortune, which was just as well because the man was Mogadon in human form. Lottie was doing her best to spend that fortune. Despite having a first-class honours degree in Commerce, she'd never had a real job – 'work gives you wrinkles,' she explained. Instead, she devoted her considerable talents to being beautiful. Lottie was blonde and taut, and she spoke like a magazine: she bought 'transitional pieces'; women 'rocked' dresses; their style was 'effortless'. In short, she was Vee with the sound turned up to eleven.

As the two strolled around Brown Thomas, Vee was swamped by temptation. She stroked skirts and jackets, fingering their delicate fabric, inhaling their expensive smell. It had been such a long time, *weeks*, since she'd had anything new. For a while, she managed to keep a lid on that temptation. She watched her friend patrolling the changing rooms, striking poses in a variety of exorbitantly priced dresses. She was practically sick with envy, but she told herself that she was strong.

It was in the shoe department that her resolve crumbled. Oh, but the sandals were exquisite: laser-cut black suede Alaïa with perfect slender heels. Just trying them on made her feel like a new person. The owner of these sandals could not possibly have a miserable life.

The pair spent the evening drinking champagne in the bar of the Shelbourne hotel. What they were celebrating, Vee wasn't sure, but Lottie was paying. It was like old times. They rounded off the night in a little Italian place where they ate bits of this and pieces of that, and drank another bottle of fizz. When Vee saw the bill she feared she'd have a seizure. It was her turn to pay, though, and that's what she did. Intoxicated from alcohol and the joy of spending, she toyed with telling Lottie about the Shine family's problems. She decided against. Word would get out, and she didn't want to risk the wrath of Gus.

Sixteen hours later, every millimetre of her head was banging. Her eyes, her ears, even her teeth hurt. Of her one thousand euro, precisely seventy-nine cents remained. How she lamented her day of pleasure, especially her clandestine shopping. When would she ever get to wear those sandals? She was also mightily put out to learn that Tara had gone to Croatia. 'Just for a week,' her mum had said when she'd phoned. 'The girl works so hard, it'll do her good to recharge her batteries.' 'It's well for her,' Vee had replied, not caring that she sounded crabby and mean.

She realised that Ferdia was asking another question. What was she going to do about a replacement car, he wanted to know.

'I've been thinking about that, and I'm convinced there's no need for any rush. I've been using my bicycle so much lately, I wonder whether I need a car at all.' The cycling had been a smart pre-emptive move. Truly, there was no end to her deviousness. Plus, there was a significant side-benefit to having no car: she couldn't accumulate any more parking tickets.

'But what if there's an emergency? And what about work – surely you'll need a car for that?'

'I hate to remind you of this, darling, but right now I don't have any work. I'm worn out looking for work – except all I get are rejections. Every bloody day, another bloody rejection.' Vee told herself to calm down. She was becoming hysterical, and the last thing she needed was a row with Ferdia. She softened her tone. 'And in an emergency, can't I use your car?'

'Hmmm,' he said as his fringe-raking resumed. 'As you mention the work issue, I've been thinking . . .'

'Oh?'

'Perhaps it's time to cast your net a bit wider. Maybe you could look for . . . well, I don't know . . . receptionist work or something along those lines.'

She frowned. 'Seriously?'

'Or, what about a shop?'

'A *shop*,' she repeated, as though he'd suggested sewer-cleaning or a few shifts in an abattoir. 'My mother worked in a shop, Ferdia. *I* have a *degree*.'

'I don't want to be pedantic, Vee, but, strictly speaking, you don't.'

He was right. Vee had dropped out of college halfway through her final year. At the time, she'd insisted she was more suited to the real world, to making contacts and cutting deals. 'I'm a net-worker, not an academic,' she'd maintained. During the boom, she'd been able to gloss over her lack of formal qualifications. Her CV claimed she had 'studied French and Art History at University College Dublin'. This wasn't a lie; if people were dumb enough to assume she'd actually *graduated*, well, that was their look-out. The trouble was, she'd been spinning her tale for so long she'd come to believe it herself. It was sobering to be reminded of the truth.

Trying to soften the blow, Ferdia gave what he probably hoped was a reassuring smile. God love him, he was a hopeless actor. 'Of course,' he said, 'when I talk about you finding work in a shop, I mean as a manager. Or, what's that job where you tell people what to wear? You'd be super at that. Super.'

'Personal shopper,' said Vee.

'Super,' said Ferdia again, as though he was trying to persuade an awkward child to eat her vegetables.

'OK, I'll give it a go. I'll be on the case first thing Monday morning, I promise.' Vee returned her husband's smile. 'My luck's got to change soon.'

There was a chance that for a moment or two she believed what she was saying.

'Ah for heaven's sake,' said Gus, 'there's no reasoning with some people.' He threw down his phone and watched it skitter across the kitchen counter.

Joan raised an eyebrow. 'Your dinner's getting cold.'

'You don't want to know who that was?'

'I'm sure you're going to tell me.'

'That,' he said, settling into the chair, 'was Christy Hanrahan.'

'What's wrong with him?'

'It's not so much what's wrong with Christy, as what's wrong with Dolores. She was looking at one of those websites where they sell secondhand stuff at knockdown prices, and what did she see – only the wedding present they gave to Vee and Ferdia. Some class of ornament. Apparently she's very upset, and he's up to high doh about it all.'

Joan put down her knife and fork. 'How does Dolores know it's the exact present she gave to Vee?'

'Christy said she went to a lot of bother over it. Apparently it was hand-made by a man down in Kerry. And then she sees it listed on the internet, in the same place as a heap of old junk.'

'If memory serves me well, Vee got quite a few presents she wasn't particularly keen on. The Hanrahan's ornament mustn't have been to her taste.'

'Taste?' spluttered Gus. 'What's taste got to do with anything? You can't go behaving like that. What'd be wrong with doing what everybody else does and sticking the thing in the spare room? Anyway, you know what Christy's like. The fellow dotes on Dolores. I got the full speech about respect and decency. He even threatened to take his business elsewhere.'

'Ah,' said Joan. 'What did you say?'

'I tried to reason with him. "Veronica's a grown woman," I said. "And there's not a whole lot I can do about what she chooses to put up on the internet. All the same, I'll have a word." Not that he was listening to me, mind. When he hung up he was still chuntering about other accountancy firms.'

Gus squared up to his liver. How he hated the stuff. It reminded him of the very worst meals of his childhood. It was cheap, though, and these days that was what mattered. Joan had drawn up a rota of inexpensive meals. 'If the children see that we're suffering too,' she'd said, 'it'll be harder for them to complain.'

For a few minutes they ate in silence. The only way that Gus could tolerate liver was to eat like a child. Every tiny morsel had to be accompanied by a big lump of potato and washed down with a substantial gulp of milk. As he thought about Vee, his irritation started to ease. Perhaps the ornament incident heralded the start of a change in his daughter. She'd spotted an opportunity to make a bit of cash and had gone for it. You could almost accuse her of being enterprising. The only shame was that she'd chosen to put Christy-bloody-Hanrahan's present on the market. Gus would have a bit of sucking-up to do there.

'Did Tara get off OK?' he asked.

Joan speared a piece of meat. 'She did indeed. It was good to see her looking so perky.'

He reached over and touched one hand. 'I'm sorry, love. I'm sure you'd like to be heading over that way too.'

'Right this minute, I'd settle for a few days in Lahinch.'

Gus pushed his plate away. 'Do you remember the summers we spent down there? Well, the summers you and the kids spent down there. I always seemed to be working.' In the eighties, when the children were small, the family would decamp to a rented house on the County Clare coast. During the week, Gus would slave away in Dublin. On Friday nights, he'd beetle down the N7 in his Ford Sierra, singing along to country music cassettes, desperate to hear their stories about swimming and sandcastles and games. 'Happy days,' he said.

'Except for when they all fell out, or when I couldn't get Vee out of the amusement arcade.'

Gus rubbed a knuckle across his chin. 'What was that thing she was fascinated by?'

'The Coin Cascade. Even when she didn't have the coins to play herself, that's all she was interested in. She could stare at the blasted machine for hours. Honestly, she'd have my heart broken.'

'Some things never change. What's for dessert?'

'Is fruit OK?'

'Tinned or real?'

'Real,' replied Joan, an apologetic note in her voice. 'Not your favourite, I know, but we've got to do what we've got to do. You'll just have to pretend you're still six years old and an orange is a huge treat.'

He chuckled. When the children were young Gus had enjoyed tormenting them with stories from his own youth. Most of his tales lost nothing in the telling. He embroidered the details, ramping up the hardship to Dickensian levels. The strange thing was, the stories that inspired the most bafflement were the ones that were entirely true. Like the story of his uncle PJ, a monsignor in Volusia County, Florida. Every Christmas, Fr PJ would send a crate of oranges and grapefruits, and the Shine kids would fall on the box like it contained treasures untold. To his own boys and girls this was unfathomable. 'Oranges?' Niall would say. 'And you thought that was a big deal?' Gus smiled at the memory.

Joan was on her feet, tidying up the debris of their meal. 'So,' she said, 'have you decided?'

'Mmmm, I think we should fire ahead.'

'Before she left, I warned Tara there might be more bad news.' Gus clasped his hands around the back of his neck and kneaded the clammy flesh. This wasn't getting any easier. 'Now's the time, then,' he said.

Chapter 14

Niall met Tara at Dubrovnik Airport with a sign fashioned from a cereal box and a smile as wide as Wyoming. *Shine* the sign said in spidery purple letters.

'Were you worried I wouldn't recognise you?' she asked.

'Nope. I've always wanted someone to greet me with one of these.' He waved his sign. 'So I figured the next best thing would be to make one for you.'

With that, he dropped the cardboard, and brother and sister hugged. As they untangled, Niall examined Tara's fellow travellers. He grimaced.

'Did they clap when the plane landed?'

'They did.'

'Ugh.'

'What's wrong with clapping?'

'It's so . . . Irish.'

Tara grinned. 'I hate to break it to you, but no matter how long you stay away you're still one of us. Oh, and there was more than clapping.' She dropped her voice. 'A few Medjugorje-bound passengers said the rosary down the back.'

Niall feigned horror. 'And Mum and Dad wonder why I won't return to Ireland.'

'Come on,' she said. 'Are we getting the bus?'

He glanced in the direction of a row of ATM machines. 'Do you not want to get some cash first?'

'I thought you'd have enough for the two of us.'

'Ha! Good one. No, as Damien might say, I'm in a state of consistent poverty.

137

'There's a surprise.'

'Remember, a euro's worth about seven kuna,' he said. 'And get enough. It's not as cheap around here as it used to be.'

Not that Tara would know what Croatia was like in the past. She'd never visited the family's apartment. For the first couple of years, she'd always been too busy for something as frivolous as a sun holiday. Later, Craig had been reluctant to stay there. 'Bad enough that we live in your parent's house in Dublin,' he'd say, 'without us spending our holidays in their gaff too.' So, with typical bad timing, she had finally made it to Dubrovnik just as the apartment was sold. The buyers were a local couple; he worked on a ship, ferrying fuel around the Pacific. 'Good money,' Tomislav Kovac had said. 'You'll have no problems there.'

The bus crawled along the clifftop towards Dubrovnik. At several points on the journey, they encountered collections of cranes. According to Niall, new holiday apartments were popping up all the time. 'Russians,' he said with a learned nod. 'They have all the money now. Or Norwegians; they're doing well too. It's a pity Ireland can't lay claim to some oil.'

Finally, the bus rounded a corner and, for the first time, the Old Town came into view. The passengers reacted as one, raising their sunglasses and gasping with pleasure. Tara pressed her nose against the window. Below them, a forest of orange-tiled roofs jutted into the glittering turquoise. The view was heart-stoppingly beautiful, the only jarring note coming from two hulking cruise liners moored to the south. She peeked at her brother, expecting to see scorn for the tourists' predictable reaction. Instead, his face displayed something close to vindication, like he was saying, 'You're just passing through. *I* get to stay here.' Convincing him to return to the grey, rain-sodden reality of an Irish summer would not be easy.

As if he guessed her thoughts, Niall released a whoosh of air. 'When does it start?'

'You've lost me.'

'The soft-soap, the coercion, the "come home, lost sheep" routine.'

Tara put her sunglasses back on. 'Not everything's about you, you know. I'm on my holidays.'

And that was where they left it.

Niall, or to be more accurate Tomislav Kovac, had found Tara a room over the beach in Lapad, on the outskirts of the city. It was perfect: white-washed walls, wooden beams, a comfortable bed, a small, red-tiled terrace. At night, three lighthouses twinkled in sequence, warning sailors that the entrance to the bay was marked by clusters of rock. She had assumed her brother was staying in the same house, and was disappointed to learn that he was down the street in more basic accommodation. Her suggestion that he move was rebuffed, not because of the expense (Tara would have paid) or through loyalty to his landlady (tourists would have filled the room ten times over) but because Seedy the cat was content in his current lodgings.

Although Seedy was a near constant presence on Niall's terrace, his appearance suggested he was a rambling cat. One ear was so bitten it looked like rats had feasted on it, and a violent red scratch ran the length of his nose. During their first encounter, he mostly ignored Tara, concentrating instead on biting and sucking his nether regions. 'Now, now, the Seedster,' Niall said eventually, 'don't be rude. Our visitor's come all the way from Dublin.' Briefly the cat looked up and gave a truculent miaow.

Tara was dismayed by how wiped out she looked. The weeks of worrying, not to mention her break-up with Craig, had taken their toll. Her skin was matte-grey, and her eyes appeared permanently swollen. How she wished she was like Vee's friends. Neither personal anguish nor professional upheaval prevented them from looking like they'd been dipped in clear varnish.

With Niall, family-related topics remained out of bounds. They did discuss Craig, and Niall groaned when told about his plans. 'Just imagine,' he said, 'being somewhere really remote, halfway up the Amazon, say, and hearing that worthless wanker's voice emerging from a clearing.' As much as Tara appreciated her brother's loyalty, she did wonder whether her family's attitude towards Craig was also a dig at her. What did it say about her judgement – her character, even – if the partner she had chosen was deemed to be such an idiot?

For the most part, Niall was a great host. He brought her to popular spots like the Old Town where tourists were herded around like particularly compliant cattle, and to quieter places like Sipan where they cycled across the island's one road to a restaurant with no menu. You ate what you were given, which turned out to be octopus salad and sea bass straight from the Adriatic.

Throughout, he provided a laidback commentary. His favourite topics included the ways in which the Croats were similar to the Irish ('You know the way we claim everybody up to and including Barack Obama? They're worse here. They maintain Odysseus spent seven years on Mljet and that Marco Polo was from Korcula'), and his reasons for giving Irish women a wide berth ('Hooking up with a woman from home would be as naff as getting plastered in an Irish bar or wanting rashers and sausages for breakfast').

On their way back to the ferry, they passed a superannuated Yugo, a squashed snake and a family picking potatoes. Swifts looped the loop, and ripening fruit scented the air. As they freewheeled into the port, Niall burst into the theme music from *Batman*, the way he had when they were kids. For the first time in a long while, Tara felt her body unclench. Always there, however, niggling and gnawing at her conscience, was the knowledge that she'd come to Croatia with a job to do.

Later that night, they gatecrashed a wedding reception, joining a host of flamingo-pink Cork people in toasting the future happiness of Barry and Gráinne. Her brother's queasiness about his countrymen rarely stopped him from enjoying their hospitality. 'Great to know that some folks still have a few bob,' he said. 'All the same, it mightn't hurt them to invest in a bottle of factor fifty.' After several beers, two pear brandies and a twirl around the dance floor with Uncle Tim from Belgooly, Tara almost summoned the courage to question Niall. Then he launched into a heartfelt rendition of 'The Lakes of Pontchartrain', and the opportunity passed.

It was three o'clock when she collapsed into bed. As she lay there, listening to the singing of the crickets and the swooshing of the sea, she cursed her cowardice.

Niall wouldn't be badgered into submission, and he didn't want anyone – especially his parents – thinking he was back for good. But it was time to go home. He was broke. No, worse than broke; he owed his landlady, Mrs Pavlovic, three weeks rent. Tara would do the decent thing there, he hoped. He'd had a preliminary chat with Tomislav who promised to take over the feeding and watering of Seedy. As he pointed out, he'd been feeding Niall for the two weeks prior to Tara's arrival, so looking after a cat was no big deal.

How to handle his sister was another question. Who would have thought she'd find the courage to dump that sponger, Craig Fitzgerald? Niall was not without self-awareness and he knew he was poorly placed to describe anyone as a sponger – pots, kettles and all that – but at least he provided value for money. Craig was as much fun as a lounge bar on Good Friday.

Niall had been right to worry about her; she was obviously still mooning after the guy. And she was obsessing over the rest of the family. She felt guilty for ignoring Vee's calls, she said. 'Ah here,' he replied. 'You can't spend your life returning Vee's calls. That's the surest route to insanity.'

She was too nice; that was Tara's problem. And too cautious. If he lacked purpose, and Vee lacked sense, and Damien needed a personality, his younger sister was in definite need of some badness. Realising that he'd made the Shines sound like characters from *The Wizard of Oz*, he laughed to himself. He'd always considered *The Beverly Hillbillies* a more fitting reference. Although they'd had the money to move to the swisher end of Dublin 6, they'd never quite fitted in. They lacked the polish, the easy assurance that only generations of plenty can bring.

Vee was most bothered by this. He remembered how she had pleaded with their dad not to hang the Limerick GAA flag out of an upstairs window. 'People around here don't do that. It's considered provincial,' she said. Gus's broad shoulders shook with the force of his laughter. 'Perhaps it's time they started,' he replied. 'Consider your old man a trailblazer.'

On Tara's last full day in Croatia, Niall brought her to his favourite island. Kolocep, or Kalamota as most of the locals called it, possessed one shop, one post office, three bars and no roads. A path ran from the port to the far side of the island. In July, that path was still dotted with the sticky remains of cherries, overhead figs were beginning to emerge, and waxy yellow flowers decorated the cacti.

The two swam in a small, sandy harbour. On one side there was an abandoned building, its walls pockmarked by small holes. A legacy of the war, Niall presumed. On the other side, there was a restaurant with a faded rattan roof and a stone floor. As they ate, Niall could tell that Tara was growing ever more anxious. Still, he couldn't stop himself from teasing her.

'What sort of madman would abandon a spot like this, eh?'

'I'll bet it's grim enough in the winter,' she replied.

'I'll have to find somewhere else before then. I was thinking of going to the States. What do you reckon?'

Tara picked up her wine and swirled the deep yellow liquid around the glass. 'Yeah, right. What are you proposing to live on?'

'The old man might have the finances under control by then,' said Niall as he watched a boy of eight or nine untie a rowing boat.

'Don't kid yourself.'

Tara began talking about the situation in Dublin, but Niall had zoned out. By now, the boy was five metres from shore. He stood as he rowed.

'Did you ever think of taking it any further?' she was saying.

'Sorry?'

'Jesus, Niall, would you not listen to me for once? I asked whether you ever considered doing more with your drawings. The cartoons and sketches you have in your room? They're really good.'

'Nah, they're just a way of making some loose change. There's no proper money in it. Plus, can you imagine Dad?' Niall adopted Gus's voice. 'Drawing pictures, is it? I don't know, Joan, what'll the fella be at next? Playing with Lego or Scalextric? By the time I was his age, I'd invented electricity and won the World Cup.'

Tara giggled. 'He's not that bad.'

'He is, you know.'

Their conversation stalled while the waiter brought two espressos. Niall lit one of the bargain cigarettes he'd bought on a hop over the border to Herzegovina.

'Anyway,' said Tara, wrinkling her nose at the smoke, 'it was only a thought. The drawing, I mean.'

'You're a great woman for trying to sort us all out.'

'That's me, right enough. I can solve everybody else's problems. The thing is, my own life's a disaster.'

'Come on now, you know that's not true.' Niall pulled on his cigarette, then exhaled a thin stream of smoke. 'You're not doing so bad.'

Tara shivered. 'What? On my own at twenty-nine? Living in my parents' house?'

'Does being on your own scare you?'

'Doesn't it scare everybody?'

Niall took another pull of his cigarette. Lord, the things were vile. 'I wouldn't say it's top of my list.'

'What is?'

'Growing up, if that doesn't sound too dumb. It's like, I don't know what I *do* want to do with my life. But I'm fairly certain what I *don't* want. I don't want to be one of those people whose existence becomes more and more bland, until even the slightest bit of upheaval scares the bejesus out of them.'

'It's inevitable though, isn't it? You get older, life becomes less about the thrills and more about the responsibility.' Tara scrunched up her face. 'Oh, listen to me, sounding so bloody dreary. Besides, I'm not nearly as organised or competent as you think.'

'Oh?'

'The one thing I was asked to do, and I couldn't even . . .' She stopped.

'Couldn't even what?'

'Ah nothing.'

'No, go on,' said Niall as the waiter placed the bill in front of him. The boy was pulling in to the shore again, his face straining with effort. They made them tough here. Even Gus would approve.

'I told Mum I'd convince you to come home.'

Niall took a last drag of his cigarette and shoved the bill across the table. 'Oh.'

'And I haven't even tried.'

'So, why don't you?'

'Very funny. It's too late now.'

'Hmmm, I wouldn't say that.' Niall tilted his head to one side.

'Are you serious?' said Tara, green eyes opening wide.

'It sounds to me like you could do with the company. And it's been too long since I gave Damien a proper tormenting.'

Tara beamed as she rooted through her bag for her purse. 'Come on,' she said, depositing a wodge of notes on the table. 'We'd better get back to Dubrovnik so you can buy a ticket. I can't risk you changing your mind.'

He gave what he hoped was one of his more appealing gormless looks.

'All right, we'd better get back so *I* can buy you a ticket.'

'Thanks, Tara. I'm not promising to stay forever, mind. Just for now.'

'That's cool. I might get tired of you after a few weeks.'

Niall got to his feet. He could tell her about the overdue rent on the ferry.

It was mid-afternoon when they arrived in Dublin. Although the sun was obscured by gauzy cloud, there was an unusual warmth to the day. Tara was looking forward to getting home. She'd kept Niall's return under wraps, and was eager to see her mum's reaction.

Packing up his belongings had taken all of ten minutes. Tara was flabbergasted by how little he owned. He proposed leaving his sketches behind as part payment to Mrs Pavlovic. 'They're good,' Tara said. 'They're not that good.' She made another trip to the ATM.

Seedy met Niall's departure with predictable *sang froid*. 'You'll miss me when I'm gone, Seedster,' Niall said while he tickled the cat goodbye. Mrs Pavlovic, patently relieved to collect her dues, promised to look after him. Tomislav Kovac pledged to keep an eye out too.

On the journey from Dublin Airport to Palmerston Park, the taxi driver detailed everything that had happened over the preceding week. Tara learned that two men had been charged with the murder of Eric 'Redser' Lynam.

'Fucking scumbags, if you'll pardon the language,' he said.

In the front passenger seat, Niall nodded. 'A horse-whipping, that's what they need.'

'A horse-whipping? Hanging'd be more like it.'

'Too good for them,' came the reply. 'Do you reckon the EU would let us introduce the electric chair?'

In the back seat, Tara sighed quietly. Niall's compulsion to stir and goad would get him into trouble one day. 'The weather's not too bad,' she said.

'And wait until you hear the forecast. It's fabulous,' replied the taxi man. 'Your heart'd go out to anybody heading off on holidays this week. A pure waste of money. Sure, where in the world can beat Ireland when the sun's shining?'

Niall nodded again, vigorously this time. 'How right you are, man. You can have your Indian Ocean or your Caribbean.

Dollymount is the spot to be. If it was up to me, the government would charge people to leave the country. A hundred euro sounds about right. That might make them wise up.'

Before he went any further, Tara dug her nails – hardened by the Croatian sun – into the back of his neck. He took the hint. She had forgotten how quickly her brother could cross the line from entertaining to irritating, from charmingly loquacious to damn nuisance. She'd also begun to question his behaviour in Dubrovnik. At what stage had he decided to come home? Had he strung her along all week?

Wherever the truth might lie, she was genuinely delighted by his decision. He planned on staying in the spare room. She'd have to pay all the rent from her already-depleted savings but, right now, she'd rather have company than money.

As the taxi crossed Dunville Avenue and sped towards home, she scrambled about for her euros. In the front seat, Niall was more alert.

'Good God, will you look at that,' he exclaimed.

A large red and blue sign had been planted on the lawn. *O'Flaherty, Mills Auctioneers*, it read. *For Sale, By Private Treaty, Magnificent Period Home.*

Chapter 15

Four chicks in a nest, necks outstretched, mouths upturned. Gus wished he could shake the image, but that's what he saw when he looked around the room. Not that he didn't love those chicks; it was just that their neediness was overwhelming. And the day felt too hot, the room too stuffy, to cope with their demands. He was nervous too. Although he'd thought about this moment, now it was here, he wished he could turn on his heel and walk away.

He had given himself a talking-to. 'Keep it brief, keep it matter-of-fact, keep it calm,' he'd said. Now, with his sons and daughters in front of him, he appreciated how difficult this would be.

Joan was in the corner of the sitting room, knitting a tiny pink cardigan. Gus wasn't fooled by her bland expression; not a word, not a nuance, not a gesture would pass her by.

'You brought the weather back with you,' he said to Niall. 'It's great to get a bit of warmth into the old bones.'

'You're right there,' said his younger son, his face suggesting he had scant interest in chit-chat about the temperature.

'The question, Dad, is why?' started Vee. 'Why sell the house now? Why not consult us? Why not even tell us? It's not acceptable that the first we knew about this was when Tara got back from her jaunt.'

Barely five minutes had passed since they'd all assembled, and this was the third barb Vee had lobbed at her sister.

'You're right, lovey,' he said. 'We should have let Tara know. The rest of you are in a different position, though. Yourself and Damien have your own places, and our friend here,' he tipped his head towards Niall, 'is only an occasional visitor to the country. We didn't even know he was going to turn up today.'

'It was meant to be a surprise,' chipped in Tara, her voice uncharacteristically sharp. 'A good surprise.'

'Obviously, it matters to us,' said Vee. 'There we are, doing our best to comply with all your rules – and, let me tell you, it's hard – and then you go and do this to us. I mean, for heaven's sake, this is *our* family home. And another thing: is now really the time to be selling property?'

Gus reminded himself of his intention to stay calm. He rose from his green chair. 'You haven't been paying enough attention to the news, Vee. All the experts say the market is on the up again. The green shoots of recovery are sprouting.'

'Oh come on, you don't buy that propaganda, do you?' asked Damien from his perch at the end of the sofa. 'Green shoots? Bloody weeds more like.'

Joan put down her knitting. 'Do any of you honestly believe we'd be doing this unless we had to?'

'Well, *have* you considered all the options?' said Vee. 'What about the houses Dad owns in Limerick and Cork?'

'On the market too. But they're small rental properties. They won't raise enough cash. You're doing your father and me a disservice if you think we haven't examined every alternative. You know how much Garryowen means to us.'

Appearing startled by the steel in her voice, Niall spoke up. 'It's all right, Mum. You're only doing this because you're in a bind; we understand.'

Vee's eyes narrowed. 'With the greatest of respect, Niall, honey, you should keep your nose out of this. We hardly see you from one end of the year to the other. You can't barge in here and claim to speak for the rest of us.'

Niall stretched out his long denim-clad legs. Gus noticed that one of his brown sandals was held together by a length of green string. 'Thanks for the welcome home, Vee. The last I checked, I was still a member of the family. If the rules have changed, maybe someone could fill me in.'

'I'm with Vee,' said Damien. 'Next we know, you'll have effed back off to Mongolia, or wherever it is the eternal hippies hang out these days.'

'What's that got to do with anything?' asked Tara, sounding irritated at the unholy alliance beside her.

'Jee-sus,' said Gus, his good intentions in trouble. 'What are ye like? To the best of my knowledge, none of you has ever expressed any interest in taking over the house when we've shuffled off. And if it's your inheritance you're fretting about, you're too late. The bank all but owns the place already. We're trying to free up whatever cash we can.'

'But—' began Vee.

'Enough!' he growled, best intentions completely shredded. 'I had hoped for a serious conversation, but you all seem determined to turn it into a pantomime. We need to sell the house, and that's what we'll do. The process may well take a few months. In the meantime, we'll look for somewhere to rent. And, if Tara has any sense, that's what she'll do too.'

Niall put on an offended face.

'Oh, and if you do plan on reacquainting yourself with the country, Niall, you'll also be in need of lodgings. No doubt, though, you're used to kipping down in all manner of places, so I'm sure you'll be grand.' He paused. 'And do something about those sandals, would you? You look like a bloody hobo.'

Monday morning saw Gus foostering around his office, fiddling with the computer, reading figures but not taking them in. He regretted losing his temper with the children. What they were going through was difficult enough without him becoming a bully. He'd gone downstairs to apologise to Tara, and to give Niall a decent welcome, but there was no response. They were out on the town, he presumed.

Damien had sauntered away, mumbling about important political business. Vee, seemingly exhausted by her petulant display, had slunk out, her mouth in a tight line. Even by her standards, she was looking thin. She had the sunken face of an elderly woman and the knobbly legs of a young fellow. He'd get Joan to have a word. He had planned on tackling his daughter about the wedding present issue. Enough was enough, though. Besides, with the help of a little schmoozing and an eye-wateringly expensive lunch, Christy Hanrahan was back on side.

Even Gus had been taken aback by the stern way Joan had defended their decision to sell the house. 'You know how much Garryowen means to us,' she'd said. Her demeanor and her tone had said much more: 'Disagree with me at your peril,' they'd yelled. The confrontation had upset her too. Yet, two days on, he had the sense that she was more at peace with their decision. That morning as he shaved, Gus had felt as old as Methuselah. Not only had the colour gone from his hair, it was leaching from his face too.

He recalled the first time they'd viewed Garryowen: 24 April 1993. On the way there, they'd listened to the news on the radio; an IRA bomb had exploded in London. From the start, he'd been hell-bent on owning the house, an enthusiasm his wife hadn't shared. 'Too difficult to maintain,' she'd said. 'Too expensive, too *everything*.' Step by step he'd won her over. All these years later, he could still see his sister, Majella, swooning over the grandeur of the building. His mother, Phyllis, had been more guarded. 'It'll take a shocking amount of cleaning,' she'd said, her tone hinting that she alone understood the significance of this.

His father had been dead for a decade by then. 'Sixty-three – it's no age,' the mourners at his funeral had said, repeating the line until it became meaningless. Neither was it young enough for Gus Senior's passing to be considered a tragedy. He was just another burnt-out man, victim of a life that was as harsh as it was narrow.

Gus had sworn that this fate would not be his, that he wouldn't be tethered by the poverty of his youth. Disappointment was a great motivator, he'd found. He'd pledged, too, that his children would never know what it was like to be on the outside. And if, occasionally, he'd had to pull a stroke or two, tell a white lie or three, wasn't that expected in business? For all this, he couldn't escape the long arm of his upbringing. Even in his most success-ful days, he'd never managed to shrug off his insecurities.

He looked at his watch. A quarter to twelve. Where had the morning gone? There was an account he needed to discuss with Rory. According to Joan, the young lad had played a role in Craig's departure. Something about him sheltering from a down-pour, and Craig getting the wrong idea. The thought gave Gus his first smile of the day. Then another thought struck; one that re-placed his smile with a frown. What if Rory was genuinely sweet on Tara? Well, he could be as sweet as he pleased, because Gus couldn't allow anything to develop there. Not right now, at any rate. He would have to remain vigilant.

Tara returned to work to find her name beside a story on house prices. Was a recovery underway? the news editor wanted to know. Were people beginning to buy again?

'You're codding me,' she said.

He gave her a bemused stare. 'Why would I be doing that? Off out with you. Nice tan, by the way.'

She wanted to stamp her foot and say, 'Have you any idea what's going on is my life? On top of all the other crap, I'm about to be made homeless.' Her impulse was tempered by the knowledge that her credit was already low, so she murmured her agreement and headed out in search of green shoots.

For the next few hours, she spoke to the usual experts ('the kings and queens of received wisdom,' as Damien called them), who gave the usual opinions. Her head was elsewhere. It was back in Garryowen, Gus prowling the sitting room, Joan icily ad-monishing the family. Story filed, she decided a distraction was needed. One of her colleagues had told her that work was under-way at St Monica's Mansions. Nothing major, just some cleaning and painting. Worth a visit all the same, she reckoned.

The early evening was mild, and the door of Carmel's flat was ajar. As Tara knocked, she was met by the sound of laughter.

Carmel's chuckle, she recognised; the other laugh was deeper, the rumbling laugh of a man.

'Come in, Tara. Come in,' said Carmel. 'That's a lovely colour you've got. Ben's not gone far. I'd say he'll be back in a mo.'

Jenelle was propped up at the table. She was colouring a picture of a clown, taking care not to go outside the lines. She gave Tara a timid smile before returning to her task.

On the sofa was a sturdily-built man with a gleaming bald head. He was wearing work clothes: a paint-spattered shirt and dusty boots.

'Victor Lennon,' he said, rising to give her a bone-crusher of a handshake. 'Delighted to meet you. I gather you're the woman responsible for bringing us over this way.'

'Victor's with the council,' Carmel explained. 'He's supervising the work.' She smiled. 'It's all go around here. Sit down there, and I'll get us a cup of tea.'

Intrigued, Tara did as she was told. Victor told her that Carmel had been a great help. 'She's a dynamo, that woman – a real inspiration. She has all the residents on board with the work. Of course, they want us to do more, only the money's not there.'

Carmel's return from the kitchen coincided with Ben's arrival home. He burst into the flat, fizzing with excitement. 'Yay, Victor! Yaay, Tara!'

'I wanted to thank you for your picture, Ben,' she said. 'It's only brilliant. I have it hanging up in my kitchen.'

'Deadly.' He grinned. In less than a month, his teeth had changed. The gaps were filling in, giving him a new, more grown-up appearance. 'Jenelle helped too . . . a bit.'

Carmel ruffled his hair. 'I'll get your tea in a few minutes, pet. Why don't you tell Tara and Victor about your day?'

He wriggled onto the sofa beside the man from the council. 'Preston Delaney's going to see Dublin playing in Croke Park. His uncle's bringing him, and his cousins are going and all.'

'That's nice for Preston,' said Carmel. 'But you're getting to do lots of good things during the holidays too. Weren't we in town the other day, and didn't you get new runners?'

'I did but . . .' His voice tapered off, suggesting that buying shoes came a poor second to seeing Dublin play football.

Victor pressed his lips together and glanced in Carmel's direction. She gave an almost imperceptible nod.

'Would you like to go and see the Dubs some time, Ben?' asked Victor.

'Aw, yeah,' he said, new teeth on display again.

'Your nan would have to be there too, of course.'

'And Tara can come,' the little boy added. 'But not Jenelle 'cos she's too young. She wouldn't understand.'

His sister, who was filling in the clown's shoes with meticulous care, ignored him.

'We'll see,' said Carmel.

Ben gave Victor a knowing look. 'That means yes.'

Carmel said nothing, just switched her gaze to the floor.

Tara couldn't be entirely sure, but she had the feeling her new friend was blushing.

Chapter 16

Damien was in a rush. He had half an hour to get from a residents' association meeting to a children's party in Rathmines. The meeting had dragged on forever, the grumpy tenants of Padre Pio Gardens demanding to know why they weren't getting the same attention as their neighbours in St Monica's. Damien cursed Tara's meddling. He would have to put an end to that.

The party business was taking up more and more of his time. As he'd feared, Amby was wringing him dry. 'One more for the itinerary, Damo,' he'd say. 'Sorry to dump this on you, but the other gobshite is off to Lanzarote for a week.' The other gobshite was called Earl. After a long stint on a soap opera, he was between jobs. He was annoyed by Damien's arrival, claiming the boss's son-in-law was gobbling up all the work. But Damien was powerless. Every time he threatened not to co-operate, Amby would belly-ache about the astronomical cost of educating three grandchildren.

So busy was he that he'd missed several council engagements. His sidekick, Canice, was growing suspicious. 'I can never get in touch with you, man,' he complained. 'I swear you must be living a double life.' 'Family commitments,' Damien replied.

Although he would never admit it, there were times when he enjoyed being a clown. To begin with, the cacophony created by a room – or garden – full of exuberant children had given him monstrous headaches. More than this, it had scared him. How would he ever keep control? Gradually, he had learned to think of his audiences as just a bunch of Rufuses. And who wouldn't want to spend time with Rufus? He was reminded of something

Canice's partner, Jacinta, had said about teaching kids of the same age. When encouraged to talk about the horrors of the job, she'd laughed. The youngsters were a delight, she said. At that age the world was opening up to them, and for every tantrum or difficult moment, there were ten episodes to make her treasure her work.

Over the weeks, Damien had extended his repertoire of tricks. Now he could make an assortment of animals from balloons. He could dance and sing a silly song or two. Often the youngsters joined in. And he'd started juggling. If he said so himself, he was quite handy at the juggling.

There was something else he had come to appreciate: the less people had, the more they were willing to spend on their children. It was as if they wanted to reassure them that life hadn't changed. Daddy may not go to work anymore, but they could still have the same treats as their friends. Lines about bread and circuses came to mind; of course they did. What could he do, though, apart from give the kids the best possible afternoon?

There were other times when he was seized by panic, and he felt like his life was coming undone. He was a clown, for pity's sake. There was no sign of Amby loosening his grip or of Gus making a comeback. His father wouldn't be selling Garryowen unless he was totally screwed.

It was just Damien's luck that the Saturday snarl-up was even worse than usual. The traffic crawled through Rathmines, every inch an achievement. The paths were clogged with grocery shoppers, lunchtime drinkers, *Big Issue* sellers and general dawdlers. Many seemed unaware of the purpose of traffic lights. They ambled across the road wherever they chose, making the tailback even longer.

Behind the wheel of his SUV, Damien wolfed down the sandwich packed by Felicity. His wife's aggressive cost-cutting continued, and the bread was filled with a watery chutney made by one of her earth-mother friends. The previous day, when confronted by the same concoction, Willow's mouth had curled. 'Nobody else has to eat this sort of muck,' she'd said.

'Well, we've no choice,' Felicity replied. 'Think of all the poor children who'd love to have your sandwiches.'

'Give me their addresses and I'll send them on,' muttered Willow.

Aifric looked up from her plate, concern etched across her peaky face. 'Are *we* poor?' she'd asked.

When and where to change into his clown uniform always presented Damien with a challenge. Sometimes, if none of the children were home, he did so before setting out for a job. This, he reckoned, cut down on the chances of party-goers recognising him. It also prompted numerous double-takes from motorists, startled that the vehicle beside them was being driven by someone with a scarlet wig and a cherry nose. More often, however, he changed in the host family's bathroom. This was what he would have to do today.

As he turned off the main road towards his destination, his phone began to buzz. The woman who'd booked him wanted to know where he was.

'Traffic,' said Damien. 'I'll be with you in a tick.'

The woman, a Mrs Keating, sighed. 'Well, do hurry up.'

In the background Damien heard what sounded like a thousand hyperactive six-year-olds. 'Should only be a minute,' he assured her. 'Twenty-five Maple Tree Lawns, isn't it?'

'Maple Tree *Drive*. For God's sake, you're on the wrong side of the main road. You'll have to turn around and go back.'

'Aw hell,' said Damien, who could feel sweat gathering at his hairline.

'Aw hell, indeed. Mr Power promised me his top man and instead he sends a blasted imbecile who can't even get the address right.'

By the time he brought the car to a juddering halt on Maple Tree Drive, Damien was in a flap. His palms were damp, his heart drumming in his ears. Felicity's sandwich lay like a block of cement at the bottom of his stomach. He gathered up his bag of tricks and dashed towards number twenty-five. There was no missing the party house; a silver balloon floated over the gate. *Six Today*, it said.

Mrs Keating, it appeared, was one of those women who emerges from her house looking like a mannequin from a department store window but leaves chaos in her wake. At the front door shoes were scattered every which way; the hall table sagged under mounds of envelopes, flyers and magazines.

'Thirty-five minutes late,' she brayed as a cat shot past. 'There's pandemonium here. Pan-duh-mo-nium. My Poppy's such a well-behaved child, but some of her friends are complete gurriers. What did you say your name was?'

'Mr Chuckles.'

'No, your proper name.'

'Um, Niall,' said Damien, giving his usual alias.

'I'll be letting Ambrose Power know about this.'

'I'd better get changed, so. The bathroom?'

'At the top of the stairs,' she said. 'Mind the toys on the landing.' A shriek came from what Damien presumed was the kitchen. 'And be quick about it.'

He started to reply except Mrs Keating had already dashed off in the direction of the shriek. Clambering up the stairs two at a time, he collided with a figure emerging from the bathroom. One long shoe bounced from his holdall.

'What the—' said a clipped voice.

'Very sorry,' said Damien to the heavy-set blonde woman in front of him.

She tipped back her head to get a better look at him. 'Do I know you?'

'I shouldn't think so.' He bent down to retrieve the shoe, and to avoid further scrutiny.

'No, I've definitely come across you before. Don't worry, it'll come to me,' said the woman as she descended the stairs.

Tara wandered down Baggot Street, past groups of tourists. Clearly expecting the standard Irish damp, they were over-dressed and confused. Who would blame them? In the sun, Dublin became a different place – noisier, more colourful. At lunchtime, office workers colonised the parks. In the evenings, crowds spilled from pub to pavement, their chatter dominated by the weather. 'Two weeks without rain,' people said. 'How much longer do you think it can last?' The smells changed too. The aroma of burnt meat hung over the suburbs. Pungent odours wafted from the city's bins. And there was that indefinable smell of warm streets that brought you back to your childhood summers.

Tara had a rare Friday off, and was due to meet her dad for lunch. At the newsagents, she paused for a quick leaf through the *Evening Post*. Feuding criminals, cranky politicians, preening celebrities: the fare was predictable. Or rather, it was predictable until she reached page five. Page five gave her a jolt. *Councillor Blasts Media Bias*, said the headline. She read on:

Outspoken city councillor, Damien Shine, has lashed biased media coverage of the city's flats complexes. The independent representative claimed some estates were getting favourable treatment because the cash-strapped council wanted to appease 'irresponsible' journalists.

'I have hundreds of hard-pressed constituents in Padre Pio Gardens who've been waiting years for vital repair work. They're at the end of their tether,' the councillor said. 'But city bosses are ignoring their plight. Instead money's being thrown at another complex just because it appeared in the press.'

Councillor Shine refused to name the flats receiving special treatment from the city coffers, but sources told the *Post* that neighbouring St Monica's Mansions is getting a pricey facelift. The Mansions recently featured in a struggling national daily. The story was written by the councillor's sister, Tara Shine.

Mum of four Mona McCarthy (47), who lives in Padre Pio Gardens, is outraged. 'I'm outraged,' she said. 'They get everything over in St Monica's, even though we all know the place is rotten with thieves and junkies.'

Another tenant, Noel Nagle (32), says the situation is a disgrace. 'It's a disgrace,' he said. 'I heard they're getting jacuzzis and all over in St Monica's, while decent people in our flats are being blackguarded.'

In a statement, council chiefs denied favouritism. A spokesman refused to comment on Ms McCarthy's allegations about the residents of St Monica's Mansions, but insisted that no jacuzzis had been installed in the complex.

For five, ten, fifteen seconds, Tara was livid. Had her brother taken leave of his senses? Then she thought some more. And she started to giggle. Before long she was laughing so much she had to gasp for air. The man beside her, who'd been taking a sneaky peek at the *Racing Post*, appeared alarmed.

'Oh, Damien,' she said, the glee still in her voice. 'Wait until they see this in the Mansions. You won't be getting too many votes there.'

The man put down his paper.

'Family, eh?' said Tara, as he scurried for the door.

'Are you buying that *Evening Post*?' asked the girl behind the counter.

'Do you know,' she replied, 'for once I think I am.'

Meeting her dad brought Tara's giddiness to a quick end. She'd been tempted to show him the article. Not long ago, he too would have laughed. But this was the new Gus; the post-crash Gus. His face was that of someone bedevilled by debt; his summer suit looked like it was stolen from a bigger man.

Lunch was his suggestion, which made her worry that yet more bad news was in store. Instead, he sat there, taking neat bites from his ham sandwich, drinking his milky tea, and asking perfunctory questions about her job.

'I'm flying,' she replied. 'Political intrigue, dodgy dealings, major scandals? I'm all over them. Scoops galore.'

'Seriously?'

Tara swallowed a mouthful of her goat's cheese and red pepper tart. 'You want the truth? This week I've covered an agricultural show, a best-dressed lady competition, a row about signposts and a man from Sallynoggin who claims he's the true inventor of the internet. I don't think I'll be troubling the Pulitzer Prize committee.'

'You shouldn't sell yourself short.'

'I'm only messing, Dad. I'm trying to let you know that everything's good. Same as it ever was. There's no need to lose any sleep over me.'

Gus wiped a crumb from the corner of his mouth. 'And the other fellow?'

'I take it you mean Niall?'

'Who else?'

This was where the conversation became difficult. What could Tara say about her brother that Gus would want to hear? He spent his time either meeting up with old friends or engaging in general idleness. No, that wasn't entirely true. He had made it as far as the dole office where they told him his entitlements were few. He'd also cut the grass and cooked a couple of slapdash meals. Tara didn't like to complain because, as flatmates went, he was highly entertaining. Plus their mum was ridiculously happy to have him back.

Only once had she come close to cracking. Three nights previously, she'd woken to the sound of drunken laughter and the whiff of hash. From what she could tell, her brother had been joined by three of his oldest pals – Murph, Dunner and Tommo – and they were reliving their glory years. The racket was tolerable enough until the singing started. Travel had extended Niall's repertoire, and while she could handle 'This Land is Your Land' and 'NKosi Sikelel' iAfrika', a tuneless 'Waltzing Matilda' set her teeth on edge.

She hauled herself out of bed and opened the door just wide enough to holler, 'Some of us have to work in the morning, you know.' The relative peace lasted for three or four minutes before someone burst into 'The Black Velvet Band'. The others gave full-throated backing. Tara pulled the pillow over her head and made a fruitless attempt at sleep.

Now as Gus sat in front of her, wearing the needy, expectant look of a cat at the foot of the dinner table, she searched for the appropriate words. She settled on something that wasn't an out-and-out lie.

'Niall? He's . . . ahm . . . adjusting.'

'Adjusting?'

'Mmmm, getting back in touch with old contacts, sorting out his affairs. That sort of thing.'

'Gah! He's loafing around the place, you mean, spending other people's money.'

'You've got to give him time, Dad. A few weeks to get his act together.'

'He's had thirty years to get his act together. How long does he need? And for fear the boy has any notion of returning to the family business, you can tell him it's out of the question. We've enough troubles as it is.'

'I don't think he'll be asking,' said Tara, lowering her voice to a whisper. Although the café radio was cranking out eighties power ballads, she had the suspicion that other customers were eavesdropping.

'OK, OK,' said Gus, running one finger down the centre of his forehead to the bridge of his nose. 'Anyway, I didn't intend on getting waylaid by Niall. What I wanted was to make sure you weren't overly upset about our plans to sell the house.'

Since Garryowen went on the market, Tara had encountered several prospective bidders. They poked, prodded, tutted and nodded; treating another family's home – another family's life – as though it was nothing more than a collection of window frames, skirting boards and light fittings. So far, none of them had expressed any firm interest, but the clock was ticking.

Aware that people would ask questions about why the house was for sale, Gus had instructed his sons and daughters to say it was too big for an aging couple. Tara figured he didn't want anyone jumping to conclusions about his finances.

'I haven't had the chance to do much about finding a new flat. I'll be on the case soon,' she said.

'Fine, only don't get too stressed about it.' He paused, the pause a beat too long. 'I . . . your mother and I . . . we wouldn't want that.'

Tara drained her Americano. She had the sense that Gus was trying to say something. If only she could decipher what it was.

'The little scut. The *nerve* of him,' said Carmel. 'And he's *your* brother?'

'I don't like to advertise the fact,' said Tara.

They were sitting at Carmel's table, the *Evening Post* spread out in front of them. Carmel saw the funny side of the article, but she doubted the other residents of St Monica's would be so open-minded.

'I know Mona Mac,' she said. 'We were in the same class at school. If the woman had brains, she'd be dangerous.'

Victor and Ben arrived. Ben had been 'helping' with the repair work and was full of chat. His blue eyes were as big as saucers.

'There he is – foreman Ben,' said Carmel with a smile.

'My best worker,' agreed Victor.

Ben sat on the old brown sofa and drew his knees towards his chest. 'It was fantastic. We went into lots of flats. And I got to see everything. Like, there was one flat where they were all sitting on the floor 'cos they didn't have any chairs. And then but, there was this other one – near Nuala's – and they had a massive telly. Like, *really* massive. Victor said it must be the biggest telly in the whole world.'

'One of them, certainly,' said Victor, with a grave nod.

Carmel showed him the paper. He read silently for a moment, then guffawed. 'What a tool.'

Tara shrugged. 'There's not much you can do about your family.'

'Never a truer word spoken,' said Carmel.

Tara had never been sure what the phrase 'comfortable in his own skin' meant. But as Victor rose to return to work, she decided he was its very definition. He was at ease with his company, his surroundings, himself. It was a state that others – like Niall and Craig – aimed for. When faced by the genuine article, she saw how short they fell.

Before he left, Victor shook Ben's hand. 'A pleasure working with you, buddy.' He turned to Carmel, a hint of a smile on his lips. 'I'll see you later.'

Tara waited until she heard the door close. 'So,' she said, 'troublesome councillors aside, how have you been getting on?'

Carmel scratched her neck. 'Ben, pet, you haven't forgotten you're staying with Nuala tonight, have you?'

'No, I remember.'

'Isn't it time you got your stuff together?'

'Oh no, there's no need yet.'

His nan fixed him with a look that suggested there was every need. 'Tara and me are going to talk girl's talk.'

'Yee-uch,' said Ben as he scampered to his room. 'Tell me when you're finished.'

'Are you off out tonight then?' asked Tara.

'Aren't you the nosy young one?' said Carmel with a wink.

Carmel and Victor had been on a couple of dates. 'Casual, like,' she said. To the football with Ben; for a drink while Nuala watched the kids. Tonight they were going to an Italian place in town. Jenelle was already in Nuala's flat. 'I need plenty of time to doll myself up,' she laughed.

'That's . . . brilliant,' said Tara. 'Honestly. Brilliant.'

'Victor's fifty,' continued Carmel, in the manner of someone who has started talking and has to keep going. 'He's divorced. His wife left him for a young lad, not much older than you. He's a nightclub DJ in the midlands, would you believe?'

'It takes all sorts.'

'He knows about Rosanna, by the way. I thought I should – what's the saying? – lay all my cards on the table. It's early days and everything but . . .' The corners of her mouth gave a telltale twitch. 'Oh, and I try not to say much in front of Ben. It's a sensitive age – seven and a half.'

Tara laughed.

'Seriously, he's like a sponge, that boy. You think he can't possibly understand what adults are saying, and then he comes out with something that floors you.'

'Does Victor have children?'

'One boy. Davy's twenty-two. He's in Australia. Not for good, though. Please God, he'll be back in a couple of years.'

Tara brought her hands together and clapped the tips of her fingers. 'Well, go you! That's what I say. I'd better get on my way, so you can put your posh gear on.'

'I wish,' said Carmel. 'My wardrobe isn't exactly overflowing with choices. I'd planned on getting a new dress or skirt, only the prices are mad. Anyway, I'll cobble something together.'

As Tara scooped up her bag and got to her feet, she had an idea. 'What size are you? A ten?'

'Yeah, I—'

'I know someone who has more frocks than Grafton Street, and she's a ten too.'

'I couldn't—'

'Of course you could. After all, as Ben might say, you've got to put your best shoe forward.' Tara was already halfway out the door. 'I'll be back in an hour.'

Chapter 17

Before she started her car, Tara called Vee twice. No answer. On her way, she tried again. Still no answer. Assuming this was pay-back for all the calls *she* had ignored, Tara left a message saying she was in need of a teeny-tiny favour. When she reached Vee's house, she made a fourth call. This time her message was even more obsequious.

After five minutes of door-knocking and four yoo-hoos through the letterbox, Tara had to accept there was no one home. Disappointed, she started back down the path. It was then that she remembered: deep in the recesses of her handbag she had a spare key. Vee and Ferdia had given it to her the previous January so she could water the plants while they were skiing in Zermatt. Briefly she thought about the rights and wrongs of entering someone's house and plundering their wardrobe. What the hell, she'd leave a note. Chances were that Vee wouldn't even notice.

Still, as she climbed the stairs, Tara did feel rather uneasy; like she should be wearing a balaclava and carrying a sack labelled 'swag'. Heart beating far too quickly, she went into the main bed-room and opened the door to her sister's walk-in wardrobe. She was met by a collage of scents. Vee regularly changed her perfume and each dress, jacket or top had a different smell. Every colour was represented, every style, every length. In places the wardrobe was colour-coded: an emerald silk dress hung beside a sea-green cotton shift hung beside a bottle-green mini dress. On another rail, black jackets jostled for space. Vee appeared to have an in-finite number of these, and to Tara's untrained eye, they all looked the same.

Elsewhere, she found a surprising amount of disarray. The very front of the wardrobe was higgledy-piggledy – skirts crammed in beside jeans, tops beside dresses – as if the coding system had broken down. At the rear, there were a number of empty hangers. Perhaps, the missing items were at the dry cleaners. The thought of Vee's cleaning bills made Tara shiver.

She knew she should get a move on. Carmel was waiting. Yet, as she flipped through the racks, Tara was hit by a memory from the recent past. The last time she'd been in this room, she'd been trying to convince her sister that something was wrong with their dad. She'd gone home and had a stupid row with Craig. Three months on, it felt like that argument was the catalyst for their split.

She didn't care what others said. Every day she questioned her decision to break up with Craig. She missed him. Might he be missing her? Despite Niall's noisy presence, the apartment no longer felt fully lived-in. She missed the DVDs pooled around the television, the teetering pile of books beside the bed, the expensive beers in the fridge. Since Craig moved out, they hadn't spoken. In May their lives were so entwined she wouldn't go to the shop without telling him; by August, all connection was gone. Surely this was wrong? She contemplated giving him a call.

Tara blinked and swallowed, then set about her task. A small selection would be best. Three dresses, say. She didn't want anyone thinking she was acting the Lady Bountiful. She pictured Carmel – not especially tall, blue eyes, dark blonde hair – and immediately chose two. The first was navy silk, quite casual, quite short. The second was more fitted. Cream and black, it had cap sleeves and a square neckline. She was on the landing when she decided to return for the emerald silk number. Call her fanciful, but if a piece of clothing could have a personality, she reckoned this one would be perpetually sunny. It would say, 'I deserve happiness'.

Before she left, Tara scribbled a note and placed it in the centre of the kitchen island. Then, dresses swinging over one arm, she stepped out into the heat and prepared to do battle with the Friday evening traffic.

*

By the time she got back to St Monica's, Carmel was in a quilted dressing gown, putting on her makeup. Ben had been safely dispatched to Nuala's flat.

'He's in a talkative mood,' said Carmel. 'Poor Nuala won't know what hit her.' She looked at what Tara was carrying and her eyes widened and her mouth formed a small 'o' shape.

'I'm sure they'll all fit, but I figured it'd be best if you had a choice,' said Tara, while she draped the dresses across the table.

Carmel ran a hand over the navy one. 'They look expensive.'

'Believe me, in Vee's world nothing is cheap. You're not to think about the cost, though.'

'And she didn't mind you lending them to someone she's never met?'

Tara did her best to sound emphatic. 'Oh God, no. She's decent like that.'

Carmel didn't look fully convinced but smiled anyway. 'Well, just you make sure she knows how grateful I am. I'll be finished with the war-paint in a minute and then I'll try them on.'

The first two were fine. No, better than fine. The navy, in particular, was lovely. But when Carmel emerged from the bedroom in the emerald dress, it was clear that this was the one. The joy on her face showed that she knew this too. Arms outstretched, head tilted to one side, she did a twirl.

'What am I like?' she said, as she came to a stop. 'Actually, I know what I'm like. I'm like a young one going to a deb's dance.'

'Nah,' said Tara, 'you're missing the dodgy hair extensions, the false nails and the geeky-looking boyfriend. Oh, and you haven't taken at least fifty photos of yourself.'

Carmel laughed. 'I forgot to look at the label on this one. What is it that the reporters say to the actresses on their way into the Oscars?'

'"Who are you wearing?"' replied Tara, adopting a perky American accent and scrunching one hand into a microphone shape.

'That's the one. So, who *am* I wearing?'

'Chloe, I think.'

Carmel froze in her tracks, and her nose wrinkled just like Ben's did when information disturbed him. 'Tara Shine! What are you trying to do to me? I know the price of those dresses. Well, I don't, but I can give a good guess. I can't go for a bite to eat with Victor in a frock that must have cost five hundred euro. What if I spilled something? Your sister would have a seizure.'

Although designer clothing was not Tara's area of expertise, she suspected that a thousand euro was a more accurate estimate. Of course, she didn't say this. 'You won't spill anything – and even if you do, the dry cleaners will sort it out.'

'No, love. Honest to God, I appreciate the thought, but I can't take the risk.'

'Aw please, Carmel. You look fabulous.'

Carmel patted her shoulder. 'Like I said, I'm really grateful. Only, I swear to you, I wouldn't enjoy a minute of the dinner for fear something happened to the dress. I'll wear the blue one. I'd say it wasn't as pricey.'

Tara almost fought on, but the set of Carmel's face suggested the battle had been lost. She gave a reluctant nod. 'Grand so,' she said. 'The blue one it is.'

While Carmel returned to the bedroom, Tara thought about her sister. She wondered when Vee had last worn the emerald dress; or whether she had ever worn it.

A mariachi band was playing in Vee's head. Their strumming and thumping was ceaseless, frenetic. She opened one eye and the room tilted. If there was no such thing as a good hangover, this one was from the outer reaches of awfulness.

Fleetingly, she wondered where Ferdia was. Then it came to her he was at his cousin's stag party in Kilkenny. That's what had given her the excuse to hit the town. If he can throw money at a weekend of debauchery, she'd thought, then I'm entitled to a quiet drink or two.

A quiet drink or two had progressed into a noisy drink or

ten. She'd been with Lottie Bond and Carly Hyland-Grey. The terrifying Carly Hyland-Grey. Vee was honest enough to realise that she was high-maintenance. Lottie was very high-maintenance. Carly was the acme of their species. She had the body of a fourteen-year-old, hair the colour of upmarket vanilla ice cream and the phoniest laugh in Dublin. Her father was a High Court judge. According to Ferdia, he'd been reluctant to accept the preferment. His barrister's practice was so lucrative that joining the bench meant a substantial pay-cut. Carly's one-time husband was also an upper-echelons barrister. During their eighteen months together, she'd had a daughter, Domino Camille. Rumour had it that after baby Domino's birth, Carly had been angsty about her appearance. Before allowing anybody to enter her room at Mount Carmel, she'd summoned her botox doctor, her hairstylist and her makeup artist.

Vee chanced a slight movement of her head. The pillowcase and duvet cover felt stiff and musty. Since she'd been forced to let her cleaner go, the sheets hadn't been the same. She should change them more often, but it was such a pain-in-the-ass job. She thought of how house-proud she used to be and winced.

She tried to remember how much her night out had cost. From what she could recall – and she couldn't recall a lot – she'd succeeded in ducking and diving, leaving most of the expense to Lottie and Carly. This was how it should be. Both were steeped in cash. Carly was fresh off the plane from her dad's villa in Villefranche-sur-mer. She'd brought her new boyfriend. Domino remained in Dublin. 'Richard and I needed time to bond,' she explained. 'And as much as I *adore* my beautiful girl, as much as I cherish her every breath, a mewling two-year-old would have got in the way. Thankfully, her granny loves having her. She just lives for it.'

In line with her morning custom, Vee made a mental inventory of her debts. Her credit and debit card issues were by no means resolved, but the car money had bought her some time. She'd avoided having the electricity cut off by bringing her Alaia sandals back for a refund. As if that wasn't painful enough, the sad man from the electricity company had had the temerity to offer her a meter. Can you imagine? She'd be in the same boat as the destitute, like the girls who thrust their babies at you on O'Connell Street, or the old women who plodded between charity shops.

Ferdia made regular inquiries about the insurance money. Fobbing him off was becoming more tricky. The same was true of her dad. 'Any progress on getting the deposit money for me, lovey?' he'd ask. 'It hardly takes the bank this long to sort things out, does it?' She used the time of year as an all-purpose excuse. 'You know nothing happens in August,' she'd say. What line she'd use in September, she didn't know.

Occasionally she considered coming clean, saying to Gus and Ferdia, 'Listen, I'm up to my tonsils in debt, and I need your help.' But that wasn't her way. She'd been getting the odd day's work with a public relations company and she'd been bombarding boutiques and department stores with her CV. Given time, she might be able to raise the necessary cash. The parking fines were another issue, but they were next on her list. Definitely next on her list.

Vee was up now, in the kitchen, coffee brewing, painkillers filtering through her system. Why did the day have to be so bright? She put on her sunglasses. That was better. Truth to tell, she hadn't enjoyed her night out. Lottie and Carly had spent an age talking about clothes, shoes and bags. What could she say? 'Sorry girls, I haven't the cash for a pair of Dunnes Stores knickers let alone a Victoria Beckham dress?'

Increasingly, Vee's four-in-the-morning thoughts turned to her shopping habit. For as long as she remembered, she'd been convinced that one more purchase, the *right* purchase, would improve her life. Usually she didn't think about the transaction in such stark terms, yet underneath, that's how she felt. As she lay there, she would imagine how an outsider might describe her life. If somebody saw how she spent her days, if they knew how much she owed and why, would they consider her hopelessly shallow and acquisitive? For an hour or more, these thoughts would loop around her brain. Some nights she would be struck by palpitations or feel weepy. Finally, she'd tip-toe to the bathroom, swallow a tablet and sink into an unsatisfying sleep.

While she drank her coffee, further fragments from the previous night came together. She remembered something Carly had said. Something surprising. She was mulling over this when she spotted a piece of paper. What was a note from Tara doing in her kitchen? The more Vee read, the angrier she became. She found her phone, listened to her sister's messages and tore upstairs. She was in no fit state for tearing, and by the time she reached the bedroom she feared she'd throw up. A flick through the wardrobe confirmed that three dresses were missing.

'You interfering bitch,' said Vee, as if Tara was in front of her. 'How dare you?'

It wasn't so much the missing clothing that bothered her as the fact than an intruder had been marauding around the house. *What if Tara had stumbled upon an incriminating letter or demand? What if she'd been actively snooping?*

Vee wanted her clothes and her key back. She pulled a pair of jeans and a T-shirt from the wardrobe, ran a brush through her hair and splashed water onto her face.

She would get on her bike and go round there right away.

Saturday lunchtime heralded the start of the viewing window. A parade of humourless couples would pitch up. Even though most of them could no more afford Garryowen than they could swim the Irish sea, they would engage in the ritual measuring and examining. Apart from the odd fleecy cloud, the sky was a seamless blue, and Tara suspected the fine day would only encourage the rubberneckers. An open air concert was taking place, music throbbing across the city. It was, she thought, an afternoon for the park. First, though, with her heart in her boots, she switched on her laptop. The time had come to look at flats.

Hardly had the screen lit up than there was a rat-tat-tat on the door.

'Are you there?' roared Vee.

Tara opened up to see a tarnished, dishevelled version of her sister. 'Holy moly, Vee,' she said. 'There's no need for all that noise. Leave the bike there and come in.'

Even for Vee, the ensuing tirade was quite something. She stood by the door and let rip. Only once did Tara intervene. She pointed out that she couldn't do jail time for entering a house when she had the key. After some minutes of uninterrupted haranguing, Niall's bedroom door creaked open and he stumbled out. His combination of boxer shorts, Pearl Jam T-shirt and matted hair suggested he'd just woken. 'Fair play to you, Vee,' he said. 'You might need to go a small bit louder, though. There may be a few folks up in Donegal who haven't heard you yet.' He went into the kitchen and returned with a litre of milk, which he drank straight from the carton.

Barely missing a beat, Vee flashed her brother a filthy look, told him he was a complete peasant and returned to her diatribe. 'So, can I have my property now, please?'

'Like I explained in my note, I lent the dresses to a friend. I'll fetch them later.' On the off-chance that Carmel might change her mind and wear the green one, Tara had left all three dresses behind in the flat.

'Which friend? Both Niamh and Stephanie are too hefty for my clothes.'

'It was someone else. You don't know her.'

'I want you to go over to her house and get those dresses. Now.'

'You're getting carried away here,' said Tara. 'I'll have them for you later.'

'Now,' repeated her sister, sounding indistinguishable from a sulky three-year-old. She was waving one arm, her fingers splayed in anger.

Niall, who was lolling beside the kitchen door, piped up. 'Let it rest, Vee. I'm sure your precious frocks will be grand.'

Vee looked from one to the other. Gradually, her face had changed from a dishwater grey to a shade bordering on maroon. 'You're some pair.' She gave a tart smile then added, 'You're so irritating, Tara. No wonder Craig gave you the shove.'

'Actually, Veronica, I broke it off.'

'Well, it hasn't taken him long to move on.'

'What do you mean?'

'I went for a drink with Carly Hyland-Grey last night. Craig's seeing her sister, Sheena. They're totally loved up, apparently. They're even talking about going travelling.'

Joan was not having a good day. She would like to have been in the back garden or, better yet, at the seaside. Instead she was showing an exceedingly grand couple – the Queallys or the Quigleys, she couldn't remember which – around Garryowen. She had the feeling their hoity-toityness was an attempt to mask their lack of money. Joan was skilled at detecting spoofers.

The afternoon was viciously hot, and she prayed that nobody else would turn up to the viewing. Gus had insisted they could handle everything without the assistance of an estate agent. Then he'd left for the office. 'I won't be long,' he'd promised. That was three hours ago.

It was fair to say, then, that as she descended the steps with the Queallys/Quigleys, her temper was not at its most even. Behind her they were wittering about the inadequacies of the kitchen. Joan turned around and gave them an insincere smile. 'What a shame you feel like that,' she said, her voice laden with syrup. 'Perhaps you won't want to see the garden apartment after all.'

The Queallys/Quigleys were adamant that they did.

'All right, then. My daughter and son might be here, but I'm sure they won't get in our way.'

She was about to knock on the apartment door when it was flung open. Vee – a wild-eyed, bedraggled Vee – was on her way out.

'Be careful that Tara doesn't steal anything from you,' she said to her mother before barging past the viewing couple. Agog, they watched as she pushed her bicycle to the gate, mounted and ped-alled down the street like a maniac.

'That was your . . .' started Mr Q.

'Daughter,' said Joan. 'But not the one who lives here. I can't think what's up with Veronica. No doubt I'll find out later. I am sorry about that. Like I said, though, the other two are no trouble.'

She ushered them in.

Tara was standing in the middle of the sitting room, a funereal look on her face. Behind her, Niall was smoking something that Joan hoped was a cigarette. The smell indicated otherwise. In his other hand was a carton of milk. He was dressed like he'd just crawled out of bed. Neither of them appeared overly bothered that their mother and two strangers had entered the room. Niall made a grumbling noise, and Tara said nothing.

Joan noticed the Queallys/Quigleys exchange a glance. She felt her own humour darken.

'This couple are here to view the house,' she explained.

'Oh,' replied Tara.

'Good for them,' said Niall.

Joan tried not to let her exasperation show. She didn't want to make an exhibition of herself. Yet she couldn't prevent her voice from rising several notches. 'Yes,' she said, 'and I'm sure they're wondering what's going on here . . . because I certainly am.'

'Oh,' said Tara, who seemed incapable of coming out with any-thing else.

Beside her, the couple were making the sort of moves that sug-gested they were keen to leave. Joan was equally keen to find out what was going on. She knew her daughter's every expression and she knew that Tara was very upset. But why? And what was Vee so het up about?

'What's happening?' she asked. 'And for God's sake, Niall, put out that cigarette.'

'Vee being an unmitigated fucking cow – that's what's hap-pening,' her son replied. 'Do you remember how she used to bore on about not being related to the rest of us? I'm beginning to hope she was right. Damien may be a bit of a pain, but she's complete poison.' He took another drag of his joint and turned to the Queallys/Quigleys, who looked like they might dissolve with embarrassment. 'You don't want to adopt a thirty-two-year-old woman, do you? I know that sounds a bit old, only she has the mental capacity of a two-year-old. No, actually, that's a slur on two-year-olds. She has the mental capacity of a . . . a bale of hay.'

'Niall, that's enough,' said Joan, whose voice had reached a pitch usually only audible to dogs and bats.

Her son gave her a quizzical stare.

'I'm not feeling well,' mumbled Tara as she left the room.

'Ahm, perhaps we'll return on a better day,' said Mr Q as he hustled his wife towards the door.

Joan rubbed her forehead. She remembered how Gus had hoped that difficult times would bring the children together. 'God bless your innocence, Gus,' she said quietly.

Chapter 18

Damien treated council meetings like an athlete treats a race. He finalised his tactics, psyched himself up, cleared his mind of distractions. Or that was what he usually did. As he made his way to September's meeting, he was fixating on his family.

A flowchart, he thought. That's what was needed to figure out who was talking and who wasn't. Perhaps there should be colour coding: red to signify a serious knock-down argument; green to suggest a minor tiff that would most likely blow over; amber to warn of potential trouble.

Tara was still in a huff over that ludicrous article in the *Evening Post*. If he'd had any idea the reporter would include those witless residents' quotes, Damien would never have called him. Both Felicity and Canice had taken Tara's side, and the St Monica's Mansions residents' committee was demanding a written apology. On top of this, Tara and Vee were engaged in a silent stand-off. Their squabble was connected to – did he have this right? – three dresses and Craig Fitzgerald. Felicity had tried to explain, except it all washed over Damien's head. Neither were Vee and Niall on speaking terms.

And then there were his parents. His mother had taken umbrage over an incident involving a couple who'd been viewing the house. 'I was so ashamed,' she'd said. 'My own children acting like a pack of savages.' But there was something else too. There was an unease about Gus and Joan, a watchfulness, that made Damien fear a serious flare-up was imminent.

With Rufus about to start school, he had taken his son around to Garryowen for a visit. He reckoned his parents would like to see the little fellow all rigged out in his uniform. He couldn't recall doing the same with either Willow or Aifric, but if the clowning game had taught him anything it was how much grandparents loved to get involved. At every party there was at least one granny or grandad, clapping and fussing and taking endless photos.

Rufus had played his part with aplomb, nattering away in the unselfconscious manner of the very young. 'Don't you wish they could stay that age?' Damien had said. Gus had smiled, but the smile didn't travel as far as his eyes. Joan responded by flapping around. She poured juice, fetched biscuits, picked up her knitting, put it down again. *Was the business in even more difficulty?* Damien wondered. *Or was something else to blame?* He hadn't seen his parents like this before. He supposed he hadn't been looking.

He was on Dame Street now, pacing past the language schools, the bookmakers and the bars. Outside Dublin Castle, he dodged a band of youngsters in navy school tracksuits. 'Keep up there. Keep up,' their teacher was saying.

It was time to take himself in hand. All this family-obsessing would get him nowhere. The elections were just nine months away, and there was a lot of work ahead. He was continuing to comply with Amby's every wish, preparing the ground for his campaign-funding pitch. Not that he'd be asking for much; a few thousand would do. The big parties would have those enormous posters where the candidate's face is so airbrushed that even their own children wouldn't recognise them. Damien had no such aspirations. At his end of the political market, ratty-looking posters were fine. They said you were authentic.

At the steps of City Hall, Damien paused – as he always did – to let the building work its magic. He'd heard colleagues claim that the Georgian building with its ornate marble and plasterwork was off-putting. 'Too opulent,' they'd say. 'Gives the wrong message to Joe Citizen.' Damien didn't agree. He liked to stand in the rotunda and soak up the history. Today, as he did this, a group of American tourists was being shown around. Their tour guide was pointing to the statues of Irish political heroes. 'There's

Daniel O'Connell – the liberator,' she said. 'And Henry Grattan and Thomas Davis . . .'

Damien stood and listened. He closed his eyes, he tried to focus, but the magic wasn't working. The guide's words slipped past his ears, and no matter how much he tried to block out non-political thoughts, the bastards kept creeping in. The scary thing was, those thoughts weren't just about his family. They were about what else he could be doing with his life.

The council chamber was not a place to dream. Its anaemic wooden benches and spindly microphones were thoroughly twenty-first century. Its debates veered from the banal to the vituperative. At the top of the room, ranks of officials were on hand to explain why nothing was possible. In the press gallery, journalists ensured that everybody was misquoted and misrepresented. Or, at least, this was how Damien saw it.

The councillors were a mixum-gatherum of wheeler-dealers and idealists, twenty-somethings and septuagenarians. Navy-suited business people sat cheek by jowl with denim shirt-wearing community activists. Their ambition drew them together. That, and their ability to talk. Damien liked to talk, but compared to some of the windbags in the chamber, he was a complete amateur.

As a novice councillor, for instance, he'd assumed that if you agreed with someone there was no need to say anything. Surely you should save your energies for the reports or motions you opposed? How innocent he'd been. It turned out that you were supposed to express your support for the previous speaker, and then put forward the same views at even greater length, and with even more vehemence. No matter that you were talking about grass-cutting or drain-cleaning, this was *your* UN General Assembly and you had to give it socks. He had the feeling that councils the world over were exactly the same.

Despite his love of politics, there were days when Damien found the grandstanding a bit tedious. This was one of those days. He had voiced the obligatory support for progressive measures and made the obligatory denunciation of proposed cutbacks, but he'd be pleased to see the end of the session. He was keen to get home and hear about Willow's first day at secondary school. She was a feisty girl (she was definitely her mother's daughter), and he wondered how she'd handle being bottom of the heap again.

Unfortunately, one of his most dogged rivals, an independent councillor called Maurice Tully, had put down a motion condemning 'unwarranted and mischievous attacks on the decent tenants of St Monica's Mansions'. A round man with a cap of mousy curls, Maurice saw himself as the darling of the disenfranchised. Never was he happier than when ramping up his *Dubbalin* accent and getting stuck into others on the left. An outsider would swear he'd grown up in a squat and made a living selling fruit from a pram. In actual fact, he was a university lecturer. He was also dangerously ambitious and exceptionally long-winded.

Still, forewarned is forearmed, so when Maurice began his speech, Damien was unruffled. The abuse was exactly as expected. 'Consorting with the capitalist media', 'a lack of empathy and understanding', 'turning the poor on the poor while the fat cats run free': Damien had used the same insults. He slumped in his seat and scratched the side of his head, as if to say, 'Is this the best you've got?'

And then, stealthily, carefully, Maurice changed direction. 'However,' he said, ' if one appreciates how busy Councillor Shine has been of late, one might start to understand how he could make such a terrible . . . such an egregious . . . error.'

Hold on a sec, thought Damien, *what's this about?*

Maurice cleared his throat. 'Most of us know what it's like . . . how hard it is . . . to keep the wolf from the door while representing our constituents. Our hard-pressed constituents. Mind you, some of us have had to do more work than others. Some of us have been more privileged than others.'

'Ah, Maurice, get a move on, would you?' said one of the councillors. 'Christmas is coming.'

Maurice threw back his shoulders and flicked a hand in the

direction of the heckler. 'I assure you this is an important matter. Of vital importance to the reputation … the good name … of this historic chamber.'

Damien was feeling slightly nauseous. A bead of sweat ran between his shoulder blades.

'It has come to my attention – and may I say it's not my intention to judge – it has come to my attention—'

'Will the councillor get to the point?' said the Lord Mayor, a man so wooden that if you broke him up you'd get a table and four chairs.

'It has come to my attention,' repeated Maurice, ' that Councillor Shine has a new job.'

Bile rose in Damien's throat.

'A new job working with young people. Now, like I said, it's not my intention to judge. But, considering the intemperate nature of his recent remarks about the tenants – the law-abiding tenants – of St Monica's Mansions—'

Damien had to intervene. 'I said nothing about the tenants. I merely questioned the council's policy on remedial works, that's all.'

'Councillor Tully, without interruption,' chipped in the Mayor.

'Thank you,' said Maurice. 'Considering his recent intervention, I wonder if the stress of this new position is getting to Councillor Shine.' He stopped and shuffled his papers. 'I also wonder about the … how shall I put this? … the appropriateness of the councillor's new career.'

A murmur of interest floated from the press gallery.

'In fact, I've been asking myself whether the position might be said to bring the council into disrepute.'

As one, the council's members sat up straight. The murmur became more pronounced. Damien closed his eyes.

Maurice Tully cleared his throat for a second time. 'I was approached in recent days by a constituent who came into contact with Councillor Shine while he performed his new duties. "Tell me, Maurice," the constituent said, "Is this permissible?" I pledged

– and I'm sure any of you would do the same – I pledged to raise her concerns. After all, are we not committed to upholding the reputation – the hard-won reputation – of this fine institution?'

Damien opened his eyes to see his foe pulling a large brown envelope from among the sheaves of paper. His movements were ponderous, but it didn't matter; the councillors, the journalists, even the officials were watching him with rapt attention. *The man is wasted here*, thought Damien. *He should be on the stage in the Abbey Theatre.*

Maurice removed two A4 colour photos from the envelope. 'Before I go any further, may I say, colleagues, that this intervention brings me no pleasure. However . . .' He hesitated. 'I have in front of me two recent images of Councillor Shine at work.'

Councillors craned their necks to get a better view. One, a short-sighted woman called Dorothy Dowdall, actually got up to take a closer look. Reporters were bellowing, 'Over this way. Hold the photos over this way.' Damien swallowed the bile and pressed his fingers against his temples.

The photographs showed him in full regalia. In one, his hands were raised high. He may have been dancing. In the other, he was goofing around with two small girls. In that instant, nobody could say for sure that the clown in the pictures was Councillor Damien Shine. But the glint in Maurice's eye suggested he had further evidence. There was no point in Damien claiming ignorance. It might only make matters worse.

'And the question I have for the chamber is this,' said Maurice. 'Should we tolerate such . . . activity? Is it appropriate? And if we do believe this is appropriate, well, what next? Can a councillor become a dancer or a stripper? An escort, even?'

'Now, hold on a minute,' said Damien, 'you're scraping the bottom of the barrel here. There's no comparison between . . . no comparison . . .' His voice trailed off. He had already lost. He was drowning. No – worse – he had sunk.

'And for fear you're wondering,' finished Maurice, his face aglow with benevolent concern, 'I do have some spare copies of these images . . . just a small number . . . if my friends in the press are interested.'

Within half an hour, the photos were on Twitter. Tara was first to hear the news. A colleague texted from the press gallery. *What's the story with your brother?* he asked.

She couldn't believe it. Simply couldn't digest it. Damien, her relentlessly serious brother Damien, was working as a children's entertainer. Not only that: he was working for Amby Power. Tara didn't know Amby very well. What she did know was that Damien had little time for him. Gus also held him in low esteem. Her dad couldn't say the man's name without using the prefix 'that scabby fecker'.

She called Damien. There was no answer, so she sent a sympathetic text. She hoped he hadn't ignored the call because of their spat over the St Monica's article. She tried Felicity. No answer either. She considered going upstairs to tell Gus and Joan, then thought better of it. Damien should talk to them first. Up and down the sitting room she marched, trying to make sense of what had happened. The more she marched, the more she realised that sometimes things didn't make sense. Crazy stuff happened all the time. Every day of the week, people did things that were illogical, dangerous, or plain daft. She thought of her job. What was the most commonly used phrase in the newsroom? 'You couldn't make it up,' they said, over and over again.

After an hour or so, Niall rolled in, full of nonsense about a girl he'd met. Tara stuck a coffee in his hand and told him. His initial reaction was surprisingly sensitive.

'The poor devil.'

'But why?' asked Tara. 'Why do something that's so out of character?'

'Isn't it obvious? He needs the money.'

'What for though? Felicity and himself aren't what you'd call flash.'

'They've three kids, Tara. Rufus was here the other day, kitted out in his new school gear. Willow's starting secondary school. And the old man's funds have dried up.'

Tara hit the heel of her hand against her forehead. 'I'm so thick. I did a story not too long ago about school fees. St Attracta's is one of the most expensive places in the country.'

'There you have it,' said Niall. 'Any idea how your man ... the other councillor ... got wind of what was going on?'

'Oh, I'd put nothing past him. Maurice Tully has a face like a reverend mother, but he'd run naked down O'Connell Street for a vote.'

A smile had crept onto Niall's face. 'It's a gas one all the same. Damien working as a clown – who would've thought?'

She squinted at him. 'You will behave yourself, won't you? You won't go stirring it?'

'Scout's honour,' said her brother.

Although she wanted to believe him, Tara worried about the mirth in his eyes. And, now that she thought about it, he'd never been in the Boy Scouts either.

The morning newspapers had a ball. Even her own paper, the staid and responsible *Irish Tribune*, allowed itself a few laughs. The tabloids excelled themselves. *Send in the Clowns, Oh What A Circus, Clowning Around, This Politician Really Is A Clown, Councillor Juggles Two Careers*. Every possible headline was there. No quip was too corny; no pun too lame. Morning radio joined in. Normally strait-laced news presenters vied to outdo each other with cracks about clowns and circuses. Councillor Damien Shine – a man previously known only to constituents, current affairs nerds and left-wing activists – had become a household name.

Tara still didn't know how her parents had taken the news. When she got a free minute – her fellow journalists were being especially tiresome – she called Gus. In a mixture of monosyllables and grunts, he suggested they meet for lunch. Before she had time to agree, let alone come up with a venue, he had hung up. She decided to trek over to his office.

A group of young men had gathered outside. One was holding up a newspaper and reading aloud. The other three were smirking and laughing. *There won't be too much laughing if my dad catches you*, thought Tara. She was about to walk past and up the steps when she realised that Rory was among them. He quickly broke away.

'Uh, hi there,' he said.

'How bad's the *Evening Post*?' she asked.

'It's . . .'

'Go on, I can handle it.'

'It's mostly the same as the morning papers.' Rory rubbed his earlobe. 'Except with added jokes. Half a page of jokes. Like, what material do you use to make a clown outfit?'

Tara lifted one eyebrow.

'Poly-jester,' came the deadpan reply.

She groaned. 'You'd think there was no real news out there.'

'You know the way it is. It'll all be forgotten about by tomorrow. It'll be somebody else's turn to be placed on the rack.'

'I suppose.' *It won't be forgotten by Damien or my mum and dad*, she thought. And it wouldn't be forgotten by Willow and Aifric. She hoped they weren't getting grief at school.

'Anyway, how are you?' Rory asked.

Recalling the last time they'd met, Tara felt her face tingling. 'OK, thanks. Muddling along.'

As if her embarrassment was contagious, Rory began examining his shoes. 'That doesn't sound great. I hope you got everything sorted with your boyfriend, after that . . . eh . . . misunderstanding.'

When she told him that she'd split up with Craig, the embarrassment became more acute.

'God, I'm sorry,' he said.

'No, no, it was nothing to do with you. It was . . . well, these things happen. It was probably for the best. Or, maybe not for the best but . . .' Tara was appalled by how inarticulate she'd become.

Rory lifted his grey eyes from the pavement. 'If you ever . . . No, what I was wondering was . . . I mean . . .'

He stalled, like he expected her to finish the sentence. Tara felt her calves tighten. He wasn't about to ask her out, was he? On today, of all days, when she had a million family issues to sort out? She looked at him. He was as skinny as a sapling, but better-looking than she remembered. There was a kind of unaffected charm about him. Then she copped herself on. *Oh, for heaven's sake*, she thought, *he works with my dad*.

Rory renewed his efforts to string a few words together. 'Like I said—'

He was interrupted by a booming voice and the clatter of foot-steps. 'There you are, Tara,' said Gus, as he descended the steps at a rate of knots. 'We need to get a move on. I've a rake of meetings this afternoon.' He stared at his employee. 'And I'd say Rory has plenty to be doing too.'

Tara didn't know whether she was relieved or irritated, but before she got the chance to say goodbye, her dad was bustling her down the street.

'Some carry-on,' he said. 'Do you know, Felicity says Damien's very good at being a clown? Not that she's ever been to have a look. "Daddy has, though," she said to me. "And Daddy doesn't give praise lightly." Amby Power doesn't give anything lightly, I wanted to say. But, sure, what's the point? He's her father, and me running the guy down won't make the situation any better.'

'Why though?' asked Tara. 'Of all jobs, why that one? And of all people to work for, why Amby?'

Gus must have spent most of the morning talking to Felicity and Damien because a great gush of explanations followed. No money had changed hands, he said, but Amby had paid the three children's school fees. Until last night only Felicity had known. The two girls were mortified; Rufus was too young to understand. They reckoned Damien was rumbled by a woman at a party in Rathmines. Oh, and Amby insisted the debt wasn't yet paid. He wanted his son-in-law back on the clowning circuit the following weekend.

Gus tore along the footpath like a man pursued by rabid dogs.

Tara trotted beside him, cursing her decision to wear her one pair of heels (the things really were the devil's work), and trying to figure out what, if anything, her dad would do.

'Have you been speaking to Damien?' Gus asked.

This wasn't the time to reveal that they weren't on speaking terms. 'I rang. He must have been busy. I've left a couple of messages.'

'He's calling round tonight so we can have a proper chat.'

'Oh.'

'I take it you'll be there.'

'I'm meeting a friend,' she lied. Tara knew she would have to talk to Damien, but given their falling-out, it would be easier if the rest of the family wasn't listening in. She would handle the situation in her own way and in her own time.

Gus came to an abrupt halt, so abrupt that a girl carrying a tray of coffees almost fell over him. The girl gave him a frosty stare, but said nothing.

'You'll be there, Tara. It's high time you all rallied around and put your family first.'

Seven hours later, Tara was still annoyed. Indignant, even. Spikes of irritation kept popping up in her head. It wasn't fair of her father to lump her in with the other three. She always rallied around. And what thanks did she get? Despite the fact that she'd got her dresses back in pristine condition, Vee remained chilly towards her. Then again, Vee was at odds with the world right now. She hadn't turned up to meet Damien, which was just as well. She wasn't on good terms with any of the family, and given her recent behaviour, she would probably only say something to foment further upset.

The rest of them were in the sitting room awaiting his arrival. Gus, tense and twitchy, shifted around in his green chair. It struck Tara that he might be feeling guilty. After all, if he hadn't lost the money, Damien wouldn't have needed to go cap-in-hand to Amby. Joan drifted in and out, doing her 'everything's grand' act.

Niall slouched beside the table of photographs, a glass of red wine in hand.

Tara wound a lock of hair around one finger. 'Any developments?'

'No,' replied her mum. 'Nothing major, anyway.'

'Aifric came home from school with a note,' said Gus. 'She slapped a girl who teased her.'

'Aifric? Seriously?' said Tara. 'I mean, if Willow had given someone a dig I wouldn't think twice about it. But Aifric's always so quiet.'

'People can surprise you,' said Joan.

'Can't they just,' added Niall.

'By the way, Damien was right about the person who ratted on him,' said Gus. 'Apparently he bumped into a woman at a kid's party. Like, literally bumped into her. And who was she, only this Maurice Tully fellow's sister. Talk about bad luck.'

'Mmmm,' replied Tara. 'He was bound to get unmasked at some stage, though.'

'True,' said her dad. 'Ideology is no match for guile.'

When the bell rang, both parents made for the door. Joan took charge. 'Stay where you are, Gus,' she said.

Somehow Tara had expected her elder brother to have changed. She had anticipated a downcast, defeated figure. Instead the man who walked in with Joan appeared to be his usual assured self. It was her own greeting that sounded tentative.

'Hi,' she said. 'I hope you're OK.'

'Thanks.'

From behind her, Niall's reedy voice started up. She turned. It took her a moment to recognise what he was singing.

Isn't it rich?
Are we a pair?
Me here at last on the ground,
You in mid-air.
Send in the clowns—

He got no further. In one fluid movement, Damien stepped forward and landed a punch right below his brother's eye. Taken by surprise, Niall fell. As he did, he caught the edge of the table. The photograph of their granny, Phyllis, went tumbling to the ground. Niall's wine glass pirouetted in the air before landing *splat* on top. The red wine sprayed across the picture then seeped onto the carpet.

Joan gasped.

'Lord, give me strength,' said Gus.

Tara watched Damien rub his fist. Niall remained in a heap on the floor. Their confrontation had been almost cartoon-like. It could have been funny.

Except, right then, it wasn't.

Chapter 19

Gus and Joan were on their way to Limerick for his mother's birthday. If you got to eighty-seven, he reckoned, you had a right to expect some family company. Joan was driving. Gus would never say it out loud, but she was the better driver. She obeyed the speed limit for a start.

Unfortunately, none of the children had been willing to make the journey. 'Visit the bold Phyllis with my face like this? Are you serious?' Niall had protested. 'Can you imagine the questions?' Damien had been 'busy'; Tara had claimed a 'prior engagement'. And Vee? She was still being antisocial. 'I'm sure you'll manage without me,' she'd said. 'Everybody else does.' Gus considered giving them all a talking-to but couldn't handle another row, so he grudgingly accepted their excuses.

Even though Niall's eye was a dark purple mess, he was attracting scant sympathy. Amiable and all as he was, the boy had had it coming. Everybody said it. Gus had expected further antagonism between Niall and Damien. Instead, they appeared to have suspended hostilities. This was largely due to Niall's admission that he'd got what he deserved.

Phyllis had seen the story about Damien's clowning job in the paper and was expecting an explanation. 'What was the lad up to? Was it some type of joke?' she had wanted to know. 'We'll talk about it when I see you,' Gus had replied. That moment was just an hour away.

'What are we going to tell Mam?' he asked Joan as they sped past the-Lord-knows-where. That was the problem with these by-passes. The country had been turned into a homogenous blur of concrete and service stations. Gus missed the place names too: the Pike of Rushall and Toomevara and Borris-in-Ossory.

'What about the truth?'

'The truth about Damien or the truth about everything?'

'Everything. There's another toll coming up in a minute, by the way.'

'Tell me more,' said Gus as he rooted in his pocket for some change.

It was Ben's birthday too. The newly-minted eight-year-old didn't want a party. 'Can we go to the seaside?' he said. 'We never go to the seaside.' So that's where they were heading. Victor drove. Carmel was beside him. Jenelle, Tara and Ben were in the back. Tara wasn't sure why she was included, but Carmel invited her and Ben chirped 'yes, yes' and, let's face it, the trip gave her an excuse not to go to Limerick. As much as she loved her granny, Phyllis wasn't the easiest of company. On a good day, she had the subtlety of a car-crusher, and would probably ask a stream of questions about Tara's love life before giving a homily about the dangers of getting married too late.

They were on their way to Brittas Bay.

'It's a great spot,' said Victor. 'Even better than Portmarnock.'

'High praise from a Northsider,' joked Carmel. Victor lived in Beaumont and maintained that everything was better on the far side of the river.

It *was* a great spot: soft sand dunes freckled with marram grass ran down to a white arc of beach. Tara knew how lovely it was because she'd been so often with Craig. His family owned a mobile home there.

In the car, Ben told her all about his presents. 'They're brilliant,' he said. 'Best ever.' He'd got Lego superheroes and a football and books and clothes and his Uncle Jack had sent money from London. 'English money,' he added. Tara put on her impressed face.

Victor played Johnny Cash. Not the dark tunes of his later

years, but funny songs like 'One Piece at a Time' and 'A Boy Named Sue'. He sang along and they all laughed. Then Ben performed a song in Irish about a sick teddy bear. He said it was a bit young for him now, but it was Jenelle's favourite. By the time he got to the final verse, the girl was humming quietly. Carmel looked around and smiled at her granddaughter.

'That'll be you soon enough, chicken. When you're in big school, you'll learn songs like that,' she said.

'I can teach her,' offered Ben, who was taking his extra year very seriously. 'Imagine, next year I'll be *nine*.'

'You'll be so grown up, I'll have to get out and let you drive the car,' said Victor.

Tara couldn't stop herself from wondering what they would all be doing in twelve months' time. By then, Rosanna might be free from jail. Presumably she'd want her children back. Or would she? The last few months had been so topsy-turvy, with surprises lurking around every corner, that Tara didn't know what to expect anymore. Who could say what would happen tomorrow, not to mind a year from now?

The mild weather had carried on into September, and that Sunday, Brittas Bay was swarming with people. Families poured onto the beach. Mostly they strolled along the sand. Some sat and soaked up the sun. Others, Ben among them, made straight for the water.

Victor said he'd bring the two children for a paddle. Tara watched as Ben, tanned and wiry, ran helter-skelter to the sea. Jenelle, pale and cautious, followed. She was such a fastidious girl. Mess and disorganisation were anathema to her. Neither, however, did she like being left out of her brother's games. Victor took her hand and they splashed about at the edge of the water.

Tara and Carmel sat down, kicked off their sandals and let the sand trickle through their toes.

'Happy days,' said Tara as she tilted her face towards the sun.

'Hmmm,' said Carmel, who had clasped her mobile phone

between her palms, as though the added warmth might bring it to life. 'I wish she'd ring.'

'It's early yet. Besides, does the prison allow them to make calls whenever they want?'

'It's her son's birthday. I'm sure they relax the rules for special occasions.'

'I bet she'll ring soon then.'

'I hope so,' sighed Carmel. 'You know, Ben hasn't mentioned his mam today. Not once. It's like he's already learned not to get his hopes up.'

'Did Rosanna send him a card?'

'Yeah, a manky-looking thing like you'd send to an old man.'

Tara shifted her gaze to the sea, watching the waves swelling and curling and fizzing to the shore. 'Ah, you're being unfair now.'

'Maybe I am, only . . .' Carmel turned the phone over in her hands. 'Have you heard about Ben's latest obsession? Telling the truth.'

'I've heard of worse obsessions.'

'You should listen to him. His new teacher gave the class a speech about the importance of being truthful. And you know what Ben's like; he never does things by half. So now, every poor devil who comes into the flat has to get the same lecture. I'm amazed you haven't had it yet.'

'I'll prepare myself for his sermon.'

'And here we all are, lying away to the boy. Telling him his mam has a fancy job on the other side of the world. I swear to God, Tara, if Rosanna doesn't ring today, I'll go round there to-morrow and . . . well, I'll probably end up behind bars myself.'

Tara saw the three figures making their way back. Ben's head was swaying, as though he might be singing. Beside him, his sister took small, careful steps. 'Does Jenelle ever mention her mum?'

'Not very often. She was too young. This is all she's known. It's mad – after Willy died, people used say to me, "You must be heartbroken, Carmel". And I'd think, "heartbroken" – what a silly, overused word. I mean, it's your head that hurts, not your heart.

Or that's what I thought. But the thing is, there are days, days like this, when I look at those two kids, and my heart could break for them. And for Rosanna too. Really it could.'

The five went for a walk through the dunes; Ben gurgling with laughter when the sand shifted beneath him; Victor telling stories about crazy things that had happened at work; Carmel joking that, unless he was careful, his tales would end up in the *Irish Tribune*. The soothing sound of the sea and the children's whoops and giggles gave the afternoon a dreamlike quality. Although Jenelle was too young to have any real interest in flowers, Tara wanted to show her the plants that clung to the sand. Once upon a time, she'd spent a day learning their names: sea holly and biting stonecrop, wild thyme and rest harrow. Craig had claimed that she'd lost her true vocation as a primary school teacher. He called her Miss Shine for the rest of the weekend.

Tara had visualised an ideal scenario for her next meeting with Craig. They would bump into each other in town. She would be svelte and groomed, surrounded by friends, exuding calm. He would be surprised, discommoded. There would be no sign of Sheena Hyland-Grey. At night she liked to lie awake, adding details to her fantasy. No one would ever believe that she had instigated the split.

When you've been with somebody for a long time – and in her book, three years was a long time – small things become imprinted on your brain. You know the sound of their footsteps; you can read their facial cues; the gait of their walk is unmistakable. And it was this, the rolling slope of Craig's walk, that told her the man in the near distance was her former boyfriend. For a second she had an urge to run, to pretend she hadn't seen him. But Craig had spotted her. He paused to say something to his willowy companion.

Tara doubted that she'd ever looked more crumpled. She was wearing a faded, wrinkled skirt, and her hair was at its windswept worst. And then there was ... Oh, she felt ashamed for even thinking this, but what would Craig make of her company?

'Hi there,' he said, like they were vague acquaintances. 'Sheena, I think you know Tara. Tara Shine.'

Sheena, all five feet ten-ish of her, gave a simpering smile. 'Sort of.'

Tara turned towards Carmel and Victor. 'Craig's a friend of mine,' she explained. Carmel quirked one eyebrow. She knew the story of their break-up.

Ben thrust a hand towards Craig. 'I'm Ben O'Neill. Tara's our friend too. Me and my nan and Victor and Jenelle. I'm eight. Jenelle's only four. Some people think she's slow 'cos she doesn't say much. She's not, but.'

Sheena's eyes held a faraway gaze, but she had the manners to shake Ben's hand. 'Uh, hi. Are you on your holidays?'

'Course not,' he replied. 'I'm back at school, and Victor has to look after all the painting and stuff. We're here for the day, on account of it being my birthday.' He thrust his hands into the pockets of his new jeans.

'Oh, cool,' said Craig. 'How old are you?'

He just told you, you dolt, thought Tara.

Victor intervened. 'Nice to meet the two of you. Grand old day, isn't it? And isn't it great to see so many people making the most of the weather?'

Carmel nodded. 'It might be lashing rain tomorrow.'

Tara watched Craig absorb the scene. Recognition flickered across his face. He knew who Ben and Carmel were, and how she'd met them. Jenelle, she noticed, had nestled in behind her nan.

'We're very lucky,' he said, draping an arm around the glacially perfect Sheena. 'We're going to Brazil on Wednesday and then on to Argentina.'

'On your holidays?' asked Ben.

'Sort of,' said Sheena. 'We're hoping to be away for a year.'

The boy's eyes were out on stalks. 'You're going on holidays for a whole year?'

Craig laughed. How Tara knew that laugh. 'We-ell, if you put it like that,' he said, 'I suppose we are.'

'Wow. My mam's been away for even longer. She'll have to come home soon, though.'

Tara's mind raced. When Vee told her about Craig and Sheena's plans, Tara had been upset. As time passed, however, she'd come to hope that her sister was lying, or at least exaggerating. That she was being vindictive. But they really were going travelling. Tara knew what would happen next. When couples returned from their round-the-world jaunt, they got engaged. That was how it worked.

'Where's your mum, then?' Sheena was asking Ben. 'Is she working abroad? And what about your dad?'

Carmel's face puckered. She turned and stroked Jenelle's hair. 'Do you need to go to the toilet, pet?'

The little girl nodded.

'We'd better leave you to it,' said Craig, his voice distressingly breezy.

'Good luck,' replied Tara, the pain in her chest as real as a heart attack.

They found a café, a place so bustling with cheer that Tara worried her very presence would sour the atmosphere. Ben and Jenelle drank glasses of milk and ate bread with blackcurrant jam and small buns with faces on top. Tara had a bitter, black coffee. More than once she blinked back tears. Carmel squeezed her hand, and Victor did his best to entertain the children.

'You probably don't believe me,' Carmel said, her voice low for fear Ben was listening. 'But you can do better than him. Way, way better.'

'Thanks,' she squeaked.

Ben leaned in towards her. 'You know that man we met – with the skinny woman? Did he used to be your fella?'

'Why do you ask?'

'You told me once that your boyfriend's name was Craig.'

'Ben, you've got an unbelievable memory. And, yes, you're right. He was.'

'Hmmm. I think they were telling lies. No one goes on holidays for a whole year.'

Despite herself, Tara smiled. 'Are you enjoying your birthday?'

'It's deadly,' he said, his face open, his voice matter-of-fact. 'And that's the truth.'

Tara closed her eyes. She hoped that when she thought about today, it was this part she remembered.

'That's about the height of it,' said Gus as he tapped the side of his mug. 'Your first proper gig is next Saturday, but you'll need to get acquainted with the job beforehand. Amby's expecting your call.'

Niall hadn't seen his father's request coming. Well, to be fair, it wasn't a request. It was an order. He was half-tempted to play the old soldier, to flaunt his war wound, but he feared this would backfire. With any luck, the clown makeup would be thick enough to cover his black eye. Anyway, he bore no malice towards Damien. The song had been a provocation too far and, in the same situation, Niall might have had the same reaction. He rubbed the edge of the kitchen table.

'And there's no payment? I'm expected to do this for nothing?'

'The payment's already been made to Damien. Amby's looking after the kids' school fees ... and a couple of other bills. You're honouring the remainder of the debt.'

'How long's this likely to last?'

'You'll have to ask Amby. He's the man who's owed the money. I gather he's in need of a good bit of help, though. One of his regular entertainers has fecked off on a touring production of *Big Maggie*.' Gus took a slurp of tea. 'All going well, you'll be free by Christmas.'

'Christmas?' said Niall. 'I'd get a shorter sentence from a judge.'

'If you find something better to do, we can look at the situation again.'

You crafty goat, thought Niall. As far as he could see, there was only one upside to taking over Damien's clowning duties: Felicity might stop pestering him. Rather than blaming her father or

Councillor Maurice Tully for her husband's humiliation, she'd decided to take her anger out on him. The fact that this was entirely illogical didn't bother her. Someone had to be the villain, and he fitted the bill. She had called several times to moan about the damage to Damien's political career. Listening to her, you would swear it was the career she was married to rather than the man.

Two months had passed since Niall's return, and he was getting fed up with mooching around the place. Oh, for a while everything was great: old haunts were visited, pals were met, women were pursued. The thing was, even his most lackadaisical friends appeared to be moving on. They were working or retraining or – shudder – settling down. How he wished he could escape, but his wings had been well-clipped. What Niall needed was something he *could* do and *wanted* to do. What that something was eluded him.

'Who came up with the idea?' he asked. 'You or Amby? Or did Felicity put you up to it?'

'You're wide of the mark there. It was your gran's brainwave. We – your mam and I – told her about the row, and she came up with a plan.' His dad chuckled. 'There's plenty of life in her yet.'

Ah hell, thought Niall. *That's all I need: the world's scariest eighty-seven-year-old on my case too.* 'All right,' he said. 'I'll ring the dreaded Amby.'

'Good man. And, for the last time, would you do something about those bloody sandals? I've seen better-shod fellas begging for coins on O'Connell Bridge.'

The court summons arrived on Tuesday morning. Accustomed to ignoring the post, Vee nearly missed it, but something about the harp on the envelope told her that this was serious. With a tremor in her hands, she ripped it open and removed a page of closely-typed instructions. She was due to appear in the Dublin District Court on parking charges. The letter referred to her as *the accused*. The bastards made her sound like a murderer or a drug dealer. How dare they!

For the hundredth time, she thanked God that by the time the post came her husband was already at work. Then she paced around the house. She wished every sort of misfortune on the clerk who'd signed the document and on the official whose orders he was following. No affliction, no pox or plague would be too awful for them. She didn't belong in court with the flotsam and jetsam of the city. When she turned on the radio, a politician was bleating about 'green shoots'. Vee picked up the machine and threw it with such force that the front popped off and its innards came spilling out.

Oh, why couldn't she find a proper job? There must be something for her. She had skills. She knew when opaque tights were acceptable and when only ten denier would do. She knew when a handbag crossed the line from 'must-have' to 'naff'. She knew where to find jeans that would make even Tara appear long-legged. Surely there was somebody who needed her expertise?

Vee looked again at the sum she owed. She didn't have enough. Not nearly enough. She pledged not to do too much thinking. Thinking only made her depressed. She would get this courts problem sorted, and then she'd come clean to Ferdia.

Chapter 20

Despite the fact that her husband was a barrister, Vee rarely thought about the courts. If she did, she saw them as being rather like discount supermarkets or two-star hotels: they served a purpose but they weren't for the likes of her. She'd been to watch Ferdia in action once or twice and had found it pretty tedious. It wasn't as though he had the starring role, and the cases had involved arcane points of law that went right over her head.

Ferdia was away at another circuit court hearing, this time in County Donegal, so fingers crossed she would be able to make her own court appearance without him finding out. She would say what had to be said, get a rap on the knuckles and leave the episode behind her. And she'd be contrite. Contrite was good.

The Criminal Courts of Justice were an alien place for Vee. Just *how* alien was apparent as she approached the cream and brown cylindrical building. The steps were littered – and she used that word advisedly – with young hoodlums sucking hard on cigarettes. *It wouldn't have killed them to take off the tracksuits and trainers for one day,* she thought. Vee clutched her handbag close to her body. She was dressed elegantly yet not flashily in a navy trouser suit. The last thing she wanted was the judge thinking she was coming down with cash. After all, she was about to explain that she hadn't paid her parking fines because she simply hadn't had the funds. She was ... what was that phrase the politicians like to use? The squeezed middle – that was it. Vee was part of the squeezed middle.

In the cavernous entry hall, she was overwhelmed by the numbers waiting for the sittings to begin. She had no idea the place would be so busy. What had all of these people done? It seemed to her that many must be regulars. They sauntered around with a surprising nonchalance. In among them were groups of black-suited men and women flipping through manilla folders. Vee hadn't bothered to engage a solicitor. For a start, they would have to be paid. Plus, Ferdia might have got wind of the appointment. Also, she genuinely believed she could handle matters herself. After all, in comparison to some of those milling around the lobby – a man with a scorpion tattooed on his neck, another man whose face was dotted with scabs – she was a minor league offender, surely?

She was shaken to see her name listed at the door of the courtroom. That was a bit too public for her liking. She reached up to remove the sheet of paper, only to feel a tap on her shoulder. A bulky policeman advised her that it would be a mistake to interfere with 'court property'. Blushing, she muttered some nonsense about wanting a souvenir and hurried on her way.

The courtroom itself was modern with a bright blue carpet and wide television screens. There were few wigs and gowns. Also missing was the reverential hush that Vee had experienced in the higher courts. Men and women hurried in and out. Behind them the heavy wooden doors squealed shut. Some of the men were talking and joking, others were sending text messages. One young guy was rolling a cigarette! How could that be right?

Amid this frenetic activity, Vee saw that on the other side of the room a man's head lolled as though he was asleep. On the bench directly in front of her, two men chatted in unnaturally slow voices. A woman, who might have been anywhere between twenty and forty, wept quietly. Another woman had a nasty gash above her left eye. Then it struck her: half of the room was strung out. There was something else too: almost everybody was thin. Disturbingly thin. Bony elbows protruded from twig-like arms; narrow faces were prematurely wizened.

Vee was trained to view lack of flesh as an attribute. Wallis Simpson's famous line about the impossibility of being either too rich or too thin was her creed. She had no reason to change her mind about the start of that quote, but the people around her proved that the second part was bunk.

While she contemplated her surroundings, an elderly man squeezed past. The stench of urine hit her like a slap in the face. She didn't know if she'd ever been in the presence of so much misery. She prayed the judge would dispense with her case quickly. Once she got out of this room, she would never be back.

Was it possible to dislike someone from the instant you saw them? Vee reckoned it was, and that Judge Walter Duffy was living proof. A well-fed man with a steel-coloured bouffant, he was wearing a stiff black jacket and a white shirt with a wingtip collar. His arrival was heralded by a female garda bellowing at the assembled crowd to quieten down. The crowd did as they were told, and the judge responded with a satisfied nod. He looked as though he was accustomed to getting his own way.

Although Vee had hoped that her case would be up first, she soon realised that the judge was following the order laid down on the piece of paper she had tried to remove. She would be there for some time. The first few cases were, she had to admit, grimly fascinating. There was a man accused of stealing two trays of deodorants from a supermarket, another man caught with three hundred euros' worth of heroin in his underpants, and a third man who pleaded guilty to reckless driving. Even though he only looked about twenty-five, he had ninety-three previous convictions.

As she waited, her thoughts slipped back to the night before. She had called around to Damien's house to offer him her sympathies. They may have had their disagreements, but he was family, and Maurice Tully sounded like a slimy so-and-so. As Vee saw it, Damien had been trying to do the right thing by his children. If only their own father hadn't gone and lost the money. Life without money was so damn complicated.

She snapped back to attention when a woman in a creased grey jacket appeared before the judge. Vee recognised her as the woman who had been crying before the sitting began. The anguish on her face hinted that her problems weren't confined to today's appearance in court. Judge Duffy was addressing her solicitor, an intense young woman with a pageboy haircut.

'How on earth did your client manage to steal seven hundred euros' worth of shoes from a supermarket?' he asked. 'I'm not in the habit of purchasing my own footwear in that particular establishment, but I understand it's not an expensive shop. Did she take every shoe in the place?'

'She says it was a moment of madness, Judge. She just kept stuffing them into plastic bags. She didn't really think.'

'You can say that again. What did she intend to do with the shoes?'

'She doesn't know, Judge. My client has been going through a difficult time. She was in a relationship which ended badly, and she's living in a bed and breakfast with her three children, one of whom is seriously ill.'

Walter Duffy rubbed his upper lip while he thought. 'I don't wish to be unduly harsh here, but this woman does have several previous convictions. It strikes me that she's travelling a dangerous road. Perhaps some time in jail might give her an opportunity to reassess her life.'

The woman gasped.

Feeling an unfamiliar sense of solidarity, Vee couldn't stop herself from commenting. 'For pity's sake, she's hardly a criminal mastermind. Look at the state of her,' she said.

'Silence,' barked the garda.

The judge peered in her direction, irritation on his face.

The woman escaped a prison sentence, but Vee got the sense that battle had been joined between her and Judge Duffy.

When her name was called, the judge turned his head to left and right. 'Who's representing this woman?'

'No one,' replied Vee, as she stood up and walked to the front of the court. She told herself to stay cool, not to be nervous. In a few minutes this would be over.

'You're representing yourself?' he asked.

'Well, it's not a big matter, so rather than wasting a solicitor's time, I thought I would handle things myself.'

'Let me assure you, Ms Shine, that I consider everything that comes before my court to be a big matter.' He studied the notes in front of him. 'I see that you have accumulated a considerable number of parking fines, and you don't appear to have made any effort to pay them.'

'The meter kept running out before I could get back to my car,' she said.

'Kept running out? In other words, you couldn't be bothered to make it back on time.'

Vee's back stiffened. The man had such an annoying face. Supercilious didn't begin to describe it. Oh, and he had a really grating voice, like marbles rolling around a colander. 'Maybe it's more complicated than that. Like, have you considered the possibility that those machines are rigged? And the traffic wardens? Well, talk about petty. I mean, what difference does an extra ten or fifteen minutes make?'

'If everybody took that attitude, Ms Shine, Dublin would be in chaos.'

'Hardly. Anyway, I've been going through a challenging time and I didn't have the money to pay the fines.'

Judge Duffy's face took on a pinker tone. 'You're telling me that your resources are so meagre, you couldn't afford to meet your liabilities?'

Vee could feel the adrenaline running through her system. 'Oh, speak English,' she wanted to say. She stopped herself in time, then shifted her weight from one foot to the other while she did some thinking. 'I suppose that is what I'm telling you. There were other bills to pay, and I ran out of cash.'

'Did you make any effort to acquire the cash?'

'I did, only there always seemed to be other priorities.'

The judge looked down his nose at Vee in a way that suggested this hadn't been a good answer. 'Do you think you're above the law? Is that what you're telling me?'

There was a peculiar silence in the court. Conscious that everybody was staring at her, Vee leaned in towards the bench. 'Can I be straight with you here? I think you'll have to admit that I'm not in the same category as most of the people in this court.'

Was it her imagination, or was her statement greeted with a hiss?

'That's where you're wrong, Ms Shine,' said the judge. 'You're in exactly the same position as the other accused persons here, except most of them have shown some respect for the court.'

As Vee's dislike of the man grew, so did her resolve. She wasn't going to be pushed around. All of her fighting instincts came to the fore. She was a crusader for justice. 'Come on,' she said, 'that's not fair. Besides, aren't cases like mine struck out all the time?'

Judge Duffy bristled. 'I don't know what gave you that idea. You'll have to pay a fine. Like I said, you are no different from anyone else.'

Vee knew the courtroom was agog, but her irritation had bloomed into anger. She hated being spoken down to, she always had. And she wasn't going to take it from this man. 'Well, if you ask me, bringing a matter like this to court is a waste of money. What's the betting it costs more to do the paperwork than you'll ever get back?'

'I should just let you off – is that your contention?'

'I didn't say that, but I still don't have the money to pay a fine.' This was true. Every cent had gone towards her other debts.

'I have to inform you, Ms Shine, that unless you pay what you owe, you will receive a warrant for committal to jail.'

Vee's stomach fluttered. 'Are you serious?'

'Indeed I am,' said the judge, his voice dripping with pomposity. 'You either pay the fine given to you by the court, or you discharge your debt by serving some time in jail.'

Although her knees were wobbling, her resolve remained firm. 'What do you mean by "some time"?'

'I think in your case a week would be appropriate.'

Vee's every impulse told her not to back down. The guy may be an unpleasant specimen, but no way in the wide earthly world would he send her to prison. Her husband was a barrister, for God's sake. 'I've told you that I can't afford a fine, so I'll have to opt for jail.'

'You're making a mistake here, Ms Shine. But if you're determined not to pay what you owe, you will in due course receive a warrant and then you'll be taken to the women's prison.'

Walter Duffy was playing with her now. She knew that. Well, he'd met his match. She ran a hand through her hair. 'Maybe I should get it over with and go today.'

The room was silent, everybody transfixed by the stand-off. Vee imagined that she was striking a blow for them all.

The judge sighed. 'May I recommend that you take a few minutes to think this through? Or perhaps the time has come for you to get some legal advice?'

'I don't need any more time.'

'Very well,' he said. 'Stay there, if you would, while we organise the paperwork. You can listen to some more of the cases before the court. They might give you pause for thought.'

While the judge rustled through his papers, a wave of noise travelled across the room. Presently, the garda shouted for silence, and the court moved on to another slew of debt cases.

As she waited, Vee's confidence ebbed. There was a swirling pain in her chest. But the fact remained: jail wasn't for people like her. Someone would intervene. After a short delay, a policeman with handcuffs swinging from his belt ushered her to the side of the court and then into another room.

'I fought the law, huh?' he said. 'You'll have to wait here. Do you want to call someone?'

Vee shook her head. He exhaled loudly. On the far side of the room, she noticed another woman. The woman was trembling, like she was going through withdrawal.

'Are you all right there, Margie?' said the policeman.

'You do know I shouldn't be here?' Margie replied. 'I've just had a bit of bad luck, that's all. People like me don't belong in prison.'

For the first time, Vee was struck by a sense of not being so different after all.

Chapter 21

When Ferdia called, Tara was watching the aftermath of a house fire. Three children had managed to escape by jumping into the arms of neighbours. They didn't yet know that their mother, who had helped them to safety, had succumbed to the blaze. A thick drizzle was falling, and a dirty, charred smell lingered in the air.

She tried to remember when she'd last been at such an unhappy scene. Last May, she reckoned: the morning after Redser Lynam's murder, and the morning she'd met Ben.

Occasionally people asked Tara if she was affected by her work. 'All that bad news,' they'd say, 'surely it gets you down?' The simple answer was, 'Well, they're not my tragedies to bear.' But the truth was more complex. Studying older journalists, Tara came to the conclusion that one event rarely changed people, but years of covering misery and skulduggery did. She remembered talking to a colleague on the day of his retirement. 'You know what this job has taught me?' he'd said. 'In the right circumstances, anyone is capable of anything.'

To begin with, Tara wondered if Ferdia had taken something funny. What he was saying made no sense, and his voice was all skittery and strange. Gradually, his words took hold. A barrister friend had called to say that Vee was in jail. Assuming this was a wind-up, Ferdia had laughed.

'Then he got incredibly serious on me,' her brother-in-law said. 'He insisted he'd never joke about such a thing. It happened two or three hours earlier, he said, but he was only telling me now because he'd had to check out all the facts. Then he began talking about the district court and non-payment of fines and discharging her debt, and I realised that what he was saying had to be true.'

Tara was walking around in circles. 'Have you tracked Vee down?'

'I've rung her number again and again and again. But there's no answer. Even if she is in jail, why can't she call me?'

'There's probably some type of misunderstanding. Maybe she's hoping to get it all sorted before she talks to you.'

A sigh fluttered down the line from Letterkenny. 'Listen to me, Tara: there's no misunderstanding. Vee's been sent to prison. My friend said she fell out with the judge.' He paused. 'Jesus, why didn't she tell me she was in trouble? Or why didn't she tell you?'

'Because we're not talking,' Tara said softly.

Ferdia wasn't listening. 'I'm upset with her. That goes without saying. But more than that, I'm worried. And it'll be hours, *hours*, before I'm back in Dublin. Can you do something? Can you pay the fine? I'm sure it's not too late.'

The reality of Vee's predicament was hitting home. Tara could understand how it happened; she could see her sister putting on a brave face, convincing herself she could fix everything on her own. And she could picture her in court, annoying the judge. 'Oh, Vee,' she said to the air, 'you and your bloody pride. Why didn't you let me know?'

Ferdia was still talking. 'Needless to say, I'll pay you back,' he was saying. 'You will help, won't you?'

A number of reporters had gathered, and a fire officer was preparing to talk to them. By rights she should go over and record his statement. Gripping the phone between her chin and neck, she clambered into the car. 'Of course I'll help,' she said. 'What else would I do?'

Tara had to get moving. Here she was, stuck over in Bray, miles and miles from the women's prison. Mind you, even if she was at the gates of the place, what could she do? Bang on the door and holler, 'Let my sister go'? She considered her parents. Their solicitor could get on the case. But Gus and Joan already had enough on their plate, so she decided to hold off for now. She reckoned

Damien would be able to point her in the right direction, only Vee wouldn't want him involved.

She watched the reporters disperse. Then it struck her: she knew a guy who worked in the prison service. Although he handled press queries, chances were he'd find a colleague who could help. In the meantime, she'd get on the road.

Jim from the prison service um-ed and ah-ed. 'That's a novel one, right enough,' he said. 'Must be the first time a reporter has asked me to spring a family member from jail.'

'I'm not looking for special treatment. I just need some advice.'

'You do know that she isn't likely to be in there for very long? The prisons are kind of busy.'

'If you'd ever met Veronica, you'd understand that even five minutes is too long. She's not exactly prison material.'

'Who is?'

Tara didn't have the time for a philosophical debate about crime and punishment. 'Jim, can you help me or not?'

'Leave it with me. I'll see what I can do. By the way, wasn't that your brother in the papers a few weeks back?'

''Fraid so.'

'Haven't you the interesting family?' he said, amusement in his voice.

When she hung up, she noticed that she'd missed two calls from the news desk. *Damn, damn, damn,* she thought, *I'll have to come up with an excuse for my disappearing act.* She decided to wait. Give it a wee while and something would come to her. She gave Vee a call. Not surprisingly, there was no answer.

As she drove, Tara cursed the row that had brought them to this point. They'd acted like a pair of twelve-year-olds. Now she saw her sister's behaviour in a new light. Even Vee wouldn't have created such a commotion over a dress if she hadn't already been in a state about something else.

Right from the start, Tara had known that Vee would struggle without their parents' money, yet she'd closed her eyes to the truth. She'd been too preoccupied with her own life; too busy inventing fantasy reunions with Craig. If nothing else, their encounter in Brittas Bay had cured her of that.

The October rain was relentless, her progress slow. With every minute, her shoulders became more tense. The pain crept up to the base of her skull. *What was Vee doing?* she wondered. She was stuck at yet another set of traffic lights when Jim rang.

'Was I right, or was I right?' he said. 'Your sister's already a free woman.'

'Are you serious?'

'One hundred per cent. She was released half an hour ago. It's always the same with these cases. The judge wants to give the fine-dodgers a warning. They process the offender, put the frighteners on them, and then let them go. Sure, the prison is jammers with junkies and the like. Where would they put Veronica? By the way, I gather she was quite a handful in court.'

The traffic began to move. 'So where is she?'

'Ah here, Tara, we can't be keeping tabs on them once they're released. We've enough to be doing. She's probably back home with a cup of tea. Emergency over.'

'If only it was,' she replied.

There was something comforting about the drizzle. It wasn't like a regular downpour where the rain slapped and stung. Rather, it wrapped itself around you, soaking you by stealth. Vee was happy to be wet. She wanted the water to drench her clothes, her hair, her skin. Perhaps, then, she wouldn't smell of prison. No doubt most people wouldn't reckon she'd been in jail at all; no sooner than she filled out the paperwork, she was released. They wouldn't understand how she could feel so grubby, like she needed to scrub herself with wire wool and Dettol.

She walked slowly, her shoes chafing against her heels. All of the other pedestrians carried umbrellas. Several shot pitying looks in her direction. In Drumcondra, she went into a corner shop and tried to buy a takeaway coffee, twenty Marlboro Lights and a box of matches. Aside from the occasional drunken puff, Vee hadn't

smoked in five years, and was taken aback at the price of cigarettes. She didn't have enough money.

'I'll have to leave the coffee,' she said to the man who hovered
behind the cash register.

'Sorry, sweetheart, once it's poured, you have to pay for it.'

'But I can't afford it.'

'You should have thought of that beforehand.'

Her eyes filled with tears.

'Go on then,' he sighed. 'You look as though you could do with
it. I'll get you again.'

She turned back down towards the Royal Canal. Through the
curtain of water, she could just about see the outline of Croke
Park; to her it had always looked more like an alien spaceship than
a sports stadium. She leaned back against the gable end of a house
and drank her coffee. The taste was brackish, yet she swallowed it
in great, greedy gulps. With no bin in sight, she scrunched up the
cup and threw it into the canal.

An enormous seagull made what sounded like a disapproving
squawk.

'Oh, bugger off,' said Vee to the bird. 'Everybody else does it.
What are you going to do? Arrest me for littering?'

Her first cigarette wasn't particularly enjoyable, but she smoked
a second one all the same. By now she was saturated. Rivulets of
water ran down her face, and her shoes made soft sucking sounds.
She was experiencing a peculiar type of pain, like her brain had
become detached from her skull. Was it caused by shame? People
thought of shame as a hot sensation. 'I was burning with shame,'
they'd say. Yet to her, it felt unbearably cold. There were pins and
needles in her arms, and she started to shiver. Strangely, she didn't
cry.

Why had she been such a fool? Why had she let her temper
and her arrogance get the better of her?

'You'll want to call somebody,' the prison officer – a woman
with deep-set brown eyes – had said. 'No,' Vee had replied, 'they'll
all be busy. I'll make my own way home.' The officer had frowned.

Imagine if she had told her the truth; if she'd said, 'Actually, not a sinner knows I'm here.' What would the officer have thought then?

Another ten minutes passed before Vee switched on her phone. Her hands had turned blue and orange from the cold, and her fingers were so numb that pressing just one button felt like an intricate operation. Within thirty seconds, the machine was pinging. Fifteen missed calls, all from either Ferdia or Tara. Six new messages. So they'd found out. Somebody must have told Ferdia. If her husband knew, how many others were in the loop? Right this very minute, were women gathering in coffee shops, swapping gossip, making knowing clucks, having a giggle at her expense?

She counted to one hundred and then listened to the messages. Four were from Ferdia, the first so garbled she couldn't understand it. By the final message he sounded exasperated. And scared. 'I'm on my way home,' he said. 'Tara's going to sort everything out. Please, let me know you're OK. Please.' Now she did cry. She didn't deserve him. She never had. When he knew the full truth, he'd see that too. She tried to blot her eyes with the sleeve of her coat, but it was solid with water.

The next message was from Tara. 'Hiya there. If you get this, will you give me a shout?' her sister asked. Halfway through her second, lengthier message, the phone began to beep. Tara again. Vee's gut instinct was to ignore the call. Then a thought occurred to her: if she spoke to Tara, however briefly, she could convince her to deal with Ferdia.

'Hello?' she said, like the caller's identity was a mystery to her.

'Vee? Thank Christ. I thought I'd never find you. Are you back home? Jim said you might be by now.'

'Who's Jim?'

'He's . . . Oh, forget about Jim. Are you all right?'

'Absolutely flying it. Never better,' croaked Vee, her throat paper-dry from smoking. Immediately she chastised herself for being a bitch. 'I'm fine. Well, that's not true, but I'll get over it.'

'You're not at home, are you? I can hear traffic. Are you outside?'

'Listen, I need you to do something for me. Do you think you could—'

'Are you still on the northside?'

'I'm in Drumcondra, near the canal. What I want you to do is—'

'That's great because I'm only down the road.' From Tara's tone you'd think she spent every day loitering around this part of the city, waiting for a family member to be released from custody. 'Promise me you'll stay exactly where you are, and I'll be with you in five minutes.'

Vee looked around. Even if she wanted to, there was nowhere to hide. Neither did she have the energy to go any further. For once, she would do as she was told.

Before rescuing her sister, Tara made a couple of calls. Ferdia, who had got as far as Omagh, sounded half-relieved, half-angry, like the ramifications of his wife's deceit were only now sinking in.

Tara's boss was full-on angry. 'You do know that fire's turning into a big story?' he said. 'The woman's brother's some class of criminal, and it looks like the blaze was started deliberately. "That's grand," says I, "we have a reporter there." Except, you know what? We don't because she's done a fucking runner. Where are you?'

Tara opted for the truth.

'I don't believe it,' he said. 'What is it with your family?'

'I'm sure you won't believe me, but most of the time they're perfectly normal. Sometimes things go wrong though, you know?'

'What I know is that you used to be the most reliable hack in the place, and now you're all over the shop. I'm sure I don't have to remind you that there are—'

'A thousand college leavers who'd sell their souls to do my job,' finished Tara.

'Seriously, you can't continue mucking us about.'

'It won't happen again. You have my word. I do need to get

going, though. It's bucketing down, and I'll bet Vee isn't properly dressed. She'll be drenched.'

'I've a feeling that's the least of her worries,' said the news editor as he put down the phone.

When they reached Mount Pleasant, Vee was still shaking. Her hair hung in sodden hanks and her clothes were heavy with water. In the car, they'd said almost nothing. Tara would have to ask about her sister's trials, but, right this minute, she didn't have the stomach for it. *Let her speak in her own good time,* she thought.

Vee flopped onto the sofa.

'Should you not get changed?' asked Tara.

'Please, Tara, don't lay the mammy act on me. Not today.' All the same, she got to her feet and wriggled out of her coat.

'Do you want something to eat?'

'Not particularly. I wouldn't mind a drink, though.'

Tara came close to giving a speech about the foolishness of drinking on an empty stomach, but swallowed the words. 'I have to get a bite for myself anyway. I'm starving.'

'You'll be lucky. I'm not sure we have any food.'

'What have you been eating?'

Her sister lifted one shoulder, but said nothing.

Again, Tara had to suppress the urge to give an opinion. Instead, she went to the shop and bought bread, cheese, tomatoes and a currant cake. She threw in a lemon and a container of cloves. She'd spotted a bottle of whiskey in the kitchen. If Vee insisted on alcohol, she could do worse than a hot whiskey.

When she got back, she found that her sister had changed into a nightdress and dressing gown. The gown looked like it belonged to Ferdia; it was bottle green with a toothpaste smear down the front and it swaddled Vee like a rescue blanket. She was sitting in the kitchen, staring blankly at the wall.

'You don't have to stay, you know.' Vee's voice was subdued. 'I'm not going to top myself or anything.'

'I promised Ferdia I'd wait until he got back.'

At the mention of her husband's name, Vee recoiled.

Tara filled the kettle. 'You mightn't want to talk to me. That's fair enough. But you'll have to talk to him. He's beside himself with worry. And I don't know what Mum and Dad will make of it all.'

'They won't make anything of it because you're not going to tell them. And neither am I. There's no reason why they should know.'

'That's right, say nothing. After all, keeping secrets has worked *so* well up until now.' She sliced the cheese with swift, angry strokes. 'In fact, as a policy, I'd say it's been a total triumph. Apart from today's carry-on, that is. But, hey, let's not get too worked up about being sent to jail. I'm sure it happens to all the best families.'

She sloshed the whiskey and hot water into two glasses. There was no reply, and it was only when Tara turned around that she realised Vee was crying. The sobs, gentle at first, gradually became more pronounced. Tara wanted to console her sister, but given their recent history, she feared being rebuffed. Then Vee started to shudder, like an electric current was running along her spine. For a long ten minutes, the two clung together. Occasionally Vee attempted to say something, but her words were little more than gibberish.

Finally, when the whimpering subsided and the tremors eased, Tara squeezed Vee's hand. 'I know it's hard, but please try and eat something.'

In the sitting room they ate toasted cheese sandwiches and drank hot whiskeys. And Vee told her story. Figuring that a mistimed intervention would plunge them back into silence, Tara tried not to interrupt. Every now and again, she muttered something bland or reassuring. The only time she absolutely *had* to comment was when she heard about the stolen car that wasn't really stolen.

'Dear God almighty, Vee, how have you managed to pull the wool over Ferdia's eyes for so long?'

'I'm good at covering my tracks, or I was until today.'

Tara finished her whiskey. 'Do you want another one?'

'I thought you'd never ask.'

'So,' she said on her return, 'what are you going to do?'

'Come clean to Ferdia, I suppose. See what he wants to do. I wouldn't be surprised if he threw me out.'

'He can't do that.'

'If the shoe was on the other foot, it's what I'd do.'

'I always assumed you told each other everything.'

'Come on, Tara, even you're not that naive. I doubt there's a couple in existence who tell each other *everything*.'

For a short while, the two sisters sipped their drinks, thought their own thoughts. For once, Tara's head was filled with nothing but good memories of Vee: how much fun she provided, how generous she was, how protective she could be. And if her tongue was sharp, couldn't that be of benefit too? Tara's teenage years had been made far easier by having a hyper-cool big sister. In first year, she'd been bullied by a girl called Ailis Hartigan. Noticing her red eyes, Vee had winkled out the truth. Tara was never bothered by Ailis again. Later, when she'd been without a partner for her school deb's dance, Vee had swung her a date with an extraordinarily suave law student called Ultan Ward. Tara could still see the envy on her more competitive classmates' faces.

As they sat there, she couldn't help but notice Vee's feet. Not that long ago, they'd been a model of elegance. Now they were callused and raw. Some of the nails wore a remnant of polish. Others looked like they might flake away. These were not the feet of a style-conscious woman.

Vee realised she was under scrutiny. 'I know what you're thinking. I reckon today was the final insult for my poor toes; I must've got trench foot.' She rubbed a thumb along one big toe and winced. 'I'm sorry, by the way.'

'What for?'

'For being such a wagon when all you did was borrow a few dresses. I'm terrible like that. Something small irritates me and – *whoosh* – my sense of perspective flies away. I hope your friend – whoever she is – had a good night.'

Tara figured it was full disclosure time. She told Vee about Carmel, Ben and Jenelle – and about Victor's arrival on the scene. She also told her about Carmel's reaction, and about her reluctance to wear the emerald dress.

For the first time, Vee smiled. 'If they'd decided to keep me today, Rosanna might have been my cell-mate.'

'Wouldn't that have been bizarre?'

'Bizarre? Seriously scary, more like. Will you take the green dress away with you and give it to Carmel?'

'Are you sure?'

'I'm certain. It never did that much for me, and at least somebody will get some use out of it. The next time I get to go on the lash, I'll probably be wearing a nice twin-set and leaning on a Zimmer frame.'

'Lord, there's an image.'

Vee played with the back of her matted hair. 'Until the money ran out, we had a good life, didn't we? "A gilded existence", I think you'd call it. And I never appreciated it . . . not really.'

'Things aren't that bad, you know,' said Tara.

'I'm sure this . . . the mess I've made of my life . . . must be incomprehensible to you.'

'Why do you say that?'

'Well, there you are, all thoughtful and high-minded, and you have such a shallow fool for a sister.'

'Pfft,' scoffed Tara. 'I'm not that high-minded, and you're definitely not a shallow fool.'

'I've a feeling most people would disagree with you.'

'Not if they took the time to think it through, or took the time to get to know you. Then they'd see that you're far more complex than that. Although, to be honest, there are times when your brainless act is pretty convincing.'

'Your own act – the boring, mousey one – isn't bad either.'

'How do you know that's not the real me?'

Vee drained her glass. 'No relation of mine could be so dull.'

It was Tara's turn to smile. 'One more?'

'Why not? Best to be well-fortified for Ferdia's return.'

'If we're both mouldy drunk, you can blame me.'

'Believe me, I will,' said Vee. She hesitated, sucked in air through her teeth. 'It's mad, isn't it? Here I am, thirty-two years old, and apart from a wardrobe of well-cut clothing, I haven't a thing to my name. Not a house or a job or a child. And I've achieved precisely . . . nothing. What have I been doing with my life?'

'The house part isn't true.'

'Yes it is. Dad gave us the cash for the deposit, and there's no way in the world we'll be able to pay him back. I'm presuming he'll want to sell this place too.'

'You've plenty of time for children, anyway,' said Tara.

'If I still have a husband . . .' Vee dabbed at her eyes with the sleeve of her dressing gown. 'Don't worry, I'm not about to start wailing again. When you think about it, it's Mum and Dad you've got to feel sorry for. They lose their money and, aside from you, we all fall asunder.'

'Don't exclude me,' Tara wanted to say. 'My life is no great shakes either.' She held back, not because she feared contradicting Vee, but because she heard the squeak of the gate and the crunch of footsteps.

Ferdia was home.

Chapter 22

'When you're ready to pick your jaw up off the floor, I'll tell you the rest,' said Tara.

'Well, well, well,' said Felicity, her eyes a touch *too* bright, 'Veruca Salt in the clink – who would've thought?'

'Don't call her that. It doesn't seem right; not at the moment,' said Damien, conveniently forgetting that he had coined Vee's Willy Wonka-inspired nickname. He was displaying an unusual level of sympathy for his sister. *Perhaps*, thought Tara, *his brush with public humiliation has softened his corners.*

'I didn't mean any harm,' replied Felicity, a wounded note to her voice. 'It's just I can't get my head around it. Vee – in jail!'

Tara blew on her rosehip tea. She still wasn't sure that she was doing the right thing. But Vee had only said, 'Don't tell Mum and Dad.' She hadn't mentioned anybody else. And Tara had already given Niall the full story.

'Does this mean she has a criminal record?' continued Felicity. 'Like, will she be barred from going to America?'

'At the minute she doesn't have the money to get as far as the airport, not to mind the States,' said Tara, 'so I doubt that's top of her list of concerns.'

'What about Ferdia?' asked Damien. 'How's he taking it?'

'He wants her to get help,' said Tara. 'Psychiatric help. As you can imagine, that suggestion went down like a snow-storm in July. "I'm not mad," Vee keeps saying, "just slightly out of control."'

'Slightly out of control?' said Felicity, as she placed her own tea on the kitchen table. 'She certainly has a gift for understatement. I'm stunned he's still with her. Think of all the lies she's told.'

'And then there's the humiliation,' added Damien with a knowing nod. 'I'll bet the story has done the rounds of the Law Library.'

'"Reputational damage", as Ferdia calls it,' said Tara. 'There's that, right enough. The poor guy is genuinely worried about her, though. And he feels like a complete fool for failing to spot what was going on.'

'How is she?'

'In a bad way, to be honest: withdrawn, teary, depressed. I know you don't always see eye-to-eye, but if you could . . . well, I'm not sure what you can do . . . but go easy on her.'

Felicity flicked back the long, fair hair that always reminded Tara of a shampoo ad from her childhood. 'Oh, please. Let's not go overboard with the sympathy here. Vee's problems are of her own making. Nobody *forced* her to spend money she didn't have. And, in case you've both forgotten, she's the woman who never lost an opportunity to bang on about personal responsibility.' The hair got another flick. 'I mean, the hypocrisy of her.'

Damien looked at his wife. 'That's a bit harsh.'

'All I'm saying is—'

'Anyway,' said Tara, who couldn't bear the thought of another row, even one as unlikely as this, 'the two of them are still together. And Vee has promised to see a counsellor . . . when she can afford one.'

The multi-coloured kitchen clock made a clunking sound, indicating that it was 9p.m. or thereabouts. Like many of Damien and Felicity's possessions, the clock's purchase had been motivated by charity rather than practicality – its creator was on death row – and it was usually ten minutes fast. Or slow. Every room was crammed with similarly impractical items: mugs with no handles, candles that refused to burn, ornaments that bore no resemblance to anything living or dead. Joan always referred to the house as 'the national junk museum'.

'What Vee needs is a job,' said Damien.

'I don't suppose Amby's hiring?' replied Tara.

He laughed. 'Nah, Niall's got that gig sewn up. He's found his true calling.'

Tara laughed too, and within seconds they were overcome, tittering and snorting like a pair of schoolchildren.

A limp smile passed across Felicity's face. 'What's with all the hilarity?'

'Ah, nothing,' squeaked Damien. 'It's just Niall, you know?'

'When we were kids,' explained Tara, 'Dad used to say to him, "You're a terrible clown".' She giggled. 'And now he is.'

'Do you remember some of the nonsense he got up to?' added Damien. 'Like the day he convinced Vee that this old lad down the road was actually an international modelling agent. She got dolled up and called around to his house. The guy nearly had a heart attack.'

'I don't think his wife was too impressed either. She came home from mass to find a sixteen-year-old girl in hot pants and a crop top sitting in her front room,' said Tara, who shook her head as she recalled Niall's antics. 'The other one I'll never forget is the time he failed a maths exam. The little pup went into school the next morning with a black eye – which he'd faked with a stick of charcoal – and told everybody that Gus had fetched him a wallop. The teacher wanted to call in the social services.'

'Perhaps we shouldn't mention black eyes,' said Damien, which prompted another wheeze of laughter from Tara. 'My favourite school story – and I'll admit, I didn't find this funny at the time – was the day Niall managed to put every single teacher's car up for sale. He had the lot of them listed in a magazine. Don't ask me how he did it, but it was a work of genius.'

Felicity remained aloof. 'Daddy says Niall's not a bad entertainer. He's quite good at face-painting, and he's started this new thing where he draws a cartoon of the birthday boy or girl.'

Tara instructed herself to stop laughing. She was fascinated by Felicity's refusal to see her father the way others did. 'At least,' she said to Damien, 'you're free again. It must be a relief to get back to full-time politics.'

Her brother straightened his back and bunched his mouth, signalling that their family interlude was over. It was like he had packed up his lighter side, popped it in a suitcase and turned the key.

'Huh,' he said, 'I don't think I'll ever be allowed to forget about Maurice Tully's trick. And if the press have their way, I'll never get to talk about anything else again either. Why are you all so obsessed with trivia?'

'After the day I've had, I'm in no form to defend the papers,' said Tara. 'I wasted two hours on a parrot whose owner claims he can recite the national anthem. Needless to say, while I was there, the damn bird abandoned his patriotism. All he would do was swear at me.'

At work, Tara's stock had hit at an all-time low. Mostly she got the jobs that other reporters dismissed as too dreary or unimportant. Anything overtly nasty came her way too. The day before, she'd been sent to the funeral of a notorious drug dealer. One of the deceased's sisters had spat in her face.

'Any sign of anyone buying Garryowen?' asked Felicity, who sounded anxious to change the subject. She'd probably had her fill of Damien's clowning woes. 'I thought you'd be on the move by now.'

'I was due to view a flat the other day,' said Tara, 'only the Vee situation got in the way. I'll have to start looking again.'

'I'm amazed the house hasn't been sold by now. Aren't you?'

'Well, there's no buyer – as far as I know.'

'And have your mum and dad found somewhere else to live?'

Tara scratched her head. 'They were looking at houses, but they didn't find anywhere that suited. Dad's pretty fussy, and he kept complaining that everywhere was too dear.'

That was where they left it. Damien launched into a story about Willow wanting a flat-screen TV because you could only see half of the picture on their 'perfectly serviceable' twelve-year-old model. 'That school is a bad influence on her,' he was saying.

'It's all, "I want, I want."' Felicity disagreed, and they lapsed into pointless married-couple bickering.

Tara had tuned out. Now that she thought of it, the numbers viewing Garryowen had slowed to a trickle. In fact, she couldn't recall the last time she'd helped with the guided tour. *Was something wrong?* she wondered.

'I hate being the last to know,' said Gus as he scooped a shovel-full of leaves into a plastic sack.

Joan, who was holding the sack, gave him one of her sceptical looks. 'If you ask me, it's all in your head. You don't know that anybody is keeping anything from you.'

Another shovel-load went tumbling in. 'Of course, I don't *know* they're keeping anything from us, but I've a bad feeling.'

Gus scanned the back garden. A mulchy carpet of brown, yellow and red covered the grass. If they stayed out here until Christmas, they wouldn't clear all of the leaves. It was at a time like this that they needed Hughie the gardener. Letting him go had been a real shame.

'You could always ask Niall,' suggested Joan.

'It'd take a better man than me to get any sense out of that fellow. I reckon I'll give Tara a grilling.'

'You're out of luck. She's gone to Limerick to see your mam. She was trying to persuade Niall to go with her, but he's up to his eyes in Halloween parties.'

'I have to say I find this Halloween carry-on hilarious. Not that long ago, it was no big deal. Now, most of the houses around here are tarted up like something out of Disney World. Everywhere you look, there's a ghost or a gravestone. I wouldn't mind, but the same people get all sniffy about a few Christmas lights or a harmless old Santa up on the roof.'

'Halloween: the middle-class Christmas,' said Joan with a smile.

Gus leaned on his shovel. 'Why's Tara gone to Limerick?'

'I told you. To see her granny.'

'Nah, there must be more to it than that. Why now, I mean?'

'Do you know what, Gus?' said his wife. 'You're getting paranoid in your old age.'

'It's an age since you last came to see me,' said Phyllis. 'Any hope of you getting married?'

Tara smiled. They would have to go through this rigmarole for the next few minutes. Her granny would sit stiff-backed and ask a torrent of questions. If anybody else voiced the same queries, you'd be tempted to clobber them. With Phyllis, you had to take it. *That*, thought Tara, *was the joy of being very old or very young: you were free to say whatever came into your head*. Her Aunt Majella, with whom Phyllis lived, agreed. 'Bring on decrepitude,' she'd laugh. Gus, who was more wary of old age, would scowl and tell his sister she was mad.

Majella was one of those women who turned cleaning into an art form, and the front room was permeated by the scent of polish and Hoover bags. For as long as she could remember, Tara had been fascinated by her aunt's eclectic range of ornaments. Waterford crystal, Aynsley and Belleek lined up alongside a collection of snow globes and holiday knick-knacks.

'Take it from me,' Phyllis was saying, 'you can only leave these matters for so long. What age are you now? Thirty? Thirty-one?'

Tara was convinced her granny knew exactly how old she was. The woman probably had a spreadsheet listing each of her grandchildren and great grandchildren with notes on their age, marital status and job prospects. All the same, she answered. 'Twenty-nine, actually.'

'Definitely time for that fellow of yours to get moving.'

'There's a bit of a snag there.' Tara explained the situation.

Phyllis dug her teeth into her bottom lip. Her old-style dentures were a touch too long, giving her a vaguely lupine appearance. 'Ah well, I was never that gone on him anyway,' she said. That was another thing about her: she wasn't hobbled by consistency. 'As long as you're not maundering around the place, feeling sorry for yourself. That's all anybody seems to do nowadays. It's a national affliction. How are Niall and Damien after their set-to?'

'I don't know that they'll ever be the best of friends,' said Tara, 'but I don't think the, ahm, incident has caused any lasting damage.'

'Ye're a terrible crowd,' replied her granny. 'I thought with things the way they are . . . your father's troubles, I mean . . . you'd all hang together. But no, you have to turn on each other like pups fighting over scraps from the table.'

'Are you telling me your own sons and daughters never fell out?'

'Of course they did. And how! I remember Rita going after Pauline with a pair of scissors because she thought her sister had stolen a boy from her. But, I'll say this for them, when the going got tough, they supported each other.'

'Sometimes families argue. It's not like there's any law saying we have to be compatible all the time. Besides, myself and Vee . . .' Tara stalled. Phyllis didn't know about her granddaughter's run-in with the law, and it was best to leave it that way.

'What's that about yourself and Veronica?'

'Oh, nothing.'

'What's the girl up to these days?' asked Phyllis.

'A bit of this, a bit of that.'

'Not very much, you mean. Still, I've always thought Veronica was more to be pitied than blamed.'

'Why do you say that?'

'You can't spend your life relying on beauty. I've seen plenty who tried, men as well as women, and it didn't end well. One morning, they wake up and the face is sagging and the hair has gone all wiry. Where are they then? No, you're in a far better position.'

'Thanks a million,' said Tara. 'It's good to know my own grand-mother thinks I'm plain.'

Phyllis tipped her head to one side and laughed. 'Ah now, I never said that. But, if you ask me, depending on a pretty face is like depending on someone else's money. You can only get away with it for so long. And when it ends, it ends badly.'

Tara pulled at the sleeve of her cardigan. 'You know what I've been meaning to ask you? The house mum and dad own near here – the one with the students: has it been sold already?'

'What do you mean?'

'I called around on my way over here, expecting to see a For Sale sign, but it was gone. I didn't expect the place to sell so quickly.'

Her granny's eyes darted left and right. The gesture was almost theatrical, like she actually wanted to look shifty. 'You'll have to ask your mam and dad about that, love. Nobody tells me anything.'

'That's a lie if ever I heard one,' laughed Tara. 'You're like a local news bureau.'

'The day you stop taking an interest is the day you're in big trouble.'

'I'll ask them when I get back. I don't like making too many enquiries, mind. It feels wrong – like I'm pestering them.'

'Do you worry about them?'

'Oh God, of course I do. Everything's changed so much. Some days Dad looks like he doesn't know whether he's coming or going.'

'Believe me, there's no point in worrying.'

'Craig used to say I was made for it.'

'It must be hereditary. Gus Senior said the very same about me. Every day that passed gave me more cause to get worked up about one or other of the children. And here I am – eighty-seven years old – and I'm still at it. And you know what? I'm only wasting my time.' Phyllis shook her head. 'Mind you, it'd be worse if I'd nobody to worry about. What would I do then?'

'You're full of wisdom today.'

'I hope you're not getting funny on me.'

'I promise,' said Tara with a grin.

'Let me give you another word of advice, then. Never think you know exactly what's going on. You could be getting yourself into a right old state over something and, down the line, you might realise you had it all wrong.'

That was another thing about Phyllis: when it suited her, she was skilled at talking in riddles. Trying to decode her was like trying to pick up mercury with a fork.

'Tell me more,' said Tara.

'I've said plenty. Go out to the kitchen and pop on the kettle, would you? All this talking has me parched.'

Chapter 23

'I'm going to be a zombie for Halloween,' said Ben. 'Halloween's the best. Jenelle's coming trick-or-treating too, only she doesn't know what she wants to be.'

'Perhaps you can be a zombie as well,' said Tara to Jenelle. The children, pink-skinned and pyjama-clad, were perched either side of her on Carmel's sofa. They'd both had baths and were waiting for their hair to dry.

'Nope,' replied Ben. 'She'll have to be something girly like a princess.'

'Who says?' asked Jenelle.

'Girls can't be zombies. That's not the way it works.'

'Your sister can be whatever she likes,' said Carmel.

'I don't think so,' said Ben in a sing-song voice.

Jenelle's face crumpled. 'I want to be a zombie.'

'Then you can't come out with me. You'll have to find somebody else.'

'Oh Ben,' said Carmel, 'I don't know what's wrong with you today.'

The boy's mouth moved slightly, like he was settling on exactly what to say. 'Preston Delaney wants to know why I don't have a mam or a dad. He says some people don't have a dad, but only weirdos have no parents at all. I told him my mam was in Australia and my dad was in a big car crash, but he wouldn't listen. He said I was lying.'

Carmel opened her mouth then closed it again. Jenelle's right hand twitched, a sure sign that she was anxious.

'That's plain silly,' Tara told Ben. 'You shouldn't pay any

attention to Preston.' She stroked Jenelle's hand, the skin as soft as talc. 'And neither should you.'

Carmel composed herself. 'Tara's right, Ben. I thought you were too grown up to listen to the likes of Preston Delaney.'

Ben peered around like he was deciding whether the adults could be trusted. 'But when's our mam coming home? She'll have forgotten what we look like. Imagine, she could pass me and Jenelle in the street and not know it was us.'

Jenelle made a small gasping sound.

'I promise you – both of you – that will never happen,' said Carmel.

'You've got a mam and a dad, haven't you, Tara?' Ben asked.

'I have. I know lots of people who don't, though.'

'They're old but. Not four and eight like us.'

Tara sensed that no matter what she said it wouldn't be enough to pacify him. It was an impossible situation. 'You've got your nan. And Victor. And all your friends.'

'I s'pose,' he sighed. 'Does your dad have a job?'

'He works in an office.'

'In Dublin?'

'Uh huh, in a place called Fitzwilliam Square.'

'Fits William Square – that's a funny name. Why's it called that?'

Carmel's voice bore the strains of someone trying too hard to be upbeat. 'Now pet, how do you expect Tara to know that?'

'Is he a good dad?' asked Ben.

'He's a good dad,' Tara replied.

'And does he tell the truth and that?'

'He does.'

'But is he very old? I mean, is he too old to understand stuff?'

'Ben!' said Carmel.

Tara was about to make a joke of the boy's questions, but the intense look on his face suggested that this would be a mistake. 'No,' she reassured him, 'my dad's not very old. I can talk to him about most things. He's good at giving advice, too.'

'I think I'd like to meet your dad someday,' said Ben.

'Well, I'm sure that can be arranged.'

Ben was quiet for a moment, like he was considering the importance of everything he'd learned. 'You know what Preston says?' he asked.

'No.'

'He says his mam calls his dad a "fucking spacer".'

Tara did her best not to laugh, while Jenelle giggled.

'Ben, now you really have gone too far,' said Carmel. 'I reckon we've all heard more than enough for one night. Are you ready for bed?'

'Nooo. Not yet.'

'Nooo,' echoed Jenelle, her eyes drooping with sleep.

'What about if there was hot chocolate first?' suggested Carmel.

'And a story?' asked Jenelle.

'The pair of you have me wrapped around your little fingers,' said their nan, but she was smiling.

When at last the children had gone to sleep, Tara and Carmel opened a bottle of red wine. In the background the TV glowed silently. Someone who may once have been in *Eastenders* was doing her best to smile at a Friday-night chat show host. Unfortunately, she'd long since lost the ability to move her face.

'Sorry about earlier,' said Carmel. 'You having to answer Ben's questions, I mean. I suppose I've been expecting him to come out with something like that, but what frightened me was the way he said it. Like he thought Preston Delaney might be right.'

Tara took a slug of wine. 'You don't think this Preston boy knows the truth, do you?'

'I wouldn't put anything past that child. He's a little scourge.' She folded her arms, as though protecting herself from Preston and his ilk.

Tara's thoughts were scattered. She was still trying to decode something that Phyllis had said the day before. There was a comment of her dad's that she wanted to hone in on too. But, no matter how she tried, she couldn't untangle what they'd told her. It was like she was doing a jigsaw where the picture consisted solely of sea and sky, and there was no way of telling what was what.

She switched her attention back to Carmel. 'How are things with you?'

'I've had better weeks. I went to see Rosanna a couple of days ago. She was full of it. Going on and on about what she'll do when she gets out and how much she's looking forward to having her kids back. She's sure she'll get temporary release at Christmas too.'

'You've got time to prepare, anyway.'

'I suppose. I know I'm a selfish bitch – and I know she's my daughter and they're her children – but I wanted to say to her, "Will you promise me you'll behave yourself at Christmas? And if you can't make that promise, will you do us all a favour and stay where you are?"' Tara must have looked shocked because Carmel quickly added, 'Obviously I didn't say that. I told her I was delighted. What else could I do?'

'What about Jack – will he be home?'

'Bless him, he rang me the other day, all excited. He plans on asking Nicole to marry him so he'll be staying in London. In fairness, he promised they'd come visiting in the New Year.' Carmel poured some more wine. 'The thought of Rosanna, myself, Ben and Jenelle cooped up together over Christmas scares the hell out of me.'

'But she's clean?'

'She is, but it's such a long time since she's seen the kids I don't know how they'll react, or how she'll cope with them.'

'Will Victor be around?'

'We had talked about spending Christmas at his house – just the four of us, you know? There's acres of space. Ben could tear around the garden to his heart's content. And I feel like it's the little fellow's last special Christmas. Next year he'll be nine and ...'

'The fat man in the red suit mightn't come visiting,' finished Tara.

'Got it in one,' said Carmel, dropping her voice to a whisper. 'You have to be careful what you say around here. Anyway, I'm not sure what we'll do now.'

'Is it just Christmas you're anxious about, or is there more to it than that?'

Before answering, Carmel raised her face towards the ceiling and took a deep breath. 'It's everything really, isn't it? But mostly it's the fact that I don't want to give the two of them back. You've seen them. They're settled and they're happy. And with every day that passes, Jenelle takes another step out of her shell.' She paused, lowered her face again. 'Of course, this is absolutely stark staring mad. It's Rosanna who's my daughter, and I ought to be doing everything within my power to make her life better. Sometimes I ask myself if I still love her, and I'm sure I do. But that's the thing: I have to ask. With Ben and Jenelle, it's like they're part of me. Honest to God, if they go ... when they go ... it'll be like someone hacking off my arms or legs.'

Tara watched a tear slip down her friend's face. 'What does Victor say?'

'He's great, genuinely great. If he had his way, we'd all move over to his house full-time.'

'For truth?'

Carmel eased a tissue from the pocket of her jeans and patted her face. 'For truth, and I'd probably go, if it wasn't for all the complications. It's like, in one way I've been so, so lucky. Meeting Victor is one of the best things that's ever happened to me, but I don't want to visit all the craziness of my life on him. When Rosanna gets out, watching her will be a full-time job. I'll have to spend my time making sure she stays off the gear and steers clear of all the trouble-makers.'

'She's an adult,' said Tara. 'Is it not about time she took responsibility for herself?'

'So you might say, but if I don't keep an eye on her, who knows what'll become of Ben and Jenelle. If anything happened to them, I wouldn't be able to manage. I feel – and again, I know this is wrong – I feel like the day I took them was the day I got a second chance. Sometimes, when I go up to the cemetery to see Willy, I say that to him. I tell him what a shame it is that he can't see them growing up. I know how mad he'd be about the pair of them.' Another tear snaked down Carmel's face.

Not for the first time, Tara felt like she was adrift without a compass; like her cosy existence had left her ill-equipped to deal with situations like this. 'Is there any chance Rosanna might agree to leave them with you?'

'Not from the way she's talking at the moment. She's like bloody super-nanny up in that prison, going on about everything she'll do for them.'

A thought came into Tara's head and she smiled.

'What's up with you?'

'I was remembering something Ben said a few months back. He asked me if I had kids, and when I said no, he told me that he didn't think he'd have time for children either. He was dead right. Everywhere I go, somebody seems to be stressing about their family. Even my granny's at it – and half of her kids have their pension books. And if my parents had any notion what my sister Vee's been up to, they'd go berserk.'

Carmel gave a watery smile. Tara noticed that *Eastenders* woman had been replaced by a former boyband singer. His hair transplant wasn't doing him any favours. She shared out the last of the wine.

'You know the way I told you about Rosanna being caught with drugs?' said Carmel.

'Mmmm.'

'I didn't tell you everything.'

'Oh?'

'If it wasn't for me, she wouldn't be in jail at all.'

'I don't follow you.'

'When I took Ben and Jenelle, I had these naive hopes that

losing her kids might bring Rosanna to her senses. Like I've told you before, to begin with she was angry, yelling abuse at me and everybody else. Then she went on an almighty bender. She was worse than ever, and I started to get seriously worried. There was no point in me coming heavy on her, and she paid no mind to doctors or social workers. She stopped caring what anybody said. She'd no interest in Ben or Jenelle either. I remember a social worker calling to the door and telling me that Rosanna wanted me to keep them. And I thought, *God above, she's going to kill herself* – either from an OD or on purpose. I knew I had to intervene; I had to do something drastic to get her out of harm's way, to give her a chance to get clean. Only I didn't know what. She'd been in rehab before and had run away. Unless they chained her to the wall, she'd only do the same thing again.'

Carmel paused. A garda helicopter buzzed overhead. There was trouble somewhere.

'So what did you do?' asked Tara.

'Around the same time, Ben told me that lots of fellas used to visit the flat. "Men come to see mammy," he said. I figured she was on the game, so I kept an eye out. I'd tell Jack and poor Willy that I was going for a walk and I'd hang around near her block of flats – she was living over in St Columbanus Gardens. You should have seen me, lurking down below like some type of nut-job.

'It took a while, but eventually I realised what she was doing: she was holding onto gear for her dealer – like a safe house. Now, this wasn't happening every day of the week or anything, but it was regular enough. Then it struck me: what if the cops happened to call when there were drugs in the flat? She'd be in serious trouble. Of course, they had to call at the right time. And who could tell them, when there was only me.' Carmel's voice petered out. 'You can guess the rest,' she whispered.

'Did you have to give your name?'

'I thought about that and I reckoned that if I didn't tell the police who I was, they mightn't bother going round there. Or they mightn't get a warrant or whatever it was they needed. So, I told them everything. But right from the off I said, "You're never to use my name, and I'm never going to give evidence." The way things worked out, they didn't need me in court anyway. They kept the flat under surveillance, realised I was on the level, and raided the place.'

'Rosanna has no idea you—'

'Oh, Christ no. Can you imagine? I wouldn't be here talking to you or reading stories to Jenelle. I'd be in the cemetery with Willy. You've got to remember: it wasn't just Rosanna who was charged. The lad who delivered the heroin was locked up as well. Even my own brothers and sisters don't know the truth. Neither does Jack. I've only told two people: you and Victor. And that's all I'm ever going to tell.'

Tara was touched by Carmel's trust in her. 'Nobody suspected anything?'

'Why would they? As soon as we're old enough to speak, we're taught not to be a tell-tale or a tout, so what sort of monster would grass up her own daughter? No, if you asked anyone around here, they'd tell you I was poor misfortunate Carmel – a bit of a God-help-us with a dying husband, a junkie daughter and two grandkids to mind. Not that I wanted their pity. It's a terrible thing, pity; it chips away at you until you think you're not worthy of anything else. But at least it was better than anybody guessing the truth.'

'OK, what you did was extreme, but it forced Rosanna to face up to her problems. If you hadn't intervened, she might be dead by now.'

'And at the time I was convinced I was in the right. I couldn't have gone through with it otherwise. I felt like I was … what's your man's name? That baldy guy on the telly?' Carmel pursed her lips while she thought. 'Dr Phil, that's it. I was Dr Phil, dispensing tough love. I was taking control.'

'And it worked,' said Tara. 'You got her off drugs. Wasn't that what you wanted to do?'

'Only it's more complicated than that, isn't it? For the rest of her life, even if she never gets into grief again, Rosanna's going to be someone who served time. I don't know how she's going to adjust when she gets out. I don't know whether she'll be able to get a job. And what about Ben and Jenelle? One day they're going to know their mammy went to jail. How will they react?' Once again Carmel reached for her tissue and wiped away a tear. 'Sure, I needed to give Rosanna a shock, but I don't know whether I thought it all through; whether I considered all the consequences. Not a day passes that I don't ask myself if I went too far.'

They sat quietly, the only light coming from the flickering of the television. Tara thought about Carmel. She thought about Rosanna and Ben and Jenelle. And, as she did, she realised she was also thinking about her own family. Slowly, the two stories became intertwined. Her dad's words, Phyllis's words, started to make sense.

It was like staring at the horizon, seeing the curve and wondering how anyone ever believed the earth was flat. The truth was that obvious.

Chapter 24

By the time Tara got home, Niall was in bed. This was a blessing because before she said a word to anybody, she needed to gather some evidence. She also needed to keep her emotions in check. She told herself to behave like she was at work: to do the job and think about it later. For most of the night she sat on the bed, notebook in hand, writing down every thought that came to her. *Why?* she wrote. Then, *Why now?* and *Why like this?* Occasionally she doubted herself. Then another piece of information would emerge from the nooks and crevices of her brain, and the doubts would flutter away. Her journalist's scepticism came to the fore; she questioned everything she'd been told. Eventually – and it must have been five or six in the morning by then – she fell asleep. She woke at ten thirty with a dull pain in her head, and a collection of knots in her stomach.

Niall was in the kitchen slathering butter and jam onto a tower of toast. He gave her a sympathetic grimace. 'Rough night?'

'No, I wasn't that late.'

'Well, you have the face of someone who had a wild old night of it. Something's up.'

Tara rubbed the ache in her forehead. 'I wouldn't mind a coffee.'

'Sit yourself down there and tell me all about it.'

'Nah, it's nothing,' she said. 'How are you?'

'Plugging along. I've a party up in Malahide this afternoon, and another one tomorrow in Castleknock.' Niall placed a mug in front of her and sat down. 'We've got to talk about finding somewhere new to live,' he said. 'Sooner or later, the old pair will get a buyer for this place. We ought to be prepared.'

'I hope you don't mind me asking but do you have the money to pay proper rent? My funds are getting kind of low.'

'You won't believe this, but Amby's agreed to slip me a few bob. Under the table, of course.'

'Good Lord.'

'Yeah, he must have got a knock to the head. We're not talking huge money, but it's better than nothing.'

'You're going to keep on working for him, then?'

'Until Christmas, anyway. I haven't enough cash to go anywhere, so I may as well keep myself occupied.' For a minute Niall munched his toast. 'If you weren't on the lash, why do you look as though you've been up all night?'

Tara finished her coffee and rose from her seat. How could she sit there having such a mundane conversation when her head was spinning with questions? 'I'll tell you later,' she said. 'I've got to make a few calls first.'

Although Niall gave her a puzzled look, he said no more.

When Tara thought about who could help, one person came to mind. She didn't have Rory's number, but reckoned she could give a guess at his work e-mail address. Her first phone call was to O'Flaherty, Mills Auctioneers. She wasn't sure who to ring in Limerick and Cork so she tried three estate agents in each city. To be on the safe side, she tried some internet searches too. The results were as expected.

By now it was almost one o'clock. An e-mail from Rory suggested he was keen to meet up. He was confused too. *I'll explain everything when I see you*, she replied. Even as she typed the words, she knew this was a lie for she couldn't explain everything. She couldn't even start.

In the shower, she turned the water up as high as she could bear. Puffs of steam filled the room. Lines jumped around in her head. What was it Phyllis had said? 'Depending on a pretty face is like depending on someone else's money,' and, 'Never think you know exactly what's going on.' But it was

Carmel's words and deeds that had crystallised Tara's thoughts.

She'd arranged to meet Rory in a local café. A glance at her watch showed she was ten minutes early. Luckily the lunchtime crowd was scattering, and she managed to get a corner seat. Even though she was already jittery, she ordered another coffee. She asked for a sandwich too – tomato and mozzarella – but knew she wouldn't be able to eat. A hard lump had formed at the back of her throat, and just swallowing the coffee was difficult. While she waited, her doubts returned. Maybe she was wildly off-beam here. Maybe Rory would consider her strange. But no, she'd got this far; all she had to do was ask a few questions. And if she was wrong? Well, wouldn't that be brilliant?

'How are you going on?' said Rory, who arrived in a flurry of activity. He saluted the guy behind the counter, grinned at a baby and waved in the direction of a couple at the far end of the room. He wore a navy woollen hat pulled down low, and when he removed it his hair stood up in small tufts.

Tara didn't know how to describe her mood. 'I'm OK,' she said.

'Good OK or bad OK?'

'That depends.'

'I'm intrigued,' said Rory, as he took off his overcoat. 'What is it I can do for you?'

'This is going to sound a bit mad,' she said, 'but I was hoping to ask you some questions about Shine and Co.'

Gus was in the sitting room, reading his *Limerick Leader*. When asked, he could never explain why he took so much pleasure from his local paper. After all, many of the stories meant little to him; he no longer knew all of the politicians or neighbourhood characters or sportspeople. Still, the week was incomplete without a rummage through his native city's stories. Often he got the most enjoyment from reading about the smallest of events. He scoured the local notes, drawing comfort from the fact that, in a world of turmoil, football clubs elected new committees, amateur drama groups performed the plays of John B Keane, and old men still played cards for turkeys and tins of biscuits.

In the kitchen, Joan was in the middle of one of those cleaning jobs that involves taking everything out of the cupboards then putting it all back in again. He knew better than to disturb her. Later they would have to have a chat. They'd been putting it off for a couple of weeks. They'd arrived at a crossroads, however, and the time had come for some decision-making.

A short time before, Gus had stood at the window and watched Niall leave for work. His bag of clown gear was thrown over one shoulder, and he listed slightly to the right. After ten minutes, Tara had left the house. She'd dashed up the street at such a clip you would swear there were wolves at her heels. This added to his sense that something was going on, if not with Tara, with one of the others. That morning, he'd tried to tap Damien for information, but his son hadn't been forthcoming. Rather, he'd done a share of shrugging and changed the subject back to Rufus's plans for Halloween and Aifric's attempts to play the violin.

Both children had been with him, but their elder sister, Willow, was 'too busy' to come visiting. In the space of two or three months, she'd gone from an entertainingly sparky girl to a perfect example of adolescent snottiness. Poor Damien and Felicity. All that effort to try and raise a non-materialistic, politically-conscious child, and they'd ended up with Willow. At thirteen, her heroes were tousled-haired pop singers and rail-thin models. She would walk over both of her parents to get to that month's most desirable boots or earrings.

'Do you know,' Joan had said, 'I think Willow's growing up to be just like her Auntie Vee.' 'It's all ahead of you, Damien,' Gus had added. 'Before you know it, your little girl will have no interest in anything apart from boys and discos.' Damien had turned pale.

Gus tried to read on, but the words danced in front of his eyes. At this time of year, with October almost over and the winter beckoning, he saw the merit in hibernation. When the clocks went back, Dublin became enveloped by darkness. Even the sunniest days had a muted, faded quality. He placed his newspaper on the floor and closed his eyes. *Just for a few minutes,* he told himself. Not a proper sleep; that was for old men.

He woke slowly to find the room half-hidden by dusk. He peered at where his watch should be, then realised he wasn't wearing it. The rain had set in again. Heavy drops were making a *rat-tat-tat* sound against the window. In the hallway, Gus heard Joan and Tara. There was something off-kilter about the conversation, and for a moment he stayed still.

'Would you not dry off first?' Joan was saying. 'You're soaked through.'

'No, I'm fine,' replied Tara. Even without seeing her, Gus knew she was worked up.

'At least take off your boots. You're scattering leaves and Lord-knows-what-else all over the carpet.'

'I'm not that bothered about the carpet.'

'What?'

'I said I'm not that bothered about the carpet. Come with me, and you'll find out exactly what I *am* bothered about.'

Gus straightened himself in the chair. As he did, a hand crept around the door and turned all of the lights on at once. The sitting room was illuminated like a police interrogation room.

'What the . . .?' he heard himself saying to Tara, who stalked across the room and stood square in front of him. Joan, a dish-cloth in one hand, was a step or two behind.

'I could pussyfoot around here,' Tara said. 'I could try and trick you – but then I'd only be playing the same game as you. Because you have been tricking us, haven't you?'

'I'm not with you.' That wasn't true. He'd always known that if anyone guessed the truth, it would be Tara.

'Answer me this: how much money have you *actually* lost? How much trouble is the business *actually* in?'

'What is it you're accusing me of?'

'How about I ask another question? Is this house genuinely for sale? Or is that all part of your plan?'

Two sharp pleats had appeared at the top of Tara's nose. Gus tried to reply, but before the words came out, his daughter spoke again. Her voice wavered around the edges. Normally she had no time for scenes – that's what her brothers and sister were for – and she looked rumpled and ill at ease.

'Here I am,' she said, 'using a polite word like "plan" when I should say what I mean. I'm pretty sure that everything you've told us over the past few months is a lie. The faltering business, the bad investments, the need to stop giving money to your family? All lies. I have my own idea as to why you've been doing this, but I want to hear what you've got to say.'

Gus found his voice. 'Sit down, Tara, and we can talk.'

To his surprise, she walked over to the sofa, her boots squelching all the way. 'All right,' she said, 'but I need to hear your explanation. And I need to hear what you're going to say to Niall and Damien and Vee.' She picked up a cushion and hugged it to her chest. 'How are you going to tell them it's all been a hoax?'

Joan cleared her throat. 'You're getting ahead of yourself here. Your father hasn't said any such thing.'

'I haven't heard either of you denying it either.'

Tara looked at Joan. Then she turned to Gus.

For a short time, no one spoke.

'Hoax is a very harsh word,' said Gus eventually.

'Why, what word would you use?' asked Tara, as her gaze flicked between her parents.

'I don't know,' he replied. 'I don't know.'

'But you didn't lose any money?'

He took a deep breath. 'No more than anybody else, I suppose.'

Tara sighed. 'What's that supposed to mean?'

Gus rubbed his hands over his eyes and down his face. His voice was barely audible. 'I'm telling you that you're right. We're not broke, and we never have been.'

Chapter 25

Tara watched them troop in. There was Niall, fresh from work, his skin newly scrubbed. Next came a tired-looking Damien. And finally there was Vee, her dark-chocolate hair in a low ponytail, her face all angles and shadows.

Three hours before, when Tara voiced her accusations, Gus and Joan had been all at sea. Talking in circles; talking over each other; conceding that their daughter was right but qualifying everything they said with, 'You've got to understand' or 'You need to look at the whole picture'. Tara hadn't been much better. She spoke in fits and starts. There was still so much to consider. Neither did she want to give too much away. It was Gus who suggested they postpone any serious discussion until the other three were present. 'Then we'll tell you everything,' he said. Warily, she had agreed.

She had prised information from Rory with a series of half-truths. 'I think Dad has misled the family about the health of the business,' she'd said. Of his possible motives or the scale of his deception, she'd said nothing. A bemused Rory gave her what he believed to be an accurate description of affairs at Shine and Co. Like every company in the land, it had experienced setbacks. In the grand scheme of things, though, they'd coped well enough. There had been no fresh problems in recent months. None of which he was aware, at any rate. 'Would you know if something had gone wrong?' Tara asked. He paused, scratched his throat, and decided he would.

As the conversation continued, Rory became increasingly perplexed. 'Listen to me,' he said, 'I'm getting the feeling I'm in over my head here. You won't tell Gus you spoke to me, will you?' Not a word, she promised. Before they parted, they exchanged phone numbers, and he kissed her on the cheek. 'I haven't a clue what's going on,' he said, 'but take care of yourself.'

Now, as her brothers and sister sat down, Tara thought again about what she knew. She wished it was possible to *un*know something, to wipe her head clean. But it wasn't, and she had to press on. She was experiencing an unsettling sensation. For as long as she remembered, she had viewed her parents as an oasis of sanity in a crazy world. And what happened? It turned out they were the craziest of all.

She looked around. Had the others any inkling of what they were likely to hear? She suspected not. Gus was already in his green chair. Joan was in the corner – just like they'd been five months previously, when her father had first spun his tale. She felt like she was in the final chapter of one her beloved Agatha Christie books, with everybody waiting for Hercule Poirot to dissect the tensions at the heart of the family before revealing the truth.

'Thanks for coming over here,' started Gus, 'especially on a Saturday night when I'm sure you all had other plans. We're going to tell you something, and I don't expect that any of you will take it well.' Vee and Damien exchanged a sharp look. 'But,' he continued, 'I'd be grateful if, for a few minutes, you'd hear me out. Hear *us* out, I should say.'

'I suppose,' added Joan, 'this all began because we were worried. Worried about the lives you've been leading, and worried that you've never had to face up to the consequences of your decisions.'

'And while neither your mam nor I have any intention of trundling off to the graveyard for a while yet,' said Gus, 'we started to obsess about what would become of you if we weren't around.'

His wife nodded. 'You're all adults. You're entitled to live your own lives in whatever way you see fit. But we came to realise that you took our money for granted. You took *us* for granted. Opportunities we would have *killed* for meant nothing to you, were tossed aside.' She hesitated and swept a wisp of hair behind her left ear. 'I've no doubt you'll accuse us of being dishonest. But what we wanted was for all of you to question the honesty of your own lives.'

Gus took up the baton again. 'Before we go any further, I, *we*, want to stress that none of this affects our love for you.'

The room was quiet, yet Tara imagined she could hear her siblings' brains pinging and whirring, while each of them tried to figure out what was happening. She was also uneasy about the amount of self-justification going on – like her dad talking about love. 'You've got to be kidding me,' she was tempted to say. She opted for a more gentle intervention. 'You told me you'd give us the truth,' she said to him. As one, Vee, Niall and Damien shifted their attention in her direction. She did her best to avoid their stares.

'I did, I did, and we're getting there,' said Gus.

'What we wondered,' said Joan, 'was what it would be like for all of you to live without the family money. To have no safety net. All around us people were having to make do with less. The entire country was cutting back. And we thought, well, for a small while, why not? Why not behave as though there is no money?'

Niall focused hard on his parents. 'So you lied?'

'We did what we had to do. We had to tell you the money was gone. If you believed otherwise, you wouldn't have tolerated us saying no. You wouldn't have understood why we were looking for you to pay your own way.'

'You can dress it up whatever way you like,' said Tara. 'That doesn't change what you did. You lied to us.'

'And you've been in cahoots on this?' asked Niall. 'Dad wasn't on his own?'

'Whatever we did, we did together,' said Joan.

It was Damien's turn to speak. 'I'm sorry, are you telling us that the last few months have been a hoax? You've been playing some sort of game?'

'Oh God, not a game,' said Gus. 'Never a game.'

Vee blinked several times in quick succession, like she'd been under water and was coming to the surface. 'I may be stupid, but I want you to say it plainly and clearly. Did you ever have money problems?'

'No,' said Joan.

Tara expected an immediate outpouring of questions and denunciations; for Vee to stamp out; for Damien to lose his temper. Wasn't that what *should* happen? Instead, there was barely a murmur. Perhaps they were too dazed for outrage.

'What I don't understand,' she said, 'is why now? What was it that changed? We're the same as we've always been. OK, we're far from perfect, but what was it that was so heinous about our lives that you were willing to do . . . this?'

'That's what we're trying to say to you,' replied Joan. 'Decisions rarely hinge on one incident or disagreement. You can forgive a thousand things. And then something – something that may seem inconsequential to others – causes you to stop and think. Did any of you do anything that was completely reprehensible? The answer is no.'

'It was something small,' said Gus, his voice subdued. 'A date that you forgot. That's all.'

Vee was the first to decipher what their father was saying. 'You did this because we forgot Mum's birthday? You reckoned that gave you sufficient motive to upend our lives?'

'That's not what we're saying to you.' Gus shook his head. 'If it wasn't that, it would have been something else.'

'Seriously?' Vee replied.

'I'm sorry, lovey, that came out wrong. It sounded too flippant, and you've got to believe us, there was nothing flippant about what we did. What I meant was this: there could have been any number of tipping points, but that was the incident that brought us to the edge, that made us think about everything.'

'I don't believe this,' said Tara. 'You can't get up one morning and say, "Oh, they're not quite the children we wanted. Let's see if a dose of misery will change them." I mean, seriously, what sort of parents behave like that?'

Joan clasped her hands together, like she was praying. 'Oh Tara, you're more intelligent than that. You know that wasn't how we thought. We just reckoned that the time had come for all of us to take stock of our lives. It's not as though we wanted to make you unhappy, but we had to make you think. Granted, we could have nudged and cajoled and nagged, only I don't believe that would have made any difference. You would have ignored us.'

Unusually, Damien – firebrand Damien – was the calmest of the four. 'Maybe I'm a touch slow, but I'm trying to get my head around all of this. Were there ever any bad investments?'

'No,' said Gus.

'Is the house for sale?'

'No.'

'What about the sign – not to mention the parade of people who came to view the place?'

'A little sleight of hand, I'm afraid. Myself and Kevin Mills go back a long way. I told him the truth, and promised that if and when Garryowen was on the market, he'd get the business.'

'You mean you duped all of those punters?'

'I wouldn't go that far,' said Gus. 'Most of them had an enjoyable hour looking around the house. And if any of them had made a really spectacular offer, we might well have accepted.'

'The houses in Limerick and Cork,' said Damien. 'Were they ever on the market?'

'No.'

'And Dubrovnik?'

'We'd been planning on selling the apartment anyway. We never got enough use out of it.'

'What about letting Edita and Hughie go? That's different. For the life of me, I can't see how you can justify that.'

'We don't have to. We're still paying them,' replied Joan. 'We said there was some family business that needed sorting, and we'd be back to them soon.'

Tara's hands were balled into fists. 'And all of the other stuff

– the two of you eating cheap dinners and the like – was that just an act?'

'We had to play our part,' said Gus. 'We had to make the story believable.'

Vee blinked again. 'Did it ever occur to you that what you were doing was totally mad?'

'Mad?' said Joan. 'Perhaps. But was it any madder than a thirty-year-old touring the world because he couldn't decide what to do with himself? Or a politician whose life was founded on contradictions? Or a woman whose existence revolved around spending other people's money?'

'Mad is one word for what you've done,' said Tara. 'I can think of others too. Like cruel.' As if to emphasise her point, a Halloween firework exploded outside. Its whistles, bangs and sizzles burst into the room. She knew the others were looking at her. Who would have expected docile Tara to be the most spiky, the most indignant?

Joan spoke a shade too quickly. 'Honest to God, it was never our intention to be cruel. Never. Neither did we find all this . . . subterfuge . . . easy.'

Gus pulled at his earlobe. 'And I suppose we hoped it might bring you together, that you might see what you had in common rather than focusing on your petty differences all the time.'

'So correct me if I've got this wrong,' said Niall, 'but the only reason you're telling us now is because Tara guessed what you were doing? Otherwise you'd have kept on pretending you were broke?'

'Even without Tara, we would have dropped the pretence soon,' replied their father.

'Long before Christmas, anyway,' said Joan.

'What was it you planned on saying? "Surprise! We're not poor after all"?' asked Tara.

'Well, we thought we'd come around to it gradually; that bit by bit we'd let you know the situation was improving.'

'How did Tara rumble what you were doing?' asked Damien.

In as much as she could, Tara explained.

'*Gran* was in on this as well?' asked Vee.

'Only belatedly,' said Gus. 'We told her a few weeks ago. She was a bit put out that we hadn't told her sooner.' He swallowed. 'Maybe that's why she started dropping hints to Tara.'

'Did you tell anybody else?' said Vee.

'No, that was it.'

Outside, another firework whooshed and crackled.

'I know this has given all of you a shock. But I hope we can talk about it rationally, and that you can have some understanding of where we were coming from,' said Joan. 'We really do regret the Councillor Maurice Tully business. Thankfully, though, it seems to have blown over without any long-term harm.'

Tara didn't believe what she was hearing. OK, her parents had to put on a brave face, but did they seriously think their deception had been a success? 'That's not the half of it,' she said. Although Vee flashed her a warning look, Tara wouldn't be dissuaded. She wanted Gus and Joan to show some contrition. 'There's something else you should know. Vee, are you going to tell them, or will I?'

Gus jumped in. 'I *knew* there was a problem. Didn't I say it to you, Joan? "They're keeping us in the dark about something," I said.'

Vee sighed and told her story. Or rather, she told *most* of her story. Some parts – like the stolen car – were glossed over.

'Mother of God,' said Joan. 'Why didn't you tell me about your debts? Why didn't you tell anybody?'

'I didn't want to worry you.'

Gus held his face in his palms and, for the first time, Tara sensed they had misgivings about their trickery. For a minute or two it was quiet, and then the clamour started. All at once, everybody had to give an opinion or ask a question. Tara let them talk. Niall, Damien and Vee were all grappling with what they'd been told.

She was rigid with tiredness. What she wanted was a hot bath and a long sleep. And she wanted to be on her own. She thought back on her innocence; on how she'd blithely spoken about trusting her family. She recalled the speech she'd given to Craig about how her family were her top priority. And all the while her parents had been fooling her.

Oh, she remembered the summer, and her dad's half-hearted attempt at reassuring her about Garryowen. 'Don't get too stressed about it. We wouldn't want that,' he'd said. But that was all the warning they had given her. For all her dutiful behaviour, they had treated her no better than the rest.

She realised that her brothers and sister hadn't yet asked the most obvious question: what now? The words were in Tara's mouth, but she swallowed them. She didn't have the energy to pursue her parents for an answer.

Chapter 26

The worst of the rain had cleared, and Vee decided to push her bicycle home. A light mist swirled around her. Halloween decorations appeared to pop up out of nowhere: here a ghostly sheet; there an eerie pumpkin. She was glad of the extra time. Before she spoke to Ferdia she wanted to do some thinking. The problem was, her brain felt too active for proper thought. She tried to focus on one new piece of information, only to find it nudged aside by another.

There was one indisputable fact: she'd been hoodwinked, good and proper. The pain of the past few months had been needless. Vee wondered what would have happened if, rather than going it alone, she had told her parents the truth. Would they have relented – or would they have maintained their pretence? She supposed she would never know.

When she got home, Ferdia was in the sitting room immersed in a legal textbook. He'd been working every hour of every day, and not solely because they were short of money. He had been humiliated by the prison episode. Everybody in the legal world knew about his dizzy, uppity wife, and he felt a need to prove his character. To show what a sober, diligent individual he was. Their relationship remained strained. How could it be otherwise? There were times when he looked at Vee like he genuinely believed she was demented. Fast-forward an hour, and they would be nattering away like nothing had happened.

Her own life had been turned upside down. Her confidence was in smithereens. When Lottie heard about her court appearance, she'd made a sympathetic call. Few others had bothered. She could picture her so-called friends claiming they'd always known she was heading for a fall. People in Vee's circle didn't like to be associated with failure. They worried that it was contagious.

'I've got something to tell you,' said Vee, as she folded herself into one of their Italian armchairs. Panic flashed across Ferdia's face, and immediately she added, 'No, not about me. Well, sort of about me . . . but not bad. Well, sort of bad.' She wasn't doing anything to ease his concerns. Finally, she said, 'It's my parents – they've been lying to us. They still have all the money.'

'Holy fuck,' said Ferdia, who was not given to swearing. His fringe flopped into his eyes. 'You've got to be joking me.'

'I promise . . . it's true,' said Vee, and she began to tell the story.

Aside from the occasional barrister-like interjection ('This really was extraordinarily risky behaviour for such a well-established businessman,' and 'Did he, at any stage, consider the legal consequences of his fabrications?'), Ferdia said little. When she reached her part in the story, however, he became more animated.

'And when they found out the worst, how did your parents react?'

'Mum got upset. I reckon she'll have us pestered for the next while. She wanted to drive me home, but I insisted I'd be fine.'

'And are you?'

'Oh gosh, I don't know. I'm all over the place – again. I mean, what they did was outrageous, but what's the point in roaring and shouting and throwing stuff around the place? I've done enough of that over the years and where has it got me?'

'The crockery's safe, then?'

'For now. I need to have a good think.'

'What did they say about the future?'

'The future?'

'Obviously we can't expect everything to be exactly the way it was before, but do you think we can rely on your parents for some help? Like, do you still want their deposit back or are we off the hook?'

'I'm sure this is going to sound crackers, but the conversation didn't get that far. Everybody was so shocked, or wiped out, or worked up that we decided to call it a night.'

Ferdia gave her an unusual smile. Although his mouth hardly moved, his eyes were warm and encouraging. 'You're all right, I understand.'

'Thanks.' Afraid she might cry, Vee looked down. There had already been more than enough crying.

'What's wrong?'

'I wish I was able to say to you, "That's it, problems solved." Only I can't, because they're not. My life's still in a heap.'

'One step at a time,' he said. 'There is one other thing, though. How did Tara take the news?'

'Like I told you, she'd already guessed. Then again, she's always been smarter than the rest of us. Or so she likes to claim.'

'But how did she react? Was she very upset?'

'I suppose she was. She's normally so agreeable, it was a surprise to hear her getting ratty. She'll be grand, though. She always is. Every time I hear somebody on the radio droning on about the "coping classes", I think to myself, *That's Tara. She could cope for Ireland.* Why all the concern about her?'

Ferdia raised his eyes to the ceiling. 'Because Tara's the one who's got the right to feel totally aggrieved. She's had to endure the same treatment as the rest of you when, in fairness, she wasn't nearly as reliant on your parents' cash. And she's always been a hard worker. If I was her, I'd be very pissed off indeed.'

Annoyed with her stupidity, Vee slapped herself on the cheek. 'I hadn't thought of it like that.'

Damien tried to remember what life had been like before. When decisions had been black and white. When telling right from wrong had seemed simple. In one way, he felt like he'd been mugged. Without actually using the word 'hypocrite', his parents had implied that it was a fitting description. But, strange as it might sound, he also had a sneaky regard for Gus and Joan. Sure, he regretted what they'd done, but he didn't believe they'd been motivated by malice.

Felicity didn't agree.

'Are you for real?' she said as she sewed the Spiderman costume Rufus would be wearing for Halloween (she was dubious about the ethical soundness of superheroes but couldn't think of a specific reason to nix the boy's choice).

For half an hour, Damien had been recounting the evening's events at Garryowen, and his wife's temper was rising. He needed to choose his words more carefully. 'I'm not saying I'm happy. I'm far from happy. I'm saying I have some understanding of where they were coming from. They were tired of being taken for granted.' He paused, before quietly adding, 'And that's something I can relate to.'

'Think about it, Damien. Thanks to your parents' antics, the children might have ended up in some God-awful school.'

'How bad would a different school have been?'

Felicity put down her sewing. 'You know what goes on in those places – bullying and all sorts.'

'You mean the sort of bullying poor Aifric had to put up with when I was in the papers?'

'That was harmless.'

'Aifric didn't think so. And while we're on the subject of schools, I can't say I'm impressed by the crowd Willow's knocking about with. I was listening to them the other day, wittering on about half-term holidays and manicures and fancy mobile phones. They're *thirteen*.'

'You sound like your father,' she said, her tone making it clear that this was not a good thing.

'There's worse than Dad.'

'This is getting ridiculous. You're defending the man who told you a pack of lies; the man responsible for your public humiliation.'

'I would have thought the responsibility for that lay squarely with your own father.'

Blotches of colour were rising on Felicity's pale face. 'Oh please. My dad expected you to work for your money. That's all.'

'Amby took pleasure in watching me run myself ragged at children's parties. And now he's taking pleasure in bleeding Niall dry. The guy's a misery, and the only person who can't admit it is you.'

'How fucking dare you?' she said. 'How dare you say that about my father when your parents have spent the past five months watching their sons and daughters fall apart.'

'They didn't know about Vee's debts. They only found out this evening and they were stunned. Besides, I can't remember you showing much sympathy for her. You said she deserved everything she got.'

Temporarily bested, Felicity picked up her sewing. She stabbed the needle into the cloth. 'I'm not going down this road. When you've had time to think, you'll realise how ridiculous you're being, accusing my father of all sorts when it's Gus and Joan who've treated us badly.'

By now the atmosphere was sulphurous. The clock did its clunking thing, indicating that it was ten o'clock or thereabouts. Damien thought about Amby. He still hadn't asked his father-in-law for election funding. He knew he should start work on his campaign, only right now, he couldn't get motivated.

'By the way,' Felicity said, 'Canice was looking for you. He wanted to know why you weren't returning his calls. I told him I didn't know where your head was these days.'

'I'm going to check on the children,' said Damien.

'You'll have a hard job checking on Willow. She's staying at her friend Béibhinn's house.'

'I'll check on the other two, then.'

'Make sure you don't wake them.'

Damien came within inches of slamming the kitchen door, but stopped himself in time. That was the infuriating thing about Felicity: she always had to have the last bloody word.

He stuck his head into the girls' room. Aifric was dead to the world. She was a great girl for sleep. A glance next door showed that Rufus had thrown off his quilt. Damien tip-toed in and leaned over to fix the bedding.

'Hello, Dad,' said a small voice.

Hoping his son hadn't heard the row downstairs, he smoothed a hand over the boy's sandy head. 'What's going on, Rufe? I thought a busy lad like you would need his sleep.'

'I was sleeping, but I woke up and remembered that nobody had read me a story.'

'Your mum's fixing your Halloween costume. She can't do everything.'

'What about you?'

'I had to go and see your granny and grandad.'

'Oh,' said Rufus. 'How about now, then?'

'Is it not a wee bit late?'

'Not really. And you're the best at stories.'

'And you're an awful charmer. It'll have to be a short one, mind. Will one of my own do?'

Damien liked making up stories. Usually they were total nonsense, but they pleased his son. A couple of weeks ago, Rufus had told Niall about his dad's tales. 'Let me see,' Niall had said, a glint in his eye. 'Once upon a time, there was a good worker. Unfortunately, he was exploited by the bad capitalist.' Rufus had given his uncle a look of unwavering seriousness. 'I don't think I've heard that one,' he'd said. Relations between the brothers were unusually cordial. Niall bore no grudge over the punch he'd received. This, in turn, made it impossible for Damien to harbour any ill will. Oh, and they had something to unite them: a mutual loathing of Amby Power.

Rufus gave his dad a drowsy smile. 'Your stories are my favourites.'

'Honestly?'

'Cross my heart.'

Perched on the edge of the small bed, Damien began a story. As he spoke, an idea that had been taking shelter at the back of his head took on new life.

Tara was packing, cramming tops and trousers and cardigans into her rucksack. Other belongings were scattered on the bed. Niall was attempting to slow her progress.

'You've every right to be upset,' he said, 'but stop and think for a minute. You can't just walk out.'

She stuffed a jumper into her rucksack and placed her hairdryer on top. 'I don't think you get where I'm coming from, Niall. Upset is too puny a word for how I feel. I'm raging. Incandescent. You know that saying, "The rug's been pulled from under me"? That describes where I'm at, only it doesn't go far enough. Forget about the rug; the underlay and the floorboards have been pulled up too.'

'I hear what you're saying. I'm not exactly thrilled about the way they lied to us either. I remember being really worried about the two of them – what a waste of time that was. But can't you ease up for a minute while we talk about this? There's no point in rushing off anywhere on a Sunday morning.'

'I've got to go to work, and I plan on bringing my stuff with me.' She was leaving most of her possessions behind. It was high time she bought some new clothes. Here she was, a twenty-nine-year-old woman in the uniform of a grunge-era student. She might even ask Vee for advice. Wouldn't that be funny?

'Where will you stay?' asked Niall.

'I don't know,' said Tara as she flung items into her washbag. 'I'll probably get a bed and breakfast for a few days, and then I'll find a flat. I'm not fussy. I've no desire to stay here listening to the pious wafflings of the pair upstairs. I've spent more than enough time under their roof.'

'You don't like being on your own.'

'I'm sure it won't do me any harm.'

'And what will I do?'

'Whatever you want. Isn't that what everybody else does? I'm the only idiot who goes around trying to please people. I presume you can stay here. Given what we now know, they can hardly charge you rent.'

In an apparent attempt to halt her packing, Niall sat on the bed. 'I'm not too impressed with Mum and Dad either, but there's nothing to be gained by haring off.' He smiled. 'There's a bit of role reversal going on here. This must be the first time I've tried to prevent *you* from leaving home.'

'Ha! Very funny. Now move over, would you? You're sitting on my belongings, and I'm running out of time.'

He refused to shift. 'Just so as we're clear here: are you annoyed with Mum and Dad because of what they did to all of us – or because of what they did to you?'

'Both,' replied Tara. She hoped her voice made it clear that she didn't intend discussing this any further. Not right this minute, at any rate. But the truth? The truth was that she wasn't just angry with Gus and Joan. She was angry with herself. 'Please get up, Niall. I've a job to do.'

Reluctantly, her brother got to his feet. 'I don't blame you for feeling betrayed. In your position, I'd feel the same. Whatever about the rest of us, you've . . . well, you've always been the model citizen.'

'The model fool, you mean?'

'You're no fool, as well you know. Listen, rather than running away in a sulk, I think you should talk to Mum and Dad. With all of the shock and the questions, last night wasn't the right time.'

Tara fastened the straps of her rucksack. 'I'm not sulking, and at the moment talking wouldn't be a good idea. I need to get away from here and give my fury a chance to die down.' She needed to do more than that. She needed to look again at her life. Despite her exhaustion, she hadn't been able to sleep. With every second that passed, her grievances grew.

She remembered Craig claiming that her brothers and sister took advantage of her and that she was happy to let them. Now she saw it all more clearly: Niall, Damien and Vee were harmless, their schemes the work of amateurs. It was her parents who had abused her trust and loyalty.

'Be careful not to do anything too dramatic. That's my advice,' said her brother.

Tara knew she should remain quiet. That was the sensible thing to do. But she'd had her fill of being sensible. 'You know what I think, Niall?'

He shook his head.

'I think that for once in my life I'll do exactly what I want to do. I don't know what you learned on your world travels, but I'll tell you what I've learnt. I've learnt that only a mug tries to do the right thing. You work and you work and you obey all the rules, and then somebody kicks the legs out from under you anyway.'

'Ah, Tara. You can't—'

She picked up her rucksack. 'And then it hits you that all of the game-players and the wasters and the posers . . . they've all prospered.'

'I hope you're not suggesting—'

'And you become convinced that you're the dumbest person on the planet. I remember a year or two back, interviewing a woman who'd lost all of her savings in the crash. And do you know what she told me? She'd never been extravagant. She'd saved for her retirement, followed the rules. And there she was, without a cent to her name. "I'm only sorry," she said, "that I was always so bloody sensible. I should have lost the run of myself while I had the chance. Now I feel like people are laughing at me." Well, that's how *I* feel now.'

'There's not much point in arguing with you, is there?'

She was almost at the front door. 'There's not.'

'What'll I tell Mum and Dad?'

'Tell them whatever you like. Actually, no, tell them I've gone away to take stock of my life. That's what they wanted, isn't it?'

259

Chapter 27

Joan had always prided herself on her equanimity. When others were flapping and swearing and making fools of themselves, she was the woman who kept her head and got things done. But she'd never been in a situation like this before.

Gus was beside himself. No matter that their subterfuge had paid dividends with Damien and Niall (that was her view, anyway), Tara's walking out had left him in a terrible state. 'You have to give her time,' Joan kept saying. 'The more pressure you put on her, the more she's likely to rebel.' He wouldn't listen. He called his younger daughter, three, four, five times a day. And every time she failed to answer. Just once had she returned his call. 'If you don't leave me alone, I'll change my number,' she'd warned. She hadn't followed through on her threat. Yet.

Of course, he had expected her to be upset. They both had. What they hadn't anticipated was the coldness of her anger, or its depth. Nor had they foreseen her moving out. Vee had always been the one for dramatic gestures. Not Tara.

Almost three weeks had passed since she had joined the dots and the truth was revealed. Not a day went by without Damien, Niall and Vee getting in touch. Questions were asked, arguments raised, disagreements thrashed out. That was good, though, wasn't it?

Niall remained downstairs. They weren't charging him rent, but otherwise he was making do with his earnings from Amby Power. Vee was getting by with bits and pieces of public relations work that she'd managed to line up for herself. Joan worried that her daughter's brief stint in jail would make it even more difficult for her to find permanent employment. Gus had told Vee and Ferdia to forget about repaying the deposit on the house; he'd even offered to resume paying the mortgage. Ferdia was having none of it. He was adamant that he'd take care of his own bills. He did ask for one thing in return. He wanted them to meet the cost of counselling sessions for Vee. Although Gus agreed, he was baffled by the exercise. 'A hundred and sixty euro for an hour of talking,' he said. 'It's a strange world, and no mistake.'

And then there was Damien. As they strolled along the streets near Palmerston Park, it was their elder son who was the focus of Gus's attention. The November sun was low in the sky, but many of the trees still had leaves to shed. This year's leaves were especially colourful, and a patchwork of red, yellow and rust stretched out ahead of them. Despite the beauty of the day, Gus hadn't wanted to go for a walk. 'It's my busiest time of the year,' he'd said. 'It's *Sunday*,' Joan had replied. After much wheedling, he had capitulated.

'So what do you think Damien's up to?' he asked. 'I used to worry about his single-mindedness, but these days he's as distracted as a three-year-old.'

'We wanted them to re-evaluate their lives. We can hardly blame them if that's what they're doing. If they were all insisting on business as usual, then we'd have real cause to worry.'

'I hear you, only it's odd to see him like this.'

Joan kicked a clump of leaves. 'Maybe we underestimated the impact of Maurice Tully's stunt. Not to mention all the rubbish in the newspapers.'

'That moron. I heard him on the radio the other day, pontificating about the poor. A bishop wouldn't sound as sanctimonious. I don't think that's the problem, though. Something else is bothering Damien.'

'Have you asked?'

'He says he'll talk to us about it, but not yet.'

She linked her arm through her husband's. 'Is this one of your regretful days?'

'Jesus, Joan, I have regrets every day. Every minute of every day. Don't you?'

Yes, she had regrets. After all, the entire scheme had been her idea. She remembered the day the idea came to her: the day of her sixty-second birthday. She had never been one for birthday fuss. Gus, however, believed in marking and recording occasions. That three of the four children should forget their mother's birthday had sent him into a rage. Her first remark had been offhand. 'Do you ever think that life would be easier if they all had to earn their own keep?' she'd asked. 'It wouldn't do them any harm to live without our money,' he'd replied. From that conversation, the plan had sprung.

Their initial planning sessions had allowed them to let off steam, to give voice to what irritated them. Until that point, they'd been slow to criticise their sons and daughters. All of a sudden it was as if they had a licence to view the four of them in the same way they would view anybody else.

It was the wasted opportunity that bothered Joan. How she would love to have been to university, to have spent days reading and learning and swapping ideas with like-minded men and women. Instead, she'd been thrust into a job she didn't enjoy with a group of women twice her age. The fact that her children had taken a college education for granted rankled with her. All four had seen it as an entitlement rather than something to be treasured. Worse, Vee had dropped out, while Niall had only scraped through.

Gus's main complaints had been Vee's aversion to work and Niall's shiftless existence. Given that his motto was 'it's better to wear out than to rust out', this was no surprise. 'How those two manage to do so little is beyond me,' he liked to say. 'They manage because we let them,' she would reply. Her husband would nod. 'And then there's the other fellow, with his socialist principles and his champagne spending.'

Joan's own father had had a PhD in finding fault. Mini skirts, maxi skirts, long hair, short hair, altar girls, the Common Market, cable television; at one time or another all of these had been blamed for Ireland's woes. But his favourite target had been the younger generation. Each and every one of them. Joan prayed that she and Gus wouldn't fall into the same trap. Oh, Gus performed his 'young people these days' act. But it was just that – an act. It was too easy to say that all youngsters were the same.

When discussing the shortcomings of their own sons and daughters, her friends invariably blamed the boom. 'They had it too easy. Way, way too easy. The world went mad,' one of them would intone. The others would murmur in agreement. 'Right,' Joan wanted to say, 'so when poor kids cause trouble, their parents are at fault, but when *our* children go wrong, it's the entire western world that's to blame?' Of course, she never said any such thing; she clucked and moaned with the rest of them.

As Gus and Joan had seen things, they were to blame for their children's cosseted existence and they were the only ones who could bring about change. Every so often, one of them would say, 'Are we deranged? Is this completely out of order?' Still, once they'd rolled the dice, they had to keep going. Sustaining a lie was tough – especially for Gus. Often he lay awake at night. No matter how still he was, Joan always knew when he wasn't sleeping.

Now there were days when she felt wretched about what they had done. The thought of Tara – angry, confused and alone – tore at her heart. Deep down, down where she didn't want to go, she obsessed about the others too, especially Vee. 'What sort of mother are you?' she would whisper to herself. It was only with hindsight that she appreciated the depth of Vee's problems. Why was she so obsessed with how others perceived her? Joan didn't know. As she saw it, you could spend every waking minute trying to work out what made somebody act and think in a particular way. You could ponder nature and nurture. You could consider their childhood, their friends, their DNA. But still you couldn't say for sure why they had become that person. This didn't prevent her from blaming herself; from trying to pinpoint what she had or hadn't done.

She gleaned no comfort from the fact that plenty of families were even more troubled. Often the news made the family home sound like the most dangerous place to be: one brother stabbing another, a woman whose toddler was covered in cigarette burns, a man strangling his wife over a petty remark. Listening to the reports, Joan wondered why some people had families at all.

Every day she wished she could think of something to repair the damage; something that would make life better for Vee and make Tara understand why her parents had chosen to lie. But nothing came to her, and she was scared that a clumsy approach would make matters worse.

All of these thoughts she kept to herself. Revealing her worries would only add to Gus's unhappiness. As it was, he slouched around the place, a hangdog expression on his face. She was also careful not to harp on about Phyllis's role in the foundering of their scheme. In truth, Joan could swing for the woman. If it hadn't been for her meddling, they would have been able to bring their charade to a gradual end. Although Gus had exchanged words with his mother on the phone, he was reluctant to fall out with her. Plus, as he pointed out, letting her in on the ruse had been Joan's idea.

For her part, Phyllis continued to maintain that her conscience was clear. 'I didn't actually tell Tara anything,' she insisted. 'I just urged her not to be worrying. What was wrong with that?'

'Are your regrets all about Tara?' Joan asked Gus as they crossed the road and headed towards Ranelagh village.

'Pretty much,' he said. 'If I could reason with her, if she'd allow me to explain, I'm convinced we could make some progress. But we don't even know where she's living.'

'In a bedsit near the American Embassy, according to Niall.'

'A bedsit!' exploded Gus, as though he was hearing the news for the first time. 'My daughter in some filthy bedsit, and Niall won't even give us the address.'

'That's because she doesn't want us calling around there. Besides, I doubt it's filthy.'

'She should come back home where she belongs.'

Joan looked at the ground. 'I think, love, you'll have to accept that that isn't going to happen. She'll be thirty next year. It's time she moved on. Before we know it, she'll have found a better flat or bought a place of her own.'

'I know, I know. Only I can't handle the way things are at the moment. It's not right.'

They hadn't given sufficient consideration to Tara; Joan conceded that. The problem was, their younger daughter had always been so compliant. While the other three were awkward and demanding, Tara was willing to occupy the space that was left for her.

Gus came to a stop. 'I reckon the time has come to go and see her.'

'Like you said, you don't know where she lives.'

'I'll have to track her down at work.'

A sudden gust swept up some dry leaves, sending them hurtling around in a circle.

Joan shivered. 'Are you sure that's a good idea? She won't thank you for calling the office. If you ask me, we've got to hunker down and wait until she's ready to talk.'

'No, I'll think of something,' he said. 'We can't go on like this.'

Tara had taken the first flat she went to see, gazumping her rivals by promising to pay in cash and by letting the landlord know what a responsible job she had. 'I can assure you there'll be no parties while I'm here,' she'd said.

Not that it would be physically possible to hold a party in so cramped a space. She was living in one room on the second floor of an old red-bricked house. From the outside, the house was similar to her family home. The interior was a different story. Although the advertisement had promised 'all mod cons', Tara guessed that the furniture and decor dated back to the eighties. The bed was flimsy and narrow, the carpet scarred by cigarette burns. The kitchen was in the corner of the room, which meant the drone emitted by the ancient fridge kept her awake. Heat was provided by a portable radiator.

Repeatedly she told herself that she had been right to leave home. Something Niall had said in Croatia came back to her, something about not wanting to be one of those people who was scared by the slightest bit of upheaval. Every day she looked at herself in the speckled bathroom mirror and said, 'I'm free to live my life however I choose.' She wanted to be bolder, brighter, braver. But this was easier said than done. In the mornings she set off for work, filled with good intentions. At night, she sloped home feeling listless and withdrawn. She was lonely yet she couldn't be bothered having a conversation with any of the other women in the building. Once or twice she wondered where Craig was now.

When she was out, she found herself listening to snatches of conversation or noticing small scenes: a man grinning while taking photos of his children, a girl arranging a date, two elderly men having a great old gossip. 'Life moves on,' she told herself. 'You'll have to adjust.' She repeated these platitudes until she was thoroughly bored with herself.

She called her friends, Niamh and Stephanie. They were all chat and friendly wishes, but they were so *busy*. Unbelievably busy.

'Oh, I know,' lied Tara, 'it's that time of year, isn't it?'

'So glad you understand,' trilled Niamh. 'We'll definitely get together before Christmas. Or early in the new year.'

Twice Rory had called. 'I was a bit worried after our conversation, so I'm just making sure you're OK,' he'd said. To begin with, she'd been scared that he knew about the family falling-out. Her worries were in vain; unless Rory was a very good actor, he was genuinely in the dark. She was half-tempted to meet him for a coffee, but the way she was feeling, she'd say too much. The whole twisted mess would come spilling out. So she was offhand, distant. He stopped ringing.

One night she went out with the gang from work. Wasn't this what the new improved Tara was supposed to do? Meet different people? Go to more exciting places? Certainly she shouldn't be sitting at home brooding over the bad behaviour of others. For the first drink or two she was fine. Then, as the conversation descended into a bitch-fest about which newspaper would be next to close and which reporter had been promoted beyond their abilities, she realised she couldn't focus on the conversation. She'd forgotten that when journalists drink, they're only capable of discussing other journalists. She decided she'd prefer to be at home in her flimsy bed.

At least she had her job, and she threw herself into it with as much enthusiasm as she could summon. That morning she was outside a low, brown-bricked building on the western fringes of the city. The building housed a large pharmaceutical company, and rumours were circulating that several hundred workers were about to be made redundant. During the depths of the crash, Tara had spent many days standing outside similar places, waiting for similar announcements.

Four reporters were stationed at the factory's steel gates. The morning was chilly, and their breath created clouds of vapour. Tara was wearing mismatched gloves – one navy, one black. Because she'd left Garryowen in such haste, her wardrobe was a disaster. She'd been left with an assortment of odd socks and outfits that didn't quite go together. She'd always had difficulty with gloves. When she was a child, her mother had knitted her a pair of special mittens with string attached so she couldn't lose them. Niall had taken to calling her 'Fr Dougal' after the character in *Father Ted* who had a similar pair. The memory made her smile.

When a familiar black car pulled up, her first instinct was to worry that something terrible had happened. Then the truth hit. She hadn't returned his calls, so he must have tracked her down.

'Eh, how are you doing?' said Gus as he shut the car door and walked towards her. 'It's not a bad time, is it?'

'Of course it's a bad time. I'm at work.'

'Do you have a minute?'

He gave her a pleading look. The other reporters were staring at them.

'OK,' replied Tara, 'but I don't have much more than a minute. I've missed a lot of work lately – because of one family crisis or another. I've got to file soon, and I can't afford to screw up again.'

'It's only ten o'clock in the morning,' said a bewildered-sounding Gus.

'I've got to do a piece for the website. It's all about the website these days.'

They walked back towards his car. The last thing she wanted was her fellow hacks eavesdropping on the conversation.

'So . . .' he said.

'So?'

'I rehearsed a speech, only now it seems all wrong.'

Finding that she couldn't look her father in the eye, Tara peered into the mid-distance. 'I don't want to hear a speech. Actually, I don't want to hear anything. I don't know why you've come here. I don't even know how you found me.'

'I rang your boss and said it was an emergency.'

'Great. He already thinks my family's completely dysfunctional.'

'Maybe he's right.'

'What was it you wanted to say?'

'For fear I didn't say it properly before, I wanted to let you know that I'm . . .' Gus hesitated then corrected himself. 'We're both sorry – your mam and I. We didn't mean to treat you badly. We didn't think—'

'That's just it, isn't it?' said Tara. 'Neither of you thought about me. You wanted to teach the other three a lesson, and I was collateral damage.'

'You can't think of it like that, love.'

He tried to touch her arm, so she moved away. 'You know what, Dad? I'm a wee bit tired of people telling me what I can or can't think. And what I can or can't do.'

'I didn't mean it like that.'

'Why don't you go and pester one of the others? I spent months worrying about you and Mum with your miserable faces and your pathetic voices, and the whole time you were lying to me. People have won Academy Awards for less.'

Gus took a deep breath. 'I don't expect you to thank me for what we did, but are you sure you're being entirely fair? OK, you've always provided for yourself, but was your life really that wonderful?'

'What are you getting at?'

'When Craig thought the family money was gone, he didn't hang around for long. And according to Vee, his new girlfriend's family are loaded.'

How much easier would it have been if there was no truth to what her father said? Even after Tara had gathered up the gumption to dump Craig, she'd almost gone back on her decision. She might well have done so . . . if he hadn't already moved on to the lovely Sheena. But knowing her father was right didn't mean that Tara could accept a dressing down from him. Not after what he and her mother had done.

'Tsk,' she said, 'I should have known that sooner or later the conversation would work its way around to Craig. In case you've forgotten, *I* broke up with *him*.'

'I know that, love, and you did the right thing.'

'Have you any idea how insulting you're being? You come here, trying to sort things out – and you think the best way of doing that is to suggest that *my* boyfriend was only interested in *your* money. Jesus!'

Gus's face collapsed. 'Oh, Tara, I didn't mean it like that.'

'That's what it sounded like.'

'Listen to me, I didn't come here to argue. I came to say sorry, and to ask you to come home. We miss you.'

Tara looked at him. For a minute or more, neither spoke. All sorts of feelings flushed through her. For a moment, she even contemplated caving in and returning to Garryowen. After all, she had a lifetime's experience of the path of least resistance.

Finally, she broke the silence. 'Thanks for the apology, but I haven't changed my mind.' Gus opened his mouth to speak. She waved at him to stop. 'There's a phrase that journalists love to use: "coming to terms". If you read the papers, the world is full of people coming to terms with something or other. It's such a cliché, I've always hated it. But I'm going to use it. I haven't come to terms with what you did. Hopefully at some stage I will. For now, though, I'm better off on my own.'

Once more he tried to touch her arm. She flinched. The other journalists must have been watching because one of them yelled, 'Are you all right, Tara?'

'Fine,' she shouted. 'Everything's cool. I'll be with you in a tick.'

'If that's . . .' Gus's voice petered out.

'Yeah,' she said. 'That's the way it is. Like I said, I reckon you're better off concentrating on the others, especially Vee. She needs all the help she can get.'

Again, there was silence.

At last, her father opened the door of the car. 'Take care of yourself,' he said.

Tara nodded.

It was only as he drove away that she remembered it was his birthday.

Tara hadn't spoken to Carmel since the night of the revelation. Every morning she resolved to get in touch, but when evening arrived she was too bone-tired to do anything apart from sleep. Often, she didn't bother to eat. Although she tried to focus on work, her family troubles tended to crowd out all other thoughts. She took to comfort reading – re-reading old books in the hope that their familiarity might provide solace.

Eventually a text message arrived: *I'm sorry you don't understand what I did*, it read. *Ben and Jenelle say hello*.

For the first time in days, Tara snapped out of her self-pity. 'Oh, Jesus,' she said, causing half of the newsroom to turn around.

She picked up her phone and tapped out a reply. *Sorry! Disappearance nothing to do with you. Are you home?*

As quickly as possible, she finished her work and headed for St Monica's Mansions. In the winter gloom, the building looked more ramshackle than ever. Another flat had been boarded up, while the stairwell felt dreary and down-at-heel. There was fresh graffiti too: Lindsay loved Dane, apparently, and Natalie was a whore.

When Tara reached the landing, Carmel, Victor, Ben and Jenelle were only a few steps ahead of her. They were on the doorstep, laden down with bags and parcels. The children had new winter hats. Ben's was a striped affair with flaps, while Jenelle's was mauve with small sticky-up ears.

'We've been doing a spot of shopping,' said Carmel, giving her a look that may not have been entirely hostile, but wasn't that friendly either.

'It'll be Christmas before we know it,' added Victor.

'Our mam'll be home then,' said Ben, his voice brimming with excitement. 'She's coming back for Christmas. She'll be here for almost a week, isn't that right, Nan?'

'It is, pet.'

'Can Tara stay for her tea?'

'She mightn't want to. She might have better things to do,' replied a wary-sounding Carmel.

Tara smiled at Ben. 'I'd love to . . . if it's no trouble.'

'Cool,' said the boy. 'Did you know I'm teaching Jenelle to read so as when she starts school next year they'll think she's very clever?'

'What a great idea. Are you a good teacher?'

'He's only fantastic. The way he's going, the school will be offering him a job,' said Carmel with a wink. The atmosphere thawed slightly.

By now they were inside, shedding their winter layers. Tara silently scolded herself for staying away. Ben and Jenelle had had enough upheaval in their short lives without her disappearing too.

She remembered the picture they'd drawn back in the summer. She'd left it in Garryowen. She would ring Niall and ask him to send it on.

'You're looking shocking thin,' Carmel was saying. 'Don't go wasting away on us. Have you a new fella? Is that why we haven't seen you?'

'Tara's got a new fella,' sang Ben.

For some stupid reason, she blushed. 'No, no, that's not it. I'm sorry I haven't been in touch. I've had a lot going on.' She glanced in the direction of the children, as if to say, 'Not in front of these two.'

Victor was first to understand her signal. 'Can't we talk about it all later?' he said. 'When we've had a bite to eat.'

Over sausages, beans and chips, they tried to put the world to rights.

'I was listening to a woman on the radio,' said Victor, 'moaning about Christmas starting too early. You hear the same old whinge every year. I wanted to ring in and say to her, "Why all the cribbing? What's wrong with a bit of good cheer?"'

'She's probably short of cash,' said Carmel. 'If you're under pressure, Christmas is the worst time of the year.'

'Well, I'm not exactly the Sultan of Brunei, and it can't begin early enough for me.'

Jenelle gave the adults a thoughtful look. 'The woman shouldn't worry. Santy will help her out.'

'You're dead right, chicken,' said Carmel. 'Victor, you should have called the radio station and told her that.'

Jenelle beamed. 'Only a small while to go 'til Santy comes.'

'And our mam comes home to see us,' chimed in Ben. 'Don't forget about that.'

Concern passed across the girl's face. Who could blame her? To all intents and purposes, Carmel was her mother. Now that Tara thought about it, Ben's recollections of his mum must be fairly hazy. She hoped the genuine Rosanna would live up to the picture in his head.

As they finished their dinner, the children chatted about their letters to Santa Claus. All the talk of Christmas made Tara uneasy. Usually the Shines piled in together in Garryowen. Joan cooked the turkey with Tara as her assistant. Would her brothers and sister be there this year? she wondered. Until now, she hadn't given any thought to her own plans. The *Irish Tribune* was published on the twenty-sixth of December, so work would probably be her salvation. *It's only a day*, she thought. *You can get through it.*

It took an age to get the children to bed. Tara knew her presence only made them more anxious to stay up and talk. Usually she welcomed this. Tonight, however, she was desperate for them to go to sleep so she could explain herself to Carmel and Victor.

'At last,' said Carmel, shutting the living room door behind her. 'Both of them are conked out.'

She sat down on the brown sofa and gave Tara an expectant look. Tara swallowed a mouthful of tea. The brew had been made by Victor and was so strong you could paint railings with it.

'The last time I was here,' she said, 'you said something that got me thinking. Not about you or the kids or Rosanna, but about my own family.'

Over the next thirty minutes, she told the full story, ending with a phone call the previous day from her mum. Tara wouldn't go so far as to call it a conversation; there had been more silences and umms and ahs than actual words. Joan had invited her daughter over for a chat. Tara had said no. She'd been left with the sense that, for now, her parents would abandon their attempts at re-establishing connection.

When she finished, Carmel and Victor stared at each other like both were stumped. He was first to speak.

'That's quite a tale,' he said. 'Quite a tale. How have your brothers and sister reacted?'

'I can't say that they're thrilled,' she replied. 'They're chastened, but they're still speaking to Mum and Dad.'

Carmel whistled. 'There was I, thinking the worst of you. "Oh, she's abandoned us," I said. "Her with her perfect family and her perfect life." Little did I know . . . I'm really sorry, Tara.'

'There's no need to be sorry. I should have called you. I've been giving my wounds a good old lick.'

Victor scratched his bullet-shaped head. 'It's true what they say – every family has its own madness.'

'Only some are madder than others,' added Carmel, with the weariness of one whose burden is particularly heavy.

'What's been going on here?' asked Tara.

'Just the usual lunacy. Like Ben told you – sorry, *kept* telling you – Rosanna will definitely be home for Christmas.'

'The little chap's up to ninety,' said Victor. 'I hope she has some stories prepared about the wonders of Australia because he has a million questions for her.'

'I hadn't thought of that,' said Tara. 'Is Rosanna still prepared to go along with the Australia pretence?'

'She is,' replied Carmel. 'And she's such an amazing liar, she'll probably pull it off too. It's other folks that have me worried. Everybody in the flats knows where she really is, and it will only take one stray word for her story to come undone. I realise the kids will have to hear the truth at some stage, but they're still too young. Besides, Christmas isn't the right time.'

'She's laying down the law,' said Victor. 'Says she doesn't want me here on Christmas Day.'

Carmel looked embarrassed. 'And I feel terrible about it, only what can I do? The last thing I need is her creating a ruckus. We'll have to celebrate our Christmas before Rosanna gets out.' She turned towards Tara. 'My daughter's gone all Holy Josephine on me. She thinks it's too soon for me to be seeing another man. "And my da only dead eighteen months. The poor man's not cold in his grave," she says. I tell you, Tara, I had a hard time biting my tongue. How easy would it have been to say, "I know where he is, love, because you put him there?" But I kept my mouth shut.'

'What does Jenelle think?'

'Bless her heart, she's addled by it all. I wish I had a decent photo of Rosanna to show her. I'm convinced that Santa is more real to her than her own mother. Funnily enough, Rosanna's the same. She's forever asking after Ben, but she rarely says a word about Jenelle.'

'I suppose she never really had the chance to know her.'

'True,' said Carmel, 'only it's going to make for one odd Christmas. I hope we all survive it in one piece.'

Chapter 28

'Do you know what?' said Gus. 'I'll bet there are men in the power station in Moneypoint doing extra shifts to keep that lot going.'

His sister Majella was a Christmas obsessive. If she could, she would keep the lights and decorations up all year round. As it was, she managed to restrain herself until the second week in December, and then - *wham!* - the house became a seasonal wonderland. This year, the front garden was festooned with blue and white lights. Multi-coloured baubles hung from the apple tree. A wickerwork reindeer sat underneath.

Joan smiled. 'We should send Vee down for a visit. She would shrivel up with horror.'

Inside was even more extravagantly kitted out: bells, beads, holly and mistletoe hung at every angle. The Christmas tree was laden with decorations from around the world. Everything had been brought back to Limerick by relatives familiar with Majella's passion.

'You'd better keep active,' said Gus to his mother, 'or there's a danger Majella will wrap you up in tinsel.'

Phyllis gave a sage shake of the head. 'She's in town as we speak, buying more. God be with the days when we made our own decorations.'

For all his mother's sprightliness, there was something about Christmas and the turn of the year that made Gus worry about her. He spent more time looking for the signs of old age. Was her voice less distinct? Were her eyes less clear? Her wrinkles more pronounced? Every December he wondered if this would be their last Christmas together. When January came, he banished his fears and looked to the future again.

He liked a traditional Christmas with as many family members as possible under one roof. He didn't care if they fell out or ignored each other: they belonged together. Damien and Felicity had promised that they would spend the big day in Garryowen. Rufus had already sent his letter to Santa Claus. He'd told his Grandad that he wasn't asking for too much because, 'Mum and Dad say it's been a tough year.' These days Rufus was the one true believer, although Aifric was a trooper and could be relied upon to play along. Niall, Vee and Ferdia would also be there for dinner. Reluctantly, Gus had come to accept that Tara would be missing.

He had made every effort to reach out to her. Joan had done the same, and Niall had made entreaties on their behalf. But their efforts were in vain. Gus felt like a man laying out sandbags when the house was already flooded.

This was their first visit to Limerick since their scheme had unravelled. He didn't plan on saying very much to his mother about her role in that unravelling; they'd already had words on the phone. She was irritated that she hadn't been in the picture from the start. 'I could have helped you,' she'd complained. Gus had done his best to mollify her: 'We didn't want to worry you,' he'd said. In truth, he regretted not involving her. He and Joan hadn't given her enough thought. He needed, however, to make some reference to her interference, so he remarked upon Tara's likely absence from the Christmas table.

'I've said it before and I'll say it again, Gus,' replied his mother. 'I was only trying to put the girl's mind at ease. If you'd been better at handling matters, there'd have been no need for me to say anything. I'm sorry to hear that she's still in a huff.'

'We've decided to give her some time to think things through,' said Joan. 'I always worried that she was too malleable, but now I see how obstinate she can be. She really is very stubborn, you know.'

'The apple doesn't fall far from the tree,' said Phyllis as she tipped her head in Gus's direction.

'Tuh,' he replied, 'I wonder where *I* got it from, then.'

'If the girl would only come down to see me, I'd put her straight, but I doubt that'll happen before Christmas. It doesn't matter how upset she is, there's never anything to be gained by sulking.'

'Go easy, Mam, please. We don't want to alienate her any further.'

'I'll say my piece. That's one of the joys of getting to this age. You can speak your mind, and nobody takes offence. They think you're in your dotage.'

She paused to drink from her whiskey and red lemonade. Joan had offered to make tea, but Phyllis had insisted on 'a little tot'. 'On account of it being Christmas,' she'd said. Gus was bemused by her frequent sermons about the benefits of being old. He wasn't sure that he'd ever share her point of view.

'What about the others?' she was asking now. 'How are they getting on?'

'Niall is still working for Amby Power,' said Gus. 'He's getting a lot of Santa Claus work at the moment. I'd love to go and have a look, but I've been warned to stay away. Vee is, well, she's muddling along.' What he didn't say was that Joan had come up with what she reckoned was a great plan for Vee. Before going public, however, they would have to put in some groundwork. 'But the big story is Damien.'

'Really?'

'Oh yes,' replied Joan. 'In fact, I wouldn't blame you if you don't believe what we have to say.'

'I don't believe you,' said Niall, as he took a large gulp from his pint. 'You're having me on.'

Damien looked up from his own drink. 'I swear to you, I'm not.'

The two were in a city centre bar. Even though it was barely past six o'clock, the place was heaving with men and women wearing Christmas jumpers and antlers. Judging by their florid faces and the amount of noise they were creating, most of them were in an advanced stage of drunkenness. Still, what else could you expect in the week before Christmas? Especially *this* Christmas when, for the first time in years, all-out gaudy celebration was not considered unseemly.

When his brother spoke about needing 'a quick chat', Niall assumed he wanted to talk about Tara's self-imposed exile. Instead, after a few minutes of banter about the sadness of office parties and the crankiness of Amby Power, Damien had oh-so-casually revealed that he planned on becoming a teacher.

'A teacher?' said Niall, his voice suggesting that Damien had expressed an interest in becoming a porn star. 'Why?'

'It was something I thought about when I was younger, only other stuff got in the way. A while ago, I started thinking about it again. The idea was niggling away at me until eventually I said to myself, *why not give it a go?*'

'I can think of a million reasons. Having to go back to college for starters.'

'It's only for a year. I've been talking to Mum and Dad, and they're willing to pay the fees. And they'll keep us afloat until I get a job.'

This part of the story was less surprising. Gus and Joan set a lot of store by 'proper jobs' and teaching was undoubtedly a 'proper job'. 'What about your political ambitions? I know it's possible to be a councillor and teach as well, but it's an awful lot to take on. And that's before you take Felicity and the kids into account. You won't know what hit you.'

'I'm giving up politics. I'll stick with the council until the summer, but I won't run again.'

Niall's jaw sagged, prompting a laugh from his brother. 'You should close your mouth. You look like a complete gom.'

'I hope you don't speak to your future pupils like that. Seriously, man, this is getting weird. Politics is your life's work. You can't turn your back on it. Don't mind Maurice Tully's chicanery.

Nobody remembers that; nobody sensible, at any rate. Dust under the chariot wheels and all of that.'

'I can't believe you're trying to convince me of the benefits of being a politician. Anyway, it's not like I've changed my opinions; I've just changed my plans. Oh, and the decision has nothing to do with the dreaded Tully.' Damien swirled the remains of his pint around the glass. 'Actually, that's not quite true. Maurice's trick did make me question what I was doing. But – how do I explain this? – it's not so much that I *don't* want to be a politician; more that I *do* want to be a teacher. And, like you said, with three children to worry about as well, I'm not sure that I'd be able for both.'

'What does Felicity think?'

'She's all for the teaching. Giving up the council she's not so happy about. I think I've talked her round, though. In fact, she's considering running for election herself.'

'Get away.'

'Why not? Maybe I'm biased, but I think she'd be good at it. There's no better woman for getting her own way. Maurice Tully should be very afraid.'

Niall thought for a moment. 'Is this about Mum and Dad? Have you been infected by their scam and all of that talk about taking stock of your life?'

Damien ran a hand through his reddish-brown hair. Now that his stint with Amby was behind him, he was letting it grow again. 'Hmmm, yes and no. If you remember, one of the things they spoke about was how no one ever made a big decision for one reason alone. And they're right. The more I thought about what I was doing, the more the reasons for change started to pile up. Mind you, if it makes them happy to think their scheme prompted my move, let them at it.'

'You're a smart boy, and no mistake. I take it you'll be doing the full family Christmas?'

'I considered staying at home, except Felicity began mutter-ing about spending the day with her parents, and I've had more than enough Amby for one year. The thought of eating Christmas dinner with him makes my skin crawl.'

'You and me both,' sighed Niall.

'So the full family Christmas it is, complete with Dad's stories about the olden days.'

'Ah, where would we be without the tale of how he got a lump of coal and one shoelace for Christmas?'

'The lace being for the shoes they shared between eight of them.'

'And they were girl's shoes, don't forget,' added Niall with a laugh.

'Another pint?' offered his brother.

'If you're twisting my arm.'

When Damien returned from the bar, Niall went outside for a smoke. Leaning against the wall and lighting up, he reflected on what he'd just heard. Damien, his dour, nay-saying brother, was overflowing with positivity. He was like a Sunday supplement in the first week in January: all opportunities and challenges and new beginnings. Niall tried not to dwell on his own situation. By rights, a seasoned world traveller should have some wisdom to draw upon, but his mind was blank.

He was stamping out his cigarette when a truly strange thought hit him: he was enjoying – genuinely enjoying – a night out with Damien. How had that happened? He smiled to himself and turned to go back inside. As he did, he noticed a man wrestling with a Christmas tree. And losing. Three young guys swayed past, crucifying 'Fairytale of New York'. A girl in skew-whiff antlers shook her head at the scene.

'All this fuss, and for what?' she said.

'You can't think of it like that,' said Niall. 'Sure, doesn't it bring people together?'

'That's exactly what I mean. People go soft in the head at this time of year.'

She had that much right, at least.

*

Vee and Joan were standing outside a charity shop in Rathmines. Vee wasn't impressed.

'The state of that window display,' she said. 'You'd want to be desperate or completely without taste to go in there.'

'Why do you think I brought you here?' replied Joan.

Vee squinted at her mother. 'Well, my taste is intact so it must be because I'm desperate.'

Chuckling, Joan took her by the arm and brought her inside, where Vee was surprised to see that some of the stock was quite presentable. The layout was all wrong, though, with tweed overcoats rubbing against lacy tops and skinny jeans crammed in beside skirts with elasticated waists. She inspected a tray of jewellery. Most of it looked like it had started life in a lucky-bag. 'Hideous,' she whispered, hoping the woman behind the counter wouldn't hear. There was, however, a scattering of attractive pieces, which, if properly displayed, would be snapped up in no time.

'Such a shame,' said Vee, her voice still low. 'They could make a go of this place. As things stand, though, it's a disaster zone.'

Joan shepherded her daughter back outside. 'Coffee?' she asked.

'OK, only you'll have to do the buying. I'm skint.'

'Don't worry, I can rise to the price of a coffee.'

'And then will you tell me what you're up to?'

Joan gave one of her inscrutable smiles. 'I have a proposal to put to you, but it can wait until we get indoors again. I'm freezing.'

With that, the elder woman took off at quite a pace, forcing her daughter to trot in her wake.

On her good days, Vee described her life as 'pared back'. On her bad days, she considered that life to be unrelentingly dull. On her really bad days, she hid under the duvet and gave in to a long self-loathing weep. She was eking out an existence on the occasional bit of PR work. Mostly, though, she stayed at home, keeping house and trying to stay out of trouble. Her only social outlet was her weekly visit to a therapist, the aptly named Dr Tim Speake. She was making progress of sorts. But then, along came Christmas. Everywhere she went, people were spending money.

Every time she turned on the television, items she couldn't afford were dangled in front of her. She was surrounded by untrammelled consumption. There was no denying it: Christmas made Vee miserable. And her resolve was fragile.

She continued to wrestle with what her parents had done. Was she angry? Of course. Was she upset? Oh, yes. Every now and again, something that Gus or Joan had said would come back to her, and she'd be reminded of the enormity of their deceit. She would mull over the events of the past few months, and she would want to cycle over to Garryowen and have it out with them. But there were other questions too. Was there merit in any of what her mum and dad had said? Did any part of her understand what they had done? If she was being fair, she would have to say yes. And then there was the most uncomfortable question of all: what right had she to complain about the dishonesty of others?

There was another consideration too: they had paid off her remaining debt. The moral high ground wasn't hers to claim. She was in no position to do a Tara and go flouncing off.

The arrival of her latte caused Vee to emerge from her reverie. In front of her, Joan was sipping a black coffee. The café hummed with sated shoppers, and Vee was on the verge of tears.

'You were a million miles away,' her mother said. 'Are you all right?'

'I'm grand. Well, I'm stumbling about a bit, you know? But I'll get through it.' Despite everything, Vee still found it hard to admit that her life was anything other than wonderful.

'That's why I wanted to talk to you, and why I wanted to bring you to the shop. I've had an idea.'

'What sort of idea?'

'I don't know how you'll feel about this,' said Joan, 'but here goes. A couple of months ago, I happened to bump into a woman I knew years ago – back when you were a teenager. She told me she was working for a charity, The Good Samaritan Trust, and that times were tough. They help out families in need, provide food parcels, pay emergency medical bills ... that type of thing.

Anyway, Annie – that's her name – said they were snowed under. There's a huge demand for their services, but donations have dwindled. People don't have the spare cash. It's as simple as that.'

'It was their shop we were in today,' said Vee.

'That's right. Well, one of their shops. They have three. There's another one in town, and the third one is in Finglas. The shops are a particular problem for them. Like you saw, they do get some decent stuff, only it gets lost among the dross.'

'And if that place is anything to go by, the window displays are atrocious.'

'That's the thing. According to Annie, they're well aware that the shops aren't appealing enough, that they could perform so much better, but nobody involved in the charity has the expertise to tackle the problem.'

'Why don't they hire somebody to sort it out?'

Joan took another sip of coffee. 'That's where you come in.'

'In what way?'

'I told her that you were the woman for the job. "Nobody has an eye like Vee," I said. "She would transform those shops."'

'There's a job?' said Vee.

'Mmmm.' Joan spoke tentatively. 'Yes and no. Annie said they would absolutely love to have you on board, except it would have to be as a volunteer. They don't have the funds to pay anyone.'

Although Vee went to object, her mother ploughed on. 'It would be fabulous experience, though. You'd be able to change the layout, totally revamp the shops. I think it'd be right up your alley.'

Vee felt her face sagging. For a minute, she had made the mistake of getting her hopes up. She should have had more sense. And anyway, what business had she getting involved in charity shops? Hadn't she always said they were appalling places where the customers were either penniless or ancient?

'I don't think so,' she replied, her voice sounding more clipped than she'd intended. 'I can't see that I'd fit in. Anyway, they should pay somebody to do the job properly.'

'They're a charity, Vee,' snapped Joan.

'I said no, Mum. I need to find a proper job, not mess around in some poky shop filled with other people's cast-offs.'

At first, Joan looked deflated. Then something closer to annoyance sparked into her eyes. Vee got the sense that her mother was about to give her a thorough tongue-lashing. She must have thought better of it, though, for all she did was sigh.

'I'm sorry, Veronica,' she said, 'I thought you'd see merit in the idea. If nothing else, I hoped it would give you something to do apart from moping around the house. Spending all that time on your own isn't healthy.'

They sat in silence. Around them, the seasonal tumult continued. The woman at the next table was having an animated phone conversation. 'I've done my best,' she was saying, 'but there aren't any left. He'll have to be told that sometimes even Santa Claus runs out of games.' She paused to listen to the person, her partner presumably, on the other end of the line. 'The woman in the shop looked it up on the computer,' she said. 'There's only one left and it's in Athlone.' Again she paused, before giving a dry laugh. 'Are you serious? If you're willing to drive all the way to Athlone, I'll call and ask them to hold onto it. You do know you're officially insane?'

Vee listened in awe. It was ludicrous what people were willing to do for their kids.

Presently, Joan picked up her gloves and slipped on her coat. She gave a tight, tooth-free smile. 'I've already paid. I suppose I'll see you on Christmas Day.'

Vee looked up at her mum. 'I'm like a punch-drunk boxer,' she said, 'fighting on instinct. Saying no is what I'm used to. If it's not perfect, I don't want to know.' She hesitated. 'You didn't just "bump into" this Annie lady, did you?'

Joan sat down again. 'Am I that easy to read?'

'I don't know how to answer that. You managed to fool all of us for months. Maybe I'm getting better at understanding you.'

'Well, you're right. The idea came to me, and I sought Annie out. I've spent so much time wondering what you can do, and I'm

285

convinced this is something you'd be brilliant at. And it wouldn't be forever. Better opportunities will come your way, I'm sure they will.'

Vee stared into her coffee. 'Dad always claimed you should be running the country, that you'd have everything fixed in no time. I reckon he was right.'

'What are you saying to me?'

She reached over and squeezed her mum's hand. 'I'm saying I'll give it a go.'

'Thanks a million for meeting me,' said Rory, as he rose from his seat in the corner of the bar. 'What'll you have?'

'Um, a white wine, please,' replied Tara.

Why they were meeting, she wasn't sure. She hadn't seen Rory since the day he told her the business was sound, and she hadn't heard from him in more than a month. When he'd called the day before and suggested a drink, she'd been blindsided and had immediately agreed. Ever since, she'd been trying to guess what was going on. Did he have new information about the business? Had he heard about the family schism? Or were they on a date? She dismissed the third option. What type of man would invite someone for a 'quiet drink' a few days before Christmas when even the most sedate suburban pub was likely to be bursting at the seams with revellers?

After five minutes, she was none the wiser. They discussed the weather (foul), her job (ticking along) and their feelings about Christmas (both were in favour). Struggling for somewhere to bring the conversation, she asked if he remembered what she'd told him about Carmel, Ben and Jenelle. Thankfully, he did.

As it happened, she said, she'd been with them the previous day. Rosanna was due to get her Christmas release later in the week and, curious as Tara was, she didn't think they should meet. There would already be enough tension in that household without her poking her nose in. So she had delivered her Christmas presents a few days early. She hadn't expected anything in return, but the children had given her a handmade card and a long woolly scarf. She knew that Carmel didn't have a lot of spare cash and she was touched by the gift.

She was tickled too by Ben's most recent artwork. A large sign reading *Santa Please Call Here!!* covered most of the front window. Carmel told her how Jenelle had been fretting that Santa might skip them out. 'Because we've no chimney,' she explained. Ben had tried to reassure his sister that this hadn't mattered any other year, and that everything would be grand. Still Jenelle worried, so he decided some specific instructions were called for. 'She's much happier now,' chirped Ben, clearly proud of his multicoloured poster. Tara told him that when she was his age she had got upset with her mum for lighting a fire on Christmas Eve. 'I was terrified that Santy would see flames leaping up the chimney, and he'd think we didn't want him to call,' she said. 'In the end my dad agreed to let the fire go out early.'

'Fair play to Gus,' said Rory, after she recounted the tale. 'I'd say Santy was delighted not to have his backside burned off. Actually, it's your old man I wanted to ask about.'

'What's he done?'

'He hasn't done anything; that's the problem. He's lost interest in work – just sits there with his chin in his boots. Oh, he tries to hide it. He's always surrounded by his beloved paperwork, but his eyes are vacant.'

Hell, thought Tara, *how am I going to talk my way around this?* 'Time of year?' she offered. 'It does make some people melancholy, you know – all this dark.'

'Nah, not Gus. He's more robust than that.' Rory fixed her with an enquiring look. He was, it seemed, not a man to be fobbed off with flim-flam.

'I suppose . . .' she started, hoping a plausible explanation would come to her. It didn't, so she attempted to deflect the question back to him. 'What do *you* reckon the problem is?'

He shrugged. 'I might be looking in the wrong place, only I remembered you asking all of those questions about Shine and

Co. So, I was wondering if there was a connection. Like, has there been a family disagreement? What sort of form is he in at home?'

'He's . . . well, he's . . .' *Dammit,* she thought, *I'll have to tell the truth; or a version of it anyway.* 'To be honest, Rory, I wouldn't know how he is because I've got my own flat now.'

'Did you buy an apartment? Fair play to you. Now's the time to get in there, according to the experts. Mind you, those experts didn't do us any favours the last time, but hey—'

'No. I'm renting in Ballsbridge. It's a poky little place, but it's all I need.'

'Right,' he said, stretching the word into three syllables. He plainly couldn't understand why someone would abandon a substantial apartment in Palmerston Park for a shoebox elsewhere.

Tara knocked back half of her drink in one go. 'We fell out.'

Rory arched his eyebrows. 'Aha! That explains it so. Your dad's bad form, I mean.'

The other half of her wine met a similar fate. 'There may be more to it than that.'

'I see. If it's awkward you don't have to tell me.' His eyes said, 'But you know you want to.'

Tara didn't want the evening to end yet. Like she'd always said, she wasn't suited to being on her own. Another evening cloistered away in the bedsit would strain her sanity. She was desperate for a night out. There was more too. Over recent weeks, she'd had cause to think about Rory's kindness. About how helpful he'd been when she was seeking information on Shine and Co.; about his phone calls afterwards. Now, here he was, doing it again. It was difficult to imagine most employees being so concerned about their boss. *Kindness.* It sounded so dull, so unchallenging. *But in its own way*, she thought, *it was more potent than charm*. She decided that if she was going to reveal the family secrets to anyone else, Rory was the man.

'Will I get you another drink?' he asked.

'Listen, the bar is filling up, and we'll probably have to start roaring to be heard.' Tara was, she realised, already roaring. 'Have you eaten?'

He shook his head.

'I know a restaurant around the corner. It's off the main street, so if we go now, we'll probably get a table.'

'You're on.'

It may have been around then that she heard her phone ringing for the first time.

Tara allowed the warm hubbub of the restaurant to wash over her. Before she began her story, she needed to relax. She also needed another glass of wine.

As she spoke, Rory remained quiet, although he did break into a laugh when she got to the part where Niall sang 'Send in the Clowns'.

'Sorry,' he said almost immediately. 'I'm sure it wasn't funny.'

'You're grand. Believe it or not, Niall and Damien laugh about it too.'

Her phone rang again, but she was determined not to be distracted.

By the time she'd finished speaking, they had eaten their pasta and were on their second bottle of wine. She feared she had drunk the lion's share, but talking was thirsty business.

'Well, now,' said Rory, 'I'm not sure what I was expecting, but it definitely wasn't that. That puts a whole new light on ... everything.'

With one finger, he stroked the back of Tara's hand. It was so long since she'd had any sort of human contact that initially she was slightly startled. *What was he signalling?* Whatever it was, she had to admit the sensation was enjoyable. Then, as suddenly as the stroking had started, it stopped. Rory withdrew his hand and began fidgeting with the edge of the tablecloth. Tara concluded that the gesture had been just that: a gesture of affection towards a friend who was all at sea. She told herself to stop over-analysing.

Craig had been right about one thing at least: she did too much thinking.

Rory was still talking. 'If you don't mind me saying so, it seems to me that you're punishing yourself as much as you're punishing your parents.'

'I don't know what to do,' she said. 'Nothing's right anymore. And I can't seem to do the right thing. I used to think that I was the perceptive one in the family, but I had the wool pulled over my eyes like everybody else.' She took another slug of wine. 'I felt like I needed to change my life, and I've done my best to strike out on my own. Only the problem is, you can't just forget about your family, or I can't, at any rate. At the same time, I don't want to go bounding back like nothing has happened.'

'That's the difficulty with families, isn't it? Wouldn't life be an awful lot simpler without them?'

'You've nailed it there.'

He gave her an encouraging smile. Tara decided that she liked his face. She also decided she was drunk.

'The thing is,' he said, 'it'd be kind of empty too. And there'd be nobody to fall out with, which might be a bit boring.'

'How did you get to be so wise?' She was a corny drunk. She suspected that Rory might be too, which was another reason to like him. *Oh, listen to me*, she thought. *This is Rory who works with my dad; I can't be making moves on him. But what if he made the move?* While he went to the bathroom, she made up her mind. If he invited her home for a coffee, she would say yes. If he angled for an invitation to her place . . . no, that was out of the question. Her ugliest grey underwear was drying on the radiator and three days' worth of washing-up festered in the sink.

Head a little foggy, Tara realised that her phone was ringing again. When she took it from her bag, she was taken aback to see a string of missed calls: five from Carmel and two from Damien. What was going on? Noticing Rory returning, she stood up and waved her phone. 'Just going outside,' she signalled.

At the door, she dialled her voicemail. There was a message

from Carmel; then another; then one from Damien; the fourth and final message was also from Carmel. By now, Tara was trembling so much she was barely able to grip the phone.

'Please, love, will you get back to me?' Carmel said, her voice all wobbly. 'We need every bit of help we can get. Ben's been missing for six hours now, and I'm frantic. We all are.'

Chapter 29

For five minutes or more after she arrived at St Monica's Mansions, Tara barely said a word; just held Carmel's hand and watched as her friend tried to compose herself. It was frightening how quickly fear could transform someone. Compared to the woman Tara had met the day before, Carmel appeared hollowed out. Her cheeks were concave, her shoulders sloped.

'I didn't think there was anything wrong at first,' she explained, 'not for well over an hour. I mean, you know what Ben's like. He's always been incapable of coming straight home from school. Why should today be any different?'

Tara nodded. She knew what Carmel meant. If it wasn't for Ben's tendency to wander, she would never have met him to begin with.

'It must have been half four before I really began to worry. It was getting dark, so I rang his friends' parents, and I asked around the flats, but nobody had seen hide nor hair of him. Sometimes he calls over to my sister, Glenda, so I tried her, but she hadn't seen him either. Next I tried Victor. Again, no joy.

'Then I wondered if he was still at school. Maybe he was involved in something and forgot to tell me. So I called the principal, only she said no, everybody was gone home. She said all the special activities, the plays and such, were on tomorrow, on account of it being their last day before Christmas. "Leave it with me," she said, "and I'll check around." After twenty minutes or so she rang back and said she couldn't find anybody who'd seen Ben since school finished.'

Carmel took a long breath before continuing. 'By that stage, I was getting fairly worked up, and the principal, Mrs Carroll, she recommended that I call the guards. Well, needless to say, the very thought of the police scared the hell out of me. But I knew she was right, so that's what I did.'

'What did they say?' asked Tara.

'A young lad took all my details. Then he asked if Ben had ever gone missing before. He wanted to know if I'd checked here, if I'd checked there. "Listen," I said to him, "do you think I'd be ringing you if I hadn't tried everywhere else?" "Fair enough," he said. "Stay where you are, and I'll have someone with you in a few minutes."' Carmel shuddered. 'By the time they arrived, Victor was here. And my friend Nuala – she was here too.'

Tara thought of all the missed calls on her phone and was struck by a twinge of guilt. If only she had bothered to see who was ringing. And if only she'd had less to drink. Although Carmel's message had shocked her back to sobriety, her mouth was coated with cotton wool and there was a sharp pain behind her eyes.

Victor took up the story. 'We had to get Jenelle out of the way before she realised anything was wrong, so she's sleeping in Nuala's flat. She thinks we've gone out for the night and that Ben's staying with another pal.'

'I hope to God she doesn't catch sight of all this to-ing and fro-ing,' said Carmel.

If the flat was unnaturally still, outside was a blur of activity. The word had spread quickly, not just around St Monica's but also to the neighbouring flats complexes and houses. That's how Damien had heard the news. On the landing, in the courtyard, and beyond, neighbours flitted around like moths. In low murmurs, they exchanged news and offered theories, all the while thanking God it wasn't their child who was missing. Others had organised search parties and were combing every inch of waste ground and every possible hiding place. Damien was somewhere among them. Rory was there too. 'I won't intrude,' he'd said to Tara, 'but another pair of legs can't do any harm.'

Theoretically, the gardaí were in charge of the search, but their manpower could never match that of a community that believes a child is in danger. Experience had taught Tara that while most of those offering assistance were doing so for good-hearted reasons, others were enticed by the possibility of bad news. They would never admit it, even to themselves, but the misfortune of others gave them a bizarre pleasure.

'What have the police said?' asked Tara.

'Not a lot,' Carmel replied. 'Like, they're helpful and everything but they simply don't know where Ben could have gone. They kept asking me if he had any reason to be upset, so I had to tell them about Rosanna. Only you've seen him . . . he's thrilled she's coming home, not upset at all. And, of course, they wanted a photo. I gave them one I took on his birthday – when we were all down in Brittas Bay.' She swallowed. 'He looks like the happiest lad alive.'

'And . . . Rosanna . . . does she know Ben's missing?'

Carmel massaged her forehead with the fingers of both hands, pressing so hard that a red mark was left behind. 'I asked the guards not to say anything for now. I pleaded with them, in fact. "Give it another couple of hours," I said. "You don't know how volatile she is. She'll blame me." They'll have to tell her soon, though.'

'Nobody will blame you. You can't go thinking like that.'

Carmel's response was immediate. 'Oh Jesus, they will. A woman whose own daughter is in jail? You can be sure they'll blame me. I can hear people already. "Why wasn't she at the school gates to meet him?" they'll say. "Why didn't she walk him home?" But Ben doesn't like me making a fuss. He always says there's no need, that he's big enough to mind himself. And the school is so close.' Tears pooled in her eyes. 'Anyway, I don't give a damn what anyone says as long as Ben comes home safe.'

Tara squeezed her hand, as if to say, 'I understand. There's no need to explain yourself to me.' The gesture offered no succour. Carmel shut her eyes and clamped her lips together. Tears spilled down her face. For a short while she sobbed onto Victor's shoulder.

When she looked up, her eyes were raw with misery. 'Answer me this, Tara: how could he just vanish?'

'He *can't* just vanish, Carmel. And that's why he'll be found. Perhaps he's with a friend you don't know, or ...' Tara wished she could offer another explanation, but although her head was whirring with thoughts, each one was more disturbing than the last. 'He could turn up at any minute, asking for his dinner and wondering what all the fuss is about. You'll see. Like you said, this is Ben we're talking about, not some kid who gets scared if he's more than fifty metres from home. He's an adventurer, and he's smart.'

'What you're saying makes sense. He's only small, though. And he's so friendly. He doesn't see any danger.' Carmel stopped, probably because to say any more would be to give voice to her fears.

Tara's mind slipped back to the previous day and her last conversation with Ben and Jenelle. As she was leaving, Ben had put on a solemn face and asked that she pass on his Christmas greetings to her family. 'Me too,' Jenelle had said. The image stabbed at her heart. In front of her, Carmel appeared to have drifted off to another world. Her eyes were open, but she didn't seem to be taking anything in.

Tara turned to Victor. 'Is there anything I can do, do you think? I'm not sure that I'm of much use sitting here. Should I be out with the others?'

'No,' said Victor softly. 'As it is, they're falling over each other out there. Not that Carmel isn't grateful. We both are. You're better here, for fear there's any news.'

'You don't mind staying, do you, pet?' asked Carmel, another tear sliding down her cheek.

'Oh God, of course not. I don't want to be in the way, though.'

'You'd never be in the way, and who knows what's going to happen over the next few hours?'

'There'll be good news, I'm sure,' said Tara, leaning in and giving her friend's hand another squeeze.

'I wish I had your faith,' she replied.

*

Later, Tara and Victor went out to the landing. The night was dank, and they needed to bundle up against the cold. Still, the outdoors provided a short respite from the flat's oppressive atmosphere. A small while before, the gardaí had decided that Rosanna needed to be told her son was missing. Carmel toyed with the idea of making the call, but Victor dissuaded her. 'Let the guards handle Rosanna,' he advised. 'She's more than you can cope with at the moment.'

For a time, Carmel had insisted that she join the search. Nobody else considered this a good idea. In the end, she'd agreed to stay put, but she remained restive. At regular intervals she paced the room. Otherwise, she sat hunched up on the sofa, lacerating herself for things she had or hadn't done. At a loss as to how best to comfort her, both Tara and Victor were relieved to see the arrival of her sister. A younger, plumper version of Carmel, Glenda provided a dry shoulder and a steady supply of Rothmans.

In the flat, there was an unofficial ban on speculation. Outside, there was more freedom to speak. Victor turned towards Tara. 'What do you think has happened to him?'

'Nothing, I hope. I pray to God there's some totally innocent explanation.'

'Me too. Only what if there isn't?'

Tara pinched the bridge of her nose while she thought. 'The obvious fear is that someone has abducted him but, you know, that sort of thing really is very rare.'

'It does happen, though.'

'Yeah, but it's more likely that Ben's had an accident or that he's trapped somewhere. Or . . .' she hesitated. 'Is the canal being searched?'

Victor shivered. 'The cops were reluctant to mention it in front of Carmel, but they're examining the area, all right.'

Wanting to be sure they remained out of earshot, the pair shuffled along the landing. Momentarily they paused outside number

424. That was where poor Redser Lynam had lived, and Tara didn't want to stop there. It felt like a bad omen.

'You may not have thought of this,' she said. 'There's no reason why you should. But if Ben isn't found tonight, there's likely to be a pile of journalists here in the morning. It's not just that he's a missing child, he's also a neighbour of the boy who was killed earlier in the year.'

'What difference does that make?'

'Rationally, it doesn't make any difference, except, grim as this might sound, it makes the story more appealing for journalists. If they've nothing to say about Ben, they can rehash stuff about Eric.'

Victor exhaled slowly. 'To be honest, I hadn't given a thought to the papers or the telly. Will you have to go to work?'

'I . . .' The words 'I don't know' were almost on Tara's tongue. Then she changed her mind. 'I plan on staying here,' she said.

'Thanks. Carmel will be pleased. She thinks you're good at dealing with people.'

'Really?'

'Well, she reckons – how should I put this? – that people are less likely to give you the run around.'

Tara gave a sorrowful shake of the head. 'Poor Carmel.'

'The Lord only knows what state she'll be in if we don't get some good news soon. As it is she spends her days berating herself for Rosanna's failings. I can't imagine how she'll manage if something happens to Ben. And it doesn't matter what you say or what I say, people *are* judgemental. We all are. If we didn't know Carmel, we might easily stand in judgement of her too.'

Bleak as his analysis was, Tara knew Victor was right. 'It's depressing, isn't it?' she said. 'People do appalling things every day of the week, and it doesn't knock a bother out of them. Yet there's Carmel, with so much to offer, and she goes through life beaten-down by guilt.'

'She deserves far, far more than life has given her,' he said, his voice sounding strangely muffled.

Tara realised that Victor – big, solid, capable Victor – was crying.

Shortly after midnight two gardaí arrived. One looked as though he was freshly-sprung from training college. The other, a woman who introduced herself as Sergeant Christine Drumm, had the hard-set face of someone accustomed to dealing with tragedy. This made Tara apprehensive. Was she a special 'bad news' officer, called in on the most distressing of cases?

She certainly didn't waste time on small talk. 'Before I bring you up to date,' she said, 'may I check something with you, Mrs O'Neill? You told us your daughter was due to begin her temporary release from the women's prison tomorrow, is that right?'

'Mmmm. She's getting six days starting tomorrow. She'll be here until just after Christmas.'

'It seems Rosanna was actually released earlier today.'

'But, hold on a minute, if that's the case, where is she? And why did they let her go early?'

'Unfortunately I can't answer the first part of your question because, the truth is, we simply don't know. As for the second part: they didn't let her go early. Rosanna was always scheduled to be released today.'

'Oh.'

Confusion engulfed the room. Victor began to say something, but the policewoman gave a wave as if to say, 'Bear with me a minute.'

She peered at her notebook. 'We've also come into possession of two further pieces of information. The first is from a boy who told his parents he saw Ben talking to a woman after school. His description wasn't precise, but he thinks she had long blonde, or maybe light red, hair.'

Carmel gave a tiny gasp.

Sergeant Drumm returned to her notebook. 'The second contact is from a woman who rang us a short time ago. She'd only just heard about a local boy going missing. Her daughter is in another class at Ben's school. And while the woman doesn't know Ben, she does know Rosanna. They may once have been friends. Anyway, she's convinced she saw her this afternoon holding the hand of a boy. He was wearing a navy padded anorak and a stripy hat. The woman said she remembered the hat because it was so cute.'

'That's Ben. That's definitely our Ben,' said Carmel. 'He loves that hat. He'd wear it to bed if I let him.'

'So, while we can't say for certain that Ben is with his mother now, it does sound as though they met this afternoon.'

As she attempted to absorb the information, Tara's mind veered one way then the next. *Was this good news or was it cause for more anxiety?*

'She's taken him,' said Carmel. 'I should have guessed. I should have seen it coming.'

'The little cow,' added Carmel's sister, Glenda, who had been silent up until then. 'She knows full well she's not capable of taking care of that child.'

The sergeant fixed Glenda with a look that suggested her contribution was less than helpful. She cleared her throat. 'I have to ask you, Mrs O'Neill – do you have any idea where Rosanna might be? And do you have any reason to believe she might hurt Ben?'

Chapter 30

In the early hours, as the searches wound down, family and friends converged on the flat. So many people passed through that Tara couldn't keep hold of their names. They all pledged to return in the morning. They all insisted the sightings of Ben were good news. 'She won't have taken him far, Carmel,' they said. 'You'll see, they'll be back here in no time.' But their reassurances were stilted, and their faces hinted at their doubts. Lingering on the doorstep as one couple left, Tara heard their true views. 'I'd say Rosanna and Ben are in London by now,' the woman said. 'I wouldn't trust her with a puppy, let alone a child,' added the man.

By three thirty, there were just four of them left: Carmel, Victor, Tara and Rory. Tara had assumed that Rory would go home. The problem was, Carmel seemed to believe they were together – as in boyfriend and girlfriend together – and kept insisting that he stay.

'You two can bed down in Jenelle's room,' she said. Tara didn't want to correct her, and Rory appeared content to do her bidding.

'That's very decent of you,' he replied. 'Maybe we should try and get a couple of hours rest. Do you think you'll get any sleep yourself?'

She patted him on the shoulder. 'I doubt it, but we'll lie down for a wee while anyway. I'll have the phone beside the bed.'

'And—' started Tara.

'And if there's even a hint of news, you'll be the first to know,' said Victor.

Jenelle's room was small and overwhelmingly pink. Before Tara had the chance to say a word, Rory voiced his intention to sleep on the floor. 'Although I've got to tell you,' he added, 'right at this moment, I'd sleep on a bed of nails.'

Tara peeled off her boots. 'I think Carmel might have . . . ahm . . . got the wrong end of the stick.'

'I hope you're not offended.' He lay down on Jenelle's Barbie rug and arranged his overcoat as a blanket.

She thought of her earlier intentions and her neck started to tingle. 'Oh Lord, no. What about you?'

'As if.'

Within ten minutes, Rory was snoring steadily. Tara didn't have the heart to disturb him. She wasn't sure she would be able to sleep anyway. For a moment, her mind shifted back to her own problems. But they felt distant, ephemeral.

She wondered whether Ben was still with Rosanna, and if so what he was doing. She wondered where he was sleeping. Or whether he was sleeping at all.

'Shush, Gus, would you?' said Joan as she waved a hand in the direction of the kitchen radio. 'There's something I want to hear.'

Joan was wearing her listening expression – head cocked, face tense – so he did as he was told. They were rarely in sync at breakfast-time. Whereas he liked to chat, his wife needed to think through the day ahead.

The newsreader was talking about a missing boy. 'Ben, who lives with his grandmother, was last seen yesterday afternoon when he left St Tiernach's National School, close to his home in St Monica's Mansions. It's believed he may be in the company of his mother. Gardaí are keen to trace them both.'

'Isn't that—' said Gus

'I asked you to shush,' hissed Joan as she turned the radio's volume to its maximum setting.

The newsreader boomed across the room. 'Sergeant Christine Drumm said local people have been very helpful and she appealed to anyone with information to come forward.' The policewoman made her appeal, the newsreader moved on to the situation in Syria, and Joan turned the radio down again.

'Yes,' she said. 'I'm sure that's the young fellow Tara knows.'

'I remember her doing a piece about those flats,' said Gus through half a mouthful of toast. 'Didn't Damien get on his high horse about it afterwards?'

'He did indeed.'

'I hope the boy's all right. It's no weather to be outdoors, that's if he is outdoors. Should we ring Tara, do you think?'

Joan squeezed his shoulder. 'We can try, only it might be another wasted call.'

'I wish there was something I could do.'

'About Ben or about Tara?'

'Both of them,' Gus replied.

In the morning, Carmel was dry-eyed, efficient, upbeat. 'There's no point in me falling asunder,' she said. 'That won't help Ben.'

She gave a smile that could have doubled as a grimace. Tara and Victor exchanged a look. They knew she was trying too hard.

Carmel had been up since six. She'd wanted to call Jack before he heard the news from anyone else. He was already on his way to Stansted airport. Jenelle was going to stay with Nuala. 'I'll pop down to her with some of her toys,' Carmel said. 'And there's a couple of things that Santy was going to bring her . . . I'm thinking I'll give those to her now. They'll help keep her occupied. Please God, Ben will be home before she realises he's gone.'

Tara suspected the police had made scant headway. Otherwise, why did they keep coming back to Carmel for names and addresses and numbers? They asked about old friends and boyfriends, about Rosanna's favourite places, even about her old dealer. They wanted to know if she was particularly friendly with anyone in prison. Did anyone else visit her? What had she said about her future plans? Carmel was dismayed by how little she knew. Her voice cracked from crying and cigarettes (until the previous night she hadn't smoked in months), she told them she'd already passed on every detail she could think of. 'You've got to understand,' she said, 'me and Rosanna, we're not exactly best buddies. If we were, well, she wouldn't have . . .' Her voice trailing away, she closed her eyes.

Tara guessed what she'd been about to say. Again, she was blaming herself, assuming that if she had a stronger relationship with her daughter, the events of the past twenty-four hours would not have happened.

The gardaí stressed that they were working at full tilt. They were knocking on doors, scrutinising CCTV footage, making calls. But Ben and Rosanna remained out of reach.

As Tara had predicted, a tribe of reporters had gathered down-stairs. They were her tribe, yet she was distanced from them. For once, she wasn't a bystander. A look at her phone showed that pictures of Ben and Rosanna were plastered across the news web-sites. The photo of Rosanna had been provided by the prison. She was smiling, but nobody would have guessed she was only in her mid-twenties. Other pictures were there too. There was an image of St Monica's looking neglected and forbidding. And then there was a photo of Ben's sign, the one that urged Santa to 'Please Call Here'.

What really stung – and she prayed that Carmel never saw them – were some of the comments posted by readers. One started, *What a rough-looking mother!! And no mention of a father. When they find that kid he should be put into care.* Another said, *If these low-lifes can't mind their kids, they shouldn't be allowed to have any.* A third read, *I pray the child is OK, but these stories never end well.* She remembered her conversation with Victor, and she re-membered something that Damien had said following his brush with notoriety. 'We're living in the era of instant judgement,' he'd complained. Tara wondered whether this was true, or whether it had simply become easier for people to disseminate their half-baked opinions and casual malice. Perhaps internet forums were just the modern-day church gate or street corner.

When Tara rang her own paper to explain her absence, the

news editor released a lengthy sigh. 'You truly are one of the oddest reporters I've ever come across,' he said. 'Do you go around befriending everybody you interview?'

'This was different,' she replied, before pledging to keep the news desk informed of developments.

Rory showed no sign of leaving. 'I reckon Gus will survive without me for one day,' he said. 'Whatever needs doing, I'm your man.' Briefly, Tara considered the possibility that *he* was one of the people attracted by misery. Then she looked at his eager face. *Oh, get a grip*, she said to herself. This was what happened when you were surrounded by doubt and suspicion: you became infected.

Damien rang to see if there was any news. She received texts from Vee and Niall. Her father called too. Her finger hovered over the answer key, but she didn't press it.

At lunchtime, Sergeant Christine Drumm arrived. She had a new sidekick, who looked to be cut from the same cloth as his predecessor. Rory had gone to fetch some coffees, so there were only three of them in the flat.

'First things first,' the policewoman said, as she shuffled through her trusty notebook. Tara had the feeling she used the notebook more as a prop than a source of information. 'We've found Rosanna.'

'Thanks be to God,' said Carmel, before quickly adding, 'and Ben? How's Ben?'

'I'm coming to that. Rosanna was in a house in Briarstown. It's being rented by the sister of a woman who spent some time in prison with her. It looks as though there was a party there last night.'

Tara knew from Carmel's puzzled expression that she'd never heard of Briarstown. This was no surprise. Briarstown was a suburb tacked onto a suburb. One of those places lashed up during the boom, its sole facilities were an overburdened primary school, a warehouse of a pub and a down-at-heel corner shop. Even in Dublin most people only knew it as a name on the front of a bus.

'Were there drugs at this party?' asked Carmel.

'It's likely that people were doing drugs in the house, yes. There's no evidence that your daughter took heroin, but she did have a lot to drink. She's been taken to hospital – just as a precaution.'

Tara could tell that Carmel was becoming more and more anxious. Her palms were pressed flat against her thighs and she was rubbing them up and down.

Sergeant Drumm continued, 'Unfortunately, Mrs O'Neill, when we arrived at the house, Ben was no longer there.'

A high note of panic hit Carmel's voice. 'Where is he, then? What's Rosanna done with him? Did somebody take him?'

'From what we can ascertain, Ben did spend the night in Briarstown. Certainly, Rosanna brought him there. We believe that at some stage this morning, when the other occupants of the house were asleep, he left on his own.'

'So where did he go? Somebody must have seen him.'

'We do have *some* information.' Christine Drumm hesitated. Tara feared this was a bad sign. Victor must have thought so too because he took one of Carmel's hands into his own. 'Now this hasn't been one hundred per cent confirmed, but it looks like Ben got a bus into the city centre.'

'If the bus driver recognised him, why didn't he call you?' asked Victor.

'The trouble is, he didn't recognise Ben at the time. He'd gone to work without seeing or hearing a news bulletin, much less reading a paper.' She gazed towards the heavens. 'Young guys these days don't seem to follow the news. And as for the passengers? Well, there weren't many of them. And those that were there must have been either half-asleep or stupid.' She paused. 'Sorry, I shouldn't rant.'

Tara had an urge to tell her she should rant more. The display of frustration made her human. But she didn't. Instead she asked whether the driver was sure it was Ben he had seen.

'Pretty sure,' replied the sergeant. 'Thankfully, there's CCTV on the bus, and we hope to check the footage shortly.'

'Why not now?' said Carmel. 'Why does everything take so bloody long? If you'd got to the house earlier, Ben would already be home.'

'I appreciate what you're saying, Mrs O'Neill. I swear to you I do. We're doing our very best to find your grandson. As we speak, officers are searching for him.'

Victor asked the question that Tara had been too nervous to voice. 'And what about Rosanna? She's not likely to stay in hospital, is she?'

'No, she'll be returned to jail. Temporary release comes with a lot of rules attached, and I think we can take it that Rosanna has broken most of them.'

'Did she say why she took him?' asked Carmel.

'She said she wanted to spend some time on her own with him. That's all. That's why she lied about her release date.'

'And did she plan on coming back here at all?'

'She's rather vague about that. I've a feeling that taking care of Ben turned out to be more work than she anticipated.'

'And he's no trouble, you know,' said Carmel. 'No trouble at all. I want you to understand that. Like, he's not some young tearaway or anything. He's as good a kid as anybody could want.'

Sergeant Drumm smiled. 'That's just what his school says too. And they say he's great fun.'

Carmel nodded. 'He's that, right enough.'

'What I don't understand,' said Tara, 'is why Rosanna didn't just ring to say she'd got Ben. She must have known that everybody would be mad with worry.'

The sergeant's face and tone suggested she would be sceptical about anything Rosanna said. 'Well, she claims she meant to, only it got too late and she thought she'd sort everything out in the morning. She says she didn't think the gardaí would get involved.'

'She never did do much thinking,' said Carmel. 'That's her problem.'

'Would you like to see Rosanna, Mrs O'Neill?' This was the

first time the garda sidekick had spoken. His voice was unexpectedly deep. 'That can be arranged.'

'God, I don't know,' said Carmel. 'Just tell me – is she OK? The thing is ... whatever she's done, she's still my daughter. She wrecks my head, but I can't stop caring about her.'

'She's fine,' said the sergeant.

After the officers left, Carmel crumbled. Despite promising that she would have something to eat, she couldn't even bring herself to drink a glass of water. When Rory returned, carrying a tray of coffees and a bag of doughnuts, Carmel shook her head. 'I'm sorry. It's like my throat's too small,' she explained. She remained on the sofa, inhaling one of Ben's jumpers, rocking slowly back and forth.

'He doesn't even like town,' she said. 'Why would he go into town?'

'Because he's on his way home,' offered Victor. 'He's no fool. He knew to get the bus into town, and then to get another one here.'

'Why isn't he here then?' snapped Carmel.

'At least you know he was well this morning.'

'But why did he leave on his own? I'm worried that Rosanna might have said something to make him run away. What if she told him the truth about where she's been?'

'There's no point in torturing yourself, Carmel. For a small fellow, Ben's very independent.'

'That's easy for you to say. Do you understand how serious this is? There's every kind of loo-lah out there. Heaven only knows what might happen to him.' She wiped away a tear. 'I'm sorry, Victor. I'm sorry. My nerves are jangling like nobody's business.'

Tara decided to intervene. 'I know this probably isn't of much comfort right now,' she said to Carmel, 'but, from what the police said, Rosanna didn't do any drugs at this party. I mean, there was probably stuff there, but she steered clear of it. That's got to be good, hasn't it?'

Carmel sniffed. 'It's something small to cling on to, I suppose.'

In the afternoon there was a deluge of visitors. Glenda returned, as did Carmel's brothers. Victor's colleagues, all large men, stood shyly by the door, asking if they could help. Ben's teacher and principal arrived to offer support. Two priests and a community worker turned up. At one point, Tara was introduced to a shrunken woman called Esther Halpin. It took her a few minutes to realise that this was Ben's other granny. Advice was dished out. Prayers were promised. Cups of tea were drunk. A bottle of whiskey appeared.

It was only when Jack arrived from London that the crowds began to thin. Tara and Rory, who were washing cups and glasses, stayed in the kitchen and watched a wave of people descend the stairs. Two or three paused to speak to the reporters. One man remonstrated with them. Carmel's son was like her: spare-framed and blue-eyed. He spoke with a touch of a London accent. If he thought it bizarre that people he knew had left while three strangers stayed behind, he didn't say.

'Mam told me about you,' Jack said to Tara. 'She said you've been good to Ben and Jenelle.'

Tara was touched that Carmel had mentioned her yet she was at a loss as to what to say in return. Glad you could come? Sorry for your troubles? She settled on, 'Your mum's very proud of you.' There was no template for a situation like this.

After considerable cajoling from the police, Carmel agreed to a TV interview. 'It'll just be the one interview,' Christine Drumm assured her. 'RTE will give the tape, or whatever it is they use nowadays, to the other media. It'll be a big help, Carmel, you have my word.'

'What'll I say?'

'You need to describe Ben and to let people know what a wonderful boy he is. And maybe you should say something *to* him, in case he sees the news. Let him know that you're desperate to see him come home. And reassure him that he's not in any trouble.'

Carmel gave her a beseeching look. 'But if this isn't on the news until six o'clock, does that mean you don't think you'll find Ben before then? Please tell me you'll find him before then.'

The garda sought refuge in her notebook. It was like she was hoping that if she stared hard enough, Ben would suddenly materialise. 'You've got to believe that we're doing everything we can,' she said.

Shortly afterwards, a TV reporter with whom Tara had a nodding acquaintance arrived. In his navy suit and box-fresh shirt, he looked as incongruous as a visiting government minister.

Deciding that it would be best to leave them alone for a few minutes, Tara and Rory went out to the landing.

'It's getting dark,' she said.

'Nah, it's just a gloomy day, and there's never any light at this time of year anyway.'

'No, it's definitely getting dark. And I feel so useless.'

Rory rubbed his chin. 'We could always go into town. Go looking for Ben, I mean.'

'Really?'

'It's what you want to do, isn't it?'

'I know we said we'd hang around . . . only Jack's here now. And if Ben is somewhere in the city centre, well, I'm more likely to spot him than someone who doesn't know him.'

'Come on, we'll explain what we're at, and then get a taxi into town.'

Within ten minutes, they were on their way. As they left, Tara saw the reporter and cameraman who had conducted the interview with Carmel. Councillor Maurice Tully was standing in front of the camera. No doubt he had foisted himself upon them. 'I've always said this is a fine community, a strong community,' he was saying. 'And we will get through this difficult time.' The journalist looked bored, the cameraman looked irritated. Tara wasn't able to stop herself. She stood behind Maurice Tully and pretended she was vomiting. The councillor was too lost in his rhetoric to notice, but the reporter and cameraman struggled to contain their laughter.

Rory was baffled. 'What was that for?'

'I was making sure he doesn't appear on the TV news.'

For the first time that day, they both laughed.

Until they reached the city centre, Tara couldn't fathom why no one had spotted Ben. 'An eight-year-old on his own – how could you miss him?' she asked. After five minutes amid the mayhem she understood.

She had forgotten what the days before Christmas were like. Herds of shoppers and party-goers had taken over the streets. People didn't walk so much as swarm, and in the mass of humanity, it was almost impossible to make out individuals, especially small ones. She kept imagining that she'd spotted a small stripy hat bobbing up and down amid the throng. But her mind was playing tricks on her.

'You know that phrase "hiding in plain sight"? It really does make sense,' said Rory. 'There could be a hundred missing children on this street, and nobody would notice them.'

Wedged in beside a wall, Tara wanted to scream with frustration. 'And even on the quieter streets, nobody sees anything anymore. They're all too busy staring at their bloody phones.'

'You'd wonder as well whether anybody sees or hears the news on a day like this. It's like we're all wrapped up in our own pre-Christmas worlds.'

Knowing he was right, Tara sighed. It was definitely getting dark now. The sky, an ugly pewter, threatened rain. She clasped her phone in one hand. There was no chance she would hear it ring, but if she kept it close she would feel its vibrations. In her other hand she carried a photo of Ben. They had planned on showing it around, but everybody was in such a hurry that this would probably be a wasted effort. Besides, it was hard to find room to manoeuvre.

The pair inched onto a side street where it was a tiny bit quieter.

'If your dad rings again, will you talk to him?' asked Rory.

Slightly irritated – *didn't they have more important things to worry about?* – Tara shrugged. 'I'll see. Why do you ask?'

'I was thinking about him. I haven't really had a chance to digest what you told me last night.'

'Like I said, I'll see.'

Just as she feared this was going to get awkward, her phone buzzed to life. It was Victor – with two developments. There was some good news and some troubling news, he said. The troubling news was the discovery of Ben's school bag behind a collection of bins in Temple Bar. It had been abandoned there. Tara recalled the first day she'd met Ben and the way he'd retrieved his belongings from the back of the bins in St Monica's Mansions. She told Victor.

'So you see, he probably stashed it away for safekeeping,' she said. 'I don't think it's bad news at all.'

The positive development was the fact that a woman had spoken to Ben earlier in the afternoon. Or rather, she had spoken to a boy who was on his own near St Stephen's Green. The boy had cheerfully assured her that he was waiting for his mam and was fine. It was only when she got back to work and mentioned the episode that a colleague decided she must have been talking to Ben.

'The guards are in both areas as we speak,' said Victor, 'but I'm sure they'd welcome two extra pairs of eyes.'

As the two set off for the Green, the clouds opened. The rain hit Tara's face like a fistful of gravel. *Oh Ben*, she thought, *I hope you're not out in this.*

Even though it was barely four thirty, Gus was the only person left in the office. Everybody was going for a Christmas drink, and he'd told them to head off early. 'I'll follow you,' he'd promised. How he would love to renege on the commitment. He wasn't in the humour for socialising; he'd prefer to go home and collapse in front of the telly. But that wasn't possible. Not only was his presence expected in the pub, his wallet was too. There was no denying it: business was on the up again. After everything that had happened, however, Gus got little joy from the upturn. He felt like his hunger for success had been sated.

Still, he would have to put on his game face and brave the crowds. He wouldn't have too much to drink; there was a danger that alcohol would make him sentimental and mawkish.

Although a glance out the window showed the rain had passed, chances were another shower would scuttle in before too long. He needed to get going. The square below was almost deserted. It was hard to imagine the chaos that waited a couple of hundred yards away. He was about to step away from the window and get his coat when, out of the corner of his eye, he noticed something move. Because of the way the light hit the glass, his only clear view was of his own reflection. To get a better look, he pressed his face against the window.

A short way down the street, a child – he couldn't tell whether it was a boy or a girl – was peering at a brass name plate. Evidently dissatisfied, the child trudged down the steps and onto the next door. Once again, he – Gus could see now that it was definitely a boy – failed to find what he was looking for.

Heart lifting in a way he wouldn't have thought possible, Gus ran out of his office and tore down the stairs. By the time he reached the front door, the boy was standing square in front of it. He wrinkled his freckled nose and gazed upwards.

''Scuse me,' he said, 'are you Tara's dad?'

Chapter 31

According to the hospital doctor, Ben was none the worse for his adventures.

'You're a hardy young man, aren't you?' he said to the patient, who nodded and asked if he could have some sleep now.

'It was kind of loud last night,' he explained. 'Even louder than Jenelle when she has her bad dreams. All the music and shouting and singing kept me awake.'

The doctor patted his head. 'You get your rest. We'll keep an eye on you tonight, but you should be able to go home in the morning.'

Ben pursed his lips in thought. 'Is my mam in the party house or is she at home in our flat?'

Carmel kissed the bridge of his nose. 'We'll talk about that tomorrow, pet.'

'OK.' He paused. 'Nan?'

'Yes?'

'I think I've lost my hat. Can you get it back?'

'I'll do my best, but we might have to get you a new one.'

'Thanks. Can I ask another question?'

'Go on.'

'Was I really on the telly?'

'You were really on the telly.'

'Very strange,' said the little boy who was already floating off to sleep.

As Carmel relayed this to Tara, Gus, Rory and Jack, her voice faltered. Victor placed an arm around her. They were sitting in a small cluster of chairs in the hospital waiting area, eating crisps, drinking grey vending-machine coffee and piecing together Ben's lost twenty-four hours. What a sight they were, thought Tara; each one more exhausted and dishevelled than the next. All around them anxious parents waited for news. Stern-faced men and women with clipboards and stethoscopes scurried past.

Tara reckoned Carmel was experiencing about twenty different emotions. Relief and joy may have topped the list, but her happiness was tarnished by darker feelings. Back and forth she swung; one moment rejoicing at her grandson's safe return, the next obsessing about how she would answer his questions. While Tara's own profession left no room for ambiguity – everything was either a triumph or a disaster – she knew that life was rarely lived in absolutes. Ben's return was a cause for celebration, but the events of the last day had shown him that all was not as it seemed. Now Carmel would have to handle the repercussions.

It was this thirst for answers that had brought Ben to Gus's doorstep. Although Rosanna hadn't told her son that she'd spent the previous two years in jail, she had poured cold water on the Australia story. When he kept coming back to her with fresh queries, she fobbed him off; told him to behave himself and go to sleep. One of her friends laughed and said she'd been 'in the big house'. What big house, he wanted to know, and where? After a restless night, he tried to rouse his mother. She wouldn't get up, so he decided to go in search of answers. He wasn't sure who he trusted to tell the truth, but in true Ben form, he remembered a conversation he'd had with Tara where she'd told him her dad was honest. 'That's why I'm here,' he'd said to Gus. 'You'll tell me the truth.'

The irony was not lost on Gus or his daughter. 'That conversation was *months* ago,' said Tara, her voice tart. She confined herself to that. Carmel had enough on her plate without having to cope with the Shine family's squabbles.

'What I don't get,' said Jack, 'is *how* Ben found you.'

Carmel's lips curved into a half smile. 'That young fella has ways and means that wouldn't occur to people three times his age.'

'To quote Ben,' said Gus, 'finding me was "easy peasy". He knew Fitzwilliam Square was somewhere in the city centre so he looked up what he called "one of the picture signs". The street map showed him that his destination wasn't too far away, so off he trotted.'

'All the same, it's quite a stretch for an eight-year-old,' said Jack.

'I think the walk might have taken a wee bit longer than he'd bargained for. He got worried at one point and asked a woman if he was walking in the right direction. He said she was "wearing a long skirt and holding magazines", so I assume she was selling the *Big Issue*. She told him he was almost there. I tell you, Carmel, if Ben ever considers a career in accountancy, let me know. He'd buy and sell most of the youngsters in our office.' He winked at Rory. 'Present company excepted, of course.'

If Gus had been surprised to see Tara arriving with one of his employees in tow, he hadn't said. Mind you, the past couple of hours had been so hectic he probably hadn't had time to think about Rory's presence. Under the harsh hospital lighting, the hollows beneath her father's eyes were more obvious, and his wrinkles were more defined. Yet there was a jauntiness about him that reminded her of the Gus of old.

Carmel fastened her coat. 'I'd better get home. Nuala rang to say that Jenelle's all worked up. She wants to know where I've gone and where Ben's gone. And she wants to sleep in her own bed. Bless the little mite, she's such a home-bird. She'll never do a runner on me, that's for sure.'

'At least you'll sleep easily tonight,' said Tara.

'I suppose. Only I have to work out what to tell Ben. Do I tell him the truth about his mam? And how do I explain to an eight-year-old that if I lied, I did it for the best of reasons?'

Gus leaned towards her. 'For now, the most important thing is that he's back. And don't worry about his hat, by the way. I know a woman who'll have a new one knitted in no time.'

*

Gus wondered if it was possible to have a more peculiar day. For sheer oddness, it would be hard to beat opening the door to a child whose first question is, 'Are you Tara's dad?' and whose next words are, 'Will you tell me the truth?'

Now he too was caught up in a muddle of emotions. One part of him ached to go back to Garryowen and reflect on what had happened. Another part was so delighted to have Tara with him, actually sitting in the back of the car, that he wanted to throw a party. On top of this, he was nervous. What would happen when they did get back to the house? Would she hare away, or would she be willing to stay for a drink? Oh, and he was curious: where did Rory fit into the picture?

Ben had been oblivious to the brouhaha over his disappearance. From what Gus could gather, his mother had maintained that everybody knew he was spending the night with her. After that, he'd been so wrapped up in his mission that he'd scarcely considered how others would react. When Gus tried to explain, the child, who was drenched to the core, had put his head to one side. 'Uh oh,' he'd said, 'my nan will be giving out about me wandering off. She's always doing that. Will you tell her not to be cross?'

Ben's other questions were more challenging. Amid a flurry of phone calls to Tara, to Carmel and to the police, Gus had attempted to reassure the boy. He was out of practice at dealing with eight-year-olds, and worried that he would only make a bad situation worse.

He was also impossibly touched by Ben's trust. Or, to be more accurate, Ben's misplaced trust. There Tara had been, telling the child that her dad was honest, and all the while he'd been lying to her. It gave her yet another reason not to forgive him.

'There are times when adults don't tell the full truth,' he said to Ben, 'but that doesn't mean they want to hurt you.'

'Why do they lie?' asked the boy.

'For a million different reasons. But, sometimes, it feels like the best option. Like the right thing to do.'

'Being an adult sounds very complicated.'

Much to Ben's puzzlement, Gus chuckled. 'You can say that again,' he replied.

Tara hadn't expected a welcoming party. When they got back to Garryowen, however, the entire family was waiting. Vee, with assistance from Ferdia, was rearranging the decorations on the Christmas tree. Joan was wafting back and forth, tending to the fire and filling drinks. Niall was attacking a box of chocolates, while Damien was fielding calls about Ben's return. They were all desperate to hear the full story.

Rory gave Tara a look as if to say, 'I'm probably out of place here,' but her father intervened.

'You'll come in for a drink,' he said as he gave his employee an almighty slap across the back.

Smart enough to realise that this was an offer he couldn't refuse, Rory nodded and said, 'Grand so.'

Gus switched his attention to Tara. 'And you'll be staying yourself?'

'For a short while.'

Almost two months had passed since she'd left, and it was hard not to be seduced by the warmth of home. Plus, she needed a proper word with her dad. No matter what had happened between them, he had been brilliant with Ben. Before the gardaí arrived, he'd given the boy a cup of hot milk and a plate of biscuits, and had chatted away to him. He'd put him on the phone to Carmel too so she could hear her grandson's voice. Victor said Carmel had been so overwhelmed she could hardly breathe. As they'd left the hospital, Gus had invited Carmel and Victor for a drink over the Christmas holidays. 'And bring Jenelle and my new buddy Ben,' he'd said. Watching him in action, Tara had felt a rush of affection – and an unsettling sense of pride.

She also wanted to talk to Rory, only he'd been buttonholed by Joan. Her mum had the thirsty-eyed look of a woman seeking information. When Tara arrived, Joan had hovered for a moment like she wasn't quite sure what to do. Then she'd cast aside her awkwardness and hugged her daughter. Her rigid smile and jittery words revealed how nervous she was. 'You're too thin,' she'd said. 'There's a first time for everything,' Tara had replied. When they separated, Tara saw that there was a misting of tears in her mum's green eyes. She couldn't recall the last time she'd seen Joan, who was always more controlled than Gus, look so ill at ease.

How did she feel about her mum now? The knowledge that she'd been Gus's co-conspirator, that the plot had actually been her idea, was hard to handle. But Tara couldn't start to forgive one without including the other. They were indivisible.

As she watched, she saw that while poor Rory was doing his best to answer Joan's questions, there was a danger he would keel over from exhaustion. She would have to rescue him. First, though, there was the rest of the family to contend with. Vee fell upon her with frightening enthusiasm.

'I feel like I know Carmel,' she said, 'because of all that carry-on over the dress. Doesn't that seem like a million years ago?'

Tara managed a quick 'yes' before being hit with a barrage of questions. What had the experience been like? Was it the same as in the TV dramas? Was there ever a point where she feared the worst? Would she be writing about it for the *Tribune*?

Mercifully, Niall had no questions. He did, however, have a brainwave. He thought Ben and Jenelle deserved a party with balloons and face-painting and magic. The full works.

'A *free* party? If Amby gets wind of that, you'll be out on your ear,' said Damien.

'You leave Amby to me,' laughed Niall, with the conviction of a man who didn't give two hoots about Amby or his job.

Damien had news of his own. Well, it wasn't news yet, but he hoped it would be. 'I've heard a rumour about Maurice Tully,' he whispered.

Intrigued by his theatrics (he was acting in a way that suggested he was Deep Throat in a Washington car park, rather than her brother in the front room), Tara listened on. She agreed that, if true, it was a good story; a story with the potential to end Councillor Tully's political career.

'I can't write it, though,' she said. 'It would come across as a family vendetta.'

Damien scowled.

'But I do have plenty of colleagues who'd be only too happy to do a spot of digging, and I'll pass all the details on to them.'

'Promise?'

'First thing Monday morning, I promise.'

'Fair play to you, Tara. I always said you'd come good in the end.'

Not sure whether she'd been complimented or insulted, she went in search of Gus.

'I wanted to say thanks,' she said. 'For finding Ben.'

'I think it was more a case of him finding me.'

'Well, I'm glad he thought of you.'

Her dad fixed her with a quizzical look. 'Did you really tell him I could be relied upon to tell the truth?'

'Like I said earlier, that was quite a while ago.'

'I see. I'm not sure what I should say. I—'

'Perhaps tonight's not the right time to say anything.'

'All right. Another time, then.' His gaze moved in Rory's direction. 'What's the story with our friend?'

Tara had guessed this was coming. 'I'm not sure.'

'I've always suspected he was sweet on you. I spotted it ages ago. It had me worried, to be honest.'

'Why were you worried?' No sooner had Tara asked the question, than the obvious answer hit her. 'Ah, I get it. You knew that if I spent any time with Rory, I'd realise the business wasn't about to go down the drain?'

Her father gave a small nod.

'Mad,' she said. 'Just mad.'

'You could do a lot worse than Rory,' said Gus.

'That's a glowing recommendation, if ever I heard one.'

'You know what I mean. He's a good lad. He mightn't be tricky enough for you, though.'

She couldn't resist a grin. 'I reckon I've had my fill of tricky.'

Gus went to say something, then hesitated. 'Listen, lovey, why don't you stay the night?'

Tara looked around the room. Vee was two paces back from the Christmas tree, head tilted, admiring her decorating skills. Ferdia was talking to Joan, who was rooting through a bag of knitting patterns. Looking for a hat pattern, perhaps. Niall, Damien and Rory were mid-discussion. Niall held his hands up, his fingers splayed, like he was making sure the others listened. Save for Rory, everybody and everything was reassuringly familiar. They quarrelled; they whinged; they wore you out. Sometimes, they ran away. But they always came back.

Her dad was still talking. 'It's a damp old night,' he was saying. 'And your room's downstairs waiting for you.'

Tara brushed his forearm. 'Thanks . . . but I have my own place now. In fact, I'm going to make tracks shortly. I'm dead on my feet.'

His face wilted.

'I'll be back on Christmas Day, though . . . if I'm invited, that is.'

Gus smiled. 'Since when did you need an invitation to come home?'

Chapter 32

Five months later

Tara tore off another wad of newspaper and wrapped it around a glass. A streak of May sunlight peeped through the window, illuminating the items in front of her. The lease on the bedsit was up, and she was sitting on the floor sorting through her belongings. For a thirty-year-old, there was a pitifully small amount to pack: some crockery and cutlery, some saucepans, clothes, shoes, sheets and toiletries. Add in a box of books, an iron, a hairdryer, her laptop and a transistor radio, and she was almost done. She had never got around to buying a television and, apart from Ben's thank-you picture, the walls were bare.

Even before she began packing, the room had an impermanent, unloved appearance. She had moved there in haste and had never intended staying for long. But, in the strange way that mind and memory work, now that she was leaving, she was already feeling nostalgic.

Beside her were two newspaper articles from the previous day. Tara would pack them carefully and file them away. Nowadays, she supposed, few people kept newspaper clippings. Wasn't everything available on the net? But these made her smile.

The first article was from the *Evening Post*. Under the headline, *Felicity Takes a Shine to Power*, it read:

> The wife of an outgoing councillor has romped to victory in the Dublin City Council elections. Independent candidate

Felicity Power-Shine sensationally topped the poll in the South Inner City ward.

A jubilant Ms Power-Shine (36) said she was thrilled by her performance. 'It proves people are tired of the same old faces and the same tired policies,' she told the *Post*.

The new councillor's husband, Damien Shine, shocked political insiders when he announced he was quitting politics. Mr Shine sprang to national notoriety when a fellow councillor, Maurice Tully, revealed he was moonlighting as a clown.

Asked if her politics were similar to those of her husband, the mum of three replied, 'That's a sexist question if ever I heard one.' She said her views were 'a good bit stronger than Damien's.'

'I ran a grassroots campaign, and I will hit the ground running,' she added.

As expected, Maurice Tully failed in his re-election bid. Mr Tully's campaign was rocked by revelations that he fraudulently claimed thousands of euro in political expenses. The money was siphoned off to build an extension to his luxury home in one of the capital's leafier suburbs.

Conceding defeat, the one-time political bigwig said he had always expected a dog-fight. He slammed pollsters and the media. 'I was written off by lazy right-wing journalists and by self-appointed pundits. These people are the enemies of democracy,' he complained.

Quizzed about his future plans, Mr Tully said he would assess the modalities as they currently pertain and exercise his options accordingly.

Among the family, Maurice Tully's trouncing provided as much joy as Felicity's victory. In fact, Tara's parents were nervous about their daughter-in-law's new role. 'She was hard work before,' Gus moaned. 'What will she be like now?' Thankfully, Damien was out of earshot at the time. He was persevering with his plan to become a teacher and had secured a college place for the autumn. In the meantime, he was back working for Amby. This time he was getting paid.

Damien had taken over from Niall, who was backpacking in Central Asia with a blue-haired jewellery designer called Caoimhe. When he announced his intention to go wandering again, Joan got all mopey and Gus practically went into orbit. For more than a week, while Gus fulminated about idiot sons who refused to grow up, Niall strung them along. Finally, he came clean: he'd actually got a new job and would be back in a month. They could hardly complain about being hoodwinked.

While working at a party, Niall had met the boss of an animation company. They had just won a big contract from a children's TV channel and needed someone to do the books, run the office and generally keep them on the straight and narrow. As Tara saw things, Niall was going to be in the right place doing the wrong job. His interest lay more in drawing characters than in totting up numbers. She suggested he return to college to study animation. 'Ha! One student layabout in the family is enough,' he said with a laugh. But she had the suspicion that this was precisely what he was planning.

Vee had thrown herself into her charity project with uncharacteristic enthusiasm. Although she was curbing her worst instincts, Tara guessed that her sister would always have a skittish, unsettled streak. But, as Niall liked to say, who would want a *totally* staid and responsible Vee? A month ago she had called them all together to announce big news: she was pregnant. Joan was giddy with pleasure. Gus claimed his wife had bought up all the wool east of the River Shannon and would be able to wrap the house in small knitted items.

That was the other big news: Garryowen was for sale. Genuinely for sale. 'It's only a house, and it's too big, too much work,' her mum and dad maintained. They hoped to stay in the same area, they said, just in a smaller place. Tara thought back wryly on the uproar they had provoked when they'd pretended they were selling up. This time, there was barely a murmur of protest. Nevertheless, the four had spent a lot of time analysing their parents' decision. 'What are they really at?' Vee had asked. 'Perhaps, they want a fresh start too,' Damien had said. 'Bah!' she'd replied, 'you've gone all happy-clappy on us.'

Tara placed the last of her crockery into a cardboard box and instructed herself to stop day-dreaming. There was still plenty to do, and she was running short of time. First, she took another peek at the second newspaper article. This one she had written herself. A small piece about a less than spectacular event, she had the feeling that most of the *Tribune*'s readers wouldn't even have noticed it. But it was close to her heart.

A Dublin boy whose disappearance made national headlines last year has won a major writing competition. Eight-year-old Ben O'Neill from St Monica's Mansions in the south inner city won the under-tens section of the competition, which was run by the Department of Children. His essay was called 'Where I Live'. The contest attracted more than five thousand entries from across the country.

The judges said Ben had an exceptional understanding of the lives of people in his community. 'He obviously has a very lively mind,' said author Jean Rawling, who picked the winner.

Ben said he was delighted to win the prize of two hundred euros' worth of book tokens. He added that he hoped to buy some books for his school, St Tiernach's, and 'something small' for his sister, Jenelle, who is due to start school in September.

'When I grow up, I'd like to be a teacher or a writer, or else have a job like my nan's friend, Victor, where I can talk all day and get to see inside other people's flats,' Ben said.

The winner also revealed that he is about to leave St Monica's Mansions. He is moving to Beaumont with his grandmother, Carmel O'Neill. Mrs O'Neill, a widow, will marry her partner, Victor Lennon, next month.

What tickled Tara was that the paper had printed the last paragraph when she'd only included it as a joke. 'Look at us with our wedding announcement in the paper,' Carmel had said with laughter in her voice. 'You'd think we were royalty or movie stars.'

Within a couple of weeks, Carmel, Ben and Jenelle would be gone from the flats. Carmel said that while she would miss the camaraderie, she wasn't sorry to be moving on. At forty-seven, she was starting over.

Not that long ago, St Monica's Mansions had been in the news again. Although the men accused of shooting young Eric 'Redser' Lynam were in jail awaiting trial, the criminal suspected of masterminding the attack had been at large. On Easter Monday, while visiting his sister in a nearby estate, he was shot dead. Popular gossip had it that a former associate was to blame. The television news reports revisited Eric's murder, every image a reminder of the cruelty of his death.

Following her Christmas escapade, Rosanna stood no chance of getting early release, so Ben and Jenelle would be living with their grandmother for another year at least. After that, Carmel didn't know what would happen. She had told Ben the truth about his mother, and he had accepted it with a stoicism that belied his years. 'Don't tell Jenelle,' he'd advised. 'She's too young to understand.' Carmel didn't reveal her role in Rosanna's imprisonment. That would have to remain a secret.

Occasionally, Ben wrote to his mum. His letters were cheery, laden with stories about school and the flats and illustrated with smiley faces. His disappointments he kept to himself. There were times when Carmel shook with worry about this. More often, she reckoned his resilience would see him through. 'It's a funny old world,' she once said, 'when the rest of us have to learn lessons in maturity from an eight-year-old boy.'

Tara checked her phone. It was twenty past two. She had time to give the bathroom a quick wipe before Rory arrived. He had already moved his own belongings into their new flat.

She had never intended for things to get so serious so quickly. Some fun, a small flirtation, that's what she'd been after. But, within a ridiculously short space of time, she was hooked. She didn't want to be with anyone else. She didn't even want to think about anyone else. How could you not fall for a man who was sharp, but never sneered? Who ate every meal as though it was his last? Who was chronically uninterested in fashion? Who could talk for Ireland – but knew when to stop?

Once or twice, she had stopped to ask herself if it was too soon for them to be moving in together. After all, they had only been a couple for a few months. But, impulsive as it was, this felt like the right decision. Tara had her low days when she couldn't stop thinking about her parents' deception; when she felt like she was still picking shrapnel from her wounds. But she needed to move on. And forging a new life with someone she loved felt like the best way of doing this. Not that long ago, Vee had asked if she ever thought about Craig. It would be a lie to say she didn't, but her memories were increasingly fuzzy. 'You know he split up with Sheena Hyland-Grey?' her sister had said. 'They're both back in Ireland – but not together.' Tara hadn't known. She was relieved by her indifference.

In September, Tara and Rory were going to India. It turned out that he had always wanted to go there too. Although their trip would only last three weeks, they were already making plans. There were so many places to see: the lake palace in Udaipur; the pink city of Jaipur; the Taj Mahal and the Ajanta Caves. Their list grew by the day.

Vee claimed they were mad to go on such a risky holiday. 'Especially for your *first* holiday,' she said. 'What if one of you gets sick or something else goes wrong? No, if you ask me, you should play it safe: find a smart hotel and laze around in the sun.'

Tara just smiled and shrugged. She would take her chances.

Acknowledgements

Before I thank the many people who helped me with *Each and Every One*, a quick word about the story and the setting. While the book is set in contemporary Dublin, I didn't want to stigmatise any particular area. To that end, some of the places featured – like Palmerston Park – are real. Others – including St Monica's Mansions – are fictional. Also, I hope that the more legal-minded among you will forgive me for taking a few liberties with the courts process, especially in Chapter Twenty.

Huge thanks to my agent, Robert Kirby, for his wisdom and encouragement. Thanks too to Holly Thompson.

At Orion, thank you to my editor, Genevieve Pegg, and also to Susan Lamb and Laura Gerrard.

I owe many, many thanks to Hachette Ireland, in particular to Breda Purdue, Jim Binchy, Ruth Shern and Joanna Smyth.

I'm really grateful to my friends and colleagues in the RTE newsroom for their support. Thanks for putting up with me!

A big thank you to Vido, Sonja and Filip Gustin.

A special thanks to my mother, Ruth, who was first to read *Each and Every One*, and to my father, Tony.

More thanks than I can say to my husband, Eamon Quinn.

And finally, my heartfelt gratitude to all those who have bought and promoted my books. There are a million novels out there, and endless reasons not to take a chance on a new author, so I truly appreciate your support and your kind words.

THE STORY BEHIND

☙

Each & Every One

YOU KNOW THAT short paragraph at the start of every novel? The one that begins, *All the characters in this book are fictitious*, and then goes on to warn that if you think you recognise anybody you are completely and totally mistaken? I should probably repeat that here because while the Shines are fictitious, their story was prompted by what's been happening in Ireland over the past few years. To be fair, if you are Irish, or know very much about the country, you probably assumed that from the start.

As a journalist, I've had to work with the big picture: the loans and the losses, the acronyms and the jargon. The problem is, you start to lose sight of the real people whose lives have been ripped apart by financial turmoil. Obviously, it was people like Carmel who lost most. Work dried up; neighbourhoods fractured; sons and daughters went abroad. But there's also been the unusual sight of the formerly wealthy traipsing in and out of the courts, trying to hold on to some part of what they thought was theirs. Like Tara says, 'For a while, every week had brought new tales of the journey from rags to riches and back to rags again.'

I found myself wondering what it's like to be at the heart of an affluent family when the funds dry up. Do you really get along, or has money been papering over the cracks? And, if you've grown up surrounded by plenty, how do you cope when you have to fend for yourself? These thoughts provided the spark for *Each and Every One*.

Of course, characters take on a life you hadn't expected at the outset. When I started writing, I didn't plan on Carmel and Ben becoming such a significant part of the story. The more I wrote about them, however, the more I saw their possibilities. And it was such a joy to write about people who soak up the worst that life can throw at them, and battle on with grace and humour. Over the years, I've interviewed numerous people who embodied this sort of resilience, and I've found that their stories remained with me long after encounters with the celebrated and powerful had faded.

One other thought: in a lot of fiction, journalists are either exceedingly glamorous or the personification of seediness. I'm sure both types exist. Just for a change, though, I wanted to write about the day to day life of an average hack: somebody like Tara, whose work can vary from the excruciatingly dull to the achingly sad. I will admit that some of her markings were inspired by my own experiences as a reporter.

Although rooted in what's been happening in Ireland, I hope that *Each and Every One* features universal questions, dilemmas and characters. Many families have a Vee or a Niall. Similarly, I'm pretty sure that most communities have their own versions of Amby Power and Councillor Maurice

Tully. Oh, and I'd like to think there are some real-life Ben O'Neills out there too. We could do with a few of those.

FOR DISCUSSION

- Damien believes that 'hypocrite' is the 'most wounding of words'. To what extent is *Each and Every One* about hypocrisy?

- 'For all this, he couldn't escape the long arm of his upbringing.' Is Gus right to say this about himself?

- How does the book contrast Gus and Joan's upbringing with that of their children?

- Are Gus and Joan's actions justified? Does their plan succeed?

- Is Carmel right to blame herself for Rosanna's failings? Was she right to take Ben and Jenelle?

- Does your view of the Shines change over the course of the book?

- How does the author portray contemporary Dublin?

- Tara says that 'only a mug tries to do the right thing'. Does she really believe this?

- Vee describes herself as a 'shallow fool'. Do you agree with her?

- According to Damien, 'If you started seeing merit in the views of others, you might as well give up'. What do you think of the portrayal of politics and politicians in *Each and Every One*?

- What do you think of the book's portrayal of journalists and journalism?